## WHO IS

The bronze giant, who with his five aides became world famous, whose name was as well known in the far regions of China and the jungles of Africa as in the skyscrapers of New York.

There were stories of Doc Savage's almost incredible strength; of his amazing scientific discoveries of strange weapons and dangerous exploits.

Doc dedicated his life to aiding those faced by dangers with which they could not cope.

His name brought fear to those who sought to prey upon the unsuspecting. His name was praised by thousands he had saved.

### DOC SAVAGE'S AMAZING CREW

"Ham," **Brigadier General Theodore Marley Brooks,** was never without his ominous, black sword cane.

"Monk," **Lieutenant Colonel Andrew Blodgett Mayfair,** just over five feet tall, yet over 260 pounds. His brutish exterior concealed the mind of a great scientist.

"Renny," **Colonel John Renwick,** his favorite sport was pounding his massive fists through heavy, paneled doors.

"Long Tom," **Major Thomas J. Roberts,** was the physiscal weakling of the crowd, but a genius at electricity.

"Johnny," **William Harper Littlejohn,** the scientist and greatest living expert on geology and archaeology.

**WITH THEIR LEADER, THEY WOULD
GO ANYWHERE, FIGHT ANYONE,
DARE EVERYTHING—SEEKING
EXCITEMENT AND PERILOUS
ADVENTURE!**

Bantam Books by Kenneth Robeson
Ask your bookseller for the books you have missed

20 and 21 THE SECRET IN THE SKY and COLD DEATH

97 and 98 SATAN BLACK and CARGO UNKNOWN

99 and 100 HELL BELOW and THE LOST GIANT

101 and 102 THE PHARAOH'S GHOST and
THE TIME TERROR

103 and 104 THE WHISKER OF HERCULES and
THE MAN WHO WAS SCARED

105 and 106 THEY DIED TWICE and
THE SCREAMING MAN

107 and 108 JIU SAN and THE BLACK, BLACK
WITCH

109 and 110 THE SHAPE OF TERROR and
DEATH HAD YELLOW EYES

Coming in June 1982 a double volume of
*According to Plan of a One-Eyed Mystic*
and *The Man Who Fell Up*

Two Complete Adventures in One Volume

# THE SECRET IN THE SKY
### and
## COLD DEATH

## Kenneth Robeson

**BANTAM BOOKS**
TORONTO · NEW YORK · LONDON · SYDNEY

THE SECRET IN THE SKY #20
COLD DEATH #21
*A Bantam Book / published by arrangement with*
*The Condé Nast Publications Inc.*

*PRINTING HISTORY*

The Secret in the Sky *was originally published in Doc Savage*
*Magazine, May 1935. Copyright 1935 by Street & Smith Publi-*
*cations, Inc. Copyright © renewed 1962 by The Condé Nast*
*Publications Inc.*

*First Bantam edition / November 1967*

Cold Death *was originally published in Doc Savage Magazine,*
*September 1936. Copyright 1936 by Street & Smith Publications,*
*Inc. Copyright © renewed 1964 by The Condé Nast Publications*
*Inc.*

*Bantam edition / January 1968*

*Bantam 2 Vol. edition / March 1982*

ISBN 0-553-20934-5

*Published simultaneously in the United States and Canada*

*Bantam Books are published by Bantam Books, Inc. Its trade-*
*mark, consisting of the words "Bantam Books" and the por-*
*trayal of a rooster, is Registered in U.S. Patent and Trademark*
*Office and in other countries. Marca Registrada. Bantam*
*Books, Inc., 666 Fifth Avenue, New York, New York 10103.*

# Contents

The Secret in the Sky      1

Cold Death      127

## THE SECRET IN THE SKY

# Chapter 1
## THE FRIEND WHO DIED

THE matter of Willard Spanner was almost unbelievable. It was too preposterous. The newspapers publishing the story were certain a mistake had been made somewhere. True, this was the Twentieth Century, the age of marvels. But—then——

At exactly noon, the telephone buzzer whirred in Doc Savage's New York skyscraper headquarters. Noon, straight up, Eastern Standard Time.

The buzzer whirred three times, with lengthy pauses between *whirs*, which allowed time for any one present to have answered. Then an automatic answering device, an ingenious arrangement of dictaphone voice recorder and phonographic speaker—a creation of Doc Savage's scientific skill—was cut in automatically. The phonograph record turned under the needle and sent words over the telephone wire.

"This is a mechanical robot speaking from Doc Savage's headquarters and advising you that Doc Savage is not present, but that any message you care to speak will be recorded on a dictaphone and will come to Doc Savage's attention later," spoke the mechanical contrivance. "You may proceed with whatever you wish to say, if anything."

"Doc!" gasped a voice, which had that strange quality lent by long-distance telephonic amplifiers. "This is Willard Spanner! I am in San Francisco. I have just learned something too horrible for me to believe!"

Several violent grunts came over the wire. There were thumps. Glass seemed to break at the San Francisco end. Then came silence, followed by a *click* as the receiver was placed on the hook at the San Francisco terminus of the wire.

The mechanical device in Doc Savage's New York office ran on for some moments, and a stamp clock automatically recorded the exact time of the message on a paper roll; then the apparatus stopped and set itself for another call, should one come.

The time recorded was two minutes past twelve, noon.

3

Thirty minutes later, approximately, the newspaper press association wires hummed with the story of the mysterious seizure of Willard Kipring Parker Spanner in San Francisco. Willard Kipring Parker Spanner was a nabob, a somebody, a big shot. Anything unusual that happened to him was big news.

The newspapers did not know the half of it. The biggest was yet to come.

Financially, Willard Kipring Parker Spanner did not amount to much. A post-mortem examination of his assets showed less than five thousand dollars, an insignificant sum for a man who was known over most of the world.

Willard Kipring Parker Spanner called himself simply, "a guy who likes to fiddle around with microscopes." It was said that he knew as much about disease germs, and methods of combating them, as any living man. He had won one Nobel prize. He was less than thirty years old. Scientists and physicians who knew him considered him a genius.

When Willard Spanner was found dead, many a scientist and physician actually shed tears, realizing what the world had lost.

When Willard Spanner was found dead, the newspapers began to have fits. And with good reason.

For Willard Spanner's body was found on a New York street—less than three hours after he had been seized in San Francisco! Seized in Frisco at noon, Eastern Standard Time. Dead in New York at ten minutes to three, Eastern Standard Time.

A NEWSBOY with a freckled face was first to convey the news to Doc Savage. The newsboy was also cross-eyed. Neither the newsboy, nor his freckles, nor his crossed eyes had other connection with the affair, except that the lad's reaction when he sighted Doc Savage was typical of the effect which the bronze man had on people.

The boy's mouth went roundly open with a kind of amazement when he first saw the bronze giant; then, as he sold the paper, his demeanor was awed and very near worshipful.

"I know you, mister," he said in a small voice. "You're Doc Savage! I've seen your picture in the newspapers."

Doc Savage studied the boy as he paid for the paper. He seemed particularly interested in the crossed eyes.

"Wear glasses?" he asked. He had a remarkable voice; it seemed filled with a great, controlled power.

"Sure," said the newsboy, "They give me headaches."

Doc Savage produced a small business card. The card was not white, but bronze, and the printing—his name only was on it—was in a slightly darker bronze.

"If I asked you to do something," he queried, "would you do it?"

"Betcha boots!" replied the newsboy.

Doc Savage wrote a name and address on the card and said, "Go see that man," then walked on, leaving the boy puzzled.

The name and address the bronze man had written was that of an eye specialist whose particular forte was afflictions such as the boy had.

More than one gaze followed Doc Savage along the street, for he was a giant of bronze with a face that was remarkable in its regularity of feature and a body that was a thing of incredible muscular development. His eyes attracted no little attention, too. They were like pools of flake-gold, stirred into continuous motion by some invisible force.

He read the newspaper headlines, the galleys of type beneath, but there was nothing on his features to show that he was perusing anything of importance.

The skyscraper which housed his headquarters was, in size and architecture, probably the most impressive in New York City. A private high-speed elevator lifted him to the eighty-sixth floor. He passed through a door that was plain, except for a name in small bronze letters:

CLARK SAVAGE Jr.

The reception room inside had large windows, deep leather chairs, a strange and rich inlaid table of great size, and an impressive safe.

An automatic pistol lay on the floor. A pig, a shote with long legs and ears like boat sails, walked around and around the gun, grunting in a displeased way.

A man sat in a chair. He was a very short man and the chair was huge and high and faced away from the door, so that only red bristles which stuck up straight on top of the man's head could be seen.

The man in the chair said in a small, childlike voice, "Shoot off that gun, Habeas, of I'll tie knots in all your legs."

With an uncanny intelligence, the pig sat down, inserted a hoof inside the trigger guard, and the gun went off with an ear-splitting report.

"Swell!" said the man in the chair. "Only you better stand, Habeas. Next time, the gun might be pointed at your posterior and there might not be a blank in it."

Doc Savage said, "Monk."

"Uh-huh," said the man in the chair. "Sure, Doc, what is it?"

"Willard Spanner was a friend of mine."

"MONK"—Lieutenant Colonel Andrew Blodgett Mayfair— lifted out of the chair. He was not much over five feet tall. He was only slightly less broad than that, and he had a pair of arms which gave the grotesque impression of being nearly as long as he was tall. Red hairs, which looked coarse as match sticks, furred his leathery hide. His was the build of a gorilla.

"I read about it in them blasted newspapers," he said, and his small voice was doubly ridiculous, contrasted with his physique. "Willard Spanner was seized in Frisco at noon. He was found dead here in New York at ten minutes to three. Screw loose somewhere."

Monk wrinkled a fabulously homely face to show puzzlement. He looked amiable, stupid, when, in truth, he was one of the most clever industrial chemists alive.

"Maybe the newspapers got balled up on the difference in time between San Francisco and New York," he added.

"All times given are New York time," Doc Savage said.

"Then the guy seized in San Francisco wasn't Willard Spanner, or the one dead here in New York isn't Spanner," Monk declared. "The bird didn't go from Frisco to New York in a little over two hours. It just isn't being done yet."

Doc Savage asked, "Any messages?"

"Ham phoned, and said he was coming up," replied the homely chemist. "I haven't been here long. Dunno what was recorded before I got here."

The bronze man went into the next room, which was a scientific laboratory, one of the most complete in existence, and crossed that to the vast, white-enameled room which held his laboratory of chemical, electrical and other devices. He lifted the cover on the telephone recorder robot, switched a loud-speaker and amplifier into circuit with the playback pickup, and started the mechanism.

Monk came in and listened, slackjawed, as the device reproduced the call from San Francisco, complete to its violent termination. The pig, Habeas—Habeas Corpus was the shote's full appendage—trailed at the homely chemist's heels.

Doc Savage examined the time stamped on the recording roll.

"Two minutes past twelve," he said.

"Was that Willard Spanner's voice, or would you know it?" Monk demanded.

"I would know his voice," Doc replied. "And that was, unquestionably, Willard Spanner."

"Speaking from San Francisco?" Monk grunted incredulously.

"We will see." Doc Savage made a call, checking with the telephone people, then hung up and advised, "The call came from San Francisco, all right. Willard Spanner appears to have been seized while he was in the booth making the call."

Monk picked the pig, Habeas, up by one oversize ear—a treatment the shote seemed not to mind.

"Then the dead man here in New York is not Willard Spanner," declared the simian chemist. "Nobody goes from Frisco to New York in not much more than two hours."

"We will see about that," Doc told him.

"How?"

"By visiting the New York morgue where the dead man was taken."

Monk nodded. "How about Ham?"

"We will leave him a note," Doc said.

APPARENTLY, it had not occurred to any one in authority on the New York civic scene that the surroundings of the dead were of aesthetic value, for the morgue building was a structure which nearly attained the ultimate in shoddiness.

Its brick walls gave the appearance of having not been washed in generations, being almost black with soot and city grime. The steps were grooved deep by treading feet, and the stone paving of the entry into which the dead wagons ran was rutted by tires. Rusting iron bars, very heavy, were over the windows; for just what reason, no one probably could have told.

"This joint gives me the creeps—and I don't creep easy,"

Monk imparted, as they got out of Doc Savage's roadster before the morgue.

The roadster was deceptively long. Its color was somber. The fact that its body was of armor plate, its windows—specially built in the roadster doors—of bullet-proof glass, was not readily apparent.

Monk carried Habeas Corpus by an ear and grumbled, "I wonder why anybody should kill Willard Spanner? Or grab him, either? Spanner was an all-right guy. He didn't have any enemies."

Doc listened at the entrance. There was silence, and no attendant was behind the reception desk where one should have been. They stepped inside.

"Hello, somebody!" Monk called.

Silence answered.

There was an odor in the air, a rather peculiar tang. Monk sniffed.

"Say, I knew they used formaldehyde around these places," he muttered. "But there's something besides——"

Doc Savage moved with such suddenness that he seemed to explode. But it was a silent explosion, and he was little more than a noiseless bronze blur as he crossed to the nearest door. He did not try to pass through the door, but flattened beside it.

Monk, bewildered, began, "Say, what the blazes? First I smell——"

A man came through the door, holding a big single-action six-gun. He said, "Start your settin'-up exercises, boys!" Then his eyes bulged, for he had apparently expected to see two men—and Doc Savage, beside the door, escaped his notice.

The man with the six-shooter was bony and looked as if he had been under bright suns much of his life. He wore a new suit, but his shirt was a coarse blue work garment, faded from washing. The tie was blue and looked as if it had been put on and taken off many times, without untying the knot. The knot was a very long one.

Doc Savage struck silently and with blinding speed. The gun wielder saw him, but could not move in time, and the bronze man's fist took him on the temple. The six-gun evidently had a hair trigger. It went off. The bullet made a hole, round and neat, in the wall behind Monk.

Monk began howling and charged for the door.

"Now ain't this somethin'!" he bellowed.

Doc SAVAGE had gone on with a continuation of the dive which he had made at the six-gun wielder, and was already through the door. The room beyond was an office with four desks and four swivel chairs.

Five persons were arrayed on the floor. The morgue attendants, obviously. They were neither bound nor gagged, but they lay very still. The odor of chloroform was heavy in the air.

Two men were on their feet. One was tall, the other short, and the short one wore overall pants and his legs were bowed. Both were weather-beaten.

The tall one held in one hand a blue revolver and in the other a bandanna handkerchief, which gave off chloroform stench. The short man had an automatic rifle from which barrel and stock had been bobbed off short.

A bundle of clothing lay in the middle of the floor.

The automatic rifle smacked loudly as Doc came through the door. But the marksman did not lead his target quite enough. He shot again. The cartridge stuck in the ejector.

"Damn it!" the rifleman bawled.

"Throw it away!" gritted the tall man. "I told you that gun wouldn't work if you bobtailed it!"

The tall man danced back as he spoke, seeming in no hurry to shoot. He waved his blue revolver, that Doc Savage might be sure to see it.

"Don't be a sucker!" the man suggested. "Behave yourself."

Doc Savage held his hands out even with his shoulders and came to a stop, but not until momentum had carried him to the center of the room.

Monk lumbered through the door. He stopped, looked closely at the blue gun as if it were some strange animal, then put up his stub-fingered hands.

"That's bein' sensible," said the tall man. "I can bust poker chips in the air with this here hogleg. Stunted, there, is a good shot, too, only he thought he knew more about that auto rifle than the gent who made her."

"Stunted," the short man, was peering into the innards of his doctored rifle.

"Aw-w," he mumbled. "I took too much tension off the spring."

Monk grunted, "What's the idea, you guys?"

"We like to look at dead people," the tall man said dryly. "We're strange that way."

Doc Savage was standing with his toes almost against the bundle of clothing. The bundle was snug, being strapped around tightly with a belt.

Doc hooked a toe under the bundle and kicked with great force.

THE human nervous system is capable of registering impressions only so fast. The tall man undoubtedly knew the missile was coming, but could do nothing. When it hit him, he recoiled instinctively.

The next instant, he was flat on his face, held there by one foot which Doc Savage jammed down on his neck.

Monk whooped loudly, rushed Stunted. Monk's fights were always noisy.

Stunted clung like a zealot to his bobtailed auto rifle, trying to get it in operation. He failed. He tried to club with the gun. Monk jerked it out of his hands as if he were taking a lollypop from a child, then dropped it.

Monk picked the short man up bodily, turned him over and dropped him on his head. He accomplished the motion with such speed that the short man was helpless. Stunted did not move after he fell on his head.

Monk blinked small eyes at his victim.

"Gosh," he said. "I wonder if that hurt him?"

The tall man on the floor snarled, "What in blue blazes kind of a circus is this, anyhow?"

Monk felt of Stunted's head, found it intact, then twisted one of the short man's rather oversize ears, but got no response. The homely chemist turned on the tall man.

"So it's a circus, huh?" he grunted. "I wondered."

"Aw, hell!" gritted the other.

Monk came over and sat on the lean prisoner. Doc Savage removed his foot from the man's neck. Monk grabbed the fellow's ears and pulled them. He seemed fascinated by the rubbery manner in which they stretched out from the man's head.

"They'd make swell souvenirs," Monk grunted.

"Cut it out!" the tall man howled. "What're you gonna do with me?"

"I'm gonna ask you questions," Monk told him. "And I'm gonna be awful mad if you don't answer 'em."

"Nuts!" said the captive.

"Has this raid, or whatever it was, got anything to do with Willard Spanner?" Monk asked.

"What do you think?" the other snapped.

Monk pulled the ears. Tears came to the man's eyes. He cursed, and his voice was a shrill whine of agony.

"I'll kill you for that!" he promised. "Damn me, if I don't!"

Monk shuddered elaborately, grinned and said, "If I had on boots, I'd shake in 'em. What did you come here for?"

A new voice said, "You gentlemen seem to be humorists."

MONK started violently and twisted his head toward the door. He gulped, "Blazes!" and got hastily to his feet.

The man in the door was solid, athletic-looking, and he held a revolver with familiar ease. He was in his socks. That probably explained how he had come in from the outside so silently: that, and the faint mumble of city traffic, which was always present.

"Get up!" he told the tall man. "Wipe your eyes. Then grab that bunch of clothes. This is sure something to write home about!"

"I'll kill this ape!" bawled the tall man.

"Some other time," the rescuer suggested. "Get the clothes. Say, just who is this big bronze guy and the monkey, anyhow?"

"How would I know?" snarled the man whom Monk had been badgering. He picked up the bundle of clothing and started for the door.

"You wouldn't leave Stunted, would you?" asked the first.

Without a word, the tall man picked up the short fellow and made his way, not without difficulty, out through the door.

The gun wielder looked on benignly. He had one stark peculiarity. His eyes were blue. And something was wrong with them. They crossed at intervals, pupils turning in toward the nose. Then they straightened out. The owner seemed to do the straightening with visible effort.

Monk demanded, "Who did them clothes belong to?"

The man said, "They'll answer a lot of questions where you're going."

Monk did not get a clear impression of what happened next. Things moved too fast. Doc Savage must have read the intention of the man with the queer eyes. Doc lunged.

The gun went off. But the man with the eyes had tried to shift from Monk to Doc for a target and had not quite made it. His bullet pocked the wall. Then Doc had a grip on the revolver.

The man let go of the revolver. He bounced back, fast on his feet, reached the door and sloped through. He was yelling now. His yells caused noise of other feet in the next room. There were evidently more men.

Doc grasped Monk and propelled him backward. They got into a rear room and slammed the door. Doc shot the bolt.

Revolver bullets chopped around the lock. Wood splintered. The lock held. A man kicked the door. Monk roared a threat.

There was no more kicking, no more shooting. Silence fell, except for the traffic noises.

Monk looked at Doc.

"That guy with the performing eyes was gonna kill us both," he mumbled.

Doc Savage did not comment. He listened, then unlocked the door. The room beyond was empty. He advanced. In the next room, one of the chloroformed morgue attendants was sitting up and acting sick.

The street outside held no sign of the violent raiders. There was no trace of the bundle of clothing.

The reviving morgue attendant began to mumble.

"They wanted clothes off a corpse," he muttered. "Whatcha know about that?"

"Off what corpse?" Doc asked him.

"Off Willard Spanner," said the attendant.

# Chapter 2
# THE HIGH-PRESSURE GHOULS

Doc Savage exited to the street and made inquiries, finding that the men had gone away in two cars. Persons questioned named four different makes of cars, in each instance insisting that their information was correct.

"They're all wrong, probably," Monk grumbled.

Pursuit was patently hopeless, although Monk cast a number of expectant glances in Doc Savage's direction. The bronze man had a way of pulling rabbits out of hats in affairs such as this. But Doc only reëntered the morgue. None of those who had been chloroformed were in immediate danger.

"We came here to see the body of Willard Spanner," Doc told the attendant who had revived.

"Sort of a coincidence," said the attendant, and managed a sickly grin which typified a peculiarity of human behavior—the fact that persons who work regularly in close proximity to death are inclined to arm themselves with a wise-cracking veneer.

The bodies were stored in bins not unlike huge filing boxes. The marble slabs on which they lay slid into the bins on rollers. The attendant was still too groggy to bring the Willard Spanner slide out after he had found the identifying card, and Monk helped him.

Doc Savage looked at the body for a long time.

"This is Willard Spanner," he said finally.

They went out.

Monk scratched his head, then said, "But the man seized in San Francisco—that couldn't have been Willard Spanner."

"The voice on the phone recorder," Doc reminded.

"You said it was Willard Spanner's voice." Monk found his pig, Habeas, and picked him up by an ear. "Could you have been mistaken about that voice?"

"I think not," Doc Savage said slowly.

They examined those who were still senseless from the chloroform, gave a description of the morgue raiders to police officers who had arrived, then walked out to the roadster.

Monk seemed to be thinking deeply. He snapped his fingers.

"That bundle of Willard Spanner's clothing!" he grumbled. "Now what in the dickens did they want with that? The police had searched the pockets and had found nothing."

"It must have been something important," Doc told him. "They wanted the garments badly enough to make quite a disturbance in getting them."

A policeman came to the morgue door and called, "You are wanted on the phone."

Doc and Monk went back, and Doc picked up the receiver and said, "Yes?" inquiringly.

A clipped, melodious voice spoke rapidly. It was the voice of an orator, and it carried the accent which is commonly associated with Harvard.

"I got to the morgue in time to observe that something was badly wrong," advised the speaker. "I followed the chaps outside when they left in such a hurry. They are now at Albemarle Avenue and Frame Street. I will meet you at the corner."

Doc Savage said, "In ten minutes," and hung up.

Monk, making for the street in a series of ungainly bounds, demanded, "Who was it?"

"Ham," Doc replied.

"The shyster!" Monk growled, and there was infinite contempt in his tone.

ALBEMARLE AVENUE was a twin groove through marsh mud on the outskirts on New York City. Frame Street seemed to be a sign, scabby and ancient, which stuck out of the salt grass. If there ever had been a Frame Street, it had long ago given up to the swamp.

Darkness was coming on when Doc Savage and Monk arrived in the roadster.

"There's Ham," Monk said.

"Ham" was Brigadier General Theodore Marley Brooks, Park Avenue fashion plate, and a lawyer, the pride of Harvard Law School. He was a slender man with the manner of a wasp and a tongue as sharp as the fine Damascus sword blade concealed in the innocent-looking black cane which he carried.

He came out of the marsh grass, stepping gingerly to avoid soiling his natty afternoon garb, the sword cane tucked under an arm.

"Hy-ah, you fashion plate," Monk growled.

"Hello, stupid," Ham retorted insultingly.

The two glared at each other. A stranger would have thought fisticuffs imminent. As a matter of fact, each of these two had time and again risked his life to save the other, although no one had ever heard one of them address a civil word to the other.

Ham opened the roadster door on Doc Savage's side, and said, "I got the note you left at headquarters, telling me you had gone to the morgue. I went to the morgue. As I said over the phone—those chaps were clowning around, so I followed them."

"Where are they?" Doc asked.

Ham pointed across the swamp. "An oyster plant over there."

"Oyster plant?" Monk grunted.

"They probably use it as a blind for whatever they are doing," Ham offered. "And, incidentally, just what is behind this?"

"It's all screwy, so far," Monk snorted. "Willard Spanner is reported grabbed in Frisco at noon, and is found dead in New York before three o'clock. Then a gang of birds raid the morgue and steal his clothing. That's all we know."

Ham said, "I'll show you where they went. They had that bundle of clothing, too."

There were a few comparatively firm spots in the marsh. The rest of the terrain was covered with water which ranged in depth from an inch to two feet, with spots which were deeper, as Monk promptly proved by going in above the waist.

A cloud bank in the west shortened the period of twilight. They were soon in complete darkness. Using flashlights would have given away their position. Making any speed through the coarse grass, without noise, was almost impossible.

"You fellows take it easy," Doc directed. "Do not try to get too close."

Monk began, "But what're you —" and did not finish. The bronze man had vanished in the darkness.

Monk listened, then shook his head. It was difficult to conceive of any one moving with such silence.

It was no casual trait, this ability of Doc Savage's to stalk quietly. He had practiced a great deal, had studied the masters of the art: the carnivorous beasts of the jungle.

The bronze man had covered not more than a hundred yards when something happened—something that was, later, to take on great significance and a terrible importance.

He heard a peculiar crashing sound. That described it more accurately than anything else. It was not a series of crashes, but one long, brittle report. It started faintly and attained, in the span of two seconds or so, a surprising loudness.

Doc glanced up. Hanging in the sky was what appeared to be a taut rope of liquid fire. This faded in a moment.

It was an uncanny phenomena.

Doc Savage crouched for some time, listening, flake-gold eyes on the sky. But there was nothing more. He went on toward the oyster plant.

The odor of the place was evident long before the low, rambling processing building showed up. It was built on the beach, with a wharf shoving out porch fashion to one side. A channel had evidently been dredged for the oyster boats. The plant was used for the sorting and opening of oysters.

Mounds of oyster shells were pyramided here and there, and were thick on the ground. They made walking difficult. Wash of waves on the near-by beach covered up lesser sounds.

Several times Doc Savage stooped and brushed away oyster shells, that he might step on the bare ground. The brittle shells would break with loud reports. The side of the building which he approached was dark. He worked around. Lighted windows appeared.

Smell of oysters was strong. Two small schooners were tied up at a wharf. The cabin portholes of one of these were lighted. An instant later, the light went out, and three men came up the companion. They stepped to the wharf. One used a flashlight, and this illuminated them.

One was Stunted. His companions were the tall man and the one with the peculiar crossing and uncrossing eyes. One carried a bundle which resembled clothing.

Stunted said, "Danged if I don't still maintain that an automatic rifle can be bobbed and still——"

"Aw, hell!" The tall man spat disgustedly. "Here we really got things to worry about, and you go on and on about that gun. Man, don't the fact that that bronze guy was Doc Savage impress you none a-tall?"

Stunted stopped suddenly.

"Look, you gents," he said. "You been cackling around like two old hens since you learned that bird was Doc Savage. Now I want you to tell me something."

"Yeah?" said the tall man.

"Ain't it a fact that with what we got, we don't need to be afraid of anybody?" demanded Stunted.

"You mean——"

"You know what I mean. You saw that streak in the sky and heard that crack of a noise, a while ago, didn't you? Now answer my question."

"Aw-w-w!" The tall man spat again. "We ain't exactly afraid of him. Only it might've been more convenient if he hadn't turned up on the spot. That Savage is nobody's cinch, and don't forget that."

"I ain't forgettin' it," said Stunted. "And quit squawkin', you hombres. We're settin' pretty. Doc Savage ain't got a line on us. And didn't we get Willard Spanner's clothing. And ain't the rest gonna be taken care of?"

The tall man burst into sudden laughter.

"Now what?" Stunted growled.

"Just thinkin'," the other chuckled. "People are gonna wonder how Willard Spanner was in Frisco at noon and dead here in New York at three o'clock the same afternoon."

DOC SAVAGE was close to them. He could have reached out and tripped any one of the trio as they filed past.

The silent man of the three, the one with the unnaturally roving eyes, brought up the rear. Doc Savage had been crouching. He stood erect. His fist made a sound like a loud finger snap on the man's jaw. The man fell. The bundle of clothing flew to one side.

A number of surprising things happened. The surrounding darkness erupted human beings. At least a dozen men appeared with magical effect. Each had a flashlight, a gun.

"Take 'im alive?" one shouted questioningly.

"Not much!" squawked another, evidently the chief.

Doc started for the clothing bundle. A man was leaping over it, coming toward him, gun spouting flame and thunder. Doc sloped aside. He twisted. Lead slammed past.

Doc hit the ground and rolled. Tall marsh grass took him in. He burrowed a dozen feet, veered left. Slugs tore through the grass. They made hoarse snarls.

A pile of oyster shells jutted out of the darkness in front of him. The bronze man got behind it. He ran a score of paces, went down in a hollow where there was soft mud, but no water, and waited, listening.

Stunted was yelling, "He's behind that shell pile! If I had an auto rifle, it would put a pill right through that stuff!"

"Suppose you use your legs more and your mouth less!" some one suggested.

The men scattered, hunting. They were in pairs, a neat precaution. The couples did not walk close enough together that both could be surprised at once, yet nothing could happen to one without the other knowing it.

Stunted shouted, "You jaspers knew he was around here! How in thunder did you know that?"

"You wouldn't understand," a voice told him.

Stunted swore at the speaker. "C'mon, feller, how'd you know it?"

"There's a bank of alarm wires strung around here," said the voice.

"Nuts!" Stunted told him. "I haven't seen any wires."

"They're underground," the other snapped. "Just barely covered. Any one walking over them changes the capacity of a high-frequency electric field enough to show on a recording device inside."

"Well, sink me!" Stunted snorted.

Doc Savage, listening, made a mental note that some one of considerable scientific ability was involved with the gang. Such an alarm system as had been described was feasible, but required high technical knowledge to construct.

The bronze man crawled away through the tall grass.

Doc did not go far, however. A score of yards, and he stopped. He spent a moment or two tensing his throat muscles, striving for a certain effect.

"Hands up, you fellows!" he said loudly, using his own natural voice.

A split of a second later, he shouted again. This time, his tone was a splendid imitation of a man greatly frightened.

"It's Doc Savage!" he shrilled. "Give us a hand over here, somebody!"

Results were instant and noisy. Men howled irately and made a great clatter in the marsh grass, charging for the spot. They were completely deceived.

Doc Savage moved swiftly, not in flight but circling back toward the oyster shell mound near which he had made his attack. He wanted the bundle of clothes.

He reached the shell pile, paused, listened. Men were making angry sounds, but not close by. Some one had dropped a flashlight in the excitement. Its beam did not play directly on the spot where the garments lay, but the backglow disclosed the parcel. It was hardly more than thirty feet away. It lay in the open.

Doc continued listening. His ears were remarkable, for he had trained them from childhood with a sonic device calculated to develop the utmost in sensitivity. He evidently caught some small sound, for he produced from inside his clothing a coil of thin silken cord to which was affixed a folding grapple hook.

That he had practiced a great deal with the grapple was shown by the accuracy with which he tossed the hook. It snared the bundle of clothing. He hauled it toward him, remaining sheltered behind the shell pile.

Stunted and other men bounded up from where they had been lying and watching the bundle.

"He slicked us!" Stunted bawled.

Doc Savage gave the silk cord a brisk yank, stooped, and caught the garments, and was off like a sprinter. Guns made whooping thunder behind him. He pitched right, then left, zigzagging. Then he doubled over and changed course.

The last was a wise move. Some type of light machine gun blared out behind him. Its lead stream sickled off the marsh grass across the spot where he had vacated. The gunman did not fan his fire, but concentrated it, and the ammo drum went empty. Violent cursing followed.

Doc was some distance away now. He heard noises of men sloughing about in mud, and enraged grunts and growls.

"Monk!" he called softly. "Ham!"

The pair were waist-deep in mud. Doc extricated them. They joined him in flight.

"Monk, the baboon, led us into that bog!" Ham complained.

Monk found his pet pig before he shouted, "That's a lie! I was followin' that overdressed shyster!"

Sounds of pursuit dropped rapidly behind, and it became evident that they were going to get clear.

"We oughta do something about them rambunctious jaspers," Monk announced.

"The police will do something about it," Doc told him.

Doc SAVAGE, Monk, and Ham were in the skyscraper headquarters when the police telephoned the results of their raid, staged on the strength of the bronze man's information.

The oyster factory, they advised, had been found deserted. The "birds" had flown.

"They must have a bally tight organization to move that fast," Ham opined. "They knew their hangout was no longer a secret, so they cleared out."

Monk lifted his pig, Habeas, by one oversize ear and swayed the porker slowly back and forth, a procedure the shote seemed to enjoy.

"What gets me," muttered the homely chemist, "is what

that streak of a thing in the sky could have been. Did you see it, Doc?"

The bronze man nodded.

Monk persisted, "Hear the funny long crack of a noise it, or something like it, made?"

Doc nodded again, then said, "The men at the oyster factory mentioned the streak in the sky and the sound, as having some mysterious connection with their own project."

Monk let Habeas fall. "Say, what's behind all of this, anyway?"

The telephone rang.

"This is the central police station," a voice stated. "You seemed to be interested in that Willard Spanner killing, so I thought we'd better let you know his body has been stolen from the morgue."

"You mean Willard Spanner's clothing was stolen?" Doc queried.

"I mean his body," said the officer. "They got his clothing first. They came back about fifteen minutes ago for his body."

"Same crowd?"

"Sure."

"They got away?"

"They did. Or they have, so far."

Doc had switched an audio amplifier-and-loud-speaker into circuit with the telephone, a procedure he commonly followed on calls in which his aides might be interested. Monk and Ham heard.

"Jove!" Ham exploded. "They made no move to take the body the first time."

"At the oyster factory, I heard them speaking of 'taking care of the rest,'" Doc said slowly. "This matter of the body must have been the 'rest.'"

Ham lifted the bundle of clothing which Doc Savage had taken at the oyster factory.

"We still have Willard Spanner's garments here," he declared. "Since those men wanted them so badly, they may possibly furnish us with a clue."

Monk got up, grunting, "Maybe the duds had papers or something sewed in them, like they have in story books. Let's have a gander at 'em, as we lowbrows say."

The garments were tied together with tarred twine of the type which seagoing men call marlin. Ham took hold of it, after trying the knot, intending to break it; but finding it much stronger than he had expected, gave it up, grimacing, snapping his strained fingers.

Doc examined the knots.

"No sailor tied those," he decided.

"They didn't talk like sailors, either," Monk offered. "What part of the country d'you figure they came from, Doc?"

"The West, or the Southwest," the bronze man said, and, with no perceptible difficulty, broke the cord which had baffled Ham. He sorted through the pieces of clothing.

"They outfoxed us," he said. "Fixed this up as a decoy by that shell pile merely to draw me back, hoping to get a shot at me."

Monk squinted. "Meaning?"

"These are not Willard Spanner's clothes," Doc said. "They are for a much larger and fatter man."

Monk groaned, "We're sunk!"

"We have," Doc corrected him, "one chance."

## Chapter 3
## THE MAN FROM OKLAHOMA

THE bronze man lifted the telephone receiver and dialed a number.

"Police headquarters?" he asked. . . . "Homicide bureau, please." There was a brief wait. "Homicide? . . . This is Doc Savage speaking. I believe it is your custom to secure pictures of murder scenes, and also photographs of the body of the victim. I wonder if you would send me copies of the pictures taken of Willard Spanner."

"You can have them," advised the voice at the homicide bureau.

"By messenger, immediately," Doc requested.

That he had been promised the photographs so readily was not remarkable, since the bronze man held a high commission, no whit less effective because it was honorary, on the New York police force. The commission was a gesture of appreciation for past aid.

Doc Savage's life work was helping others out of trouble—those who deserved aid. It was a strange career, one with few financial rewards. But the bronze man did not need money, for he had access to a fabulous treasure trove. He followed his career for the return it gave in excitement and adventure. And he had five aides who followed it for the same reason.

Monk and Ham were two of the five. The other three were, at the moment, in upper New York State, where Doc Savage maintained a remarkable institution for making honest men out of such criminals as he caught, a treatment which entailed brain operations and which wiped out past memories. A course of vocational training followed the surgery.

Monk frowned, demanding, "How in the heck are those pictures gonna help us?"

Doc Savage did not answer, seemed not to hear. Monk showed no resentment at not getting an answer. It happened frequently. The homely chemist went out and came back with late editions of the leading newspapers.

"Lookit!" He pointed at headlines.

### UNPREDICTED RAIN OF COMETS
### SCIENCE CANNOT EXPLAIN

Those residents of New York City, particularly those residing near the marsh section of Long Island, were treated to the sight of a comet to-night. Many reported a loud crack of a sound and a streak of fire in the sky.

Inquiry develops that such phenomena have been reported within the last few days, from various sections of the United States.

Monk said, "And they kindly neglected to state just where the other comets were seen."

"Telephone the newspapers," Doc requested.

Monk went to the instrument, made several calls, and hung up, wearing a puzzled expression.

"The comets have appeared within the last two weeks," he reported. "Several were seen around San Francisco. That kinda hooks in with this Willard Spanner killing. But most of the comets were seen in Oklahoma, around Tulsa."

Doc Savage was examining the bundle of clothing.

"Come here," he said, and pointed at the label inside the coat.

### THE OIL MAN'S TAILOR
#### Tulsa, Oklahoma.

Monk grunted, "That'll bear looking into."

Doc Savage put in a long-distance telephone call, and because it was late, some time was required in obtaining the information which he desired. In the interim, a messenger arrived from police headquarters with a parcel of pictures. Finally, the bronze man secured from the Tulsa tailor, the name of the man for whom a suit answering the description of the one in the bundle had been made. It was a suit distinctive enough to be remembered, being rather loud in color.

"The garment was tailored for Calvert R. Moore, who is more commonly known as 'Leases' Moore," came the report from Tulsa.

"Just what do you know about this man Moore?" Doc asked.

"He is very wealthy." The Tulsa tailor hesitated. "He is also considered a bit sharp as a business man. Nothing crooked, you understand. Merely, well—a man who misses few bargains."

"What else?"

"He has disappeared?"

"He has what?"

"Disappeared."

"A kidnaping?" Doc demanded.

"There has been no indication of that. Leases Moore merely dropped out of sight two weeks ago, on the same day that Quince Randweil vanished."

"Quince Randweil?" Doc asked sharply. "Who is he?"

"The owner and operator of a local dog-racing track," explained the tailor.

"There is no indication of what became of these men?" Doc persisted.

"None."

"Have either of these men been considered crooked?" Doc asked.

"Oh, they ain't neither one been in jail, that anybody knows of," said the tailor, who seemed to be a frank and talkative individual.

MONK squinted at Doc when the conversation ended. "More angles?"

"Two men named Leases Moore and Quince Randweil vanished mysteriously in Tulsa, two weeks ago," Doc told him. "Leases Moore's clothing turned up in that bundle."

The bronze man now scrutinized the pictures of Willard Spanner's body. Spanner had been shot to death. Two bullets had hit him in the chest.

But it was another wound, a wrist cut, upon which the bronze man concentrated attention.

"This was not a new cut," he pointed out. "You will notice marks made by adhesive tape, indicating it was bandaged. The manner of the tape application indicates the work of a physician. The man would hardly have applied the tape himself in this manner. I observed this fact at the morgue, but unfortunately, not close enough to be sure."

Monk looked surprised. It was not often that the bronze man had to go back over ground he had already covered for information.

"But where's this getting us?" asked the homely chemist.

"Our problem is to ascertain whether the man seized in San Francisco was the one found dead in New York," Doc told him. "On the face of it, that seems an impossibility—for less than three hours elapsed."

Doc resorted to the long-distance telephone again. He first called San Francisco police. They gave him the name of the hotel at which Willard Spanner had been staying. Incidental was the information that Spanner had arrived in San Francisco only the previous day.

The call to the hotel was fruitful. Willard Spanner had slipped in the hotel bathroom, struck his arm against a glass shelf over the washstand, and the shelf had broken, cutting his wrist. The hotel physician had dressed the wound, which was undoubtedly the one the pictures showed.

"*Whew!*" Monk exploded. "Willard Spanner *was* seized in San Francisco a little over a couple o' hours before he was found dead in New York!"

Ham flourished his sword cane. "But it could not happen!"

Monk stood up. "The telephoning has taken time. There oughta be fresh newspapers out. I'll go get some."

He was back in a few moments. He looked excited.

"Lamp this!" he barked, and exhibited extra editions.

The headlines were large, black.

### SEEK SPANNER RANSOM IN FRISCO—$50,000 DEMANDED

A San Francisco newspaper editor late to-day received a note stating that Willard Spanner, reported slain in New York this afternoon, was alive, and would be released upon the payment of fifty thousand dollars.

There was more of it, but the opening paragraph told the substance of the story.

Monk eyed Doc. "Hadn't we better look into this? Ham or me can go."

"We will all three go," Doc told him. "We will leave a note advising the other three members of our outfit to do what investigating they can, when they return from up-State. They can handle the New York end."

"What about the Tulsa, Oklahoma, angle?" Ham queried.

"We will stop off there," Doc advised.

TULSA likes to call itself the capital of the oil industry. Oil men do much flying. The Tulsa municipal airport is a source of local pride. Facilities and appointments are excellent.

Floodlights fanned brilliance as Doc Savage dropped his big speed plane in for a landing. The night force of mechanics stood about and stared. Some one ran to a near-by flying school, and shortly afterward there was a stampede to the tarmac of aëronautical students in all states of partial dress. It was not often that a plane such as the bronze man was flying was seen.

The speed ship was trimotored, and all three motors were streamlined into the wings until their presence was hardly apparent to the eye. The hull breasted down so that the plane could be landed on water, and the landing gear was retractable. The cabin was as bulletproof as was feasible, and inside were innumerable mechanical devices.

One individual did not seem interested in the bronze man's remarkable craft. He was a pilot in greasy coveralls who tinkered with the motor of a shabby-looking cabin monoplane over near the edge of the field.

He had dropped into the airport two hours before, and had been tinkering with his plane since. He had given short answers to the field mechanics, and thereafter had been left severely alone. It was now not long before dawn.

Doc Savage taxied over near the covered pit which held the gasoline hoses and cut all three motors. He stepped out of the plane and glanced into the east, as if seeking the sunrise.

"I've heard a lot about that bird," a flying student said,

unconscious that his whisper carried. "They say he designed that sky wagon himself and that it's the fastest thing of its size in the world."

Over at the edge of the field, the motor of the shabby cabin monoplane came to life. It roared loudly.

A small crowd surged around Doc's speed ship. They were flying men, greatly interested in a sample of the most advanced aërial conveyance. Most of them were interested in the layout of navigating instruments, in the robot pilot.

"I've heard this bus can take off and fly herself, and can be controlled by radio from a distance," a man said. "Is that a fact?"

One man was interested in the tail structure of the plane. He found himself alone back there. He flashed a long knife out of his clothing, ripped and gouged, and got open one of the inspection ports through which the control connections could be examined.

The man was thin; his movements had the speed of an animal. He whipped a series of three packages out of his clothing. They were connected by wires, and none were extraordinarily large. He thrust all three inside the inspection port, then closed the flap. Then he backed away into the darkness.

He blinked a small flashlight four times rapidly.

Motor a-howl, the cabin monoplane scudded away from the edge of the field. It headed straight for Doc's ship.

THE bronze man had to all appearances been occupied entirely in answering questions. But now he flashed into life, and seemed to know exactly what he was doing.

"Run!" he rapped at those standing about. "Get away from here! Quick!"

His great voice was a crash. It was compelling. Three men turned and fled without knowing why. The others retreated more slowly. They saw the oncoming cabin plane.

"Runaway ship!" some one howled.

Monk and Ham had stepped out of Doc's speed craft. They whirled to clamber back inside. But Doc Savage was ahead of them. He banged the cabin door in their faces, then lunged to the controls. The big motors whooped out at the first touch of the starters, and because they were hot, instantly hauled the speed craft into motion.

There was a tense second or two. Then it became evident

that Doc's plane was going to get clear. The men scattered from the path of the oncoming cabin monoplane. It went bawling past, doing no harm, except to give an aviator student a bad fright.

All who looked could see by the floodlight glare that the cabin was empty.

"Where's the pilot of that trap?" yelled the night field manager. "Such damned carelessness——"

He swallowed the rest. An unexpected thing was happening. A weird thing.

The old cabin ship had gone on, but instead of crashing into the fence at the edge of the field, as every one expected, it was turning—swinging as if a hand of uncanny skill were at the controls. It arched completely around and cannoned after the speed plane of Doc Savage.

The onlookers gasped, unable to believe what they were witnessing. They saw the pig, Habeas Corpus, come hurtling from the cabin of Doc's speed ship. Then they saw the bronze man appear in the cabin door.

He seemed to be trying to reach the tail of his plane, for he dropped off and sought to seize it as it went past. But the streamlined metal surface offered no grip. He was knocked aside and the ship went on.

Doc scrambled to all fours, seized the pig, Habeas, and fell flat with him. He lay there.

The shabby cabin ship charged in pursuit of the speed plane. The two ships approached at an angle. They met. The whole world seemed to go in blinding white.

The tarmac jumped, quaked. Windows fell out of operations office, hangars, the flying school buildings across the paved road. The side of one huge hangar buckled inward, and the roof came down as if a giant had stepped upon it.

The noise of the blast thumped and rolled and finally went into the distance like a heavy salvo of thunder.

Out where the two planes had met, there was a hole in the earth which would require two days to fill.

# Chapter 4
## OKLAHOMA ACTION

Doc Savage heaved up from where he had lain after failing to reach the tail of his plane. He ran—not toward the blast scene, but toward his men. Monk and Ham veered out to meet him, Ham unconsciously knocking dust off his natty raiment.

"Why'd you quit the plane?" Monk gulped. "Why didn't you take it into the air?"

"We were low on gas," Doc clipped. "That other ship probably had full tanks. It would have caught me. Come on!"

"But there wasn't nobody in it!" Monk exploded as he ran.

"Radio control," Doc told him, racing toward the edge of the flying field. "The ship was loaded with explosive!"

Monk and Ham pounded in his wake. The pig, Habeas, trailed.

Monk puffed, "But no radio control would——"

"This was a device which would send the plane toward a sending set operating on a designated frequency," Doc advised over his shoulder. "It is merely an adaption of the robot pilot which keeps planes in the path of a beam radio."

Monk yelled, "But there wasn't no sending set in our bus!" He ran with the waddling gait of a scared bull ape.

"On the contrary, there was," Doc rapped. "A fellow stuck a tiny portable set inside the empennage shortly before the excitement started. I saw him. There wasn't time to grab him."

"Where'd he go?" Monk roared, and put on more speed.

"This way," Doc said, and vaulted the metal fence which surrounded the field.

Ham tried to use too much care in mounting the fence, with the result that he slipped, caught his immaculate afternoon coat on the barbed top strand and left the entire back of it behind.

"Where'd the pilot of the plane go?" he gritted.

"This way," Doc said. "He and the fellow who planted the decoy radio transmitter probably intended to meet."

They covered a hundred yards. Weeds about them were tall. The rotating beacon at the airport flashed white light at regular intervals. The airport floodlights were still on, making a great glow.

Doc Savage stopped, breathed a "Listen!"

Monk and Ham both strained their ears. They heard crickets, sounds of distant automobiles and voice murmur back at the flying field, but nothing else.

"The two are heading a bit to the right," Doc decided.

Monk and Ham showed no surprise, being aware of the bronze man's almost superhuman ability to hear. Countless times, they had seen him employ the sonic device with which he had developed his aural organs over a period of years.

Weeds became more profuse, then ended suddenly at the edge of an evidently little used road. There was a fence which they managed to keep from squeaking while climbing it. Clouds were making the night darker than before. They crawled up an embankment, evidently some kind of dike. Hulks like gigantic pill boxes loomed ahead. The night air acquired a definite odor.

"Oil tank farm," Ham decided in a whisper.

"Not being used," Doc added.

Ham asked in a surprised tone, "How can you tell?"

"The odor," Doc told him. "The smell of fresh crude oil is lacking."

Off to the side, a smaller, squarer hulk appeared. A light came on suddenly and whitened soiled windows. Inside was the gleam of dull gray machinery and brasswork which needed cleaning.

"The pump station," Monk grunted. "They must be using it for a headquarters."

Ham offered abruptly, "Doc, what say the missing link and myself circle and watch the rear, while you are reconnoitering?"

"Do not get too close," Doc requested.

Ham eased away in the darkness, Monk on his heels. The pig, Habeas, trailed them. They made half a circle and were behind the pump station. There was a pile of pipe there. They eased behind that.

Two men arose from the darkness and put guns against their backs.

"What the——" Monk began.

"I know it's a shame," said one of the men. "You two boys must have thought we were pretty dumb."

Monk and Ham turned around. There was not much light, but they did not need light to observe that the guns were genuine, and of large caliber. The hammer of each weapon was also rocked back.

Habeas, the shote, faded away into the night with the soundlessness of a shadow.

Monk jutted his small head forward to peer more closely at the two who had sprung the surprise.

"You'll get eyestrain," one of the men admonished. "We're the two yahoos you followed here from the airport, if that's what's worryin' you."

The speech had been in whispers, unconsciously. Now Ham decided to speak aloud, hoping to advise Doc of their predicament.

"You two—*ugh!*"

He doubled over painfully. His mouth flew wide, and breath came past his teeth with such force that it carried a fine spray with it.

The man who had jammed a gun into Ham's middle with great force hissed, "We know the bronze guy is around in front. You try to tip him again and you'll spring a leak just about the third button of that trick vest!"

The other man said, "We hate to part you two from that big bronze shadow, but we fear we must. Shake a leg."

They backed away from the pump station, came to a path, and went down it. Monk and Ham were searched expertly as they walked, and relieved of the only weapons they carried— the small supermachine pistols which were Doc Savage's own invention.

"What's the idea?" Monk demanded.

"A gentleman wants to see you," one of the two replied.

"Who?"

"A man whom I'm more than half convinced is one of the cleverest gents in the world," said the other. "And mind you, partner, I know all about the rep of this Doc Savage."

"The guy who thought up that bright idea of fixing the plane bomb so it would chase a radio transmitter, and who also rigged up that burglar alarm at the oyster plant in New York?" Monk hazarded.

"Sure," said the man. "He's thought of some other things that would surprise you, too."

"Shut up!" advised the man's companion. "Some day you'll talk yourself inside a wooden jacket, and they'll sprinkle some nice clean dirt on you."

They went on in silence. There was roadway underfoot now—a dirt road, hard packed by heavy traffic.

"What about Doc?" Ham demanded.

"We ain't ambitious," said one of the captors. "We'll dispose of *you* first. He'll get his later."

They rounded a bend fringed by scrub oak and came suddenly upon a truck waiting. The truck was large and had a flat bed, the type of machine employed in hauling pipe and oil-field supplies.

A stubby man came forward, also a tall, thin one and a man who had, when flashlights were turned on, eyes which turned inward at intervals. It was Stunted and the rest of the coterie from New York.

"It's a regular reunion," Stunted chuckled.

"You got that sawed-off auto rifle to working?" Monk asked him.

"You bet," Stunted retorted. "I worked on it all the way from New York."

"You made a quick trip," Monk suggested.

"Sure," said Stunted. "We came in a——"

The man with the uneasy eyes whipped forward and slapped Stunted in the face. The force of the blow sent Stunted reeling back.

"What in blue blazes was the idea?" he snarled.

"You got a head like a toad," the man with the weird eyes snapped. "You was gettin' set to tell this monkey how we came back!"

"Huh!" Stunted fell silent, his mien sheepish.

Two pairs of greasy overalls and two equally soiled jumpers were produced. Menace of gun muzzles persuaded Monk and Ham to don these. They were compelled to sit on the flat bed of the truck, legs dangling over, and the machine got into motion.

Some of the captors stood erect on the bed platform. All

wore work clothing. They might have been some pipeline crew, bound into the fields.

"Let out a bleat and we'll certainly weight you down with lead," Monk and Ham were advised.

"Deuced boorish treatment," Ham said primly.

Some one laughed. The truck had a rear and gear grind and the sound went on and on, like something in pain. There was little traffic on the road, passenger cars for the most part. Once two policemen on motorcycles went past with a violent popping, but did not even glance at the truck.

Later, a ramshackle delivery car ran around the truck with a great clatter, cut in sharply and went on.

"Durn nut!" growled the truck driver.

Hardly more than ten minutes later, there was a loud report from a front wheel. The truck began to pound along in a manner which indicated a flat tire. The driver pulled over to the edge of the road. He began to swear, making no effort to get out and start repairs.

"You waiting for it to thunder, or something?" Stunted demanded.

"No spare tire along," said the driver. He alighted and used a flashlight until he found a large-headed roofing nail embedded in the tire. He kicked the nail and swore some more.

Down the road, a light flashed.

"Who's that?" a man demanded.

One of the men advanced down the road, keeping in the darker shadows beside the ditch. He returned soon.

"Delivery truck with a puncture," he reported. "It's that nut who passed us. He must've picked up another of them nails."

"He got a spare tire?" Stunted demanded.

"Seems to have," said the other.

Stunted chuckled. "Old Nick takes care of his own, eh, boys?"

Two guns were kept jammed against Monk and Ham. Three men went forward. There was a wait, during which pounding noises came from the delivery truck, then a sharp exchange of commands. One of the men called back, "Come on, you birds."

The guns urged Monk and Ham forward. They came to the truck.

The driver was an unusual-looking fellow, having a tremendous girth and a right leg which twisted out in grotesque fashion. His face was puffy. He had a swarthy skin and dark hair.

"This Mexican has kindly consented to give us a lift," chuckled Stunted, and flourished his sawed-off auto rifle at the swarthy driver.

The driver wailed, "Señors, my poor car——"

"Shut up!" advised Stunted. "You just drive us carefullike. We'll tell you where to go."

An hour later, they were traveling where there seemed to be no road at all. The sun was rising, but not yet in view.

"Turn right," Stunted advised, and they pulled down a precipitous bank and took to the gravel bed of a dry stream.

The swarthy driver complained, "Señors, my poor car will never run back over thees road. Tell me, how shall I return?"

"You'll find out all about that," Stunted told him.

"Hey!" one of the men barked. "Lookit!"

They craned necks. After a moment of that, they all heard a long, rending crack of a sound, and a weird streak of luminance appeared in the reddening sky. It seemed to stretch in an arch away into the infinite reaches of the heavens.

"Now, what?" Stunted grumbled. "Could that mean that——"

"Shut up, stupid!" the man with the peculiar eyes rapped.

The streak in the sky died away quickly, vanishing completely.

The rickety truck went on. In spite of the deserted appearance of the region, it was undoubtedly a road of sorts which they traveled. Twice, when they crossed sandy stretches, the men alighted and, with leafy boughs, carefully brushed out their tracks.

"Don't want 'em to look too recent," Stunted grinned.

The driver showed alarm. "What ees thees mean, señores?"

"In about three minutes, you'll know," Stunted leered.

The driver reacted in a fashion which was the more surprising, since he had previously shown a surprisingly small degree of backbone. He lashed out a fist toward Stunted.

It was a terrific blow. After it, Stunted's face would never look quite the same. Stunted fell out of the seat.

The driver emitted a blood-curdling yell and took to the opposite direction. He had chosen his spot well. A narrow rip of a draw entered the creek bed at that point. The dark man dived into that. His game leg seemed, if anything, to add to his speed. He disappeared.

The truck unloaded in roaring confusion. Wild shots were discharged. The men rushed into the gully. Some climbed the steep sides. After the first excitement, they used flashlights and searched more thoroughly. They found no trace of the fugitive.

"One of that guy's ancestors must have been a rabbit," Stunted grumbled.

They consulted for a time. There seemed to be little they could do about it.

"That Mex won't know what it's all about, anyhow," some one decided.

They got in the truck, and it had rolled hardly less than half a mile before it pulled out on a flat and stopped before what seemed to be literally a mansion.

It was a great brick building, two stories in height, with flanking wings and a garage capable of housing four cars. Situated on the outskirts of a city such as Tulsa, the mansion would have aroused no more than admiration, but located here in a wilderness of scrub oak and hills, with no roads worthy of the name near by, it was a startling sight.

The headlights played on the place at closer range, and it became evident in the early morning light that many of the windows were broken out, that the woodwork needed painting, that the lawn had not been trimmed in years. Yet the place could not, from the style of architecture, have been more than ten years old.

Monk asked, "How did this dump come to be here?"

"Osage Indian," Stunted leered through his smashed face. "Heap oil, catchum many dollars. Build um brick tepee. Then Osage, him turn around and croak. Tepee, him go pot."

"You're quite a smart guy, ain'tcha?" Monk growled.

They unloaded beside the mansion. A lean, brown man stepped out to meet them, squinting in the headlights. He had a rifle.

"We got two visitors for the chief," said Stunted.

"The chief just left," said the man with the rifle.

"Oh," said Stunted. "So it was him in——"

The man with the queer eyes screamed, "Damn you! All the time about to let things slip where these guys can hear!" He slugged Stunted heavily with his right fist.

Stunted's face was already sore from the blow landed by the swarthy delivery truck driver. The new pain maddened him. He went down, but retained his grip on his rifle, rolled over and lifted the weapon.

Men shouted, and sprang forward to prevent bloodshed.

Ham kicked Monk on the shins. Monk bellowed in pain and knocked down the handiest of his captors.

"The house!" Ham yelled. "They'd shoot us down before we could get across the clearing."

The house entrance was not more than a dozen feet away. They dived for it. A rifle slug tore an ample fistful of splinters off the edge of the door as they went through.

## Chapter 5
## FLAME THREAD

THE door was of some rich dark wood. Paint had peeled off, but the panel still retained its strength. Monk tossed out one long, hairy arm and slammed it. Echoes of the slam echoed through the house, which seemed virtually devoid of furniture.

Monk snarled, "You didn't need to kick me!"

"It was a pleasure," Ham told him. "I mean—I had to get you in action."

"Yeah!" Monk hit a door at the end of the reception hall where they stood. It was not locked. Momentum sent him across the chamber beyond on hands and knees.

There was a table at this side of the room. It had been thrown hastily together from rough wood. But there was nothing crude about the apparatus on it. Black insulating panels, knobs, and switches glistened.

Monk veered for the apparatus.

Ham yelled. "That won't help us!"

"Heck it won't!" Monk began fumbling with the dials. "This is a bang-up radio transmitter-and-receiver."

"I know it." Ham was making for another door. "What good will the bally thing do us?"

"Bring help." Monk made a fierce face. "Trouble is, I gotta figure out what knob does what."

Glass crashed out of a window, a rifle smashed, and the high-powered slug clouted completely through the walls, missing Monk by something less than a yard.

"Take your time," Ham told Monk dryly. "You only have to get that thing working and call until you raise a station. Five or ten minutes should be all you need."

Two more rifle bullets came in, showering Monk with plaster dust.

Monk made another fierce grimace and gave up working with the radio mechanism. He followed Ham into another room—which held numerous boxes, all of them of stout wood, none of them bearing markings which might have hinted at their past contents.

Monk upset a box, found it empty, and began heaving the containers against the door to block it. Rifle lead went through the boxes with splintering ease.

"Them high-powered guns kinda complicate things," Monk grunted.

They retreated, finding an empty chamber, then one with cheap canvas camp cots on the floor. Blankets were piled carelessly on the cots. Odds and ends of clothing lay about. Cigarette stubs spotted the floor.

Monk scooped up an armload of the clothing.

"Maybe there's something in the pockets that'll tell us things," he said.

He carried the clothing as he lumbered in the wake of Ham. The latter peered through a window, rubbed dust off the pane, looked again, and began knocking glass out with quick blows.

"Sure, we can just walk away," Monk told him sourly. "They'll stand by and sing us a bedtime story, or something."

"Look, you accident of nature!" Ham pointed an arm. "There is a car behind the house, which we failed to sight before."

Monk looked and saw that the car was large and powerful; it was inclosed. He helped smash the rest of the glass out, let Ham jump down to the ground, then followed, retaining the clothes and grunting loudly as he landed.

They reached the car together and crowded each other getting inside. Monk threw his right hand for the switch, then made a fist of the hand and struck the instrument panel.

"Blast it!" he grated. "They *would* take the key out!"

He flopped down on the floorboards, tore a fistful of wiring bodily from under the instrument panel, took one rather long second in sorting them over, then joined the ends of two and the motor whooped into life.

"Handy to know how these cars are wired," Monk grinned.

The machine moaned and pitched in second gear, making an ample circle around the house. Ham drove recklessly, shoving his head up at intervals to ascertain their course. Brush switched the underside of the car. A loud clanking sound came from one of the windows, and Monk squinted at a spidery outline of cracks which had appeared magically in the glass.

"Glory be!" he snorted. "This chariot has bulletproof glass! There sure is a Santa Claus!"

Ham sat up, drove more carefully, and they pitched into the obscure roadway by which they had arrived. Ham was overanxious. He put on too much speed and the car skidded, went into a ditch and stopped. He looked outside.

"We can back out," he said.

Then he sat very still, for he had felt a small spot of metallic coldness come against the back of his neck. He had felt gun muzzles on his bare skin on other occasions.

"We should have looked in the back seat," he told Monk.

The homely chemist reared up and peered around. The gun was removed from Ham's neck and shoved almost against Monk's flattened nose. It was a single-action six-shooter of tremendous size.

A young woman held the gun with one hand.

She was a lean, tanned young woman with a few freckles, not at all hard to look at. Her eyes were a rather enchanting blue, and she showed teeth which would have graced the advertising of any dentrifice. It was not a smile which showed her teeth. Rather, it was a grimace intended to convey fierceness.

"These are hollow-point bullets," she advised. "They would just about remove your head."

Monk swallowed. "Now, listen——"

"Shut up!" she requested. "I never saw you before, and don't know you. Maybe you don't know me. But you've heard of me. I'm Lanca Jaxon."

"Oh," said Monk.

"You've heard enough to know I'd as soon shoot you as not, or sooner," said the girl.

"Two-gun Lanca Jaxon," murmured Monk, who had never before heard of any young woman with such a name.

"A wise-cracker, like the rest of them," the girl said, frostily. "I never dreamed there could be so many alleged humorists in one gang of crooks."

Monk said, "Young lady——"

"Quiet!" she snapped. "One of these bullets won't be funny. You two sit still. I'll get out and then you get out. I'll tell you what to do next."

She got out.

Three men came from the adjacent brush. Their arrival was so sudden that it was evident that they were men who had scattered to the edges of the clearing surrounding the house when the action had started, that they might be in a position to shoot down any one attempting to cross the open space. Each of the three held a gun.

"We'll take it over now, Lanca," one said.

The young woman looked at them very hard. She seemed to be trying to make up her mind about something of great importance. The gun was perfectly steady in her hand. She shrugged at last, and one of the men came over and got the gun she had wielded.

"You helped us a lot," he chuckled.

The girl said nothing.

Puffing and growling at each other, the remaining members of the gang arrived shortly. They surrounded Monk and Ham. Discussion followed. Three of them favored shooting Monk and Ham immediately. Others held saner convictions.

"Let the big boss decide," suggested the man with the peculiar-behaving eyes.

They walked Monk and Ham back toward the house.

The man with the queer eyes linked an arm with the girl, and said, "My dear Lanca, would you explain just how you happened to be in that car? And with a gun, too? It was Stunted's old six-shooter, wasn't it?"

The girl managed to say nothing in a very vehement manner. The man's eyes seemed to shift more queerly than usual. He conducted the girl into another part of the house.

Monk and Ham found themselves in the room with the radio apparatus. One of the captors went out, came back with a lariat of the cowboy variety, and they were bound with expert thoroughness.

"What'll we do with 'em?" Stunted asked, nursing his bruised features.

"I'll find out," said one of the men, and went to the radio apparatus. He switched the mechanism on. It was apparently of all-wave construction, because an ordinary broadcast program began coming from the receiver. It was a newscast. The commentator had a pleasant voice, rapid enunciation.

"—weird phenomena reported from various sections of the nation," said the voice from the radio.

The man at the apparatus started to turn knobs.

"Wait!" Stunted barked. "Get that!"

THE man reset the dial to the broadcast station.

"Some of the reports state that long ribbons of flame were seen in the heavens, accompanied by a weird crashing noise," said the radio newscaster. "Others insist they saw balls of flame. Astronomers, for the most part, insist that the phenomena witnessed are not meteors, as was at first believed. In no case has it been reported that a fallen meteor has been found."

One of the men laughed harshly, said, "It's got 'em worried."

"It'll have 'em a lot more worried before it's over," Stunted muttered.

"The last streak of flame in the heavens was reported over north-central Oklahoma and over Kansas," said the broadcaster. "This was hardly more than an hour ago——" The voice stopped coming from the radio. During the pause which ensued, crackle of papers in the distant radio station could be heard.

"Flash!" said the broadcaster, an undercurrent of excitement in his voice. "Here is an important item which just arrived."

"Aw, turn it off!" growled one of the men in the room. "Somebody has shot somebody else in Siberia or somewhere, probably."

Stunted snapped, "Nix! Get the news before we contact the chief."

They fell silent. The broadcaster was still rattling papers. He began speaking:

"It has just been announced that the explosion heard in

downtown Kansas City, and which broke studio windows in this station, was a blast which thieves set off to enter the vaults of the city's largest bank," said the newscaster. "The raid was on a gigantic scale, and daringly executed. At least ten men participated. Bank officials have not been able to make a check, but estimate that the thieves could have escaped with nearly three million dollars."

Stunted seemed to forget all about his facial injuries. He grinned from ear to ear and slapped a palm resoundingly against a thigh.

"Boy, oh boy!" he chortled. "Get that! Get that!"

"Shut up!" some one told him.

They were all intent on the radio now.

"A few minutes after the robbery, one of the strange streaks of fire in the sky, which have so mystified the nation, was sighted," said the radio announcer. "Police are investigating a theory that this might be connected with the robbery of the bank."

Stunted said, "They begin to smell a rat."

"This concludes our news broadcast," said the loud-speaker voice. "We will be on the air later with more details of the sensational robbery."

One of the men shifted the radio control knob, *clicked* a switch and got down on short-wave bands. All of the men looked suddenly and extraordinarily cheerful.

The man at the controls made adjustments, switching on the transmitter. Then he picked up a microphone and a small notebook, evidently a code book of some kind.

"Calling CQ, calling CQ," he said into the microphone. "Station W9EXF, calling CQ."

Monk blinked as he heard that. It was the accepted manner in which amateur radio stations took the air and sought to establish connection with other amateurs. The "CQ" was merely the radio "ham" manner of stating that the station wanted to talk with anybody who would answer.

Out of the radio loud-speaker came an answer.

"Station W9SAV calling station W9EXF," the voice said.

The man at the apparatus grinned, winked. He consulted the code book.

"I have two headaches to-day," he said, obviously using the code. "How are you feeling?"

"The two headaches you were looking for?" asked the distant voice, which was somewhat distorted.

"That's the two," advised the man in the room.

"Have you tried diagnosing them?" asked the voice from the loud-speaker.

The man at the apparatus consulted the code book.

"Sure, I diagnosed them," he stated. "But they ain't the kind of headaches that tell you things."

Monk scowled darkly as he listened. There were thousands of amateur radio stations on the air all over the country, and a conversation such as this would not arouse suspicion. The code was simple, so simple that any one knowing it was code could guess what many of the statements meant. But a casual listener would not catch the hidden significance.

The radio conversation continued.

"You talked about a big headache that you felt coming on, the last time we hooked up," said the distant voice. "Any sign of that one?"

"Nope," said the man in the room. "But I may get it yet."

Monk decided they were referring to Doc Savage.

"Otherwise, you are all well?" asked the loud-speaker voice.

"Nothing to complain about." The man at the transmitter hastily thumbed the code book. "How is your case of ptomaine—the one you got out of a can?"

"All cleared up," chuckled the radio voice.

Another look at the code book. "What do you suggest doing for my two headaches?"

"I'll see what the manual says," replied the far-away speaker.

The man at the transmitter laughed; then there was silence, during which Monk concluded that the "manual" referred to must be a cipher word designating the mysterious chief of the gang.

"The manual says to use two pills," growled the radio voice.

Grim expressions on the features of the men in the room as the radio conversation terminated showed Monk that they all knew, without referring to the code book, what a "pill" meant.

Stunted stood up, scowling.

"I don't like that," he said sourly.

"What's eating you?" the man with the queer eyes snapped.

"I ain't exactly a puritan," Stunted grunted. "But croakin'

these two guys in cold blood don't come in my bailiwick. If they've got a chance—sure! But just to plug 'em, feed 'em one of them pills a piece, which we all know darn well is the boss's word for a bullet—not me!"

"Turned champion of defenseless manhood?" the uneasy-eyed man grated.

"Nuts!" Stunted glared at him. "I ain't forgot that pop in the kisser you give me, you cock-eyed gazoo!"

"Cut it out, you two!" a man barked.

Stunted continued to glare. The eyes of the other man crossed, uncrossed; then he shrugged.

"Aw, the delivery-truck driver getting away had me fussed up," he said. "I guess I shouldn't have smacked you."

Stunted said, "We'll let it go at that, then."

The man with the unusual eyes drew a revolver.

"I'll take care of the pill doses," he said. "I'm not as finicky as some."

He shoved Monk and Ham, propelling them before him through the door. They staggered about, helpless to do more than voice threats, which had absolutely no effect. The lariat bindings on their arms were painfully tight, securely tied.

One of the men left behind in the room called, "Say, what about that delivery-truck driver?"

"We'll look for him after I take care of this," said the self-appointed executioner.

They passed outside. The man with uneasy eyes did not close the door. Evidently he was calloused enough to want the others to hear the shot.

"Walk!" the fellow snarled. "You guys make one move and I'll let you have it here, instead of outdoors."

Monk and Ham walked. They could hear the tread of the man behind them. It was heavy, regular, betraying no nervousness, and there was in it the quality of doom.

Then the tread stopped. Monk thought afterward that there was also a faint gasp about the same time that the tread ceased. But he was never quite sure.

It was a long moment before Monk, apprehensive lest their captor shoot, turned. The homely chemist's little eyes flew round. His mouth came open.

The delivery-truck driver stood spread-legged in the passage. He had the uneasy-eyed man gripped by the neck with both hands. He held the fellow off the floor with an obvious ease, and the victim was making no outcry, hardly twitching.

Monk ogled the delivery-truck driver. The latter had changed appearance vastly, although he still wore the same garments and his skin and hair were swarthy. But the limp was gone, and the stature and fabulous strength identified the man.

"Doc Savage!" Monk gulped.

# Chapter 6
## TWO GENTLEMEN OF TULSA

DOC SAVAGE was not choking his prisoner, but rather, working on the back of the man's neck with corded bronze finger tips, seeking out certain sensitive nerve centers on which pressure, properly applied, would induce a state of paralysis lasting some time.

When the man was completely limp, with only his eyes and breathing showing that he still lived, Doc lowered him to the floor.

Monk and Ham stood immobile while the lariat was untied. Doc's finger strength managed the knots with ease.

"You hear anything that was said in that room?" Monk whispered.

"Practically all of it," Doc told him. "After using the ruse of the delivery truck I——"

"You sprinkled nails in the road?" Ham interjected.

"Exactly," Doc answered. "I hired the truck from a fellow who chanced to pass, and his clothing as well. He was carrying some roofing material, and the nails came in handy. The make-up material I always carry on my person. It was largely dye and wax for the cheeks."

Monk and Ham shook off the ropes.

"Where's my hog?" Monk demanded.

"Back at that old tank farm," Doc said. "I had to leave him behind."

Monk waved an arm. "What do you make of this mess, Doc?"

"Their chief obviously robbed that Kansas City bank," the bronze man pointed out.

"Sure. But what about those streaks of fire in the sky? They've got a connection with the gang. And why'd they kill

Willard Spanner? And who is that girl and what's she doing here?"

"Always thinking about women," Ham told Monk sourly.

"She acted queer," Monk said. "This whole thing makes me dizzy."

Doc picked up the gun which had been carried by the man with the roving eyes. He fired it twice. The reports were ear-splitting.

"To make them think you have been executed," the bronze man breathed. "That should give us a moment or so respite."

They eased back through the house until they encountered a door which seemed to be locked. Ordinarily, a lock offered Doc Savage few difficulties. But this was a padlock and hasp—on the other side of the door.

"We will try it through the basement," the bronze man whispered.

The basement stairs were behind an adjacent door and squeaked a little, but not too much, as they went down.

The room below had once been a recreation chamber and held a huge billiard table, the green covering mildewed and rotted. The table must have been too ponderous to move away. Adjacent was the furnace room. Grimy windows afforded faint illumination.

Monk stopped the instant he was inside the room.

"Lookit!" he gulped.

Two men were handcuffed to the pipes which comprised the heating system.

ONE man was long and lean, and his body looked as if it were made of leather and sticks. He grinned at them, and his grin was hideous because he must have had false teeth and was not wearing them now. His clothing was fastidious. When he tried to beckon at them, it was evident that the thumb was missing from his right hand, making that grotesque, too.

"I dunno who you are, but you look like angels to me," he said thickly. "You don't belong to this crowd. Turn us loose, brother."

The second man was a sleek, round butterball, entirely bald. Not only was his body round, but his head, hands, and his arms were like jointed, elongated balls. He wore a ring which had once held an enormous setting, but the stone was missing now and the bent prongs of the ring showed it had been pried from place, possibly without removing the ring from his fat rounded fingers.

"Yuss," he said, and his words were a mushy hissing. "Turn us loose." His "loose" sounded like "lush."

Monk lumbered forward, asking, small-voiced, "Who are you birds?"

"Leases Moore," said the leathery man with the missing teeth and thumb.

"Quince Randweil," said the man with the rounded anatomy.

"Oh!" Monk squinted. "The two missing men from Tulsa?"

Ham snapped, "It was Leases Moore's clothing that we got hold of in New York!"

Leases Moore made a leathery grimace. "How do I know what they did with my duds? They took 'em when they grabbed me and Quince, here, out of my car."

"A bulletproof sedan?" Monk demanded, thinking of the machine in which they had tried flight.

"Sure," said Leases Moore. "Are you gonna turn us loose, or not?"

Doc went to the handcuffs, examined the links, and found them of no more than average strength. The pipes formed an excellent anchorage. He grasped the links, set himself, threw his enormous sinews into play and the thin metal parted with brittle snappings.

"I'm a son of a gun!" Quince Randweil made it "gunsh." "That tells me who you are."

Doc said nothing. He finished breaking the cuffs.

"I heard them talking about you," said Randweil. "You are Doc Savage." The way he said it, the name sounded like "Savvash."

"We had better get out of here," Doc said. "We will try that bulletproof car again."

They moved for the grimy window.

"Why were you being held?" Monk asked Leases Moore.

"That," Leases Moore said promptly, "is the blackest mystery a man ever went up against. They wouldn't tell us."

"Ransom?"

"They never mentioned it."

"Know their names?"

"Only that runt Stunted," said Leases Moore. "I never saw any of them before. Neither has Quince, here."

The rounded man bobbed all of his layers of fat in agreement.

"What is their game?" Monk asked.

"Search us," replied Leases Moore. "That's another mystery."

Doc Savage was working on the window, and now it came open with only minor squeaks of complaint.

"Out," said the bronze man, and boosted lean, leathery Leases Moore out through the aperture, after first taking a look around.

Quince Randweil was helped out next. He and Moore ran for the car, which had been wheeled back into the clearing and stood not many yards from the house. They ran boldly, with more haste than caution.

"The dopes," Monk growled. "They oughta be careful until we get out."

Then his jaw fell, for Leases Moore and Quince Randweil had started the car and were racing wildly away, the engine making a great deal of noise.

"Why, the double-crossers!" Monk gritted.

THE homely chemist had one pronounced failing. When he got mad, he was inclined to go into action without forethought of the consequences. Now he gave every indication of intending to climb out of the window and pursue the two fleeing men.

Doc dropped a hand on Monk's shoulder and settled him back on the basement floor.

"Wait," said the bronze man.

Upstairs, there was excited shouting. They had heard the car's departure. Guns began going off.

"They may not see who is in the car, and think we have escaped," Doc said. "That will give us a chance to prowl about this place, and possibly overhear something that will give us a better line on what is going on."

There was a staccato series of deafening reports, undoubtedly the voice of Stunted's cherished automatic rifle from which the barrel had been bobbed. Six guns made noises more nearly resembling firecrackers, and a shotgun boomed deeply.

There was a general charge of men from the house. They had obviously found in the hallway the senseless man with the queer eyes. Their wild rage might have been ludicrous under other circumstances.

Doc had gotten the soiled cellar window shut. They watched the excitement from behind its semiopaque screen.

Monk grinned. "Wonder how many of 'em was around?"

"I was unable to ascertain," Doc told him.

"Looks like more'n a dozen pulling out after that car," Monk offered. "Bet they're all leaving."

Doc Savage nodded, admitting, "Now is as good a time as any to look around."

They left the basement. The stair squeaking as they went up seemed louder than before, for the house was very silent.

"I didn't see that girl leave," Monk whispered. "Maybe we can find her and ask questions."

"And probably get shot," Ham said pessimistically.

They listened. Outdoors, in the morning sunlight, birds were making sound. Wind fluttered scrub-oak leaves.

Then they heard a voice. It was a steady, well-modulated voice, and it came in spells. There was also an answering voice, this one metallic and difficult to distinguish.

Monk breathed, "The radio! Somebody is using it!"

They made for the room which held the radio transmitting and-receiving apparatus. The door was open. One of the gang crouched over the mechanism, code book in one hand.

"So you think the weather should be warmer out in San Francisco," he was saying. "Yes, old man, that's probably true, and if, as you say, the manual says Frisco is a good place to be, we'll go——"

Behind Doc Savage and his companions, Stunted yelled, "Get them lunch hooks up, you three guys!"

Stunted, for all of his villainy, seemed to have some of the spirit attributed to old-time Western bad men. He disliked shooting down his victims in cold blood.

Had he, having come back unheard, or possibly never having left the house, started shooting without warning, Doc Savage or one of the pair with him, possibly all of them, would have died then. As it was, they reacted unconsciously to the command. They pitched forward into the radio room.

THE man at the radio apparatus cried out in excitement and went for a gun. He was infinitely slow.

Doc Savage, lunging across the room, sent out a fist and

the man bounced from it to the apparatus table. His weight ruptured wiring, and sparks sizzled and blue smoke arose.

The fellow had succeeded in freeing his gun from a pocket, and it bounced across the floor. Monk got it.

Out in the corridor, Stunted bawled, "You guys ain't got no sense a-tall! Come outa there! This cannon of mine'll throw lead right through them walls!"

Monk lifted his captured revolver, then lowered it, grimacing to his companions. "Maybe he won't shoot if he thinks we're unarmed."

Stunted lifted his voice, yelling for assistance. He did not enter the radio room. His bellow was ample to carry to his associates.

The man on the radio table fell to the floor, but did not move afterward. A spot on his coat was smoking where it had been ignited by an electric arc.

Ham went over and rubbed the smoulder out with a foot.

Doc threw up the window, making ample noise for Stunted to hear. Then he listened. Stunted had fallen silent. Doc picked up a chair and dropped it out of the window. Hitting the ground outside, it sounded not unlike a man dropping from the window.

Stunted swore, and they could hear him rushing for the door which led outside.

Doc led his two men out of the radio room—not through the window, but back into the corridor which Stunted had just vacated. They found a window on the opposite side of the house. It was open, and they dropped through.

Some distance away, men were calling excitedly. They had heard Stunted's yell. The latter answered them, advising what had happened. Doc and his men began to run.

It was the bronze man's sharp ears which ascertained that Stunted was running around the house and would soon glimpse them. Doc breathed a command. They all three slammed flat in the coarse grass.

Stunted came puffing around the corner of the house, and stopped. His breathing was distinct, loud. He muttered in a baffled way.

Doc and his men were perfectly motionless. It seemed incredible that they had escaped discovery so far. But Stunted was certain to sight them. Monk held his revolver expectantly.

Then a clear feminine voice called, "Stunted! They went around the other way!"

Doc and his two aides eyed the house. The girl who had said her name was Lanca Jaxon was leaning from a second-story window, looking down at Stunted and waving an arm around the building.

"They got out of a window on this side," she cried excitedly. "They ran around when they heard you coming. Hurry up! They may be getting away!"

Stunted hesitated, growling. Then he spun and sprinted around the house, deceived by the girl.

THE young woman looked at Doc Savage and his two men. She could see them plainly, looking down from above as she was. Her arm waved sharply, gesturing that they should take advantage of the moment to escape.

They did so.

Scrub brush hid just as a flood of men poured into the clearing which held the strange mansion. Monk had underestimated the numbers of the gang, for there was nearer two dozen than one, and all were heavily armed.

"What say we stick around and bushwhack with 'em?" Monk queried.

It was an idea which Doc Savage seemed to favor, but which proved unfeasible, for the gang found their trail and followed it with a rapidity which indicated that a skilled tracker was numbered among the enemy. Doc and his men were forced to retreat, closely followed.

A small stream, rocky of bottom, gave them respite. They waded along it—first going up and making a false trail on the bank, then reentering the water and wading downstream. They turned back toward the house, confident the pursuers would waste much time untangling the tracks.

"That girl," Monk breathed wonderingly. "She helped us! But before, she stopped our getting away."

"You know," Ham said slowly, "it strikes me that when she held us up the first time, it might have been an accident. She might have thought we were with the gang."

"But what was she doing in the car?" Monk countered.

Ham shrugged. "I don't know. Possibly trying to get away herself."

Monk looked at Doc. "What about this girl?"

The bronze man said, "That is why we are going back."

Their flight had taken them almost two miles before they encountered the stream, and now, going back, they were cautious. They spread, separating from each other by the space of a hundred feet or so, in order that if one were discovered, the other might be clear to render assistance.

IT was Ham who, some ten minutes later, stopped in a clearing and squinted intently. He could see a building, a large shack of a structure, through a rent in the scrub-oak thickets. The obvious newness of the building intrigued him. He veered over to find Doc.

He was surprised, and a little chagrined, to discover the bronze man had already sighted the structure and had climbed a small tree in order to view it more closely.

"Think it has any connection with this gang?" Ham asked.

"They have been around the building," Doc said. "All of them just went inside. They had that girl along."

Ham exploded, "But I thought they were tailing us!"

"They gave that up some minutes ago," Doc advised him.

The bronze man whistled a perfect imitation of a bird common to Oklahoma, giving the call twice. It was the signal which they had agreed upon to summon each other, and Monk ambled up shortly, his small eyes curious.

"That shed of a building," Doc told him. "All of our friends seem to have gone inside it."

Monk swung up a small tree with an ease that could not have been bettered by one of the apes which he so closely resembled. He peered for a moment.

"That thing don't look like an ordinary shed," he said. "It's kinda round, for one thing."

The scrub oaks were thick, and down in a small valley which they found it necessary to cross, briars and small thorny bushes interlaced to form a barrier that they penetrated but slowly. On either side of the defile trees grew high, so that view of the shed was cut off completely.

They were still in the arroyo when they heard a long, brittle crack of a noise. It was distinct, and very loud, with an utterly distinct quality. They had heard that noise before—in New York City, and in Oklahoma. It was a noise such as had been heard, according to newspaper and radio reports, by many persons in various parts of the United States. Always, it had been accompanied by threads of flame in the sky.

Doc and his two aides looked upward. There was no trace of a fiery ribbon in the heavens.

"Come on!" Doc rapped. "Let's get to that shed."

They raced forward. A moment later, Monk emitted an excited howl.

"That shed!" he bawled. "It's afire!"

THE shed must have been soaked with some inflammable compound, some substance which burned even more readily than gasoline, for it was a crackling pyre of flame when they reached it.

Trees, ignited by the terrific heat, were bursting into flame as far as a score of yards from the structure.

Doc and his men circled the spot. They saw nothing, heard no screams which would indicate human beings inside the burning structure. They would have been dead by now, anyway. There was nothing for the bronze man and his aides to do but to stand by and extinguish such of the flames as threatened to spread and become a forest fire.

Eventually, they went back to the house where they had been first attacked. Their attackers had flown thoroughly. The radio transmitting-and-receiving apparatus had been smashed. The odds and ends of clothing were gone.

Doc Savage had no finger-printing outfit with him, but managed to improvise one by employing a mixture of ordinary pulverized pencil lead and burned cork on white surfaces in the kitchen regions.

He examined these, using the bottom which he broke from a milk bottle for a magnifier. He looked intently for some time at the prints thus brought out.

Monk and Ham watched him. Both were fully aware of the facility with which the bronze man retained a mental image. They were willing to bet he could run through a finger-print classification days later and pick out any prints which matched those he was viewing now.

They searched for some time, but the house offered nothing more to solve the mystery of what was behind the murder of Willard Spanner, and the robbery of some millions of dollars from a Kansas City bank. Neither was there a clue to the meaning of the streaks in the sky and the accompanying cracking noises.

They went back to the shed, which had burned itself down. Poking through the hot embers was a procedure more fruitless than the search of the house. The incredibly hot fire had consumed everything inflammable, had melted together such metal work as there had been inside, making it unrecognizable, except for what apparently had been two large and excellent metal-working lathes.

"We're drawing blanks fast," Monk said.

Ham was sober. "I wonder what happened to that gang and the girl? Were they burned to death?"

Doc Savage said nothing.

They found the pig, Habeas Corpus, on their way back to Tulsa.

## Chapter 7
## PERIL IN FRISCO

THEY spent four hours investigating in Tulsa. Interesting things came to light.

The revolver which Monk had secured from the man knocked out in the radio room of the strange house in the brush, had been sold to Leases Moore a year previously. Further inquiry brought to light the fact that Leases Moore had purchased a number of firearms, revolvers, shotguns, and automatic rifles, during the past six months.

"Which makes me think of Stunted's bobtailed automatic rifle," Monk growled.

The house in the hills had been built by an Osage made wealthy by oil, who had later died. This fact, corroborating what the gang had told Monk, Doc Savage secured from a rather remarkable "morgue" of personal sketches maintained by a feature writer on the *Graphic*, a Tulsa morning newspaper.

The feature writer was a dresser whose sartorial perfection rivaled that of Ham, and he was a mine of information. It seemed that he kept in his morgue bits of information about all persons of importance in and about Tulsa.

Doc Savage was enabled, through the morgue, to make an interesting scrutiny of the careers of Leases Moore and Quince Randweil.

Leases Moore was a broker of oilfield leases; in popular parlance, a "lease robber." He had never been in the penitentiary. That was about all that could be said for his business tactics. He was sharp, squeezing and scheming, qualities, it seemed, which had made him a millionaire.

Quince Randweil had started life as a small-time gambler, had trafficked in liquor during prohibition, and had later taken over the local dog-racing track, a profitable affair indeed. He was also reported to be the undercover gambling czar locally, and not above turning a dishonest penny now and then.

But, like Leases Moore, he had never been convicted of a crime more serious than overtime parking, speeding, parking without lights and even jay-walking.

Of these trivial offenses, there was an incredible array of convictions. Doc Savage asked about that.

"The police tried to ride him out of town by picking him up on every conceivable charge," advised the sartorially perfect *Graphic* feature writer. "That was two years ago. It didn't work."

The really important development of the investigation came from the local airport. Monk turned it up when he perused the list of passengers taking planes that morning. He was excited when he got Doc Savage on the telephone at the *Graphic*.

"The Frisco angle is getting hot, Doc!" he declared.

The bronze man queried, "Yes?"

"Leases Moore and Quince Randweil caught the morning plane for San Francisco," Monk advised.

Doc Savage did not hire a fast plane for the trip to San Francisco, as might ordinarily have been his course. There was a regular airliner due shortly, and it was faster than anything available for a quick charter. When the liner pulled out, he and his two aides were aboard it.

The plane had a radio. Doc communicated with New York, consulting his three aides who were there—"Johnny," "Long Tom," and "Renny." They had turned up nothing of importance in connection with the death of Willard Spanner.

At the first stop, Doc bought newspapers. There was much news concerning the flame streaks in the sky. Police were beginning to connect the phenomena with criminal activities, for in three distinct cases, in addition to the bank robbery in Kansas City, profitable crimes had been committed shortly before the weird streaks appeared in the heavens.

Doc and his two companions read the headlines while the plane was being fueled, and punctuated their reading with munches at sandwiches secured at the airport restaurant. Perhaps that was why they failed to notice a lean, neatly dressed man watching them.

The lean man was careful to keep his scrutiny furtive. He had boarded the plane in Tulsa, along with three other passengers in addition to Doc's party. He had two suitcases—one of medium size, one very large. He had seated himself well forward in the plane and had not once looked in Doc Savage's direction with anything bordering more than usual interest. He was doing his watching now from outside the airport restaurant window.

After the fueling, the man was first to enter the plane. He stooped over quickly, opened his small suitcase and took out an object which at first might have been mistaken for a bundle of tightly wound steel wire. He walked back and tucked this in one of the baggage racks where it would not be observed.

He left the plane, went hurriedly to the restaurant, and put in a long-distance call to an Arizona city. The promptness with which the call was completed indicated the other party had been awaiting it. The man consulted a code book.

"The weather is perfect," he said.

"Swell," said the voice over the wire. "We will pick you up, understand?"

"I understand," said the man.

He hung up, returned to the plane, and resumed his seat just before the giant craft took the air, motors making high-pitched sound outside the sound-proofed cabin. The air was rough, and the ship pitched slightly.

Below was an expanse of terrain not especially inviting to the eye, being composed mostly of sand and sagebrush, with here and there a butte, hardly impressive from the air, to break the monotony. The plane flew for two hours. The afternoon was well along.

The lean man stooped over and opened his large suitcase. It held a parachute. He had some difficulty wriggling into the harness, bending over as he was in order to avoid notice. When he had the harness almost in place, he lifted his head to see if he had attracted attention.

He had. Doc Savage was already in the aisle, and coming forward.

The lean man dived for the door. He had difficulty getting it open against the force of the propeller slipstream, but finally succeeded and lunged through. The face was triumphant. But the expression changed quickly. A hand—it felt like the clamp of some metal-compressing machine—had grasped his ankle.

The man cursed shrilly. He hung down from the plane, smashed about by the terrific rush of air, only the grip on his ankle preventing him from falling clear. His body battered the hard plane fuselage. Then he was slowly hauled upward toward the plane door.

Desperate, the man whipped out a gun. He was not unlike a rag held in a stiff breeze, and his first shot went wild. Then, grasping the edge of the cabin door, he took deliberate aim.

Doc Savage let him fall. It was the only move that would preserve the bronze man's life.

THE lean man fell away behind, turning over and over in the air. That he had made parachute jumps before was evident from the way in which he kicked his legs to stop his gyrations in the air. Then he plucked the ripcord and the silk parachute blossomed out whitely.

The plane was in an uproar. Passengers yelled excitedly and crowded to the windows on the side of the door, upsetting the equilibrium of the plane and causing the pilot to do some howling of his own.

Doc Savage lunged to the side of the pilot.

"Follow that man down!" he rapped.

Such was the quality of compelling obedience in the bronze man's remarkable voice that the pilot obeyed without stopping to reason out why he should.

Monk charged forward, reached Doc and demanded, "Why'd that guy jump?"

Doc Savage sent one glance fanning the horizon and saw nothing to cause alarm. There was no signal visible below.

"Search the plane!" he said crisply.

Passengers objected strenuously to having their baggage rifled, and there was no time for explanations. Ham lost his temper and knocked out a young salesman who tried to defend a stout black case which, when Ham opened it, proved to contain a small fortune in gem samples.

Monk lost numerous of the red bristles which served him

as hair to a fat woman who had no idea of seeing her fitted case opened by the simian chemist.

The pilot still fought the controls. The associate pilot and the hostess trying to do their bit toward restoring calm, only added to the bedlam.

It was Doc Savage who found the bomb that the lean man had hidden. He smashed a window and heaved it overboard. Whether the missile exploded when it hit the hard earth below, or slightly before, was difficult to decide, but a sizable cloud of smoke and débris arose—enough of a cloud to prove that the plane would have been blown into fragments.

THE pilot had followed the man with the parachute only until the balance of his plane had been affected by the shifting passengers, and in the ensuing excitement, he had forgotten the bronze man's orders. The ship was now some distance from the parachute.

The white silk lobe was only a spot on the desert floor. It had settled into a canyon, they saw.

Doc advanced again and spoke grimly to the pilot, and that worthy, suddenly apprised of the bronze man's identity and shown a small card, hastened to send the plane toward the parachute.

The card Doc displayed was one directing all employees of the air line to put themselves at his service upon request, and had been issued partially because Doc Savage, a man of more wealth than any one dreamed, owned a goodly portion of the air-line stock.

It was impossible to land in the canyon. The nearest terrain for a safe descent was fully a mile distant. The pilot put his ship down there.

"Armed?" Doc asked the pilot.

The flier nodded.

Doc, Monk, and Ham raced for the canyon. It was rough going. Mesquite prongs raked their clothing and cactus prodded painfully. Once a rattlesnake *whirred,* and shortly after that Monk made a loud gulping noise and stopped. He said something.

Whatever he said was lost in a loud, rending crack of a noise which seemed to come from the direction of the canyon.

"There's that thing again!" Monk growled, and searched the sky in vain for some trace of a flame thread.

They ran on.

Then they heard the crack of a noise again, and once more listened and searched with their eyes. Again, they saw nothing in the sky.

The perusal of the heavens might have been an omen——they found no trace of their quarry when they reached the canyon. They did locate the parachute where it had been abandoned. Tracks in the sand showed where the would-be killer had fled. They followed these.

The tracks terminated in inexplicable fashion in the midst of an expanse of sand which bore every imprint with amazing distinctness. But where the tracks vanished there was a queer disturbance, as if a small and terrific whirlwind had sucked up the sand, then let it sift back.

Monk, frowning, insisted that some of the sand already floated in the air.

They hunted for an hour before they resigned themselves to conviction that, in some manner as yet unexplained, the one they sought had managed to vanish.

"This thing has had a lot of dizzy angles so far," Monk grumbled. "But this one takes the cookies."

## Chapter 8
## THE DEAD MAN'S BROTHER

It was foggy in San Francisco. The air was full of moisture. The newspapers which Monk brought into Doc Savage's hotel room were soft with wetness. Monk seemed baffled, and he waved the papers.

"It's all over 'em!" he complained. "Here we've been in Frisco less than two hours and it's all over the newspapers. Now what I want to know is who told 'em we were here?"

Doc Savage said, "I did."

Monk shook his head. "But we generally keep out of the papers all we can."

"We have few clues to go on," Doc said. "None, in fact."

"Don't I know it!"

"So if these men come to us, even with the intention of

getting us out of the way, it will put us in contact with them, at least," Doc said.

Monk grinned doubtfully. "Well, that's one way of doing it."

Doc Savage took one of the newspapers, but gave only brief attention to the story concerning his arrival in San Francisco. The item indicated, among other things, that the bronze man was on the West coast to investigate the murder of his friend, Willard Spanner. Or had there been a murder?

There was another story concerning the Willard Spanner affair. The newspaper publisher who had received the first letter demanding a money payment for Spanner's release, had received a second missive, insisting that Spanner was still alive and demanding money for his safety.

"This may be a newspaper publicity stunt," Monk suggested. "I've known some of the wilder papers to stoop to things like that."

Doc Savage lifted the telephone and got in communication with the publisher who had received the missives. Doc made his identity known.

"I would like to see those notes," he said.

The publisher tried to bargain.

"In return for them, you'll have to let us write up your movements exclusively in our paper," he said.

"We will do nothing of the sort," Doc said promptly.

"Then you can whistle for the notes," he was told.

The bronze man showed no emotion.

"Suit yourself," he said.

The publisher sounded less certain when he asked, "What are you going to do about it?"

"Tell the other newspapers what you are doing," Doc advised. "The fact that you are going so far as to block efforts to find Spanner, if alive, for the sake of a story, should make interesting reading. I also have a Federal agent's commission. The Federal authorities will be interested in your refusal of information and coöperation to an agent. I may think of other measures. For instance, the majority stock in your sheet is owned by a chain of which I am a director."

"You win," said the newspaperman. "I'll send the notes over."

Doc had hardly hung up when the telephone rang. It was the clerk downstairs.

"A Mr. Nock Spanner to see Doc Savage," he said. "Mr. Spanner says he is a brother of Willard Spanner."

"Send him up," Doc said, and replaced the receiver.

THE bronze man advised Monk and Ham that a visitor was coming up, and told them his name.

"Willard Spanner's brother!" Monk exploded. "I didn't know he had a brother!"

"He has," Doc said.

"Ever met him?" Monk asked.

"No," Doc said. "The brother is a military expert, and has been in China for a number of years."

There was a knock at the door, and Doc arose and admitted the visitor.

Nock Spanner was a hard-bodied man of more than average height. Although his hair was slightly gray at the temples, his age was probably not much past thirty. On his left hand he wore a rather large wrist watch, the band of which was composed of Chinese coins, linked together.

"I read in the newspapers that you were in San Francisco, investigating the mystery about my brother," he said in a crisp voice which held a hint of the accent sometimes acquired by Americans spending a period of years in a foreign land. "I just arrived this morning."

"Have you any idea why your brother was in San Francisco?" Doc queried.

Nock Spanner turned the wrist band of Chinese coins, which seemed to fit a bit too tight for comfort.

"To meet me, of course," he said. "We had not seen each other for seven years. I had finished my work in China and was coming back to the States to live."

"You have any ideas about this?"

Nock Spanner straightened the wrist band. "I have made enemies in China. I did not think, however, that they would strike at me through my brother."

"You think that possible?"

Nock Spanner shrugged. "I am at a loss to think of anything else. Of course, I knew little about my brother's connections in the States. He might have made enemies of his own. Or some one may merely want money. If so, I am willing to pay. Fifty thousand was the sum demanded, so the newspapers say."

"You have it?"

Nock Spanner nodded. He took a large automatic with a thin barrel from a pocket. Then he brought out a roll of bills, tapped them and returned them to the pocket.

"I can pay," he said. "But I want to know if my brother is alive. I want the writers of those notes asked a question. If they answer it correctly, I will know my brother is alive."

"Is it a sure-fire question?" Doc asked.

"It is. I'll ask him my middle name, which I haven't used since childhood, and which I'll guarantee no one but my brother knows."

"All right," Doc told him. "The notes will be here shortly."

A messenger brought the notes. They were printed on rough brown paper, the hardest kind of material to identify, and there were no finger prints on them. They were simple and intelligently worded, stating that Willard Spanner was alive and would be released upon the payment of fifty thousand dollars in small bills. The last line gave the method of communication:

WILL TELEPHONE YOU WHEN WE JUDGE TIME PROPER

"They're taking a chance when they use the telephone," Monk offered.

"They can call from some remote spot and depart quickly," Doc replied.

The telephone rang.

"Yes," Doc said into the mouthpiece.

"That newspaper guy said to call you," stated a voice which held a deliberate, artificial shrillness.

"About what?" Doc asked.

"About Willard Spanner," said the voice. "I'm one of the guys who's got him."

Using the hand with which he was not holding the telephone, Doc Savage made small, rapid posturing motions. Monk watched these, reading them—for the gestures were those of the accepted one-hand deaf-and-dumb sign language, and the homely chemist was being directed to trace the call.

Monk departed hastily.

"We have to know for certain that Willard Spanner is alive," Doc said. "It is reported that his body was found in New York somewhat less than three hours after he was seized in San Francisco."

"How we gonna do that?" the shrill voice asked.

"Ask Willard Spanner for his brother Nock's middle name," Doc advised. "The answer will tell us if he is alive."

"Sure." The other hung up.

It was some five minutes before Monk entered the room, wearing a downcast expression.

"Too fast," he said. "The connection was down before we could trace it."

"Instantaneous tracing of telephone calls is successful in fiction," Doc told him. "In actual practice, there are slips."

Nock Spanner had stood by, fingering the tight band of Chinese coins about his wrist during the last few minutes. Now he stepped forward.

"Just so there won't be any doubt," he said, and got a sheet of paper and an envelope from the room desk. He wrote briefly on the paper, standing so that none could see what he was imprinting, then inserted the sheet in the envelope, sealed it and gave it to Doc Savage.

"The name is written inside," he advised. "Unless they come back at us with that name, they haven't got Willard."

The telephone rang. It was the voice with the disguising artificial shrillness.

"The brother's middle name is Morency," the voice stated.

Instantly afterward, the other receiver clicked up. There had been no chance to trace the call.

Doc Savage opened the envelope handed him by Nock Spanner. There was one name printed on the stationery inside:

MORENCY

"Willard is alive," said Nock Spanner. "This proves it to me!"

JUDGING that there would be future calls from the men who claimed to be holding Willard Spanner—if, incredibly enough, he was still alive, as it seemed now—Doc Savage made preparations.

He got in touch with the telephone company and, after some discussion, succeeded in having the entire testboard crew set to work watching such calls as might come to his hotel. They were to trace each call instantly. With luck, they might succeed.

It was fully an hour later when the call came. The same disguised voice made it.

"You will take the money, get in an automobile and drive out of San Francisco on the main Los Angeles road," the voice directed. "Watch the fences on your right. When you see a piece of green cloth on a fence, throw the money overboard. We'll turn Spanner loose."

There was a momentary pause while the other took a deep breath.

"And listen, Doc Savage," he continued. "You're supposed to be a tough guy, but if you cross me, it'll be tough for you and Willard Spanner both!"

The other receiver clicked.

Doc Savage kept his own receiver to his ear, and not more than twenty seconds passed before a briskly business-like feminine telephone operator came in on the wire and said:

"That last call was made from 6932 Fantan Road."

Doc's arrangement for the immediate tracing of incoming calls with the telephone company, had worked.

Nock Spanner waved his arms wildly when the bronze man started for the door.

"But aren't you going to do what they demanded?" he barked.

"No," Doc informed him. "The voice on the telephone was not sufficiently anxious about the money."

Spanner blinked. "What do you mean?"

"I mean simply that the thing smells like an ingenious scheme to draw us to this 6932 Fantan Road."

Monk and Ham were following the bronze man.

"A trap?" Nock Spanner exploded.

"Possibly," Doc agreed.

"What are you going to do?"

"Oblige the gentleman on the telephone, to some extent," Doc replied.

Nock Spanner trailed along behind them, looking very uneasy.

FANTAN ROAD started auspiciously with fine mansions and new asphalt, but that was down in the five and ten-hundred-number blocks, and when Doc Savage had followed the thoroughfare out to the sixties, it had dwindled to the remnant of some high-pressure subdivision realtor's bad dream. Finally, there was no pavement at all, and not much road, only two ruts in sand and weeds. Even the telephone line draped slackly from poles which were not all of the same length. It had been a long time since they had seen a house with a number on it, and just why there should be numbers on a dwelling out this far, without a rural designation attached, was a mystery.

Doc Savage made no effort to pull their rented car off the road, but stopped it and cut the engine.

Nock Spanner stood up in the seat—the car was an open phaeton—and peered about. The radiator made boiling noises.

"Darned if I see a house," he said.

"It should be less than half a mile ahead," Doc told him.

They left the car with its hot, sobbing radiator and advanced, walking through sand that repeatedly filled their low shoes, a circumstance which moved Monk to take off his footgear and pad along barefooted.

"The jungle ape in you coming out," Ham commented.

Monk only grinned and kicked sand back against the overlong snout of the pig, Habeas, who had paused to harass a large, black, frightened beetle. On either side there was woodland, the trees thick and large, sprouting from a mat of brush.

Doc Savage watched the road closely and discerned the prints of tires. They were not many. At one point, he noted in which direction spinning wheels had tossed sand. Before long, he had concluded three cars had traversed the road recently—two rather, for one had come and returned, and the other, its tires of a different tread and state of wear, had gone only one way. All of the tracks had been made that day. Night dew has a way of altering the appearance of a trail.

Doc Savage left the other three abruptly, without explanation, and went ahead.

"What's his idea?" Nock Spanner demanded suspiciously.

"He does that regular," Monk explained. "He's gonna look things over. We'd better take it easy."

Doc Savage did not follow the two ruts along the sand that was the road, but turned into the undergrowth and moved there. It was uncanny, the silence with which he traveled. There was no sign of a house as yet. But the telephone people had said there was a dwelling here, so there must be one.

The bronze man was traveling downwind from the road, and was scenting the air from time to time. Years of training had not quite given him the olfactory organs of a wild animal, but his senses were developed far beyond those of ordinary ability.

He caught the odor of tobacco smoke. He trailed it up wind, and if his caution had been remarkable before, it was miraculous now. He made no sound in coming upon two figures crouched beside the road.

They were men. They were arguing.

"I tell you I heard a car," one said. "It stopped down the road. That's suspicious!"

"You're always hearing things," said the other, sourly.

Possibly the hearing of both was a trifle deficient, for it was hardly reasonable that neither should know of Doc Savage's presence until the giant of bronze hurled down upon them; but such was what happened.

Doc had calculated his leap carefully and nothing went amiss. He landed with a hand on the back of each man's neck, and the shock of that drove them down, burying their faces in the gritty earth. They struggled. One man managed to bleat out a cry. He sounded like a caught rabbit.

Terrific pressure, skillfully administered, began to tell, so that the pair groveled with less violence, finally becoming limp and all but unconscious. Doc turned them over.

They were Leases Moore and Quince Randweil.

# Chapter 9
# MURDER SPREE

THE piping bleat—Quince Randweil had emitted it—had been loud enough to carry to Monk, Ham, and Nock Spanner, and they came up, running on their toes for greater silence.

"Ah, the two gentlemen of mystery," Ham said dryly.

"They were watching the road," Doc told him.

Doc Savage had not induced the remarkable paralytic state which he could administer by pressure upon certain spinal nerve centers, so Quince Randweil and Leases Moore soon revived enough to speak. They behaved in a manner somewhat unexpected.

"Boy, I'm glad to see you!" said Leases Moore, who had

put false teeth in his mouth and now did not look unhandsome.

"You said it!" echoed Quince Randweil, making it sound like "shedd."

"Oh," Monk leered fearsomely, "so now you're glad to see us! Yes, you are!"

"Truly we are," lisped Quince Randweil.

"And why in blue blazes shouldn't we be?" Leases Moore demanded sourly.

"We made a bad move and we know it now."

"I see." Monk made his leer more impressive. "An explanation for everything, I bet."

"Nuts!" said Leases Moore, and began to look mad.

"Now, now!" Quince Randweil lisped excitedly and made admonishing gestures. "It will not do good to get all bothered. Of course you gentlemen are aggravated with us!"

"That's a mild word for it," Monk told him.

Randweil lisped on as if he had not heard, saying, "It was our rugged individualism which made us act as we did. Yes, our rugged individualism."

Individualism was a strange sound the way he said it. He made it, "inniwissilissim."

He continued, "You see, we were mad. *Very* mad. We had heard that our enemies were coming to San Francisco, to this house at 6932 Fantan Road. We overheard that. So, being very mad and wanting to get even, we came out here. But we have not been having such good luck."

Monk said, "It's a good thing lightning don't strike liars."

"You don't believe it?" Randweil sounded hurt.

"Sure I do," Monk replied, as sarcastically as possible.

Randweil looked at Doc Savage. "Do you believe me?"

Doc Savage asked, "By now, have you any idea of what is behind all of this—the murder of Willard Spanner, the queer streaks in the sky, and the rest?"

"Not an idea," declared Randweil.

"And that's the truth," echoed Leases Moore, rubbing the knob which was his missing thumb.

"Of course," Monk agreed, more sarcastically than before.

Leases Moore yelled, "It is, and all of you can go chase yourselves! I'm not a guy you can horse around!"

Monk looked at Doc hopefully. "Shall I do some of my exercises on this guy?"

Doc replied nothing.

Monk registered cheerfulness, told Leases Moore, "There'll be more than your thumb and teeth missing when I get through with you."

"Hold it," Doc said, "while I look around a bit."

THE bronze man employed his usual caution in advancing through the brush, and when he had traversed a hundred feet, paused and listened at great length, in order to ascertain if any one were approaching, drawn by the noise made when Moore and Randweil were seized.

He heard nothing suspicious.

Birds had fallen silent, quieted by the sounds of the brief scuffle, but now they became noisy. So furtive was the bronze man's progress that not often were the feathered songsters disturbed.

The timber became thicker, with less brush and higher, more sturdy trees. Underfoot, the brush gave way to moss and dead leaves. Ahead, Doc Savage caught sight of a building of some kind.

The crack of a noise came then. Its note was the same as on other occasions—sudden, strange, a noise unlike anything else Doc Savage ever had heard.

The bronze man whipped for the handiest tree. His climbing was amazing. He had picked a tree of somewhat thin foliage. A moment later, he was high up in it. His eyes roved overhead—and riveted there.

There was a strange thing in the sky. No ribbon of weird fire. It looked like a ball of some dull, glassy substance. In diameter, the thing approached a score of feet, and its surface was not all of the same obsidian nature, but freckled with lighter and darker spots in an even pattern.

The fantastic ball was hanging back where Monk and the others had been left. It appeared to be little more than a hundred feet up. Nor was it perfectly stationary, but bounced up and down slowly, as if it had just landed on an invisible rubber mat.

The thing was surrounded by a faint haze which resembled steam—and *was* steam, Doc surmised an instant later: water particles in the mist being vaporized against the ball, which had been made hot by its terrific rate of passage through the air.

The ball was an aërial conveyance obviously, a thing of new and amazing design, a vehicle along lines utterly at variance with those on which aëronautical engineers commonly worked.

Most surprising, of course, was the lack of streamlining to be expected in a device capable of such unearthly speed. It bore no resemblance to the fish-bodied conformation sought after by designers. It was a perfect globe.

There was an explanation, somewhat startling in its possibility. The planets in space, the stars, moon, sun, were round or nearly so, and this, some scientists maintained, was a result of the application of the mysterious gravitational forces.

Was some machination with gravity responsible for the amazing powers of this ball?

There was another explanation for the lack of streamlining, a bit more sensible. The ball seemed capable of moving in any direction without turning. Was not a spherical shape the most perfect attainable streamlining for a body which must move in any direction?

Doc drove a hand inside his clothing, where he carried a small, powerful telescope. But before he could focus the lenses, the amazing ball dropped with eye-defying abruptness, and was lost back of the trees. Judging by the swiftness of its descent, there should have been a loud jar as it struck, but there was no such sound.

Doc Savage released his grip on the limb to which he had been clinging. He dropped halfway to the ground before he grasped another bough, held to it long enough to break his fall, then plunged on to the ground. He sprinted through the growth.

At first, he was cautious. Then something happened which led him to surrender silence to speed. He heard a loud, agonized bawl; unmistakably Monk's voice. Some one cursed. Doc ran faster. He heard brush crashings ahead.

Then came the cracking sound. It was something different this time, starting with a whistle of something going with terrific speed—and the crack followed, long and mounting frightfully, then dying away, as if betaking itself into the distance.

At the first note, Doc halted, stared. His scrutiny was on the sky. He thought he saw something. He was not sure. If anything, what he glimpsed was a blurred streak which arched upward until it was entirely lost. It was no fiery ribbon, however. The bronze man went on, seeking the party he had left shortly before.

He found Monk, Ham, and Nock Spanner, but not Leases

Moore and Quince Randweil. The first three were stretched out motionless in the brush.

There had been a terrific fight, judging from the violence done and the state of the victims. Monk had two ugly cuts on the head, Ham one. Spanner had evidently been slugged in the face, for his lips were stringing scarlet over the green leaves of a bush which he had mashed down in falling.

Doc Savage listened. There was a leafy shuffling, and the pig, Habeas, came out of the brush, looked at Doc with small eyes, then turned and went back into the undergrowth. There was no other sound. Even the birds had fallen silent.

Doc Savage bent over the victims. Ham was already mumbling incoherently and endeavoring to sit up. Doc gave attention to Monk, and was working over him when Ham's head cleared.

The dapper lawyer stared at the prostrate, apish chemist. A horrified expression overspread his features as he saw the gore about Monk's head wounds.

"Monk!" he gasped. "Is he dead?"

Doc Savage said nothing.

Ham staggered up and wailed, "Monk—is he all right? He's the best friend I've got!"

Without opening his small eyes, Monk mumbled, "Who's my friend? I ain't got a friend, except Habeas."

Ham switched his anxiety for a black scowl and came over and kicked Monk, far from gently, in the side.

"I was not talking about you," he snapped.

The pig, Habeas Corpus, came out of the brush again, looked at them queerly, then turned around exactly as he had done before and entered the brush.

Monk sat up and began administering to himself, and Doc gave attention to Nock Spanner, chafing his wrists, pinching him to induce arousing pain, until finally Spanner rolled over and put both hands to his bruised mouth.

The instant Spanner was cognizant of his surroundings, he whipped his hand from his mouth to the pocket in which he carried his money.

"Robbed!" he screamed. "Fifty thousand dollars! Gone!"

He began to swear loudly, his profane remarks growing more and more shrill and violent until they were almost the utterings of a madman.

"That won't help." Monk put his hands over his ears. "Besides, I ain't used to such words."

"My life savings!" Spanner shrieked. "And you crack wise! It's no joke!"

"With this head of mine, nothing is a joke." Monk growled. "Only, bellowing won't get it back."

Habeas Corpus came out of the brush and went back again.

Doc Savage said, "The pig is trying to show us something."

Monk swayed erect, weaved a small circle and fell down; groaning, he got up again. Nock Spanner stared, realizing that the homely chemist had been badly knocked out. For the next few moments Spanner was silent, as if ashamed of his own hysterical outburst.

They went through the brush slowly, for the three who had been attacked were in no shape for brisk traveling.

"What happened?" Doc Savage asked them.

"It was that thing in the sky," Monk said hoarsely. "We heard a crack of noise, and looked over here"—he pointed ahead—"and there it was. It looked like some kind of hard, funny glass——"

"A new and unique terrestrial space ship," Doc interposed.

"Yeah?" Monk frowned.

"Globe shaped," Doc elaborated. "It can move in any direction. It's actual propelling machinery, I do not yet understand, except that it is almost soundless."

"Soundless!" Monk exploded. "That crack of a noise——"

"Did you ever have a bullet pass very close to your ear?" Doc asked.

"Have I?" grunted Monk.

"What did it sound like?" Doc persisted. "Was it a whine?"

"Heck, no," said Monk. "It was——" He stopped, mouth open, understanding coming over him.

"Exactly," Doc told him. "A body moving through the air at terrific speed pushes the air aside and leaves a vacuum behind, and the air closing into this vacuum makes a distinct report. That accounts for the noise these terrestrial ball ships make."

Monk sighed mightily.

"Well, if a devil with two spikes on his tail had jumped up, we couldn't have been more surprised when we saw this ball thing, ship or whatever it is," he mumbled. "I was goggling at the thing when the lights went out for me."

"Leases Moore picked up a stick and hit you," Ham told him. "About the same time that Randweil struck me, knocking me senseless."

Nock Spanner chimed in, "And they both piled onto me. Randweil held me and Moore used his fist. That was the last I remember."

Monk said soberly, "Funny thing."

Ham snapped peevishly, "Everything seems funny to you the last few days!"

Monk shook his damaged head as if he did not want to squabble.

"When I was struck down, I didn't go out immediately," he said, speaking slowly, as if the information he were giving was painful. "I was in kind of a coma, or something. And just before I passed out, I'll swear that I saw the girl."

Ham demanded, "What girl?"

"The one in Oklahoma," Monk elaborated. "Lanca Jaxon."

"Hallucination," Ham said, skeptically.

"Maybe," Monk nursed his head. "But she was coming through the brush with that runt Stunted. Then she turned around and went back toward where that ball of a thing had been hanging in the sky."

Doc Savage stopped. "It was no hallucination."

"I didn't think it was," Monk told him. "But how do you know?"

Doc pointed at the sandy ground underfoot. It retained the impression of a foot—narrow, high of heel, unmistakably feminine.

"I wish we could talk to that young lady for a while," Ham said grimly. "She could deuced well explain a number of things."

They caught sight of the pig, Habeas. The shote's enormous ears were thrown back in order that they might not be scratched by the thorny undergrowth, and if actions were any indication, he had been waiting to see if they were following him.

Nock Spanner said, "That is the most remarkable hog I ever saw."

"He's been trained for years," Monk grunted. "Say, that ball of a jigger was hanging over here somewhere."

They stepped forward more briskly and came out in what amounted to a clearing, although the place was furred over with short brush and tall grass. This growth was mashed down over a spot a dozen feet across, as if something heavy had come to rest upon it.

At the edge of the area where the brush was crushed, there lay three dead men.

## Chapter 10
## DEATH ZONE

DEAD bodies have a certain distinctive grotesqueness which indicated their condition, and these three were certainly dead. Bullets had finished one of them, knives the other two.

The knife victims were not dressed as expensively as the one slain by lead, their clothing being cheaply made, nor did they seem as intelligent a type.

Doc Savage and his aides had seen the two knife victims before.

"Members of the gang!" Monk exploded.

"Worthics who were with the crew in Tulsa, and in New York," Ham said more precisely.

Doc glanced at Nock Spanner. "Ever see them before?"

Spanner shook his head. "Strangers to me."

Doc Savage bent over the victims, searching, but with little expectation of finding anything, for he had already seen that the pockets were turned inside out, indicating the unfortunates had been previously gone over.

The garments of the bullet victim held no label. These had been cut out carefully.

There were labels in the clothing of the other two, and these indicated, not surprisingly, that the suits had been purchased from a department store in Tulsa, Oklahoma.

Doc returned his attention to the man who had been shot.

"Been dead at least ten hours," he said.

Monk and Ham showed no surprise at that until Monk, watching the knife victims morbidly, suddenly perceived that scarlet still oozed from their wounds.

"Hey!" he exploded. "These other two——"

"Were killed only a few moments ago," Doc told him. "Probably while that mysterious ball of a thing was resting here."

Doc Savage gave more attention to the body of the victim who had been dead the longer period. He unscrewed lenses from his telescope, and these served as excellent magnifiers; in proper combination, they afforded magnification which could be surpassed only by the more expensive of microscopes.

"Finding anything?" Ham asked.

Doc did not reply, and Ham showed no sign of being offended, for he was accustomed to the bronze man's manner of lapsing into unexplained spells of apparent deafness, usually when questioned upon points about which he had formed no opinion definite enough to voice, or when asked about something which he wished to keep for himself, possibly to spring later as a complete surprise.

Monk nursed his gashed head and complained, "So far, I don't make heads or tails of this. It's the dizziest dang thing I've run up against!"

Nock Spanner waved his arms and growled. "What about my brother? What about that house we came out here to investigate? We haven't done anything about that yet."

Doc Savage reassembled the parts of his telescope and pocketed it.

"We will have a look at the house," he said.

"If any," Spanner muttered.

"There is one," Doc told him. "I saw it through the trees just before this—interruption."

THE house was about what might be expected. It was old. Once, when this had been a more remote region, and before some over-enthusiastic real-estate promoter had gotten hold of the region, it had been a fruit ranch. It looked as if it had not been lived in for a year or two.

They came upon a path that lay about a hundred and fifty yards from the structure, and Doc Savage at once moved ahead, voicing no word of explanation. The others were too concerned with their own hurts to be overly inquisitive.

The path turned. For a brief time, Doc Savage was concealed from the others, and during that interval he went through some rapid motions. A bottle came out of his clothing. It held a liquid which resembled rather thick, colorless sirup, and he sprinkled this over the path.

The bottle was out of sight when the others came in view.

They walked through the sticky substance on the path without noting its presence. Doc said nothing. They went on.

Behind weeds that grew thickly along the fence of what had once been a corral, they waited and used their cars. Monk and the other two heard nothing, but aware of the bronze man's super-trained hearing, they glanced inquiringly at him.

"Apparently no one around," Doc said.

They eased toward the house. Its decrepit nature became more pronounced. Portions of the roof had no shingles at all. Most of the windows were gone.

Monk suggested, "Wonder if we hadn't better scatter out, in case something happens. If it's a trap, we don't want 'em to nab us all in one bunch."

"Good idea," Nock Spanner agreed, and when Doc Savage did not veto the proposal, they separated, flattening out in the weedy cover.

"I will go in," Doc said.

He left the others, worked ahead on all fours, and gained the door. Only the top hinge supported the panel. No sound came from within. Doc entered.

Plaster had fallen off walls and ceiling and was in lumpy profusion underfoot. Powdered spots indicated where the stuff had been stepped on recently. Doc made a closer examination. Men had been in the house very recently. He went on to another room, equally as cluttered up, and stood listening.

There was sound now, rather strange sound—a faint, high-pitched singing noise. It did not undulate, but came steadily, proof that no cricket was making it, although the note did sound vaguely like that insect.

Doc whipped for the source of the noise—an adjacent room. The instant he was through the door, he saw what was making it.

A portable radio transmitter stood on the floor. It was in operation. Near by was another, slightly larger box of apparatus, and from that ran wires which progressed through cracks in the floor.

Doc hurriedly examined the second box. The workings of the thing were intricate, but not so complex that the bronze man's scientific skill failed to perceive their nature.

The box was a delicate electrical capacity balance, an

instrument constructed to register, by having its capacity balance upset, when any new object came near it. It was merely a development of the old regenerative radio receivers which howled when a hand was brought near them—only this, instead of howling, actuated a sensitive relay which in turn set the radio transmitter to sending a steady oscillating signal.

Exactly such a device as this must have been employed back at the oyster plant in New York to detect the approach of Doc Savage. Here, it had served the same purpose, except that it started the radio transmitter in lieu of actuating some other signal.

Doc spun about, raced out of the room. There was furious haste in his movements. The instant he was outdoors his powerful voice crashed a warning.

"Get away from here!" he rapped. "It's a trap!"

Monk heaved up instantly from among the weeds. Ham appeared a short distance to his right.

They waited.

"Spanner!" Doc called.

Nock Spanner did not show himself. Doc called again. Only silence answered.

"Blazes!" Monk snapped. "That's blasted strange!"

"WHERE was Nock Spanner when you last saw him?" Doc Savage questioned.

Monk pointed. "Over there."

They went to the spot. There was a trail where the leaves had been mashed down, the weeds crushed. But it only led for a short distance before it became difficult to follow.

"He was heading back toward the brush," Ham said dryly. "Now I wonder what his idea was?"

"Might have seen some one," Monk said, in a tone which indicated he doubted the prediction.

Doc Savage dug a small flat flask out of his clothing. It was filled with greenish pellets hardly larger than common rice. He began shaking these out on the ground, and the moment they were exposed to the air they began turning into a rather bilious-looking vapor. This was swept away quickly by the wind.

But the strange vaporized pellets did one remarkable thing to the surrounding growth and the ground: They brought out tracks—tracks that showed with a distinct, sinister yellowish tint.

Monk gulped, "Well, for——" He looked down and saw that he himself was leaving the yellowish footprints wherever he moved. Ham's tracks likewise showed. Only Doc Savage left no trail.

"A sticky chemical I let you walk through," Doc explained. "This vapor causes a chemical reaction which makes your tracks visible."

Ham clipped, "Then you suspected that——"

"Just a precaution," Doc told him. "Hurry! We've got to find Nock Spanner and get away from here."

They began following the remarkable trail which Spanner had unknowingly left.

"Any sign of Nock Spanner's brother, Willard?" Ham asked.

"No," Doc replied.

They were in the woods now, away from the corrals, the rickety sheds. The tracks became farther apart, as if Nock Spanner had started running here.

"Darn his soul!" Monk ejaculated. "I can't understand what got into him."

"Listen!" Doc ripped suddenly.

He said only the one short word, but it was hardly out of his mouth before their eardrums all but collapsed under a terrific, rending crack of a report. Instinct made them look up. Surprise put expressions of blankness on their faces.

A fantastic, glistening ball of a thing was suspended above them. It was not the same ball they had seen before. This one was smaller, its color slightly different. And stretching from it and away into the sky was a trail that might have been left by a fast-moving skyrocket.

The ball was hot. They could feel its heat against their faces—heat which undoubtedly came from the friction of the air against its shiny hull at tremendous speed. As gusts of particularly damp mist struck it, the gleaming skin threw off faint wisps of steam.

"Under cover!" Doc shouted.

They lunged under the trees, and a fractional moment later, the ball dropped, hitting with a pronounced jar where they had stood.

"Blazes!" Monk gulped. "It's a stout thing!"

The ball seemed to be cooling off rapidly—more rapidly than was quite natural.

"Probably has an inner and outer shell, heavily insulated against heat," Doc said grimly. "Otherwise, it would get too hot inside for human life, and that in only a short period of traveling. And from the way it's cooling off, I judge that much of the heat is absorbed by refrigeration from within."

The ball lifted slowly and hung suspended in the air, unpleasantly like a fantastic bird of prey.

Monk, scrambling through the undergrowth, rasped, "The darn thing is trying to mash us!"

The ball floated back and forth and, peering closely, Doc and his men discovered what might possibly be periscopic windows, showing outwardly as little more than big lenses, at various points on the skin of the thing. There were not in one spot, but were located on top, bottom, sides.

"Got eyes all over, like the head of a fly," Monk complained.

The terrestrial ship leaped to a spot above them. As it moved, it left a distinct trail of what resembled glowing red sparks.

"That explains the fire streaks in the sky!" Monk barked.

Doc Savage nodded. "The luminous particles are exhaust from whatever mechanism propels the thing."

"But some of the balls don't leave a trail!" Monk pointed out.

"Possibly more perfected specimens," Doc told him grimly. "They may have equipped some of the ships with digestors which eliminate the luminous exhaust!"

That was a rank guess on the bronze man's part, a guess which, later developments showed, was accurate.

Doc and his men began to run, seeking to keep under cover. It was difficult, almost impossible, for the woodland here was open, and the fabulous bulb sank itself in the trees and turned slowly, as if it were a fantastic organism, with eyes, brain, and perceptive senses all in its round, gleaming torso.

Then it lifted a little and drifted over Doc and his men where they had been spied out.

There was a clicking noise and a small metal blob dropped earthward. It thudded into the dead leaves and popped itself open not unlike a large and very rotten egg. Exactly the same thing happened a bit to the other side of Doc's party.

"Gas!" Ham shouted, then coughed violently, stood up very straight, grasped his throat with both hands and pulled at it as if trying to free something lodged there. He was still pulling at his throat when he fell over.

Monk tumbled over beside him.

Whether it was due to his superior physical resistance, or to the fact that he held his breath, Doc Savage was able to run some distance and probably would have gotten away, except that the gas seemed to be assimilated through the pores of the skin almost as effectively as through the lungs.

Doc fell down a full hundred yards from the others.

WHEN Doc Savage awakened, the voice of the short man known as Stunted was saying, "I didn't figure I'd live to see this day. I sure didn't!"

When the bronze man opened his eyes, it was to see Stunted standing over him, a sawed-off automatic rifle tucked under an arm.

"No, sir, I didn't think we'd ever get you," Stunted told the bronze man.

Doc moved his arms over an area of a few inches. They were limited to that motion by handcuffs, huge and strong, one pair with oversize bands located above his elbows, three more pairs above his wrists.

He shifted his ankles. There were three more pairs of manacles there, and his knees were roped together and the knots wired.

"We're getting cautious," Stunted told him.

Doc moved his head. Monk and Ham lay near by, both handcuffed, Monk with nearly as many pair of manacles as secured the bronze man. Neither Monk nor Ham were conscious.

"They'll come out of it," Stunted said. "That gas wasn't the kind that kills, according to what the chief told us."

The man with the queerly behaving eyes came over scowling, shoved Stunted away and said, "Still working that mouth overtime!"

Stunted glared at him. "My rope's got an end, fella."

The lanky man with the queer eyes ignored that, and frowned at Doc Savage.

"Where did Leases Moore and Quince Randweil go?" he demanded.

"That," Doc told him slowly, "is something I also should like to know."

The other blackened his frown. "So they were around, huh?"

"They were."

The man swore, and the nature of his profanity indicated he had lived some of his past on a cow ranch.

"The two locoed jugheads!" he finished. "We found two of our boys dead out in the brush, where one of the balls had landed. Leases Moore and Quince Randweil killed them and took charge of the ball, didn't they?"

"The thought has occurred to me," Doc admitted.

"Just the thing we've been trying to prevent!" the man snarled, and his eyes crossed horribly.

Doc asked, "Who was the third dead man? The one who had been dead some time?"

The other man opened his mouth as if, in his absent-mindedness, he was about to make a correct answer, then his eyes suddenly straightened.

"Never mind that," he snapped.

"Where is the girl?" Doc queried.

Stunted said dryly, "Them two skunks, Moore and Randweil, must've kept her alive. They would. Gonna use her the same way he was."

The man with the roving eyes yelled, "Looks as if only a bullet will cork that trap of yours!"

Stunted advised, "Any time you feel lucky, you can try to put the cork in."

Instead of taking up the challenge, the other wheeled and stalked away.

THE man with the uneasy eyes was back some five minutes later. He looked rather happy.

"You must have had a drink," Stunted suggested.

"Nuts!" The other grinned evilly. "I been in touch with the boss. We all get an extra cut for nailing our big brass friend here."

"When you bear such tidings, all is forgiven," Stunted told him.

"The boss is gonna handle the rest," the thin man said.

"What rest?" Stunted questioned.

"Doc Savage has three more men in New York," said the other. "Guys called Long Tom, Johnny and Renny. They've got to be taken care of."

# Chapter 11
## THE FARMER GAG

RENNY had big fists. A medical authority had once claimed they were the biggest fists ever known on a man, including those of the Cardiff giant. Renny was not a boasting man—except on one point, and that was the claim that there was not a wooden door made the panel of which he could not batter out with his fists.

Renny, as Colonel John Renwick, was an engineer with a reputation that extended over much of the world. He did not work at that profession much these days. He loved excitement, and to get it, he was a soldier of trouble in Doc Savage's little group.

Renny sat in Doc Savage's skyscraper headquarters in New York City. There was a newspaper on his lap. Under the newspaper and hidden by it, was one of the bronze man's supermachine pistols capable of discharging many hundreds of shots a minute.

There came another knock on the door.

"Come in," Renny invited.

The man who entered was a tower of bones. He blinked at the newspaper, then fingered a monocle which dangled by a ribbon from his lapel.

"Your demeanor instigates apprehensions," he said in a scholastic voice.

"Didn't know it was you, Johnny," Renny rumbled, in a voice that had the volume of an angry bear in a cave. He pocketed the machine pistol.

The newcomer was William Harper Johnny Littlejohn, a gentleman with two loves—excitement, and big words. That he was considered one of the most learned experts on archaeology and geology was incidental.

"Has Long Tom communicated with you in the preterlapsed hour or so?" Johnny asked.

Renny blinked. "That one got me."

"Long Tom called me," advised Johnny in smaller words.

"He indicated he possessed information of equiparable import."

"I see," Renny said vaguely. "No, he didn't call me."

Johnny stalked into the library, appearing thinner than any man could possibly be and still live, and came back with a book only slightly smaller than a suitcase. He opened it and began to pore over the pages of fine print.

It was a book on the life habits of the prehistoric pterodactyl, which Johnny himself had written.

"Brushing up?" Renny asked.

"I left something out," Johnny explained. "A matter of ponderable consequence, too, concerning the lapidification, or progressive lapidescence, of the oval——"

"Spare me," Renny requested. "I've already got a headache. Any word from Doc?"

"No," Johnny said shortly.

The door burst open, admitting a pallid wan man who looked unhealthy enough to be in a hospital. He was hardly of average height, and his complexion had all of the ruddiness of a mushroom.

"Something important!" he yelled, and waved a paper.

He was Major Thomas J. "Long Tom" Roberts, electrical wizard extraordinary, and he had never been ill a day in his life.

THE paper bore typewritten words:

I know you're a right guy and know you're interested in This Willard Spanner killing. Go to 60 Carl Street and you may learn something. Be careful, though. I'll look you up later and if you want to do something for me for tipping you off, that's all right, too.

Buzz.

"Who's Buzz?" Renny rumbled.

"Search me," said Long Tom. "But this is worth looking into, simply because the public don't know we're interested in the affair. This man knew it, so he must have gotten a line on something worth while."

"It's eminently plausible," Johnny agreed.

Renny, after making remarkably hard-looking blocks out of his great fists, grunted, "Wonder what kind of a place this Carl Street is?"

It was a swanky residential thoroughfare. They found that

out when a taxicab carried them along Carl Street half an hour later. The street was lined with apartment buildings, and it was necessary to look nearly straight up to see the sky. The buildings looked new.

No. 60, when they passed it, was one of the most imposing buildings, its apartments having large windows, and there were two uniformed doormen under the canvas canopy, instead of the customary one.

"What shall we do?" Long Tom pondered aloud. "That's a large place. Must be three hundred apartments. And we don't know what we're looking for."

"Charge in and start asking questions," Renny suggested.

"Aboriginal reasoning," said Johnny.

"Sure," Long Tom agreed. "We wouldn't get to first base, and maybe scare off our birds."

"It won't hurt to take a look," argued Renny. "I'll turn up my coat collar and go in."

"Where'll you put them fists?" Long Tom snorted. "I'll do the gumshoeing."

They directed their taxi around the corner and got out. Long Tom stood on the curb, scratching his head.

"It's just as well not to walk in too boldly," he declared. "These birds may know us by sight."

A bright idea apparently seized him then, for he left the other two, dodged traffic across the street, and entered a telegraph office.

Renny and Johnny waited. Five minutes passed, and the waiting pair became impatient. They were on the point of investigating when a messenger came out of the telegraph office. He was directly before them before they recognized Long Tom.

"Gave a kid two bucks to loan his uniform to me," the electrical wizard grinned.

HE went into the apartment building carrying a telegraph company envelope which was empty, and when one of the doormen tried to stop him, he glared and said, "Nix! You guys don't gyp me out of the tip for delivering this!"

Long Tom walked on in, and over to the directory board which displayed a list of the tenants, office-building fashion. This last was an unusual custom for an apartment house, and a break for Long Tom.

Long Tom took one look; then he wheeled, walked out.

Excitement was on his pale face when he joined the others.

"Guess what!" he exploded.

"Blazes!" grunted Renny. "That's some way to start out. What's eating you?"

"Willard Spanner had a laboratory and room down on Staten Island," Long Tom said. "The police searched it, but found nothing to indicate why he was murdered. Am I right?"

"Right," Renny boomed.

"Yet Willard Spanner is listed in that apartment house as having an apartment there," Long Tom advised.

Renny lumbered forward. "There may be something to this angle after all. What number is this apartment?"

"Apartment 2712," said Long Tom.

FIFTEEN minutes later, Renny and Johnny appeared at the service entrance of the apartment building carrying a large wooden box which bore the designation, "Apartment 2712" on its sides in black crayon. Their scheme did not go far without hitting a snag. It seemed that the apartment house had a service department which delivered packages.

"We were to install this thing," Renny rumbled, and tapped the box. "Don't bother ringing the apartment. We got the keys."

A service elevator took them up, and, grunting a little, they carried their big box down the corridor. They stopped at the door and listened, heard nothing, exchanged glances, then rang the bell. There was no reply.

From a pocket, Renny removed a sizable array of skeleton keys. These he had brought from Doc's headquarters. He tried almost twenty of them, and his long, sober face was registering some anxiety, before one of the keys threw the tumblers.

Inside was a modernistic reception room done in black and shining chromium. Renny eyed it appreciatively. He was a connoisseur in modernistic apartments himself, possessing one of the most extremely decorated apartments in the city. He and Johnny skidded their box inside with little regard for the polished floor. They closed the door.

"Hello!" Renny called tentatively.

Only echoes answered.

They passed through the first door. If the reception hall had been modernistic, this chamber was an extreme in the opposite direction, being fitted up in early Twelfth Century style. There were great broadswords over the fireplace, the table was massive and hand hewn, and two suits of armor stood at opposite ends of the room. Mounted boar heads set off the scheme of decoration.

"Not bad," Renny said.

They advanced.

The two suits of armor moved simultaneously. Each turned a steel gauntlet over, revealing a small automatic pistol which had been hidden from view.

"You walked right into it," said a voice back of a slitted helmet.

Renny broke into a grin. It was a peculiar characteristic of Renny that when the going got tough, he seemed to become more cheerful. By the same token, when he looked most sad, he was probably happiest.

"You took a chance," he rumbled.

"Oh, we figured you wouldn't ring in the police," said the man in the armor. "Doc Savage's men don't work that way."

Four other men now came out of the rear regions of the apartment. They carried guns. Two of them searched Johnny and Renny thoroughly.

"Lock the door," one suggested.

A man went to the corridor door and turned the key, then came back juggling it in his palm.

"Get us out of these tin pants," suggested one of the pair in the armor.

This was done.

JOHNNY and Renny said nothing, but studied their captors, and the appraisal was not particularly cheering, for the six were not nervous, and their manner was hard, confident, while the clipped unconcern of their speech indicated that they were no strangers to situations involving mental stress. They were the kind of men who could be thoroughly bad; none of them looked soft.

"Well!" snapped one. "How do you like us?"

"You'd look better with a black hood over your head," Renny said dryly. "That's the way they fix you up before they put you in the electric chair!"

"Aha!" The man waved an arm. "He threatens us!"

Another said dryly, "We got Doc Savage in California, and now we collar these three. Strikes me we've about cleaned up our opposition."

"The boss worked a sweat up for nothing," said the first. "This Doc Savage wasn't such hot competition."

"It was that damn Willard Spanner," grumbled the first man. "He was tipped off about the thing, and asked to get in touch with Doc Savage. We had to smear him."

"It wasn't so much the smearing," the second man corrected. "It was the way we had to grab him in Frisco at noon, then croak him here in New York a couple of hours later, when he tried to get away."

The first speaker nodded. "But he had mailed all of the dope to his New York apartment, and we had to bring him here and make him get the letter for us."

Renny did not ordinarily show surprise. But now his eyes were all but hanging out.

"You came from San Francisco to New York in less than two hours?" he exploded.

"Sure," sneered the other. "Ain't it wonderful?"

"I don't believe it!" Renny rumbled.

Johnny put a question which had been bothering him. "Was this ever Willard Spanner's apartment?"

"Heck, no," the other chuckled. "We just fixed that up as a kind of sugar coating on the bait."

Then the man snapped a finger loudly. "Blast it! There's one of these guys loose yet! The one who looks like he's about ready to die. Long Tom, they call him."

The man who seemed to be in charge consulted his watch.

"We'll take care of him later," he decided. "They start unloading the *Seabreeze* in just about an hour. We'll have to move fast."

The men now began handcuffing, binding and gagging Johnny and Renny, working with swift ease, a hard tranquility in their manner, as if they were perfectly sure of their ground and expected no interruption.

They were more than mildly astounded when Long Tom said, from the modernistic reception room door, "Everybody stand very still."

Behind Long Tom was the box in which Renny and Johnny had carried him upstairs—against just such an emergency as this.

THE six sinister men in the apartment had been calm before, and their composure did not desert them now, for they merely turned around, saw the supermachine pistol in Long Tom's pale hand, were duly impressed, and made no exciting gestures.

They slowly held their hands out from their sides, let their guns fall on the carpet, and raised their hands over their head.

"Hold that position," Long Tom advised.

He went forward and freed Renny and Johnny, who in turn searched their prisoners thoroughly, disarming them. The search was not as productive as they had hoped, the pockets of their captives holding nothing but money; the labels inside their clothing had been cut out carefully.

"Tie them up," Long Tom suggested.

This was done, curtain cords, wire off floor lamps, serving as binding.

Long Tom frowned at them, asked, "What was that I heard about *Seabreeze?* What's *Seabreeze?*"

"A race horse," said one of the men promptly.

Long Tom shook his head. "You said something about unloading——"

"Sure!" The other shrugged. "The horse just came in from the South on a train. We gotta unload him."

Renny boomed, "That's a lie!"

The man looked hurt. Long Tom lifted his brows inquiringly.

"The *Seabreeze* is a new ocean liner," Renny said. "I read about it in the newspapers. It comes in to-day, and there's a lot of gold bullion aboard. The stuff is being shipped over from Europe."

"So!" Long Tom glared at their prisoners. "What's going to happen to the *Seabreeze?*"

No one said anything.

"It's just a coincidence!" growled one of the gang. "*Seabreeze* is a race horse."

"We'll see about that." Long Tom waved at the door. "We're going down to the pier where this ocean liner is docking."

"Somebody's gotta watch these birds," Renny boomed.

"You can have the job," Long Tom told him. "You thought of it."

They argued briefly and it ended by them matching coins, in which procedure Renny lost; so, grumbling and looking very solemn, he took over the job of guarding the captives while Johnny and Long Tom went to the pier where the liner *Seabreeze* was docking, to see if it had any connection with the present affair.

Long Tom and Johnny were jaunty indeed as they rode down in an elevator and hailed a taxi in front of the apartment building.

They would not have been as cheerful had they chanced to note the actions of a man at that moment in the act of parking his car down the street a score of yards.

THE man in the car bent over hastily, so that his face was concealed, and when he bobbed up to watch Long Tom and Johnny out of sight, he held a newspaper before his features in a manner which was casual, but effectively shielding.

When the man got out of his car, he had a topcoat collar turned up and his hat brim snapped down very low. He walked rapidly and entered the apartment house, managing to keep his face averted from the doormen.

In his free hand, the man was carrying a small case which might have contained a physician's tool kit.

An elevator let him out on the twenty-seventh floor. He waited until the cage departed, then glided to the door of the apartment to which Long Tom, Johnny, and Renny had been decoyed.

The man opened his little case. First, he took out a rubber mask which fitted his face tightly. The thing was literally a false face, padded so that it now appeared that the man had bulging cheeks, a crooked nose and more than one chin.

The case also disgorged a tin can with a screw top, and a funnel, the lower end or spout of which was flattened out. The man inserted the flattened portion of the funnel under the door. He poured the contents of the can into the funnel, and the stuff, a liquid, ran into the apartment.

The man stepped back hurriedly, and it became apparent that he was holding his breath. He went to a window at the end of the corridor, opened it and stood squarely in the stiff breeze which now blew in. He breathed deeply.

He stood there fully five minutes, consulting his watch. Then he turned and went to the apartment door, drawing a key from his pocket. Fortunately, the other key had not been left in the apartment door when it was locked from the other side, so the man with the rubber mask admitted himself readily.

The stuff on the floor had evaporated. The man held his breath until he had opened the windows, then went outside and waited for the apartment to clear of the gas which he had poured under the door.

Renny and the rest of the men in the apartment were now unconscious.

## Chapter 12
## MAN IN THE RUBBER MASK

THE man in the rubber mask seemed to know a great deal about the effect of his gas, and how to revive its victims, for he went to work on the late prisoners, first unbinding them, and transferring a number of the ropes to the person of Renny.

It was not long before inhalation of certain bottled compounds caused the men to blink and moan themselves awake. The masked man shook one of them violently.

"What happened?" he snapped.

The sound of the voice—it was not a particularly unusual voice, yet distinctive enough to be readily recognized—snapped the man who heard it into wide wakefulness.

"The big chief!" he exploded. "But what're you wearin' that mask for? You look like a goblin!"

The man in the mask ripped out, "I asked you what happened here! I didn't ask for any wise-guy stuff!"

The story of the raid by Doc Savage's three men came out—the narrators doing their best to gloss over the parts unfavorable to themselves, but, judging from the angry snorts of their leader, not succeeding very well.

"Fools!" the man yelled. "You do things just like a herd of donkeys! Where did Johnny and Long Tom go?"

The one telling the bad news looked as if he had found a worm in his apple. He hesitated. He had neglected to tell about the *Seabreeze* slip.

"It's bad," he groaned, and told the rest of it.

The masked leader proceeded to have something approaching a tantrum. He swore, and kicked those who were just regaining consciousness, so that they awakened more hurriedly and scrambled erect to get the more sensitive portions of their anatomy out of foot reach.

"You bunch of nitwits!" the man choked. "You should have told me that first! It may be too late now."

He charged into another room, grabbed a telephone, and could be heard snapping the dialing device around madly. When he got his number his voice dropped. Those in the other room did not hear a word he said, except for a final sentence which showed the man had been speaking in the strange private code which the gang employed.

"The cake should be baked half an hour earlier," was his last sentence.

He came back into the room looking somewhat less mad than before, and said, "Maybe I managed to get the bacon out of the fire."

"How?" he was asked.

"I contacted the boys and told them to go through with it half an hour earlier than planned." He consulted his watch. "That means right away. They may get it done before Johnny and Long Tom arrive on the scene."

The man eyed his watch again. "Half an hour should see the job done."

At about the same moment, Long Tom was examining a thin wafer of a watch which had cost the electrical society which had presented it to him a small fortune. "We won't make that pier much before the half hour," he said to Johnny.

However, they had secured a driver who was willing to take chances, and by stopping a traffic policeman and exhibiting their police commissions—they, too, held them, as well as did Doc Savage—they persuaded the officer to ride the running board.

The results were remarkable. Traffic split for them. Their horn blasted steadily. They chopped fifteen minutes from Long Tom's time estimate.

"There's the pier," Long Tom advised.

Johnny craned his long neck.

"The situation has certain aspects of a premonstration," he said.

Long Tom looked puzzled. "A what, did you——"

From ahead came a sound as if a snare drum had been

beaten hard for a short interval. The driver stopped the cab so suddenly that the wheels skidded. He heaved out of the seat, took a good look.

There was a crowd ahead, an excited crowd. At the snare-drum sound, the crowd showed an abrupt tendency to leave the vicinity. Many policemen were running about. Police-car sirens made an unholy music.

"This is as far as I go," the taxi driver advised. "There's a young war ahead!"

Johnny and Long Tom were already getting out of the machine. They forgot to pay the driver, and he in turn did not think of collecting. They ran forward. Men and women passed them. Two men led a woman who was having hysterics.

"They killed fifty men or more!" the woman screamed. "The bodies were everywhere!"

Johnny registered incredulity, and gasped, "A Brobdingnagian exaggeration, let us hope."

The snare-drum sound—surely a machine gun—rattled out again. Smaller firearms cracked. Shotguns went off. Gas bombs made rotten-egg noises.

A burly policeman loomed up and yelled, "Hey, this ain't no show! Get back where it's safe!"

Long Tom and Johnny showed their police-commission cards.

"What's going on?" the feeble-looking electrical wizard asked.

"Pirates!" said the officer. "They're cleaning out the *Seabreeze!*"

Going on, Long Tom and Johnny rounded the corner and came upon a surprising sight.

THREE very large trucks were backed up to the pier at which the bright, new liner *Seabreeze* was tied. The van body of the outer truck had been shot away over a small area, and it was evident that the interior was lined with thick steel. The truck tires were ragged where bullets had struck, but had not gone flat, indicating they were of solid rubber.

The engine hoods and radiators also seemed to be armored, although the engines were of a type which sat inside the cabs, and thus were difficult to shoot into.

A man—probably a news photographer—was getting pictures on top of a near-by building. A machine gun snarled from behind one of the trucks, and he dashed for cover. A fresh burst of firing started.

Possibly fifty policemen were in sight. Others were arriving. They had set up a regulation Lewis gun, and its drumming uproar burst out.

Johnny got his bony length down behind a row of parked cars. Windows were shot from some of the cars. Trailed closely by Long Tom, he worked to the side of a police sergeant. He asked questions.

"The *Seabreeze* is carrying gold bullion," the officer explained. "They're looting her. Must be thirty or more of them."

The sergeant drew the pin of a gas bomb, drew back and hurled it.

"Won't do any good," he added. "Them birds are wearing masks."

"Using regular army tactics," Long Tom growled.

"We'll get 'em," said the cop. "We got men taking their pictures with telephoto lenses. We're blocking every street leading away from here."

It became evident that the ship raiders had thrown up a barricade of sand bags, probably unloaded from the trucks, behind which they could crawl to load the trucks. Only rarely did one of them show himself above the barrier. Each lapse of this kind drew a fusillade of bullets.

Long Tom unlimbered his machine pistol, as did Johnny. They joined the police besiegers. There was little else they could do.

"Consummately unbelievable," said Johnny, referring to the whole affair.

"It does seem to be about as big a thing as was ever pulled in New York," Long Tom agreed. "Hey! Something's gonna happen!"

The truck engines had been turning over steadily. Now they roared. The huge vehicles began to move.

This was the signal for the police. Everywhere, officers leaped up, emptying their guns. Crash and roar of firearms was terrific. Bits of siding fell off the trucks.

The giant vehicles did not turn up or down the street, as expected. They continued straight across the wide waterfront thoroughfare. They were aiming for a large wooden door in a building. The first truck hit the door. It was of very thin wood, and caved in. The truck vanished inside. The others followed.

AN instant later, it was evident that a stout steel door had been put up from the inside of the building in place of the wooden one. A great roar of gunfire came from the building as bricks fell out of the walls here and there, exposing loopholes obviously prepared aforehand.

The police retreated. Occasionally, one fell, wounded.

The officers began to yell for ladder wagons from the fire department, in order that they might scale the roofs of the buildings.

"There's a court behind that building," a bluecoat shouted. "Try to get into that!"

"They're trying," he was informed. "The gang has the walls covered."

Some fifteen minutes passed. The vicinity began to take on the aspect of a battlefield. Out in the bay a tugboat maneuvered, a light field gun, secured from the fort in the bay, on its after deck. Police in number had grown to several hundred. White-clad ambulance attendants were thick.

Then something happened that knocked every one speechless. There was a rending crack—it really started with a whistle that might have been made by some body going at terrific speed. The throng gazed, stupefied, at the sky, scarcely believing what they saw.

"A big ball!" a cop gasped. "It come up out of the court behind that building and went away so fast you danged near couldn't see it!"

WHILE they still goggled at the heavens, there was another echoing report, and a second ball sailed upward, visible at first, but rapidly gathering speed until it could hardly be followed with the eye.

No more balls arose. Shooting from the building had stopped. Policemen stormed the place.

"They'll find exactly nothing, is my guess," Long Tom prophesied.

He was right. The officers found the trucks, badly riddled. They found one bar of gold which had somehow been overlooked in the excitement. Considering the magnitude of the theft, and the roaring manner in which it had been executed, it was remarkable that only one gold bar had been overlooked.

Six million dollars had been taken. The *Seabreeze* purser gave out that information. Not quite a dozen men had been killed, although one excited tabloid newspaper placed the estimate at two hundred. Altogether, it was the most spectacular bit of news which New Yorkers had experienced in a long period.

Most stunning of all, perhaps, was the manner in which the thieves had vanished. When last seen, they were fast-traveling specks in the sky. Nor was another trace of them discovered.

Of course, every one now connected the streaks in the sky—at first thought to be peculiar comets—with the mysterious balls. There was one point which caused confusion. At first, the balls had made streaks in the sky. Now they made none.

Long Tom and Johnny discussed that as they rode uptown, baffled and a little sheepish because they had been of practically no assistance in preventing the robbery.

"I don't understand it," Long Tom said. "Maybe the streaks weren't made by balls, after all. And what kind of things are these balls, anyway? How do they work?"

They got out of their cab in front of the apartment building where they had left Renny guarding the prisoners. Paying the fare took a few moments. They turned to go in.

"Look!" Long Tom exploded.

Renny sat in a car across the street; his head and shoulders showed plainly, so that there was no doubt about it being Renny.

"What the heck's he doing down here?" Long Tom quipped.

The next instant, one of Renny's huge hands lifted and beckoned to them, indicating that they should come over.

They ran across the street, unsuspecting, hands far from the armpit holsters which held their supermachine pistols.

Two men came from behind a parked car on the right. They flourished revolvers. Three came from the left, also with guns. They were members of the gang who had been in the apartment.

They said nothing. They did not need to, for their manner was fully explanatory of their intentions. Long Tom and Johnny put their hands up.

A small man got up from the floor of the car beside Renny. Crouched down there, out of sight, he had grasped Renny's arm and waved one of the engineer's big hands, thus giving the summons which had deceived Long Tom and Johnny.

Renny, it became apparent, was unconscious.

THE gang was using three cars, all large sedans of somber color. In not more than twenty seconds after the first man with a gun had appeared, the cars were in motion—Long Tom in one, Johnny in the other.

A woman had been hanging with her head out of a near-by window. Now she began to scream. Her shrieks were so piercing that a baby in a perambulator up the street burst into loud crying.

One of the men stuck a gun out of a car window. The weapon sent thunder along the street. The woman's head disappeared.

Another man in the car snarled, "We ain't killing women, you louse!"

"Who's killing women?" the other snorted. "I shot out a window twenty feet from where she had her head!"

The cars did not travel swiftly enough to attract attention. After a dozen blocks, they stopped in an alley. No one was in sight. A shift was made to three other cars of entirely different color and model. These separated.

Long Tom squirmed about as they began to bind his arms securely with bits of cotton rope. There was little he could do.

"What are you going to do with us?" he demanded.

"Plenty," a man informed him.

Long Tom managed to grab a wrist and twist it, causing the victim to cry out in pain, and, as he flounced about, his gun was dislodged from his waistband, where he had stuffed it.

Long Tom had been contriving at that. He tried mightily to get the gun. They beat him down and kicked him soundly for the trouble he was causing.

A long time later, the car stopped in a woodland. Long Tom peered out and discovered that the other two machines had also arrived by other routes. Far away, through the trees, the electrical wizard caught sight of a gleaming object.

"What next?" asked one of the men.

"The chief says to get Doc Savage and all of his men together," replied the man in charge.

"Risky, ain't it?"

The other shrugged. "We're going to do some tall question asking. Chief wants to know just how much Doc Savage has learned about us, and whether he has left a written record of what he has dug up."

Squinting at the gleaming thing through the trees, Long Tom suddenly decided it was a ball—a large globe of some obsidian material.

One of the men came over, took a bottle and a handkerchief from his pocket, poured some of the contents of the bottle on the handkerchief and suddenly pounced upon Long Tom, clamping the saturated cloth to the electrical expert's nostrils.

Long Tom held his breath as long as possible, but they punched him in the stomach until he had to take air.

The first whiff brought the odor of chloroform. He coughed, flounced. He managed to get a lungful of fresh air. Endeavoring to make them think he had succumbed, he tried to fake oncoming unconsciousness while holding his breath again.

"Full of tricks, ain't you?" snarled the man, and hit him just above the belt.

Long Tom inhaled the anaesthetic in gobbling haste, and, before long, felt it take hold. His last impression was that of Johnny and Renny fighting against handkerchiefs being pressed against their nostrils.

## Chapter 13
## SINISTER ORGANIZATION

THE room was dark, so very dark that it seemed filled with something solid. At one point only did a trace of light show, a small faint glow which, on closer examination, would have been ascertained to be the luminous dial of a wrist watch.

After a while, there was noise of a door opening, and a flashlight lunged out whitely, picking up a prone figure. The beam collapsed. The motion of the watch-dial light patch indicated the man was being lifted and borne into another room, equally dark, but into which jangling sound of a radio speaker penetrated. He was dropped heavily, and those who had borne him stalked out.

Doc Savage's trained voice asked, "Who is it?"

The man who had just been carried in said, "Nock Spanner."

From elsewhere in the room, Monk's small voice spoke up, "How did they get you? And why'd you run off from us at that old ranch?"

"Oh, that?" Nock Spanner made a disgusted noise. "I saw somebody and followed them. At first, I wasn't sure it was some one. You see, I just saw a movement. Then, when I did make sure it was some one skulking, it was too late to turn back and get you. I wish I had. They grabbed me a little later."

Ham said from close by, "I am getting very tired of this."

Nock Spanner asked, "You all tied up?"

"Like mummies," Monk growled. "And handcuffs galore."

The radio ground out music steadily.

"What do you think they'll do with us?" Nock Spanner asked.

"No idea," said Monk.

"Have you—learned if my brother is still alive?" Spanner questioned.

Monk hesitated, then admitted, "No."

The radio stopped jangling music; there was a station announcement, then a news broadcaster with a staccato manner of speaking took over the microphone.

"Our affair of the flaming comets seems to be taking on the complexion of one of the most gigantic criminal rings of all time," he said, the radio loud-speaker reproducing each word distinctly. "At least half a dozen crimes of importance can be attributed to the Comet Gang so far to-day, the largest being the fantastic robbery of bullion from a ship at a New York City pier, only a short time ago. In addition to this, a jewelry concern was rifled in Chicago, and banks robbed in various other cities. In each case, it is certain that the robbers were members of what is now being called the Comet Gang, and escaped in the fantastic ball vehicles, which scientists admit to be some new type of terrestrial ship capable of traveling at terrific speed, and of handling with remarkable facility."

The radio commentator went on, and his broadcast became dryer and dryer as he ran out of concrete information and began generalizing.

"He's been on the air steady, pretty near," Monk grumbled. "Boy, am I getting tired of that voice!"

Nock Spanner said, "It is evident that we are entangled with a gigantic criminal ring which has perfected this terrestrial ship, or whatever you would call it, and are using it as a get-away vehicle in the commission of huge crimes."

The radio in the other room suddenly went silent.

"They cut the speaker into their private transmitter-and-receiver hookup when they communicate with each other," Monk said in a stage whisper. "Listen to what they say. They've sure got an organization!"

SHORTLY afterward, the radio in the next room went into operation. Evidently a call had been picked up on a supplementary receiver, and the large speaker cut in for convenience in operation.

"This is W2OLA coming back at my friend in California," said the faint speaker voice. "This is W2OLA in Corona, Long Island, New York City, coming back to California. I just got all of the tubes in the box, old man. Your system for doing it worked splendidly. All three tubes are thoroughly boxed. Yes, sir. I am going to deliver them now. So long—and seventy-threes, old man."

That was all from the radio.

Monk muttered in the darkness. "I'm getting able to pick out the general meaning of their code," he grumbled. "Take that conflab just now. It meant they've got something done in New York, something involving three——"

He left the words hanging. Silence was thick. The ticking of the watch with the luminous dial was audible.

"Go ahead—say it," Ham suggested. "That radio talk might have referred to Renny, Long Tom and Johnny."

"Yeah," said Monk, "that's what I was thinking."

Nock Spanner snarled, "Ain't there any way of getting out of this?"

"I wouldn't worry too much," Monk told him.

Spanner swore joyfully. "Then you have a plan?"

"No," Monk told him. "But Doc, here, is something of a magician."

Spanner muttered, "If the police only knew where to look for us. Why in Sam Hill didn't we leave a note or something, telling what we had learned, or what we intended to do?"

Monk advised, "Like lots of good ideas, that one comes too late."

Time passed. It could not have been much more than an

hour and a half. They heard a cracking noise characteristic to the arrival, departure, or passage of one of the mysterious aërial globes. Then there came a voice.

There was something familiar about the voice. It took them a moment to place it. Then Ham gasped incredulously.

"That voice—the same one was on the radio from New York not over two hours ago!" he said sharply.

No one said anything for a while; then they heard the voice of the newcomer again, and within a few moments, other voices and the tramp of feet. These approached. Scuffling quality indicated men carrying heavy burdens. They came inside.

They bore Johnny, Long Tom, and Renny, all of whom were unconscious. The trio were deposited in the darkness.

"You birds enjoy yourselves," a voice said. "We're going to hold a party later."

The men departed.

Doc Savage heaved up and strained mightily against the handcuffs which held his wrists. There was no hope of breaking them. It was doubtful if, even with his incalculable strength, he could have broken one of them, for they were very heavy.

And three manacles held his arms. In addition, there were many turns of rope. It was against this that he struggled, and he was loosening it, getting a little play into his arms.

A stirring indicated that either Johnny, Long Tom, or Renny was reviving. It was Johnny's voice which first broke the silence.

"I'll be superamalgamated!" he mumbled.

The word was a favorite of Johnny's. He used it to express disgust, despair, surprise, or any other violent emotion.

"Feel all right?" Doc asked.

The ropes on the bronze man's arms had loosened somewhat, enabling him, by squirming mightily, to reach the row of buttons on the front of his coat. He tore one of these off, got it between his fingers, slipped it down between his manacled ankles, and began to work with it.

Johnny mumbled gloomily, "I feel like a valetudinarian."

"A man who can think of a word like that can't be so bad," Monk told him.

Doc Savage had managed to unscrew one half of the button from the other half; a threaded joint permitted this, although so skillfully done that no casual examination would have disclosed it. He carefully tilted the button and let the stuff in the hollow interior trickle on the handcuff links. He did this most painstakingly.

Nock Spanner growled hopelessly, "Isn't there some chance for us?"

Long Tom and Renny had both regained their senses now. Voices anxious, they made sure Doc and the others were unharmed. They noted the luminous dial of Nock Spanner's watch and asked the time. He told them.

"Holy cow!" Renny boomed. "We were brought from New York out here to California in not much more than two hours!"

Nock Spanner demanded desperately, "Didn't you fellows leave some sort of a trail by which the police may find us?"

"No," Renny said.

Doc Savage had taken four more buttons off his coat, carefully unscrewed them, and emptied the contents on the cuff links. Try as he would, he could not reach the others. He waited. The radio in the next room had not been switched on. Silence was deep.

Once, Monk pondered aloud, "I wonder what happened to that girl?"

"And Leases Moore and Quince Randweil," Ham echoed.

It must have been more than an hour later when voices became audible in one of the adjacent rooms.

"There's nothing more to hold us up," a voice said. "The balls are perfected to the point where they don't leave luminous trails at night, as did the first ones. We can go and come, and no one on earth can stop us."

Monk, in the intense darkness of the inner room, muttered, "So that's why there were streaks in the sky at first, but none any more."

"What about the prisoners?" a voice from outside queried.

"We'll get rid of them now."

Stunted's voice spoke up, saying, "I tell you jaspers, I don't like the idea of shootin' down anybody in cold blood."

"Aw, don't be a sissy!" he was advised.

The door had been locked. Now the fastenings rattled, and the panel opened. Men came in cautiously, spraying light from flashes. They cast the beams about.

"Look!" one of the men howled suddenly. He raced the

white funnel of his flashlight. Stunned profanity came from those with him.

Doc Savage was missing from among the prisoners. The bronze man was not in the room.

Stunted ran over and howled at Monk, "How long has he been gone?"

"I dunno," Monk said, truthfully.

The man with the queer eyes dashed inside, heard what had happened, and snapped out a revolver. Stunted shoved against him heavily.

"Use you head!" Stunted snapped. "With those birds alive, Doc Savage will come fooling around, trying to get 'em loose. That way, we'll have a chance at him."

"You have got a brain, after all," growled the cross-eyed man, and pocketed his weapon.

The man went over to the spot where Doc Savage had been lying. He stooped, picked up a bit of metal, and examined it. The thing was a portion of a handcuff link.

- The man touched a finger to it, then cried out in sudden pain and wiped the finger frantically on a handkerchief. He threw the handkerchief away.

"What is it?" Stunted demanded.

"Some powerful chemical of an acid nature," the man growled. "That infernal bronze fellow must have had it hidden somewhere on him, and put it on the handcuff chains. It weakened them until he could break them."

Stunted mumbled, "That's a new one on me."

DOC SAVAGE could hear the voices—rather, hear the murmur of them, for he was not close enough to distinguish the words. He was in the gloom just outside the old ranch house. He had been free something like ten minutes, but had not left the vicinity for more than one reason. It was essential that he free the others. And he wanted a look at one of the fantastic ball conveyances.

There was one of the mysterious vehicles off to the right; its rounded hulk was vaguely distinguishable. Fog was making the night very dark. Doc eased toward the thing.

The size of the ball became more impressive as he drew close. He touched its smooth surface. It felt like glass. He moved around it, noting the polished nature of the covering, probably made thus to reduce friction. Even then, the heat generated must be tremendous.

He came finally to a door, barely large enough for him to wedge through. The door operated like a plug. The walls were thick—almost four feet, he judged.

Inside the thing, a small electric bulb glowed, furnishing illumination enough to get an idea of how the shell of the vehicle was constructed.

The outer surface, some compound resistant to friction and heat, no doubt, was only a skin, and under that was layer after layer of asbestos, interlaced with cooling pipes and wires and tubes and mysterious channels having to do with the operation of the contrivance.

The interior chamber was roughly circular, literally a bit of open space completely surrounded by machinery. There were devices on the walls, even the ceiling. Remarkable indeed was the fact that the control room seemed to have neither top nor bottom, as far as arrangement of the mechanism went. There were polished pipes, crisscrossing, their purpose hard to explain.

Doc examined the machinery. The first device he came to was an electrical mechanism for producing tremendous degrees of cold, a contrivance utilizing liquid air as its cooling element, in place of the more common ammonia.

This, then, was what kept the ball cool when in motion.

The liquid air-cooling device was a commercial product in part. Trademarks of the manufacturer were distinguishable. Doc read the plate.

REFRIGERATING, INC.
NEW YORK

The bronze man passed that up as not being of chief interest. How was this device propelled? What gave it the fantastic power to rip through space without benefit of propellers, or, as far as could be seen, rocketlike discharges.

Certain it was that the luminous exhaust which some of the balls exuded when in motion was not discharge of a rocket nature, as some had at first thought.

Doc Savage began going over the largest and most intricate mass of apparatus. He had already gathered an infinite respect for the brain which had conceived all this. That respect became infinitely greater as he surveyed a set of huge motors which utilized a compressed gas as fuel. The things were of fabulous horse power for their size. There were, as far as Doc knew, no others like them in existence.

The exhaust of the motors explained the streams of sparks which some of the balls left. The burned gas came out of the exhaust in the form of flame. In this ball, the exhaust led through a digester which cooled it. Without the digester, the ball would leave a trail of the still-burning vapor.

The motors operated compact generators which undoubtedly delivered great voltage. Wires from the generators led into a metal-covered receptacle which undoubtedly held the secret of the whole incredible propulsion method. This was locked. Doc went to work on the locks.

He had operated only a moment when he heard voices outside. Men were approaching.

"We'll clear out of here before Doc Savage can come back with help," Stunted's voice said.

Doc's flake-gold eyes whipped about. Interior arrangement of the ball was fabulously compact. Only a locker device to the left seemed to offer concealment. Doc lunged for it, got the metal door open.

The place had evidently been intended as a storage place for loot. It was empty, now, but yellowish marks on the rough metal showed where heavy gold bars had reposed—no doubt loot from the liner robbery in New York.

Doc closed the door. There were slits for ventilation, and through these he could look, if he were not discovered. He waited.

Men clambered up the narrow channel that led through the thick hull. The door was evidently heavy, for they closed it mechanically, then spent some moments with wrenches, connecting the pipes from the door to the cooling machine. Stunted was among them.

Under an arm, Stunted carried Monk's pet pig, Habeas Corpus. He had muzzled the porker to discourage biting tendencies.

"Let's go," Stunted said.

PROFUSE and strange experiences had come Doc Savage's way in the past, including many that bordered on the incredible, the fantastic. But this was one which was to stand out always in his memory.

His great metallic frame seemed to grow suddenly and mysteriously light. He lifted an arm instinctively, and the effort was incredibly easy. And once the arm was up, it did not drop back to his side. It seemed to possess no weight. The effort made him start a little, so that he lifted from the floor. He hung there, in mid-air. It was necessary to push himself back to the floor.

Out in the control room, things were happening which would have driven a superstitious person into a frenzy. Men were walking on the walls, the ceiling, adjusting the controls, and throwing switches.

The crisscrossing tubes, which had seemed so useless before, now advertised their use. They were hand rails, employed in going from one place to another. A man ran up one, spider fashion, body seeming to float in the air, then released his grip and floated where he was.

Doc Savage moistened his lips. He rarely showed excitement, but he was animated now.

Here before his eyes he was seeing demonstrated the product of a fantastic scientific discovery, a discovery so advanced that even the bronze man, for all of his learning, was somewhat dazed.

If he correctly interpreted what he was seeing, the creator of this aërial device had discovered how to nullify that type of force generally designated as momentum, as well as various forms of attraction, gravitational and otherwise.

No unschooled person could hardly have been more amazed than the bronze man. Here was inertia, gravitational attraction in all or most of its forms completely stifled. Some incredibly keen brain had penetrated one of the scientific fields probably least known to man. Modern science in general was not even quite sure what gravity was. Here was one who had mastered the subject.

The ball must be in motion. The machinery was making a great uproar. Shouted orders could not be heard. The men were communicating by gestures. One man in particular watched a bank of electric thermometers which registered the outer temperature of the shell and warned of increasing friction heat generated by their passage through the air. This man made a sudden gesture when the needles crept too high, and the speed of the ball was evidently slowed.

Other men glued eyes to periscope devices which evidently permitted them to look outside. Two more worked frantically with radio direction finders, evidently keeping track of their position by spotting well-known broadcasting stations on the earth below.

It was superscientific travel in its superlative degree, and Doc Savage could only stare and marvel. He was getting a vague idea of how the ball was made to move. No doubt gravitational force was nullified on top, on one side, creating in effect a vacuum in the lines of force which sucked the ball along.

It was a vague theory, capable of many refutations according to known scientific data, but it was the best solution the bronze man could assemble until such time as he had an opportunity to inspect the power plant itself.

The ball seemed to be arriving at its destination. Men made gestures. Others jerked levers, opened switches, and turned valves.

So completely was momentum nullified that even their stop, abrupt though it must have been, was not apparent. The noise of the mechanism ceased.

Doc Savage was conscious of an abrupt return of the normal heaviness of his limbs. He was conscious of something else, too—a terrific force which hauled him against the locker door, so that the door, unfastened as it was, fell open, and he came crashing out into the control room.

Too late, he understood what had occurred. The ball had stopped in a different position, so that the locker was now on what had become the ceiling. With the mechanism turned off, he had simply fallen out.

## Chapter 14
## OSAGE RENDEZVOUS

STUNTED saw the bronze man first. Stunted, knowing what would happen when the ball stopped, was holding to one of the crisscrossing bars. He let out a howl, dropped from his perch, and lunged for his sawed-off automatic rifle, which he had tied to a stanchion with a bit of stout cord.

"The devil himself!" Stunted bawled.

Two other men had gotten the hatch open and were

making it fast. The opening was now on the side. They swung around, but were in a bad position to fight.

Doc lunged at Stunted. The latter was having trouble with the cord that held his rifle. He had used a cord too strong for him to break. He gave it up, retreated, and threw a wrench at Doc.

The bronze man dodged it, leaped upward and caught the crisscrossing bars. He made for the men at the hatch.

Doc was a master at this method of fighting. Where the others had to move slowly, supporting themselves, the bronze man whipped about with infinite agility. One man at the hatch dropped away. The other held his ground, maintaining a grip with one hand, trying to fend Doc off with the other.

That was a mistake. An instant later, he slammed heavily down on the metal plates beneath. A bronze, clublike fist had knocked him senseless.

From his vantage point under the hatch, Doc saw that he had a moment's respite before any of them would be in a position to use a gun. The bronze man was curious about where the ball had landed. He decided to look, and bobbed his head up.

What he saw changed his whole plan. He had intended to fight, overpower the men, take the ball, fathom its secrets. But he could never do that because, outside, there was a high concrete fence, and inside that, four other balls and something near two score of men. If the bronze man escaped, it would be a miracle.

A bullet smacked the rim of the hatch as he vaulted out. Stunted had gotten his rifle loose and fired it. The pig, Habeas, squealed shrilly.

Doc poised on the hatch edge, hanging by his fingers. There were men below, many of them. It was too dark for them to make out details, however.

Doc Savage exerted all of his powers of voice imitation and sent out a sharp, excited shout.

"Something's gone wrong!" he yelled. "This thing may blow up! Get away! Run!"

It was Stunted's voice which he imitated, and the shout held an edge of terror and warning which sent those below surging back.

Doc dropped down. The ruse would give him not more than a second or two. Less than that, it developed, for

Stunted's real voice swore out from inside the ball, advising his fellows of the deception.

Doc ran for the wall. It was high, too high for him to leap. But it had been poured in a rough plank form, the planks stepped in toward the top for a narrowing effect. It could be climbed.

The bronze man leaped, caught hold, climbed, slipped, then gained the top just as a spotlight caught him and guns began crashing. He went over safely.

The other side, he discovered, was camouflaged with brush and transplanted vines. He carried some of the stuff with him as he went down. Then he ran. It was infinitely dark. He kept hands out before his face, in case he should run into something. Behind, they were organizing a pursuit party.

Then, to the left, a feminine voice called, "Over here, whoever you are!"

It was the girl, Lanca Jaxon.

Doc Savage found her a moment later. "We had better leave here," he told her.

"Oh, it's their big bronze trouble!" She sounded relieved. "You are supposed to be dead!"

"According to whom?" Doc asked.

"Leases Moore and Quince Randweil," she replied. "Listen to that uproar! We're going to have some trouble."

The shooting from inside the concrete compound had lost its confused note. A great many hand searchlights had appeared. Men were assembling outside the inclosure.

Doc found the girl's arm, and they began to work through the undergrowth. Timber here was thick, many of the trees large. Fallen logs made travel difficult.

"Three of the balls just arrived," said the girl. "I guess you were in one of them. Where are your men?"

"Prisoners," Doc said. "I suspect they are in the other balls."

"How did you get away?" she asked.

Doc told her, very briefly, making it sound rather simple, and finishing his recital with a question, "What are you doing here?"

"Leases Moore and Quince Randweil let me out of their ball," she replied. "They were afraid I would make trouble at the wrong time."

"Where do they hook into this?"

The girl laughed harshly, without humor. "They were slated for suckers."

Doc was ahead now, his superior agility and keener senses making for faster progress. Even at their best, they could hardly hope to distance those behind.

"The man who invented the balls got Leases Moore and Quince Randweil to finance him," said the girl, resuming. "Their idea was to do what they are doing: organize a gang and use the speedy balls for get-away vehicles in the commission of big robberies. But Leases Moore and Randweil were greedy. They demanded too big a cut. The gang grabbed them and held them. They were prisoners when you found them."

"And you?" Doc prompted.

Brush through which they traveled made swishing noises. There seemed to be no night birds. Evidently these had been frightened away by the arrival of the balls.

"They've been holding me out here for six months," the girl snapped. "I own the land around here. They're using it. And they've ordered all of the materials with which to build those balls, in my name, the idea being that I was the goat in case the law found out where the construction work had been done."

She gasped as a bough whipped her.

"It's too bad I didn't know who your two men, Monk and Ham, were when I tried to escape in that car yesterday," she said. "We might have gotten away. As it was, I ruined their break."

A bullet whistled through the branches, making sharp, ugly sounds, and the shot noise itself followed, thumping and echoing from the surrounding hills.

"This is the most deserted place in Oklahoma," the girl murmured. "Nobody will hear that shooting."

THE girl was breathing heavily now. She had fallen before, but she was falling more often now, and more heavily. She was slower getting up.

"I haven't slept for days," she said. "I guess I'm tuckered out."

Doc Savage picked her up, found what felt like a large tree, and moved out until, by jumping, he located a branch. With the grip of only one hand, and still carrying the girl, he swung up. He mounted with surprising speed.

"Take it easy," Lanca Jaxon said, uneasily. "This stuff might do on a circus trapeze, but I don't care for it here."

"We will wait here," Doc told her quietly. "If they miss us—excellent! If not, we'll try something else."

The bronze man waited, listening. With his free hand, he tested the dryness of the bark on the tree. Then he sniffed the air. It seemed that there had been a rain recently. That meant they had left footprints.

The rapidity and sureness with which their pursuers approached indicated they were following a trail.

"They'll come right to this tree," the girl breathed.

"Let me have your shoes," Doc requested.

She began, "Now, what——"

Doc whipped the shoes off her feet without more argument. Carrying them, he dropped downward and expended some moments locating the exact limb which he had seized from the ground in starting his climb. From there, he went on.

He used the girl's shoes, one in each hand, to make tracks beside his own footprints. Light and time for a finished job was lacking. He did the best haste permitted.

Men with searchlights and guns came up rapidly. They drew near the tree which held the girl. Just before they reached it, Doc grasped a dry limb and deliberately broke it. The cracking noise rattled through the timber.

"They're ahead!" Stunted roared, and the gang charged past the tree which held Lanca Jaxon, without dreaming of her close presence.

Doc found another tree and climbed it. He took a chance on the spreading boughs interlacing with other trees. They did. He went on. Reflected glow from the pursuing lights occasionally dashed palely among the treetops. Using that illumination, Doc picked the spreading limb of another tree, and with a tremendous swing through space, reached it. A professional gymnast would have been proud of that feat.

Shortly, the gang came upon the spot where Doc had gone aloft. They wasted much time probing the treetops, then spread out slowly, searching fruitlessly. But, by now, Doc was safely away.

The pursuers were persistent. It required fifteen minutes

of hunting to disgust them, and then all did not favor giving up.

"Aw, we'll wait for daylight," advised the voice of the man with the uneasy eyes.

They turned back.

Aware that they might have left spies behind, Doc Savage was more than ordinarily cautious in returning to Lanca Jaxon. So silent was he that she gasped out sharply when he dropped to the limb beside her.

"They've given up!" she breathed. "When they passed under me, I thought sure——"

"I did not get to ask you the most important question of all," Doc told her. "Who is the individual behind all of this—the inventor of the balls?"

"I don't know for sure," she said.

"You have an idea?"

"That man with the shifting eyes," she said. "I have overheard things. If he is the big chief, not all of the gang know it."

"What did you overhear that led you to that idea?" Doc asked.

"The man with the crossing eyes was arranging with some of the others about murdering the one they call Stunted," she said. "He's to be killed whenever they have a chance to make it look like you did it."

"So they're going to kill Stunted," Doc murmured.

A moment later, the bronze man was gone into the darkness.

Doc Savage traveled swiftly, overtaking the party which was returning slowly toward the camouflaged compound which held the four weird ball craft, and the workshops where they had been manufactured.

The men were traveling without haste. All of them seemed to be tired. They walked around logs rather than over them, and their conversation was gloomy.

"This is sure a swell kettle of fish," Stunted said gloomily. "Right when we're set for a clean-up."

"Quit grousing!" snapped the man with the queer eyes.

Stunted stopped. He put out his jaw. His sawed-off automatic rifle shifted slightly under his arm.

"So you're still tryin' to push me around!" he gritted.

The other snapped, "Pipe down, you sawed-off runt!"

Stunted had ordinarily seemed a cheerful soul, inclined to keep control of his emotions even when aggravated to the point of desiring to shoot someone. But now he seemed changed. He glared. The gun moved under his arm; his hand dropped back to the trigger.

The other men saw the signs. They sprang forward, growling angrily, and got between Stunted and the man with the uneasy eyes.

"Cut it out, you two!" one ordered. "You're going to ride each other until one of you winds up picking lead out of himself!"

Stunted, glaring, said nothing. Shortly afterward, he permitted himself to be urged on ahead. Some of the group accompanied him. Others remained behind with the shifty-eyed man. These dropped well to the rear, and there was something deliberate about their behavior.

"We got a chance to talk now," one muttered. "Them guys ahead won't hear us. What're you gonna do about this bird Stunted?"

"I'll get him!" gritted the man with the roving eyes. "But I gotta be careful."

"Did you talk to the chief about disposing of Stunted?" a man asked.

"I did!" The other's eyes crossed and uncrossed evilly in the flashlight glare. "And what do you think?"

"What?"

"The chief said that if anything queer happened to Stunted, he'd croak me," gritted the conspirator.

"That's one for the book!"

"Uh-huh." The cross-eyed man turned his flash off. "It's kinda queer. Stunted seems plumb worthless to me. Him and his sawed-off rifles! Blah!"

THEY were silent a while, listening, evidently to make sure no one was near, then they dropped their voices a little and began to discuss something which was obviously of greater importance.

"You found out for sure who the big chief is?" a man asked.

The one with the restless eyes cursed.

"No. He wears that mask all of the time. You know—that rubber hood of a business."

There was a meaningful pause.

"Our plan still goes, eh?" one growled.

"Sure." The uneasy-eyed man swore again. "We croak this head guy. We do it in a quiet way, see? Then we just tell the boys that I'm really the guy who invented the balls, and they won't know the difference. I'll get the chief's cut. You gents get yours."

"Swell!" said one. "When?"

"Soon as we can."

They went on, walking rapidly now, as if their tiredness was gone, overtaking the others.

Doc Savage clung to them like their own shadows. He had been close during the conference, and what he had heard was interesting, refuting as it did the girl's conviction that the man with the peculiar eyes was the actual mastermind.

They drew near the compound. A shrill, anxious challenge ripped out.

"Who is it?"

"Us," said the man with the uneasy eyes. "Retune that capacity alarm to compensate for our arrival."

Doc Savage heard that and moved even closer to the others in the darkness. One of the delicate capacity-balance alarms was in operation here, it seemed, and by adding or subtracting capacity at the controls, the operator managed to maintain a balance which would show the arrival of even a single man in the vicinity.

Doc's plan was to get close enough to the other that his own presence would be allowed for. He seemed to succeed.

The men filed through an opening in the high compound wall.

Doc did not follow them. That was too risky. The bronze man tackled the high wall, and covered by the noise of the others' arrival, managed to surmount it.

He lowered himself slowly down the other side, utilizing the indentations left in the concrete by the original plank forms.

## Chapter 15
## PLANS SINISTER

THERE was some faint light inside the compound. Men who had been working had moved over to the entrance—a gatelike affair flanked on one side by a building and on the other by a round tank. Evidently they were interested in how the search had come out, and being informed on that point, they scattered and busied themselves making the balls secure.

Doc Savage glided back through the shadows, reached one of the balls, and got under it, undiscovered. He was interested in getting inside, in examining the mechanism.

A stepladder evidently led up to the hatch. He climbed it, being careful that the ladder did not squeak. At the top, he explored with his fingers, but felt only the smooth, rounded, obsidian chillness of the hull. The hatch was there, its outlines barely traceable. But it was fastened, and there seemed to be no lock visible.

Feet scuffed the hard earth. Doc dropped from the ladder, scrambled behind the ball and crouched there. Men were approaching.

Stunted led them. The short man's chest was out and he looked pleased with himself. He came to the ball and climbed the ladder. Flashlights were turned on him.

From a pocket Stunted took what was unmistakably ordinary copper wires, a telegraph key and a battery, hooked in series. He touched the wires to two portions of the ball hull, where there were evidently contacts, held them there; then, covering the key with his coat so no one could see just what combination he tapped out, he manipulated the key.

The hatch was evidently operated by some electrical combination, for it opened. Stunted clambered inside, replacing his unique battery "key" inside his clothing.

He came out a moment later with a box larger than a suitcase. He handled this with great care. He passed it to those below.

"Watch it!" he snapped. "This is the heart of the invention.

111

Take that away and there ain't nobody can figure out how these balls work."

He descended the ladder, closed the hatch—which locked itself—then visited the other balls, and from each removed a similar case of mechanism.

"What's the idea of taking these out?" he was asked.

"Don't we always do it?" Stunted demanded. "Supposin' that Doc Savage would get inside one of them balls? That'd be a swell howdy-do! We'll put these pieces of apparatus where we can watch 'em every minute."

Very gently, they carried the boxes to the large building beside the gate. All lights in the compound were now extinguished by way of precaution against being sighted by some nocturnal plane. They seemed surprisingly careless in the matter of a guard, too, evidently placing full dependence in the capacity alarm.

Doc Savage was not foolhardy enough to try to get into the building by the door. He moved to the right, felt along the rough concrete wall and found an open window.

An instant later, he was inside.

IN the murk, a generator made shrill hum. Over to the left, something hot glowed. Doc studied it, and decided it was a forge with a banked fire.

Directly ahead, ranging along the side of the interior, was a partition perforated with doors, and some of these apertures were lighted. The men were toward the front.

Doc approached them. There was enough machinery to hide him—big drill presses, lathe beds, and other metalworking devices. Little expense had been spared in equipping the shop for the manufacture of the ball conveyances.

Stunted was saying loudly, "Everybody stay here and everybody stay awake. You can sleep later."

"What's up?" some one asked him.

"The chief is coming," Stunted said. "He told me to tell all of you that he wanted you on hand when he got here. He's gonna outline our next job, and it's to be bigger than anything we've pulled before."

"Since when did you become the chief's mouthpiece?" demanded the man with the shifting eyes.

Stunted grinned.

"Does it hurt?" he asked.

He was sworn at. Some one, evidently an admirer of Stunted, laughed. The man with the uncontrollable eyes got off by himself and mumbled.

Doc Savage eased closer. He was seeking his five aides and Spanner. A moment later, he saw them—all except Nock Spanner. Monk and Ham were tied together, probably because one of the gang had overheard them squabbling, and had mistaken their vocal hate as genuine.

Renny was by himself, trying to work his big fists through handcuff links. Long Tom and Johnny were barely discernible.

All five prisoners were in the room with the gang. Possibly twenty of the latter were present, every one armed. If Doc Savage had any impulse to charge in and attempt a rescue, he suppressed it carefully. He took chances, but never suicidal ones.

He moved back from the door as the lean man with the restless eyes came out of the lighted room, accompanied by two others. They lighted cigarettes, then strolled off.

"Stick around," Stunted called.

"We'll be in the radio room," one of the trio growled.

Doc Savage noted the direction they were taking—toward the monotonous hum of the generator. He put on speed himself, cutting in ahead of them, reaching the door of the room where the generator ran. He sought the corner by the door, and got down behind what was evidently a spare motor-generator unit.

The man with peculiar eyes came in. He cast a flash beam about.

"They're all with Stunted," one of the pair with him grunted.

"Watch the doors." The cross-eyed man went to the radio apparatus and turned on a light with a green shade. The radio was very modern. The man seemed to know a great deal about it, for he adjusted knobs and watched meters intently, then picked up a microphone.

The other two were at the door.

"No one coming," they advised.

Their leader's eyes crossed and uncrossed, and he spoke into the microphone, saying, "Hello—hello—hello," three times very rapidly, with pauses between, as if it were a signal.

Out of the loud-speaker came a lisping, hissing voice.

"How are things coming?" The voice made "things" sound like "thingsh."

"Slow," said the man with the roving eyes. "But we'll get the big shot to-night. He's due here before long, Stunted just said."

The lisping voice came over the radio again. Doc knew it; he could not be mistaken. The speaker was Quince Randweil, who must be cruising the skies somewhere near by in the stolen ball.

"Leases and me just loaded a few hundred quarts of nitro," said Quince Randweil.

"What's the idea?" demanded the man at the radio.

"If it comes to that, we can blow that dump down there off the map," imparted Randweil. "Here's what we'll do if everything else fails: You and the guys working with you clear out and leave the others. Before you go, turn this radio transmitter on, and leave it turned on."

"I don't get this," said the man with the roving orbs.

"We'll use a direction finder on the radio," said Randweil. "That'll guide us to you. Then we'll use this nitro. That'll clean up the gang and wipe out their chief."

"But it'll mess up the balls," the other objected.

"We've got one," said Randweil, shortly. "That's enough. We can duplicate it if we have to."

"O.K.," agreed the man at the radio.

He laid down the microphone, switched off the apparatus, laughed once and walked out, followed by his two companions.

DOC SAVAGE gave them time to join the others. He had plenty to think about to keep him from being impatient. These men were not conspiring alone, as it had at first seemed, but were associated with Leases Moore and Quince Randweil. Moore and Randweil, in turn, were proving more canny than hitherto.

Doc Savage left the radio room. He did not go too near the door beyond which the gang awaited—the room which held the prisoners. The bronze man stationed himself to the side of the gate, against the tank.

The tank was large, and smelled as if it held gasoline, possibly fuel for engines that ran the machine tools. The night had quieted down remarkably, and the cries of nocturnal birds had resumed.

There came a faint scraping from the gate.

A voice—it was the man with the peculiar eyes—demanded, "Who is it?"

"Me," said another voice shortly. "The chief."

There was a short scuffling sound, a blow, ugly but not loud, followed by a cry, a wispy, hideous thing that never really got started.

Doc Savage whipped from his cover, took half a dozen steps, then halted. Sane reason had told him he was late.

By the gate, a man laughed. The sound was strained. Some one lighted a cigarette.

A man put his head out of the workshop door and yelled, "Was that the chief?"

"Hell, no," said a man at the gate.

"Cut out the smoking," said the workshop voice. "Might be seen from the air."

"Sure, sure!"

The head withdrew into the workshop.

A moment later, Doc Savage heard three men coming from the gate toward the tank. They were infinitely furtive and walked as if burdened. Doc retreated slowly before them, and as they came around behind the tank, one displayed a flash beam cautiously.

It was the cross-eyed man and his two conspirators, and they carried the limp form of a fourth. The latter wore a long topcoat and a dark suit.

Seen in the flashlight glow, the limp individual's face was covered by a grotesque mask of flexible rubber; it could be seen plainly that the mask was padded so as to alter the apparent contour of the wearer's features.

"It's the big shot—the brains," the flashlight wielder grunted. "Let's have a look at that kisser of his."

They yanked off the rubber mask. Then they stared. They looked as if they were about to fall over. One dropped the flashlight.

The uncovered face was that of the girl, Lanca Jaxon.

# Chapter 16
## DEATH RODE THE SKY

THE cross-eyed man didn't hear Doc Savage coming, didn't dream of his near presence, probably never did know exactly what happened. His two companions knew. It helped them little, for there was not time to do anything about it.

They heard a jarring *thump*, and awakened from their surprise to see their chief collapsing under a tower of bronze. Then went for their guns. They carried the weapons in the open, in low-slung holsters, and old-time Western badmen could not have gone for them in more accepted style. One gun barely left its holster; the other stayed in the leather.

The two struggled a bit, madly. Their tongues ran out, and their faces purpled, even if they were not being choked. Nothing they did loosened the clutch on the backs of their necks, a grip of awful fingers which kneaded about as if searching for something down close to the spinal cords. After a while, the pair went limp.

Doc dropped them. He yanked the topcoat off the girl. The topcoat was big, loosely made, and Doc was just able to get into it. He picked up the mask. The rubber was of good quality, and it stretched. He got it down over his metallic features. He had some difficulty with the eyeholes.

The girl was limp when he picked her up. But there was life in her. She had been struck over the head, probably.

A man came out of the tool house. He was not excited.

"I heard something else," he said. "Was it the chief this time?"

Doc Savage stumbled toward him with the girl.

"Quick!" yelled the bronze man. "Doc Savage is in here!"

The other jumped as if a firecracker had gone off under his feet. He hit the ground with a gun in either hand, running. The fellow had nerve.

"Where'd he go?" he bawled.

Doc Savage was not using his normal voice, but a shrill, nondescript tone which might easily be mistaken for the unknown leader. He did not risk speaking now, but wheeled and leveled an arm toward the gate.

More men came out of the workshop, their wild exodus somehow remindful of the comic movies wherein a lion is discovered in a filled room. They saw Doc Savage, and since the bronze man was crouching to shorten his apparent stature, they mistook him for the mysterious leader whom they were awaiting. Doc's leveled arm sent them toward the gate.

"Where'd you get the girl?" one man yelled.

"She *was* with Savage," Doc said. And that was no lie.

Doc Savage looked into the room which held the prisoners. There were two men on guard, both pressing close to the one window, watching the pursuit conducted by their fellows.

The two were lax at the moment, whereas, a bit later, they would have been alert. But the moment was sufficient. Doc put the girl down, rushed them. They saw him just as he descended upon them. It was too late.

During the brief struggle, as the bronze man accomplished the by no means easy feat of holding a man with each hand and making them senseless simultaneously, Monk began to thrash about on the floor, and the pig, Habeas Corpus, came out of a corner, where he had been secreted.

Monk and his pet had recognized Doc.

WHEN the two men were unconscious, Doc lowered them. He leaped to the prisoners and began working on their bindings. He loosened their legs first. Wrists would have to wait, for they might need to move fast.

Monk got the gag out of his mouth. He was only handcuffed at the wrists, and hence could move his fingers.

"What happened?" he gulped.

"Help me loosen the others," Doc rapped.

Renny, ankles loosened, heaved erect.

"What do you think?" he boomed. "What do you think about that Nock Spanner?"

Monk growled. "Aw, you can't hardly blame Spanner."

"They promised Spanner that if he'd tell them what all we had learned about them, they'd turn him loose," Renny growled. "So he told them we hadn't learned much of anything, and they did turn him loose, back there in California, before they brought us here in them infernal balls."

"Spanner wanted to save his neck," Monk defended. "You

can't blame him. That runt, Stunted, made the deal with Spanner. I think Stunted didn't want any more killing than was necessary. I think he got Spanner turned loose."

Ham got up and wrenched his gag out, then snapped, "I've been wondering if that Nock Spanner couldn't really be the chief of the gang?"

Doc Savage made no comment on that, a circumstance which caused Monk to look suddenly suspicious.

"Where did they put the apparatus that is the heart of those balls?" Doc asked.

"They've got a big iron safe in the next room," Monk explained. "Locked 'em up in there."

Doc Savage left the prisoners to free each other and lunged into the adjoining room. He found the safe. It was big, modern, and the lock was evidently similar to the electrical devices on the balls, for there was no knob visible.

The bronze man began to work at the door, seeking a method of opening it.

It was a baffling problem. He had no special tools. The vault was as burglarproof as science could devise.

Doc backed away and went into the workshop, searching for a cutting torch. There was almost certain to be one around. Eventually, he did locate one, but the tanks were disconnected and he had to assemble them, and the torch he had selected did not function properly.

He was working madly when two shots ripped out noisily and a man shouted. Doc lunged to the door. Three men had returned through the gate and discovered that something was wrong.

An instant later, Renny's big hand appeared in a window. It held a gun, evidently one taken from the guards. The gun went off four times so swiftly that it required a sharp ear to distinguish the reports.

One man fell down, then dragged himself out of sight, shot through the legs. The other two bounded back through the gate.

There was shouting from the woods. It did not come from very far away. The searchers were coming back. Against such a force—almost forty men—Doc and his group had little chance. The bronze man ran out into the open.

"We'll have to get out!" he shouted.

Renny bounded into view, still carrying the revolver. Long Tom, Johnny and Ham followed, supporting between them the girl, Lanca Jaxon, who seemed to be regaining consciousness. Monk did not appear.

"Monk!" Doc called.

There was a pause and no answer.

"*Monk!*" Doc made it louder.

The homely chemist popped through the door. He had his pig.

He gulped, "If I only had a minute or two more——"

"Come on!" Doc clipped.

THEY did not run for the gate. The men outside would make exit by that route difficult. They moved back to the rear, and climbed the wall. Doc assisted in getting the girl up and over. She was able to help herself a little. Five revolver bullets made the final stages of their climb exciting.

Going down the other side, they carried much of the camouflaging along. Renny produced a flashlight.

"Found it on the floor!" he boomed. "It's sure gonna help!"

"It will," Doc agreed. "It may save our lives."

They used the flashlight as little as possible at first, not wishing to draw more bullets.

The girl dropped alongside of Doc Savage. She fell down frequently. Her voice was hoarse.

"I made a bad move," she said. "I got tired of waiting in that tree. I was worried about you."

Doc advised, "You should have stayed there."

"I know it." She took a header, got up at once. "I climbed out of the tree and went toward the compound, and pretty soon I heard some one. He used a flashlight and I saw it was their chief, wearing his rubber mask. So I got a stick and clubbed him."

"Kill him?" Doc asked.

She gasped out, "No! He was still alive! I felt of his pulse."

Doc queried, "Then what?"

"I put on his regalia," she said swiftly. "I thought maybe I could get in and help you, or free some of the other prisoners before they got wise. I can make my voice hoarse. Listen."

She made her voice hoarse, and it sounded almost masculine as she continued, "I got as far as the gate, and was coming in when some one must have struck me down."

"I saw that part," Doc told her.

She sobbed once.

"I've made an awful mess," she wailed. "I've got men killed and everything."

"Got men killed?"

"Two of them," she elaborated. "The first was one of the gang, whom I bribed to send a message to Willard Spanner. You see, I knew Willard Spanner, and knew that he was a friend of yours, and I wanted you on this affair, and thought I'd get you through Spanner."

"So that's how it was." Doc helped her. Pursuit was overtaking them.

"They must have spied on the man who took the message, made him tell about it, then killed him," she said. "Then they killed Spanner, first seizing him in San Francisco, then taking him to New York and making him get a letter telling the whole story, which he had mailed to his New York address, in case anything happened to him. He marked the envelope so it would be turned over to the police if he did not appear to claim it. I heard them talking about it."

Monk howled, "We're gonna have to travel faster than this."

Doc Savage stopped very suddenly. "Listen!"

They halted.

"I heard it, too," Monk muttered.

# Chapter 17
## HOLOCAUST

"IT" was a faint moan of a noise, and seemed to come out of the sky far above, persisting only a moment before it died away.

Doc Savage, listening, made a faint, exotic trilling noise, a sound which he made under profound emotion, surprise, sometimes puzzlement. It was an indistinct tone, eerie in quality, and covering a large range. Then, with a snapping leap, he was at Monk's side.

"What's wrong?" Monk gulped.

"What were you doing back there when we called you?" Doc rapped.

"Why—uh—I was in their radio room." The imperative tone of Doc's demand had taken the homely chemist's breath.

"Why?" Doc barked.

Monk let his pet pig fall. Something was up.

"Uh—I thought I'd send out an SOS," he explained. "Somebody might have picked it up and notified the cops. We need all of the help we can get. I intended to tell you about it."

"Did you leave the transmitter on?" Doc queried with a studied calm.

"Sure. Why?"

It was a long moment before the bronze man answered, and during that interim, it was noticeable that sounds of pursuit had ceased, indicating those behind had also heard the moaning sound in the night sky and correctly interpreted its meaning.

"Leases Moore and Quince Ranweil had an arrangement with their friends in the gang to drop nitroglycerine on that inclosure if the radio was turned on and left on," Doc said.

Monk said cheerfully, "Well, that oughta wipe the place off the map. Good riddance, I'd call it!"

But Doc Savage seemed to have other ideas. He listened. Shouting of their pursuers was faintly audible.

"Leases Moore and Quince Randweil are above us in their ball!" a man yelled. "We'd better get back to the pen."

"Sure!" barked another. "We'll rig our own balls! It'll be daylight soon. Then we'll chase this Doc Savage in the balls and use gas on him. We may be able to spot Moore and Randweil, too."

Doc Savage left his own group suddenly, and went toward the pursuers. He moved swiftly. Sounds told him they were going back.

"You fellows!" he called sharply.

They stopped. Silence held them. Then one shouted suspiciously.

"Whatcha want?"

"This is Doc Savage," Doc told them.

"We know that voice," one barked. "Whatcha want?"

Doc hesitated. He had faced this problem before—whether to guarantee his own safety and the safety of his friends by permitting others to die. But it was against his policy, a policy to which he adhered rigidly, to see human life taken needlessly if there was any possible method of avoidance. He reached the decision he had known he would reach.

"Do not go back to that compound," he shouted. "Leases Moore and Quince Randweil may drop nitroglycerine on it!"

Stunned silence fell over the darkened timberland.

THE quiet held for some moments, and toward the end of the interval, Doc was not looking at the spot where the foes stood in the darkness, but at the sky above the compound.

The compound was lighted brilliantly now, illumination having been switched on during the excitement. The lights were very bright. They threw a glow upward some distance.

A gleaming object was outlined above the compound. It poised there, bobbing up and down a little, its presence marked only by the vague rays from below. The ball vehicle of Leases Moore and Quince Randweil!

"It's a trick!" a man shrilled. "The bronze guy is trying to keep us away from the pen!"

They ran back, and although Doc Savage called out again, it had no effect. Doc fell silent, and stood there, unpleasant expectancy gripping him.

Renny came up, splashing a flashlight beam.

"Didn't do much good," he said dryly.

Doc made no reply; the others of his party gathered nearer. The ball was still above the compound, swaying up and down, as if the control device was not perfected to a point where the thing could be held absolutely stationary.

Then a rifle smacked. Others followed. A machine gun made rapid stuttering sounds.

From within the compound, they were shooting at the ball, striving to drive it away. The gunfire became a continuous volley.

Suddenly, a round spot of light appeared on the undersurface of the ball. A port had been opened.

Below the ball, dropping swiftly, came something small and black. It fell lazily. In size, it was like a beer keg. Another of the articles appeared, then a third—a fourth—a fifth. All five of them were in the air—when the first hit the ground.

The world turned blasting white as the nitroglycerine struck, and the earth heaved and tumbled and trees fell over. Bushes lost their leaves. The wind of the explosion, reaching as far as where Doc and his party stood, upset them, and the ground, shaking, tossed them about as if in an earthquake.

From the compound, there was no screaming. Possibly no man lived to scream after the blasts. Flame and débris were in the sky, and the ball, fantastic thing that it was, had backed up into dark nothingness until it was now invisible.

Débris falling back, made a great roar; it added more fuel to the flaming compound, and slavering copious quantities of black smoke kited upward.

"The gasoline tank!" Lanca Jaxon said hoarsely.

After that, no one said anything.

The balls in the compound had been shattered. They could not see them. The smoke spread, mushrooming, and the light of the flames jumped above it and played like scarlet goblins on a black toadstool.

Doc said, "We had better see if we can do something."

But before they could move there came a sobbing noise from above, as of a gigantic bat in swift passage, and the ball of Moore and Randweil was suddenly above them.

"They're gonna attack us!" Monk shouted.

THEY were standing in an open space, plainly lighted by the flames. They had been seen. Doc sent out an arm, and started them for the cover of the nearest tree. The girl was past running swiftly, and he carried her.

As soon as they were under the foliage, such of it as still stuck to the trees, the bronze man urged them sharply to the left. Fallen limbs were thick on the ground.

"Get down under this stuff and crawl," Doc directed.

They did that. A minute passed. Two. Then the earth heaved under them, a fabulous crash set their eardrums ringing, and there was white fire in the air, as if lightning had struck. Débris fell all about, making sounds like fast running animals.

"Nitro!" Renny howled. "They're trying to finish us!"

The branches under which they lay had shifted a little, and Doc Savage, looking up, could see the ball, the open hatch like a round, evil red eye. It bobbed toward them, something hideous and incredible in its movement. They could hear the noise of machinery inside.

A man had head and shoulders over the hatch opening. He was a plump, rounded man—Quince Randweil, no doubt, and he was looking down. They could see him waving an arm behind his back. He had seen them, was directing Leases Moore, at the controls, to bring the ball directly over them.

Then Quince Randweil drew back for a moment, and when he showed himself again, he was gripping a container of nitro as large as a beer keg. He had some difficulty holding it, and, leaning down, made ready to drop it.

Monk said in a dry, shrill voice, "Ham, if we're gonna die now, I want to apologize for riding you."

Ham mumbled, "You big ape——"

Doc Savage rapped, "Renny! That revolver you are——"

A revolver went *bang!* beside them. There was a louder report overhead, so infinitely much louder that it beggared description.

Doc Savage, who was looking directly at the ball and Randweil, knew the nitro Randweil held had exploded. One instant the ball was there; the next it was not—and the bronze man's eyes held only pain, and knowledge of terrible danger from exploding parts of the aërial vehicle.

He did not know how long afterward it was that some one spoke. It was Renny's voice.

"I didn't intend to do that," Renny said.

He was shifting his revolver from one hand to another, as if it were hot. He looked at Doc.

"What else could I do?" he mumbled.

"Nothing," Doc told him.

"I didn't intend to hit the nitro," Renny groaned. "Honest, I didn't. I figured on shooting past that Randweil bird and scaring him into dropping the stuff before he reached us. But no man can shoot straight in this light."

"You didn't do bad," said Monk, who was inclined to be the bloodthirsty member of Doc's crowd.

"No man can shoot straight in light like this," Renny grumbled again. "I should've let Doc do it. You were asking for the gun just as I shot, weren't you, Doc?"

"Yes," said the bronze man. "Come on. Let us see what we can do at the compound."

THEY could do nothing. That was evident when they came close. The blast of the nitro had been terrific, and had shattered, not only the four balls, but the workshop and the tank as well.

One missile must have landed directly on the workshop— possibly more; for hardly a trace of the place remained other than twisted steel and blasted woodwork. Even the compound walls had been broken into surprisingly small pieces.

Doc Savage gave particular attention to where the safe had been. Hope that it had survived faded, for he distinguished one side and back standing where the flames were hottest. The floor of the workshop had been low, and the ruptured gasoline tank had poured it contents into the depression.

There was no hope that the "hearts" of the weird aërial balls, the mechanism which was the secret of their amazing performance had survived.

"Holy cow!" Renny said gloomily. "It looks like nobody is ever gonna know how them things worked."

Doc Savage nodded slowly. He would investigate, of course, but it was doubtful if the secret could be solved. Some new theory must have been stumbled upon, by accident. But he would work on it, work hard for the next few months, he resolved.

Monk took his eyes from the flames and looked pained, as if something had just stung him.

"We should have thought of it before!" he exploded.

"What?" Renny boomed.

"Lanca Jaxon, here, knocked out the mastermind, the bird who invented these balls," Monk explained. "She said she left him unconscious. Maybe he's around somewhere. If so, we can grab him and make him tell——"

"No use," Lanca Jaxon said, hoarsely.

"Why?" Monk eyed her, puzzled.

"I left him close to the compound wall," she said. "He was killed with the rest. I am sure of it."

Monk returned to gloomy depths, but almost at once started again, seized by another thought.

"Who did you knock senseless?" he asked.

"Stunted," said the girl. "That runty fellow—Stunted."

Renny made some comment that had to do with the way things had come out. His voice was a throaty roaring as Doc Savage listened to it.

It might have been a forewarning of what the future held.

But Renny, not having been gifted with the ability to fathom what the future held, went on with his roaring-voiced conversation.

## COLD DEATH

# Chapter 1
## HAND IN A CROWD

Doc Savage knew a hand had touched his pocket. There was a swift, wraith-like movement of fingers. Then the hand was gone.

The touch was fleeting enough, but Doc Savage knew it had not been for the purpose of robbery. The fingers had not been explorative. They had merely deposited something in Doc's pocket.

Doc Savage did not pause. Nor did he make any effort to apprehend the man who had touched him. It would have been simple to have laid hands upon him, corded bronze hands, to have trapped him.

Doc knew the man was not a thief. He was aware nothing had been removed. Doc pressed the back of a hand on the outside of the pocket and felt a square white card.

The man who had placed it there had slipped aside in the crowd. No doubt, he believed he had succeeded in delivering his message without being detected. If he had known Doc Savage better he would have known this to be an impossible feat.

It was Doc's principle to avoid public encounter unless the circumstance was compelling. He contented himself with a second's glimpse of the man who had touched him. He saw the back of a head.

The hair was scraggly, unshorn. This strung from under the frayed brim of a disreputable hat. The neck was scrawny. Little more than a bony upper spine with skin wrapped around it.

Doc Savage removed the card from his pocket. He did not slacken his speed. He had been moving through the Wall Street crowd with the easy movement of a jungle animal. Though there was a press on the sidewalk, it being five o'clock, it was amazing how this bronze-skinned man avoided contact with others.

Doc was careful to hold the card by its edges. The hands of the scraggly man had been bare. There should be finger-prints.

Doc cupped the card. His eyes flicked across it. Doc's eyes were like flaky gold with stirring whirlwinds in their depths. The whirlwinds seemed to move more rapidly now.

For a few seconds there was a haunting, trilling note. Those who might have been watching the smooth, bronze face of Doc would have detected no movement of his lips. There were many thus watching, for the man of bronze was a marked figure.

The trilling seemed to emanate from all of his huge, symmetrical body. It was a sound of which Doc himself was hardly conscious. It might presage danger, or that the man of bronze was upon the eve of a discovery.

The message on the card in his hand was brief, but explicit:

TO CLARK SAVAGE, JR.:—IF YOU WOULD PREVENT DEATH, DANGER TO THOUSANDS, CALL UNION 0-1214 TO-NIGHT AT EIGHT.

The words had been printed with a leaky pen. There was no signature. But the back of a man's head was all the signature Doc would need. Intuitively, he knew he would see the man again. Perhaps many times.

Doc Savage continued through the Wall Street crowd. Now he moved with greater speed, but still he touched no one.

The man of bronze had an errand in Wall Street. He completed his brief business before returning to his head-quarters. But his mind was busy with the problem the card in his pocket might represent.

Because of his amazing adventures, his world-wide assis-tance to those in trouble and his punishment of crooks, Doc Savage was always besieged with appeals. A few merited his attention.

And he was likewise a target for many who feared him. Even this small card in his pocket might be the bait for a trap.

When he had returned to his laboratory, Doc set about reading what he considered vastly more important than the mere printed words on the white card. This laboratory, on the eighty-sixth floor of Manhattan's most impressive skyscraper, was most amazing in its equipment.

Not even the latest equipment of the police or the Federal department of justice equalled the means here for scientific investigation. In addition, as the man of bronze had entered, the doors of smooth, chrome steel closed him in. No locks appeared on these doors. But their electroscopic fastenings made them possible of opening only to Doc and his five companions in adventure.

Doc first dusted the card bearing the mysterious message. The distinct imprints of a thumb and forefinger appeared. The card was a trifle grimy. The hand delivering it had been that of a man who worked. The soiled spots had a brownish tinge.

The bronze man dropped a colorless liquid upon these spots. The reagent brought out a definite greenish color.

For the time, Doc made no further tests. He had arrived at one conclusion which was significant. The hands placing the card in his pocket had been those of a working chemist.

THE bronze man placed the card carefully in a glass case. The voice of a man was speaking from the library adjoining the laboratory. It was fretful and complaining.

"You danged shyster! I waited where you said, but you didn't show up! Daggonit, you won't get the chance to stand me up again!"

The speaker was Lieutenant Colonel Andrew Blodgett Mayfair. His voice was shrill and childlike. But his appearance was that of an ungainly ape covered with reddish-brown hair. Because of this, he was known as "Monk." He was one of the world's leading industrial chemists.

Monk had been speaking into the telephone. The man he had called a shyster was Brigadier General Theodore Marley Brooks, otherwise known as "Ham." He was the legal luminary of Doc Savage's group.

Hearing Monk's voice, Doc Savage removed the card from the glass case. He came into the library and laid the card on the table before Monk.

"I received this about three hours ago," Doc stated. "Those greenish spots were brown."

Monk touched the edge of the card.

"The No. 7 reagent brought out the green."

Then he named a little-known chemical which had an acid reaction.

"That is correct, Monk," the bronze man approved. "The card was placed in my pocket."

A huge man with a melancholy face peered at the card and frowned solemnly. He was Colonel John Renwick, the engineer of the group. The hand "Renny" extended toward the card lacked little being the size of a ham. He read the words gloomily.

"Union Exchange, huh?"

The third man in the library said, "That's over in Jersey. And every time we have business with Jersey there is trouble."

This man had an unhealthy pallor. He was small, compared to the others. But many larger men had been sharply surprised by his strength and fighting ability.

He was Major Thomas J. Roberts, electrical wizard. His appearance had given him the name of "Long Tom."

As Long Tom finished speaking, a clock started chiming with musical notes.

Doc Savage crossed to the desk and picked up the telephone. The clock chimes touched the final stroke of eight o'clock with a harmonious lingering.

"Union 0-1214," said Doc, when he had the New Jersey connection.

A voice started to speak from the other end.

Without preliminaries, the voice said, "You're Doc Sav——"

Then it seemed as if the receiver had exploded. The voice was sliced off. No reverberation followed. There was no lingering roll of sound, such as could have been expected if the instrument had remained even for a few seconds in service.

"That was a powerful blast," Doc said. "The phone was torn out. The man who tried to talk was an old man."

Doc didn't explain further. He didn't waste more time in speech. He had thumbed the receiver bar. Two minutes later, he was given a trace-back on the Jersey call.

"Blind number," he said to the others. "It's off the Newark-Trenton highway in a marshy strip."

Doc moved ahead through the outer door. His three companions paused only to make a swift collection of a few special devices they might need. The bronze man did not seem hurried, but the others were compelled to move fast.

Doc's special elevator dropped with the speed of a rocket. It slowed with a cushiony rebound, when it reached the bronze man's private garage in the basement. Doc's long low car, with its extra-powerful motor under the long hood and its windows of bulletproof glass set in armor steel, glided toward the Holland Tunnel.

## Chapter 2
## THE HOUSE IN THE MARSH

SHORTLY before the eight o'clock telephone call made by Doc Savage, a battered old roadster turned off a paved New Jersey highway. Headlight beams laid ghostly fingers across a foggy strip of marshland.

When he was perhaps a mile and a half from the main highway, the driver abruptly switched off the lights. He parked the little car in concealment of bushes beside a crooked lane.

Climbing from the car, the driver walked cautiously ahead. Dim lights made a blur in the fog. They indicated some habitation.

Close up, this might have been seen to be an old log house. It appeared to squat gloomily in the murky depths of the Jersey marsh. The bulk of its presence was marked only by faint illumination from an upper window and one slanting finger of dancing, vari-colored light emanating from what seemed a mere slit at ground level.

From the basement, or some underground chamber, came a low throbbing. A trained observer would have said delicate machinery of some sort was being operated. Apparently, there was but one outside watcher. And his figure was only a furtive shadow among other sinister shadows cast by this strange, penetrating light.

At times, the escaping light gave forth a rainbow glow.

A rutty, obscure road that was little more than a twisting trail through overgrowths of waving swamp grass apparently was the only traffic communication between the old house and the highway of civilization, some two miles distant.

Across the swamp a pair of telephone wires had been strung along available trees, most of them gaunt-limbed and dead.

In the upper story of the old house there was no movement. Except for the faint light at the one window, there was no evidence the structure was then occupied by a living person.

THE man from the roadster apparently feared something or some one within the old log house. As he walked, it might have been observed he was a vague, catlike figure. He kept to the tall marsh grass beside the road, pausing every few yards to listen intently.

In the swamp at a point off the road, some considerable distance from the old house, was a single glowing eye of fire. The man hissed an oath under his breath. He crossed the soggy, yielding ground with such quick lightness his feet seemed to leave no imprints.

Before he reached the spot, the red eye of fire winked out.

"Hunter maybe," the man murmured. "Well, he's picked a poor spot for a camp."

As if the possible presence of another human no longer interested him, the luminous-eyed man retraced his steps. He glanced at the radium hands of a wrist watch.

"The time is near," he mumbled, "if old Jackson hasn't been having hallucinations."

Picking out a slightly higher, dry spot some two hundred yards to one side of the house, the thin figure became a motionless part of the deeper marsh shadows. His thin lips continued to emit whispered words.

"The great Doc Savage will be calling at eight o'clock, or old Jackson has guessed him wrong."

Again he glanced at his watch. It lacked five minutes to eight o'clock. There was no doubt but he had some objective which was closely related with the phone call Doc Savage had been requested to make from Manhattan.

"It won't work out," he muttered suddenly through gritted teeth. "And Doc Savage saw me. I could feel him looking at the back of my head. I never really touched him, but somehow I believe he knew I was there."

The radium hands of the wrist watch showed two minutes to eight o'clock. To the watcher's apparently raw-nerved senses, the lonely marsh had become alive with voices. His teeth chewed nervously at his lower lip.

He glanced at a dead-armed tree. It seemed almost as if he were waiting to read the message that might go out over the wires he knew were strung there. The thin threads of communication between this eerie desolation and the teeming modern heart of Manhattan.

One minute to eight o'clock. The spear of multi-colored light piercing the slit of the underground window of the squatting old house winked out. The wind moaned a little, as if the withdrawal of the rainbow gleam were a signal.

The catlike man became rigid. He glanced over his shoulder. The red eyes of fire deeper in the marsh had not reappeared. Perhaps this unexpected camper was no longer in the swamp.

Eight o'clock.

From the heart of the marsh, from no definite direction, came a low whirring sound, vicious as the warning of a poisonous rattler.

The cat-eyed watcher had reared to his feet. He had turned and was running away. The soggy ground of the swamp rocked and swayed. The earth heaved with a convulsive, shuddering blast.

THE explosion started at the place of the old house. A knife of giant flame shot upward and moved with ripping effect across the marsh.

The fleeting man was twice hurled from his feet. Each time, his face and clothing were befouled by the ooze in which he fell.

The man staggered at last to the side road. The slicing destruction that had seemed almost to be racing with him, had died as swiftly as it had come. The blast had been accompanied by an expanding phosphorescent glowing of steely blue light.

As the fugitive from his own apparent terror reached the spot where he had concealed his roadster, darkness again had enwrapped the silence that was of itself, by contrast, terrific. Over all of the marsh, the air had taken on an icy chill.

The dank, sulphuric odor of death permeated the country

for many miles. Shuddering, the man leaped into the roadster. He glanced only once at the place where the old log house had squatted evilly in the marsh.

Only blackness, emptiness was there. There was no light of any sort. Not even the deeper, bulking shadow that had been the house.

Something like hatred twisted the man's thin face. His lips slavered and his eyes burned. Then he turned the old roadster and sent it leaping away over the rutty side road toward the main highway.

## Chapter 3
## THE CANAL OF DEATH

THE mysterious watcher had ample time to get far from the scene of the explosion before State police were aroused to investigate. The narrow lane to the old log house was some ten miles from the city of Newark.

Some time, therefore, elapsed before the tearing jolt of the blast had been definitely traced. But cars of the State police were blocking the marsh side road when Doc Savage drove into it.

"Holy cow! What a job!" growled Renny. "Look, Doc! It's a canal, straight as if it was laid out with instruments and this was intended for a feed reservoir!"

Renny saw everything from an engineer's point of view.

"It does seem to have remarkable symmetry," replied the man of bronze. "It's the first explosion I ever came upon that seemed to have been done to a geometrical pattern."

"Howlin' calamities!" muttered squat Monk, his homely, apelike features showing puzzlement. "It's about the completest mess I ever bumped into!"

"Complete's the word, all right," assented Long Tom. "And it looks as if it wiped out some high-class electrical machinery. Look here, Doc!"

They were then beside a deep, rounded crater. It could be seen from a few remaining foundation stones imbedded in the earth that this had been the site of a house. But underneath it the ground had been scooped out as if by the swing of a giant shovel.

On three sides of the cavernous hole in the spot where the house had stood, the explosive force had apparently lifted directly upward. An ordinary powder blast, if of sufficient strength and buried deeply, could have done this.

But Doc was coming to some startling conclusions, as he glanced along the fourth side of the explosion crater. Instead of spreading in a mushroom burst, the blast had been definitely directional.

Passing up, for the moment, the smashed electrical equipment Long Tom had pointed out, Doc led the others away from the blast's place of origin. They saw the explosive force had moved laterally along the ground, cutting through the marsh by reason of the road having curved in a wide bend more than two miles in extent.

The great ditch that had been cut was as evenly grooved along its sagging banks as if a steam shovel had heaved out the soggy mud. Where the house had been, this canal was its exact width. As Doc and his companions made their way along the sucking marshland, the cut gradually narrowed.

They had proceeded about a fourth of a mile, when Renny grunted, "Doc, would you look at this!"

A man lay at the edge of the knifed-out ditch. The torso, head and arms were there. The legs were missing. The man had been sliced in half. It was as if a giant cleaver had suddenly descended.

A shotgun and a pack showed the victim had been a hunter. Doubtless, he had made his lonely camp, waiting for dawn and the first flight of fowl. Ashes of a dead fire were near by.

Doc examined the explosion cut more closely under his generator flashlight. The character of the clean incision in the soft earth and the phenomenon of the hunter's body having been neatly severed in the middle were supplying him with information.

Long Tom said, "There's a busted electrical machine back there. Something must have gone up accidentally. But that would mean tremendous voltage. Giant generators would be needed to create the energy for a lightning blast like that. Unless——"

"Unless," said Doc, "the secret of cracking the atom has been coupled up with transmitted electromagnetic force, or something similar to that."

A short distance from the dead man, possibly a mile from the annihilated house, the canal cut petered out. It terminated in a rising indentation only a few inches wide and an inch or two deep.

Doc had placed the warning message card in his pocket. Now he led the others rapidly toward the site of the greater explosion. In all that mass of scattered wreckage, the State police had passed up the thought of discovering fingerprints.

Doc produced his own outfit. He had noticed every detail of the wrecked electrical machine indicated by Long Tom. A polished copper ball had fallen to one side. With State police watching curiously, Doc dusted the gleaming surface.

The lines of a forefinger, then of a thumb, took form. Under a powerful glass, Doc studied the grimy message card, then the convolutions and whorls of the lines on the copper ball.

Returning the card to his pocket, he said, "One and the same man, a scraggly little fellow with the prehensile type fingers."

A State police sergeant stared at him.

"You're Doc Savage, aren't you?" he inquired.

"Yes."

"Wouldn't worry any more about those prints then," said the sergeant. "If he was in there, he isn't much use to anybody now. Come over here, Mr. Savage."

The man who had been in the house would neither be a menace nor a help to any one again. Only one foot remained, the leg severed roughly at the top of a high-laced boot such as a man might be wearing in the marshy ground.

Doc only glanced at it.

"No," he said, "this wasn't the man. It's some other person. I think this may be the one who was on the phone."

Doc's final words were addressed in a low tone for his own companions only to hear. Doc was piecing together the scanty material he had.

Some one in the house in the marsh must have known he was under a sentence of death. At least he was aware of some menace hovering over him. This other man, he of the scraggly person, had been sent with a message.

That might be it, but Doc was not thoroughly satisfied. Perhaps the person, or persons, responsible for the gruesome tragedy might have a reason for bringing him to the scene. This thought stuck with him strongly.

He pondered the possibility of this having been a demonstration. The messenger might have intended to have him on the telephone when the blast was set off. He would be sure Doc Savage would go directly to the scene. Then his purpose had been fulfilled.

No more likely evidence appeared in the wide-flung jangle of house wreckage. The booted foot was all that told a man had been in the house. Doc led his men to his car.

DURING the investigation of the explosion, an automobile had been playing hide and seek with State police and other cars arriving at the scene of the great explosion. Several times, the automobile was swung into side roads as sirens screamed warnings that forces of the law were arriving.

At last, the police having passed, the elusive car came into the main highway and sped northward toward Newark.

A motorcycle patrolman who had remained watching the highway was hidden around a curve as the speeding auto flashed by. He immediately swung onto the concrete and gave chase.

The motorcycle forged abreast of the auto's rear fender. The driver of the car jammed his foot suddenly on his brakes. The auto swayed and rubber squealed. When it skidded, the motorcycle patrolman hadn't a chance.

The motorcycle catapulted into the air. It turned over three times. The policeman became only a limp bundle in the ditch.

The driver of the car glanced along the highway. No other lights were showing. The man talked rapidly for perhaps a minute. It was peculiar behavior, for he seemed making some sort of a speech.

Then he climbed from the car. He kicked around in the loose soil a few yards from where the motor cop lay motionless. The driver then got back under the wheel and the car sped toward Newark.

By this time, some of the State police were returning from the scene of the explosion.

When Doc Savage and his men reached this spot, a State police car had just discovered the policeman in the ditch. The motor cop was beginning to revive. He had only been knocked out.

He was able to say it was a car of well-known make that had wrecked him. The license plate had been smeared with mud.

Doc eased from his car.

Two other police cars stopped. Passing motorists halted their machines. Soon there was a small crowd around the motor cop. The man's face was badly slashed.

From the last of the civilian cars to stop, three men got out. None noticed the driver of this car turn off into a nearby side road. At this moment, the small group around the injured patrolman had frozen to silence.

From the wall of foggy darkness over the marsh beside the highway, floated a high-pitched voice.

*"Doc Savage beware! Do not seek more information! I cannot be overcome! I control the world's most terrible force of destruction! I will not brook interference! For I am—Var!"*

The mysterious voice ceased abruptly.

"Holy cow!" grunted Renny. "What is it, Doc?"

Doc had scanned every foot of the near-by ground. It had been much trampled. The flashlight produced nothing.

"We'll have a look along the edges of the marsh," advised Doc. "You might try kicking around a bit in the loose grass."

Monk's short body with his gorilla arms trailing vanished in the fog. The chemist peered closely from the eyes deep-set in rolls of bristly gristle.

"Dag-gone it!" he growled. "I did hear it!"

He was not referring to the sepulchral tones coming from nowhere on the highway. Monk had heard another faint voice. It had sounded like a man's hoarse cry for help. Where any one needed help, there might be a fight. Monk pushed forward hopefully.

Separated from his companions, Monk decided he would rather handle this alone than wait and miss it. Pushing deeper into the marsh, he saw a man waist-deep in the sucking mud of a bog. The man was sinking deeper with each second.

"Keep your chin up, fella!" Monk called, and started to wade into the mire.

From the tall grass, figures sprang upon him. There were

three of the men. They had Monk at a disadvantage. He was already knee-deep in the bog. One man hurtled through the air and landed on Monk's back. It was his mistake.

Monk's long arms snapped up and back. His clasped hands hooked behind the other man's head. Monk's shoulders barely twisted and the man turned over twice in mid-air before he splashed face down in the mud.

Unable to release his mired feet, Monk whipped a fist into another man's face. The man sat down with a whoosh! The third man had been more wary. He had held back. When he moved, a thick, heavy club swished down upon Monk's unprotected skull.

Monk fell as if he had suddenly sunk in the quagmire. Oozing mud and water choked his mouth and nostrils.

AFTER several minutes of fruitless searching for the origin of the spoken warning, Doc, Renny and Long Tom came back to the highway. They waited ten minutes, but Monk did not appear.

A big car, with a rear trunk compartment opening under the wide seat, came from the side road a hundred yards away. Unnoticed, it wheeled into line with the parade of cars now returning to the city from the scene of the explosion.

Doc and the others combed the marsh for more than an hour. Then Doc summoned Renny and Long Tom.

"They've got Monk," he said. "I found the place in the swamp where they fought it out."

Doc had retrieved Monk's muddy hat.

# Chapter 4
## GHOST VOICE AGAIN

"FURTHER search here would be useless," announced Doc Savage. "Monk's captors undoubtedly have returned directly to the city. I judge that, for the present, he will be unharmed. We are confronted by an organization in control of a hitherto unknown force."

In a remarkably brief space of time, Doc's car was piloted

down the ramp of his special garage under the skyscraper headquarters. When they had ascended, the bronze man apparently had arrived at some definite conclusion.

For some time, he said nothing. His smoothly corded hands were assembling some small, but powerful, electrical amplifying coils. His knowledge of explosive forces, especially of electromagnetic energy and powerful rays and waves surpassed that of any other living man.

When he spoke, Doc's words had little connection with what his hands were doing.

"There is a woman in the strange happenings of the night," he said, calmly.

"Holy cow!" exploded Renny. "I didn't see any evidence of one!"

"Yes, there is a woman in it," stated Doc. "She was speaking, only a murmur, but perhaps arguing with this man who calls himself Var. All of us heard a ghostly voice in speech. I was listening to two voices."

Renny exhibited no further surprise. Doc's auditory perception was maintained by his daily two-hour exercises on a specially devised scale of vibrations. His hearing was selective.

"You're planning some form of new electrical detector," Long Tom remarked, watching Doc's skillful bronze hands assembling some wound copper coils and a series of tiny, but powerful, generators to be combined in a single power unit.

"Hardly that," stated Doc. "The explosion was brought about most likely by the accidental unleashing of tremendous electrical force. A hitherto undiscovered means of producing high voltage seems to have been involved. The day is close when we shall find vast explosive energy confined in small, compact machines."

THE special device established in the elevator corridor of Doc's headquarters gave a warning buzz. In the square of glass at one side of the laboratory a figure appeared, walking from the elevator toward Doc Savage's door.

He was a youthful, smiling-faced telegraph messenger. His expression seemed proof he was somewhat awed, but much pleased, at this opportunity to visit the headquarters of the famed Doc Savage.

The messenger stood by as Doc signed the book and opened the yellow envelope. The message read:

HAVE UNEARTHED BONES OF PREHISTORIC PLATY-
PUS WHICH PRE-DATES PALEOZOIC MAMMALS STOP
WILL BE DOMICILED AT CASPER FOR FORTHCOMING
FORTNIGHT IF YOU SHOULD DESIRE TO COMMUNI-
CATE

JOHNNY

"Johnny" was William Harper Littlejohn. He was the archaeologist and geologist of the Doc Savage group. For several weeks, he had been in Wyoming investigating a new discovery of prehistoric bones.

When the book was signed, the messenger reddened a little and stammered, "M-Mr. Savage—c-could I just have one look into your laboratory—p-please?"

Absorbing the telegram, Doc said, "Certainly. Stand here by the door."

The youthful messenger gasped as he gazed upon the hundreds of glittering devices of polished metal and glass within the big room.

"Gee!" he exclaimed. "Gee!"

He turned and walked toward the outer door, crossing the office as if he were a little dizzy from what he had seen. At this instant, the ghost voice came again, thin but strident.

"*Doc Savage—I am too strong even for you! I have your man Monk! Keep out of this or he will be destroyed without a trace! One by one, your other companions will be taken! You, too, must die if you persist! Nothing can stop me before my purpose has been accomplished, for I am—Var!*"

The messenger boy stopped an instant, eyes widening. He looked at Doc and his two companions. None of the three had spoken. The messenger turned and fled toward the elevators.

"Holy cow!" growled Renny. "They've planted something here while we were out! Come on, Long Tom!"

Long Tom joined him in the beginning of a search. They were pulling out desk drawers. Long Tom started to lift a corner of a rug.

Doc picked up the telephone. He gave the number of the nearest telegraph office. In a few seconds he replaced the instrument.

"We won't tear up the place," the bronze man announced, calmly. "The voice walked out with our smiling messenger boy. I could have stopped him, but just now, perhaps, it is better to permit this Var to play his hand a bit farther. There has been no telegram sent from Johnny."

"No message?" grunted Long Tom. "Then this fellow who calls himself Var must know all about us and what we're doing."

"That's it," Doc said, grimly. "Var not only has remarkable scientific knowledge, but he is clever-brained in other directions. Brothers, we are opposed to perhaps the most dangerous mind of our experience!"

A BUZZ of the desk phone interrupted further speech. Doc picked up the instrument.

"This is the police commissioner. Doc Savage? . . . Well, there's Hades popping! You're probably the only man who can be of help. This is something too big for my men to grapple with."

Doc said, "What is it?"

"It looks as if that explosion over in Jersey wasn't any accident," said the commissioner.

Doc said nothing, waiting.

"And we're up against something else," continued the commissioner. "The next blast is scheduled for Long Island. It's due to happen any time! You know J. Afton Carberry, the fellow who made millions lending money in South America and Europe?"

"I know him," said Doc. "Retired after the depression trimmed many other financiers dealing in foreign stuff. Disappeared for a year. Announced he was writing a book on cellular origin of the human species. Quite a smart chap."

"You know everybody," grunted the commissioner. "But Carberry isn't so smart, right now. He's scared green! Called in a few minutes ago. Had a crazy warning, he said, from some sort of a voice where there wasn't anybody. Carberry's lost his head!"

"What was the message?" interposed Doc. "Did it fix a time?"

"Nearly as he could repeat it, the message said: 'You have forty-eight hours to accede to my demand and place your fortune at my service. Other financiers will be quickly forced to follow your lead. I have a force none can oppose. Before dawn, you will see a demonstration of it. You can't combat me, for I am—Var.'"

"I shall be awaiting you at Carberry's home," stated Doc.

The bronze man delayed only to direct Long Tom to carry out the electrical experiment he had begun. The electrical wizard returned reluctantly to the laboratory.

"You'll accompany me, Renny," Doc instructed.

Renny, who had gathered part of the phone conversation, already was inside a special bulletproof vest of Doc's invention.

The bronze man flowed toward the rocket elevator. They dropped with the speed of a falling plummet to the basement garage. Doc's powerful, armored car threaded through the thinned traffic of the darkened streets.

While he drove, Doc was considering the possibilities of the threat against J. Afton Carberry. Doc's amazing, many-sided brain also was recalling all known forces which might be employed to give explosive energy a definite path of destruction.

## Chapter 5
## MONK IS SILENCED

AT the moment Doc Savage and Renny were speeding to the home of J. Afton Carberry, Monk awoke in a coffin-like space. His long arms and short body were folded and cramped. A hard metal wall jammed his head down upon his thick neck. His feet were drawn up.

For once, Monk was thankful his legs were shorter than his arms.

"Dag-goned if I ain't dead an' buried!" he grunted, trying to wedge himself into an easier position. "Nope, I ain't dead. My head must've been busted wide open."

Monk breathed with laboring lungs. His mighty chest heaved with the effort to extract a supply of ozone from the foul air in the confined space. Strength flowed back into his body.

"Anyway, I ain't in the graveyard yet," he muttered, "or I'd 'a' been smothered. An' by the calamities, I ain't staying here!"

Monk's body, housing the strength of half a dozen ordinary men, began to swell. He filled his lungs to capacity and his iron chest heaved. Elbows levered against the walls of his metal prison.

The maker of the trunk under the rear seat of the automobile had not designed it to withstand any such concentrated dynamite. The metal clasp and the brass tongue of the lock snapped. The curved upright lid of the underseat trunk flapped open with a bang.

Monk's landing was in keeping with his apelike contours. He hit on his feet. Low growls of warning, amazement, impinged on his hairy ears. A man uttered a low curse and hurtled toward him. Other figures converged in a rush.

THEY were in a dimly lighted concrete garage. Monk saw it was apparently in the basement of some larger building. Heavy iron doors were closed and barred. Monk lithely evaded the first rushing figure. With an incredibly fast sweep of one arm, he gripped the man's thick neck. His assailant was heavy, but Monk's iron muscles contracted with the force of an immense rubber slingshot.

His attacker was lifted from his feet. His body traveled a short arc through the air. The man's head deeply dented the metal back of the car above the flapping lid of the trunk. He collapsed to the floor without a groan. The human skull was never designed for withstanding such an impact.

A jungle bellow issued from Monk's throat.

"C'mon, you yella rats!" he growled. "Come an' get it!"

Three men, relying on strength of numbers, accepted the invitation.

Both of Monk's fists made definite, sickening contact with flesh and bone. One of his feet twisted between the third man's legs. He sprawled on top of his two companions. Others were coming at him, but Monk glimpsed one man standing back.

This man was short of body, broad of shoulders and face. His small eyes glittered piglike in rolls of eye-rimming fat. In his moon face the mouth was a small aperture. Set above a double chin that was adding a third roll of lard above his collar, the tiny mouth gave him a grotesque appearance.

Monk saw he was badly outnumbered. Leaping clear of the floor on his short legs, he projected his body between two more men. The backs of their heads cracked the floor. Another man hit Monk a dizzying blow behind the ear with some blunt weapon.

Monk staggered. He was facing the moon-faced fellow with the little rat-hole for a mouth. The man had a polished piece of metal in one hand. It was shaped like the round box for holding steel tape. From this box a slender stream of sizzling vapor shot into Monk's face.

Monk gritted his teeth against the pain. It was an ammonia gun. Blinded, scarcely able to breathe, Monk went to his hands and knees under a rush of bodies. A minute later he was firmly bound about the arms and was being propelled up a stairway.

Monk's captors placed him in an elevator operated automatically. Eyes smarting from the burning fumes of the ammonia gun, Monk could only guess at the number of floors they ascended. Then he was led along a hallway.

One of the men swore and muttered, "Where's that button, Wheeze?"

Though he was only beginning to see dimly, Monk knew it was the moon-faced man who was called "Wheeze."

"Right under—*siss*—that little picture—*siss*—by the molding, dumbhead!" came the reply in the wheezing voice. Wheeze talked like a chronic case of asthma.

Monk could see enough now to know they were in the room of an elaborately furnished apartment. A panel in the wall swung open. It revealed a spiral stairway. The mean snout of an automatic was pushed into Monk's back.

At the top of the stairway they emerged into a vaulted room of lavishly rich fittings. The walls of the room were odd. They were covered with paintings in oil. All of these represented some of the lower forms of marine life. In spite of his ticklish position, Monk was intrigued by this unusual display of art.

"Nobody but a nut'd ever lived in this dump," he muttered.

He heard one of the men address Wheeze by another name. It was McGovern, apparently his last name.

"Soft pedal the titles, Smoke," rapped Wheeze. "Stick to the handles the chief tacked on."

By that, Monk judged the chief of this gang was not among those present.

Monk was pushed into a chair. Wheeze came and stood before him.

"So you're the big ape Doc Savage uses for some of his chemical tricks!" he stated. "Well—*siss*—there's one or two little tricks we want to find out. Also, mister, you're going to tell us something about Doc Savage's set-up. There are several things we need to know."

"Try an' make me!" gritted Monk.

Wheeze's little mouth puckered and his small eyes gleamed wickedly.

"I gather from all those misfit words, you imagine you're not going to talk, eh?" he sissed at Monk. "Well, we'll see. Smoke, is the convincer all set?"

The man called "Smoke" smiled genially.

"The convincer's always ready," he put forth. "Right this way."

A single wide glass door was opened at the side of the room.

MONK was pulled to his feet and propelled into the adjoining space. This was a bare, small room with enameled walls and no furnishings. The single man occupying it required no chair. He was of shining armor metal and he stood erect in the middle of the floor.

The binding cords suddenly fell from Monk's arm. But two men with automatics poked the snouts into his ribs.

"We try to avoid shedding the blood of any person," Wheeze sissed in a sanctimonious voice. "Every man's blood must be on his own head. So we——"

Monk was shoved close to the armored figure. He saw the contraption was some sort of robot. It appeared to be hollow, and large enough to admit the person of a very large man.

Monk's still-smarting eyes blinked at the robot's half-bent arms. For in the metal fingers were clutched two long-pointed knives. These were directed inward toward the robot's gleaming breast. It looked as if the metal man was thinking of taking his own life.

In one enameled wall was a black switchboard. It contained a complicated array of electrical switches, coils and other gadgets. In its center was what seemed to be the circle of an enlarged microphone.

"Everybody quiet!" ordered Wheeze. His companions instantly became silent. None even moved. "Now watch, you wise ape!"

One man stepped to the switchboard and turned a button. When he stepped back, Wheeze spoke in a low tone.

"Do your stuff, big boy," he said.

Slowly, the metal arms of the robot moved inward. The

pointed knives approached two slits in the armored breast. The movement was so slow as to be almost imperceptible.

Slowly, chillingly, even though the shining figure was but cold metal, the arms continued to bend. The points of the knives disappeared into the shell-like cavity of the robot's chest. A minute, two minutes passed. Monk growled in his throat.

Both knives at last were buried to their hilts. The mechanism ceased to whirr.

"Just one little word will do it," murmured Wheeze. "One little whisper, or a sneeze—and the mike picks up the sound and starts the robot. We're going to leave you with the convincer. After I've attended to some special business, we'll come back. If you've kept that big yap of yours quiet that long, maybe you'll be about ripe to loosen up with some conversation!"

"That's what you think!" barked Monk. "You'll get nothin' outta me!"

"That'll be just too bad—for you," sissed Wheeze, softly.

THE automatics crowded Monk's spine, then his stomach, as the metal robot opened on oiled hinges. Helpless to resist, he was shoved inside. His long arms were forced into the bent hollow of the robot's arms. The torturing device was swung shut.

The speech control button on the switchboard was off while this took place. Wheeze looked up into Monk's orbs blinking through the armored eye-holes of the robot.

"Now you can talk your head off—or your heart out," grinned Wheeze. "Ready, Smoke! Everybody out! Click 'er on!"

Wheeze followed his men through the single door of glass. It closed silently. Monk could see the men outside talking, gesturing. He could not hear their voices. He was alone with the robot and his thoughts in the soundproof room.

Monk glanced over at the round disk of the big microphone. He could see the long knives inverted directly toward his heart. Many things came to Monk that he would have liked to have said.

But he took it out in thinking.

# Chapter 6
## COLD LIGHT STRIKES

MONK was confident Doc Savage would pick up his trail quickly. He would have been much more downcast had he known that Doc and Renny were at this moment rushing along a Long Island road.

The man of bronze was even now scrutinizing a lowering sky over Little Neck. This exclusive residence section just within the boundary line of New York City, was sleeping. Great elms spread protective arms over the homes of millionaires.

At the terminus of a scattered row of ornate dwellings, was set the colonial-style mansion of J. Afton Carberry. Unlike the others, the Carberry pile of architecture was ablaze with lights. When they were half a mile from the place, Doc and Renny could see this glaring illumination against the trees. The light was reflected with a dull glow upon the low-flying clouds.

"Holy cow!" grunted Renny. "You'd think a smart guy like this Carberry would have more brains than to light his house up like a Christmas tree! Suppose this Var fellow happened to be flying around upstairs? What a swell target that would make!"

"Good guess, Renny," approved Doc. "That's the way it may come this time. We'll see what we can do about it."

Police were thickly spotted in the Carberry grounds. The white gravel of the driveway showed like a winding serpent among the trees. It was perhaps two hundred yards from the entrance gate to the illuminated mansion.

Doc drove about fifty yards along the gravel. His own powerful motor was only a whispering song under the car's long hood. The humming drone that swiftly increased to a drumming throb among the scudding clouds, was distinctly audible.

"And there you are——" Renny began to say.

A NARROW band of blue-steel light shot from the murky sky. Like a long silvery knife, it stood out against the night. Its point touched the driveway only a few yards ahead of Doc's car. But it was moving swiftly, swinging directly toward the car itself.

Doc pulled the steering wheel around, swerving the car into the trees. With a swift movement, he pushed Renny to the outside.

Renny's big body was through the door. Doc slid from under the wheel. His heels crunched in the gravel. With gliding speed, he moved to one side. His direction was toward the house.

"The thing can't miss it!" Renny yelled. "All those lights would——"

It was one of the few times in his life that Doc Savage failed to hear distinctly. The drums of his ears suddenly thundered. It was as if a gigantic knife of ice had been thrust all the way through his body from his brain to his toes.

Doc's arms and legs were instantly numbed. His motor nerves refused to respond to the bidding of his brain. His keen sight was dimmed by a frost that seemed to rim his eyes. He felt himself falling forward.

"Cold Light," was Doc's instant thought. Like the illumination created by the inhabitants of The Land of Always-Night. Only their light was cold and harmless. This was deadly, more like a bath in liquid air.

Doc was temporarily paralyzed. He tried to warn Renny to keep away, but the words issued from his constricted throat. He felt consciousness fading. Then he was suffused with a vast warm wave. By comparison, it was like a fire that set his skin prickling and brought waves of jerking pain to his muscles.

Slowly, Doc got to his feet. Overhead, the airplane was flying low. It carried no riding lights, but the descending spike of cold light revealed it as a small dark object.

RENNY had whipped out his super-machine pistol and was shooting into the air. His fire was futile. The plane was beyond the reach of the mercy bullets. Renny was beside Doc again. Police surged toward the house.

"Get back, all of you!" warned Doc. He hadn't raised his voice. He never did. The peculiar quality of Doc's calmest words always carried to those listening.

The rare, mellow whistle filled the space around him. The sound may have come from his lips. But it seemed an aura of vibration that always thrilled its hearers with the imminence of deadly danger. Doc guessed what was coming.

The air sucked away. Renny and the nearest coppers felt as if they were standing in a vast vacuum. Their mouths opened and their chests heaved as they gulped for breath. The air seemed to have been snatched from the depths of their lungs.

Doc's eyes were fixed upon the Carberry mansion. He expected to see the million-dollar mass of architecture disintegrate. But the residence remained intact.

From the thicker woods well back in the wide estate came the roar as of a rushing wind. The sound was of cyclonic intensity. In the hurricane hiss of displaced air came the crackling report of great trees being snapped off.

The long spike of blue steel flashed off. It was as if a switch had been thrown in the midst of chaos. The rolling reverberation of the long explosion abruptly died. Only the trembling ground, the hissing, sighing echoes across the countryside, the heavy bumping and plopping of falling trees and shorn branches remained as an aftermath of the blast.

POLICEMEN were climbing to their feet, dusting off their clothes. For a minute, no one moved, either toward or away from the scene of the bursting Cold Light. That is, none but Doc Savage.

Instead of heading for the spot where the blast had taken place, he was moving toward the Carberry mansion. Doc's stride was unhurried; but Renny, who immediately followed, was forced to shuffle into a trot to keep up with him.

The drumming of the plane was dying away. It was flying out over Long Island Sound. With the stoppage of the Cold Light, the pyramid of blue flame had suddenly disappeared. It had seemed to ascend for half a mile or more. Doc wondered if the Cold Light had remained on, would the flame have reached the plane.

Renny was at Doc's shoulder. They passed the policemen guarding the Carberry doors. Inside, Doc instantly identified the financier, though he had seen only his photographs in the news.

Carberry's face was the color of gray chalk. The area of color denoting his terror extended up his high, narrow forehead into the baldness between strangely thick tufts of graying hair.

The man was so tall, he was compelled to bend and droop his narrow shoulders to hold a shivering, sobbing woman in his arms. Doc, for the moment, believed this woman to be the financier's daughter. She appeared to be only about half the age of the retired capitalist.

The woman was wearing a lacy negligee. Her skin was smooth, velvety. Renny paused admiringly. The woman's face was white as polished ivory. All color had been drained from it. Apparently, she had just come into the room, aroused by the explosion.

"Darling! Oh, what is it? What is it?"

The hand of the financier on the woman's shoulder was blue-veined and thin. It trembled as he gently patted the woman's alluring, rounded arm.

"It's—it's nothing much—dear," the man quavered, hoarsely.

Doc walked toward them. Carberry stared at him an instant, then his lips parted in a half fearful smile.

"You're—Doc Savage," he said, controlling his voice with an effort. "The commissioner said he would call you. I've never met you, sir."

"And you are Mr. Carberry," Doc stated.

"Yes; and this is Mrs. Carberry, Doc Savage."

The woman gave him a tremulous smile. Her slight body shivered.

BEFORE Doc could acknowledge the introduction, another voice interrupted. At its first note, Carberry stiffened and his arm fell away from his wife's shoulders. His slightly protruding eyes of a light-bluish shade roved quickly, desperately about the room. Doc was reminded of some scared animal in a trap.

"Holy cow!" ejaculated Renny. "It's coming from——"

The bulky figure of the engineer barged across the room in the direction of the wide chimney. Doc laid a hand on Renny's arm.

The voice had addressed itself to J. Afton Carberry. Now it spoke with a sibilant, ghostly cadence:

"*Carberry—now you have seen a demonstration of my power! You have forty-eight hours! I shall communicate with you at the expiration of that time! I shall find you wherever you are! I need your millions! I know the police have appealed to Doc Savage! This time, he will fail. For I am—Var!"*

Renny's keen instinct for direction had been correct. The voice was coming from the fireplace, from the chimney. A log blazed between the tiled sides.

Heedless of the blaze, Doc thrust his body into the chimney opening. Looking upward, he had the glimpse of a head silhouetted against the sky, a shadowy, shaggy head.

Showering ashes and fire as he emerged into the room, Doc was at the outside door in a flowing stride. The policeman at the door gaped after him. He had hardly seemed to move, but he was already at the corner of the house nearest the chimney.

From there, Doc seemed almost to float up the wall of the house. The residence, with its many slight projections, was like a smooth road to the bronze man.

Doc bounded onto the roof. As he came erect, lead pounded the overlapping slates at his feet. An automatic was spitting fire from the opposite end of the mansion center gable. But fast as the attacker had been, Doc was far to one side as the remaining slugs came higher in a searching stream.

Then Doc pivoted. The ground was thirty feet below. He poised only an instant, then sprang outward. He alighted with the cushioned ease of a body set on coiled springs.

Gliding toward the corner of the house, Doc encountered two city coppers in uniform. One was holding an automatic that still smoked. He was saying, "I think I got the guy! He fell off the roof!"

Doc halted the two men. "You just shot at a man on the roof?"

"Sure!" said the cop. "I al—good gosh! It's Doc Savage! Was that you up there?"

"I was on the roof," observed Doc. "Did you see another man come down, or running away?"

"I heard a noise up there," said the cop, "but it must have been you I shot at. I didn't see any other man."

Renny was inside investigating the chimney. The log fire had been drowned. No marks appeared to show that anybody or anything had been in the chimney aperture.

Carberry was sitting on a couch. His wife still clung close to him.

"What would you advise us to do, Mr. Savage?" Carberry asked.

"I'd take Mrs. Carberry and go away as secretly as possible," Doc advised. "Make it a point not to inform even your servants of your destination. I hope within forty-eight hours we may have something more definite on this man who calls himself Var."

Doc and Renny departed from the house. Doc slipped under the wheel of his car. His intended destination was the nearest airport. He had little hope of tracing the Cold Light plane, but believed communication with some of the airports might give him a lead.

Renny exclaimed, "Look at this, Doc!"

The engineer had noticed the leather flap of the side pocket was open and lifted as if to attract attention. Renny held two square white cards. One was small, the other large. The larger card showed a printed message under the pencil ray of Doc's flashlight.

The small card bore words plainly written with bright blue ink. There was no attempt to disguise the hand of the man who had written it:

Admit bearer with password to inner circle. I am—Var.

"What do you make of it?" said Renny.

"Read this," replied Doc, passing over the larger card.

Go at once to Washington. Yellow house in 14th block on K Street. Third from corner. Do not delay. Var will be there at 4 a.m. this morning. They will not kill Monk until he has talked with you. The password for the card is "Rav Rules." Var's name reversed.

The card was unsigned. Under the pencil ray it showed stains of a brownish tinge. Doc was sure the fingerprints would be the same he had encountered twice before. The man whose fingerprints were on the polished copper ball at the death house in the marsh, had escaped the explosion.

# Chapter 7
## MONK SNEEZES

MONK, at this moment, would have been relieved if he could have known of the new cards in Doc Savage's possession. But no hint had been given he was not to die before he talked with Doc.

The enlarged microphone on the black switchboard seemed to wink at him ominously. Monk could almost hear it speaking with its own diaphragm.

"Talk, go on and talk! Why don't you say something?"

The thing seemed to be mocking him. Monk not only had no desire to talk now. He was fairly sure he never would talk again. He had no especial fear, but he couldn't avoid looking at the two pointed knives. He kept recalling how slowly they had been pushed into the slits that now faced his own gorilla-like breast.

Monk could see the movements of the men in the larger room with its unique oil paintings. Wheeze McGovern had been giving orders for nearly half an hour. Monk was sweating, wondering how long this phase of the little game was to be continued?

Like Doc and his other companions, Monk could read the lips of others. When the men were facing him, he could understand what they were saying as well as if they had been beside him. So, he understood when Wheeze picked out six of his men and ordered them to Washington.

WHEEZE picked up the telephone. He was facing the glass door of the soundproof room.

Monk read Wheeze's lips. The moon-faced boss of this group of men was calling a telegraph office. Monk saw that he called himself Doc Savage. Wheeze was giving a message. It was addressed to Theodore Marley Brooks.

Wheeze recited the message slowly. Monk quickly realized

156

a trap was being set for his bickering lawyer companion, Ham. The message, as it was being given, was telling Ham to go at once to Washington. There he was to meet Doc Savage in a yellow house on K Street. The house was designated as the third house from the corner in the fourteenth block.

Even as rage fairly sizzled through his veins, Monk made a mental note of the address. He was amazed at the knowledge possessed by this Wheeze. It struck Monk that Doc and his friends must have been under some malevolent eye, or rather many such eyes, for considerable time before to-night's flashing events.

For Wheeze had the name of the hotel in Manhattan where Ham was attending a gathering of noted legal personages. Monk knew it, because Ham had ditched him on a theater date to go to this distinguished affair.

Monk came then to the brink of apoplexy. It was more than the big chemist could endure, trying to maintain silence and keep his hide unpunctured.

The surge of blood to his head brought a sudden, fierce desire to sneeze. His huge arms were tightly locked in the robot's terrible, hollowed sheets of armor.

Monk's sneeze exploded loudly in the soundproof room. The robot's armor instantly vibrated. Somewhere close beside him, a motor had started.

The fearful knives began their cruelly slow descent toward the slits over Monk's heart. Their needlelike points gleamed with wicked menace.

Monk felt the arms of the metal man slowly drawing inward. Silence being no longer of consequence, he released a flood of choice language.

Slowly, slowly, the knives pushed inward toward the slits over his heart. The motor, pulling the inexorable arms with torturing delay, kept up a steady whirring. In the other room, Wheeze was standing with the gloating smile of some vile beast of prey.

Two men remained with Wheeze. Because of the soundproof doors, Monk's unfortunate sneeze and his following outburst had been unnoticed.

At that instant, the inwardly moving knives entered the slits. Their needle points touched Monk's shrinking skin. They became painfully penetrating agony which he could no longer evade. Two or three minutes would be required before the slicing edges touched a vital spot. When they did, they would release a scarlet flood which could never be stopped by human agency.

But the knife points were never destined to reach Monk's heart. The first touch freed all the electrifying rage so long pent up in the big chemist's huge body. His sudden bellow might have come from the snarling throat of some trapped jungle beast.

Monk drew gallons of air into his capacious lungs. His body swelled. The mammoth shoulders were bowed and braced. The long arms contracted and then expanded.

The slender rods of universal jointage necessary to operation of the robot's arms were of strongest steel. But, after all, they were, by the requirements of space, very slim. Monk's giant arms, driven by his released fury, were gigantic in their expansion.

"Hold 'er, Ham!" he bellowed. "Dag-gone it, shyster! I'm comin'!"

He voiced the truth. The rods of slender steel were snapping. They made cracking sounds, as if a man's finger joints had been bent backward. The ribbed fastenings of the metal man snapped asunder.

MONK did not heed the rake of the knife points across his hard-muscled breast. He did not even pause to regret the absence of his special bullet-proof vest, because he did not feel the slicing of his flesh. The trickling of blood also went unnoticed.

For Monk had torn loose the robot's jointed arms. He swung one in each ponderous hand.

Wheeze and his men had been turned from the glass door of the soundproof room as the instant catastrophe overtook their torturing metal man. They wheeled on their toes only when the ape-like shape of Monk crashed through the thick transparent plate.

One of the men whipped out an automatic and fired point-blank. Steel-pointed slugs played jangling sparks of fire from one of the swinging metal arms in Monk's hands. Chewed lead stung one of the enraged chemist's hairy ears.

A shot from the blazing automatic flew across the room and scarred one of the oil paintings. It completely erased a fantastic conception of nonexistent marine life. The thing was a slimy creature on oils, half human, half crab.

Monk did not observe this despoilation of weird art. One of his armored weapons had cracked the forearm bones of the man who had been shooting. He was a giant of a fellow, but he howled in agony and fell writhing to the floor.

Wheeze's other companion hurled a heavy vase off a table. The improvised weapon shattered to bits across Monk's iron-hard forehead. A little blood trickled into the chemist's eyes. His other armored weapon struck this man's thigh bone. He joined his broken-armed partner in howling on the rich Oriental rug.

Wheeze had slipped through the smashed glass door. Something on the switchboard crackled with lurid blue flame. Short-circuited wires blanked out. The rooms were plunged into Stygian darkness.

Monk found his special generator flashlight. The beam was pointed as a pencil. He sent it roving about. There was no sound. Then in the distance somewhere, was a wheezing laugh. A door slammed shut.

Wheeze had escaped.

Realizing the tricky affair of the concealed stairway they had used in bringing him in the house, Monk at once decided pursuit would be useless. Besides, more important business confronted him. He must get a warning to Doc. Perhaps he could head off Ham from starting for Washington.

Vainly, Monk jiggled the receiver bar of the phone. The wire was dead. Wheeze had thoughtfully removed this means of communication. His flight had been solely in the interest of saving his own hide.

APPARENTLY the battle in the penthouse—Monk had discovered his prison quarters to be such—had been unheard by the residents of apartments in the twelve-story building. The apartment directly underneath was vacant, though its furnishing were rich. The shorted wires from above had also plunged this place in darkness.

Monk found and employed the concealed stairway. He buzzed for an elevator. The car was automatic. Monk made the street with a blank-faced doorman staring after him.

Monk noted the apartment building was a block west of Central Park. Covering blocks with his rapid, ungainly stride, Monk reached Columbus Circle.

Though it was well after the hour for the Broadway deluge of humanity at theater closing time, Monk found himself caught in a flowing river of men and women. He marked this was not the usual after-theater crowd of dressy individuals.

It was a crowd with a distinct disharmony of apprehension, of fear, in some their voices approaching terror.

A husky-voiced newspaper vendor threaded through the human stream.

"Read all about it!" he bawled. "Big explosion in Manhattan! Var will blow up whole city block! Read it!"

Monk plowed his way to the man. He snatched a paper.

"Howlin' calamities!" he squealed. "I've gotta get to Doc!"

Monk headed for a public phone booth. He dialed the number of Doc's headquarters.

Long Tom's voice came impatiently. A call had instructed him to stand by for another message from Doc. The bronze man had said he would have some plans for Long Tom to work out in connection with a new machine he called an "ex-neutralizer."

If it could be made to work, Doc wanted it to combat the Cold Light ray. Long Tom saw a night of work ahead. He wished the bronze chief were here to direct him, instead of sending his instructions by phone.

He was relieved, however, to hear Monk's voice.

"WHERE'VE you been?" demanded Long Tom. "What happened?"

"Let it ride," said Monk. "Where's Doc?"

"Headed for Washington," replied Long Tom. "But here's Renny. He'll talk. I've got a job to do."

"Where in time have you——" Renny began.

"Dag-gone it!" interrupted Monk. "Tell me something! What's going on, anyway?"

"This fellow who calls himself Var has turned all Hades loose," obliged Renny. "The latest is his announcement with that ghost voice of his that he's blowing up a whole city block in uptown Manhattan at nine o'clock in the morning. That's to-day. Turned the voice loose in one of the newspaper editorial rooms. The big town's gone batty over it!"

"You tellin' me!" grunted Monk. "Where's this blow-up comin' off?"

"Over in the upper East Side," said Renny, giving an address only two blocks from the East River. "This Var warned the police to clear the whole block of those who wanted to keep on living. He said the blast would rock the town and destroy everything directly in its path. Said he doesn't want any loss of life."

"Dag-gone it, Renny!" rapped Monk. "What are we——"

"Coming to that, Monk. Doc's in a Red Arrow transport plane. Called in by radiophone. Said if I found you, we're to get into that block Var is planning to shoot off and see what we can find. I don't know what we're to look for. But it'll take me an hour to fight my way over there and——"

"See you when you get there," cut in Monk. "I'm on my way."

MONK reached a taxicab by the simple expedient of hulking his ponderous body directly into the crowd.

News bulletins were running in the lights around a building near Times Square:

VAR ANNOUNCES THE EXPLOSION IN MANHATTAN WILL TAKE PLACE AT 9 A.M. HE SAYS IT WILL BE CUT LOOSE FIVE MINUTES AFTER THE PASSING OVER MANHATTAN OF THE WASHINGTON-NEW YORK PASSENGER-AND-MAIL PLANE.

Monk's cab pulled away.

# Chapter 8
## TRAIL OF A SHADOW

WHILE Monk was on his way to the menaced block in Manhattan, following Doc Savage's instructions to his headquarters, the man of bronze had taken up another trail. Rather, Doc had put himself directly in the way of a shadow he believed was watching his movements closely.

Word of the new threat of the Cold Light over Manhattan had caused the bronze giant to send Renny to join Long Tom at headquarters. At this time, Doc knew nothing of Monk's escape.

The ray of Cold Light causing the explosion at the home of J. Afton Carberry had given the bronze man something definite with which to grapple. Doc's intricate knowledge of all forms of electrical energy had taught him that some of the most potent electromagnetic forces could be lessened, or neutralized altogether, by the setting up of other similar but opposing rays or waves.

He had left Long Tom working upon an electrical experiment. It came to him how a possible neutralizing force could be created to combat the mysterious Cold Light. As ex-neutralizer. That would be it.

As Doc worked out this idea, he was speeding toward the Red Arrow passenger airport. He had instantly decided to follow the bidding of his mysterious messenger and go to the yellow house in Washington. Ordinarily, the bronze man would have used one of his own fast planes for the trip.

But he judged he was being closely shadowed. By going directly to the passenger port of the Red Arrow, he would be followed. Doubtless the emissary or enemy of Var, whichever he might be, also would become a passenger on the plane.

From a concealed vantage, after booking his seat, the bronze man waited. He saw all other passengers go aboard. He smiled grimly as he watched the last man to take his seat.

Then Doc himself vanished into the wash room. In a few seconds, the plane would be taking off. When it took the air, no person remotely resembling Doc Savage was aboard.

In Seat No. 7, on the right-hand side of the Red Arrow passenger plane, sat an ugly specimen of humanity. Nature had been unkind, apparently, in the beginning of the man's career. He had been endowed with ropy, tow-colored hair and washed-out, pale-blue eyes.

In size, the man was of magnificent proportions, except for the hunching of one shoulder and a malformation of his neck. Added to these marring features, the man's nose had been broken and badly set. His cheeks were puffed and had an unhealthy pallor.

In the No. 2 seat, on the left-hand side of the plane, a little man sat hunched into the big collar of an overcoat. Only the peak of his slouch hat was visible. For more than half an hour, this passenger had not moved.

The bucking of the plane in many of the airpockets was trying even to some of the veteran passengers. Suddenly, in the recovery of a level keel, something of minor importance happened in the pilots' cabin. A service wire in the passenger cabin was short-circuited for the fraction of a second.

The mishap was sufficient to blow out a fuse. Gasps came from women passengers.

"Never mind," came the calm voice of the trim stewardess. "It's only a fuse. The co-pilot will fix it."

The co-pilot, pushed his way along the aisle. In Seat No. 2, the collar-concealed head of the little man slowly turned. The movement brought a little scream from one of the women who had been chewing gum.

The homely mug in Seat No. 7 was watching with interest.

The shock to the timid woman was amply justified. For the eyes of the man in Seat No. 2 glowed in the darkness with the luminous fire of a predatory cat prowling the night. In them, one other man in the plane read hatred colored by fear. Such as might cause the beady eyes of a rat to shine with desperation when cornered.

When the fuse was replaced and the lights came on, the ugly mug from Seat No. 7 got up and followed the co-pilot toward the control room.

"What do you want?" growled the co-pilot. "Passengers have got to stay in their seats! Hey! Nobody's allowed up in——"

The ugly mug calmly disregarded the admonition. Pushing past, he went through the little door. Inside, concealed from the passengers, he murmured a few words directly into the ear of the pilot at the controls.

"Never mind! Skip it!" barked the pilot at his scowling partner. "Take a seat in back a few minutes! It's O.K.!"

The puzzled co-pilot went back and slipped into Seat No. 7. The pale-eyed, broken-nosed passenger had slipped into the co-pilot's seat and pulled on the radio earphones.

For the space of some eight or ten minutes, this strange substitute for the regular man at the secondary controls seemed very much at home. As he talked into the phone, his gloved hands played automatically on the control wheel.

Any person would have supposed he was a flier. The veteran Red Arrow pilot was not even supposing. He knew well enough the man with the broken nose was a better flier than he would be if he lived a couple of centuries. His conversation to the ground finished, the ugly mug relinquished his place.

"Thanks," he said to the pilot. "I'll remember the favor."

The co-pilot still scowled, as he came up to swap places with the extraordinary passenger who could so readily make hash of all the rules. But the passenger did not notice this. He was, without seeming to do so, absorbing every visible detail of the little man in Seat No. 2.

From this position, it could be seen that the man whose eyes had been luminous in the darkness was rather an inconsequential personality. Every article of clothing appeared to have been worn to the point of dissolution. His hat brim was soiled and frayed. His overcoat collar was faded and threaded out. The man's collar looked saw-edged.

This scraggly appearance was continued to the man's person. His hair was stringy and uneven. His face was hatchet-thin, with an oddly turned-up nose. The chin was long-pointed and stubbly with beard. The man's Adam's apple rambled up and down.

He displayed no interest in what was transpiring in the plane. In his now normal eyes was a disappointed look. The man he had come aboard to find had not appeared.

The scrambled-faced passenger returned to Seat No. 7. When the cabin radio started staccato bulletins of the menace hovering over Manhattan, the man seemed to have dropped into a doze.

THE scraggly little man in Seat No. 2 was the last person to alight from the plane at the Washington airport. He scrutinized each of his fellow passengers hopefully, as they passed him. With a grunt of disappointed resignation, he climbed from the plane.

Walking over to the information desk, he inquired, "Has any other passenger plane or private crate from New York landed in the past hour?"

"Yes, a White Liner came in, half an hour ago," the girl said.

The little man's face brightened some. He went toward the taxicab stand with short, hopping steps. Entering a taxi, he rode only to the first darkly shadowed avenue.

Leaning forward, he handed the driver a dollar, and said, "Keep moving. I'm leaving you here."

He was back among the trees when another taxicab came from the direction of the airport and turned the corner, following the first car. The luminous eyes shone more brightly as this cab passed.

"Had me fooled, all right," he muttered. "But I guess this puts me one up on him."

When the first of the taxicabs stopped and turned after proceeding a couple of blocks, the broken-nosed man in the second cab observed that it was empty.

"Expected he would do that," the man remarked to himself. "All right, driver. Take me to Dupont Circle. I'll walk the rest of the way."

The open radius known as Dupont Circle was not far distant from a yellow house in the fourteenth block on K Street.

THIS yellow house in Washington was, before the day was very old, to become a rendezvous for several mysterious figures. With Doc Savage already near this house in a guise which had passed him on the Red Arrow plane, Ham summoned by a fake telegram and Monk aware of the trick, the identity and intentions of the scraggly little man remained an enigma.

And while Monk was delaying a possible effort to assist Ham in order to investigate the threat of a new explosion in Manhattan, still another puzzling figure was planning a trip to Washington.

This last man had been pacing the floor of a palatial apartment during the greater part of the night. He was walking restlessly up and down at the time the blast shook the home of J. Afton Carberry.

This apartment was near the west side of Central Park. The man was known as Charles Arthur Vonier, noted explorer.

Vonier had heard radio announcements of the Carberry explosion. There had been a police report saying that even the redoubtable Doc Savage was baffled; that the police commissioner believed the blasts were planned by some scientist who was remarkably sane.

Vonier had switched off this report impatiently.

"And I'd counted on Doc Savage to——" He broke off the muttered phrase.

Vonier was an emaciated, seemingly bloodless man. His thin, sensitive nose was a single arching bone with tautly drawn skin covering it. His eyes were set under projecting caverns of his bony skull. But they were intensely blue, and coldly direct. Even now, under apparent stress that made his bony hands fumble, the eyes were unflickering.

A spread newspaper on the table headlined the New Jersey

log cabin explosion. Vonier opened a library table drawer and drew out a sheet of paper. On it were scrawled words in bright blue ink.

The explorer sucked his lips between teeth protruding from his skeleton-hard jaws. He folded the paper and placed it in his pocket.

Picking up the desk tray of pens and ink, he selected a bottle. The tray was of old, soft gold done in finely wrought hand carvings. It was reminiscent of the workmanship of one of the lost, though highly civilized, mountain folk of Indo-China.

Vonier let a single drop of the ink fall from the bottle on a square of white paper. The color was brightest blue.

"The strange trick of circumstance sometimes will involve the most innocent," he murmured. "Doc Savage's microscopic eyes never would overlook a detail like that."

He replaced the bottle, with his smile becoming whimsical. Apparently, a vein of humor lay under the explorer's unappealing exterior.

A woman's dress rustled. Vonier arose to greet his wife.

"I'm glad you came in, my dear," he said. "I can delay no longer. It is necessary that I make personal contact with Doc Savage, at once."

The woman's voice was throaty but calm.

"Do you think it's best?" she said. "I can't quite understand why you must see him."

Mrs. Vonier was slender of figure, as revealed by the silken gown of scarlet. Her features were clear-cut and regular.

"I've discovered it is always best to strike the first blow, to meet an enemy before he gets himself set," stated the explorer. "I have been busy. Doc Savage will be on his way to Washington. I shall see him there."

"You will be careful?" the woman pleaded. "After all the dangers you have——"

"Bosh!" interrupted Vonier. "Doc Savage must have the message. The news will have it that the bronze wizard is baffled by these strange explosions. As usual, the news is undependable!"

Vonier called a private air field. It was apparent he was ordering one of his own planes tuned up for a quick takeoff to Washington. As he was preparing to depart, the phone buzzed.

The call was long distance. It was from Washington. From Vonier's words, some special emergency had arisen in his affairs. Before he replaced the receiver, he said, "I shall take care of that. I am just preparing to leave for Washington."

## Chapter 9
## MONK'S SWEET TOOTH

ABOUT the time the plane of Charles Arthur Vonier was being prepared for a quick flight to Washington, Monk was impatiently pursuing his investigation on the East Side. He had discovered the warning of the threatened explosion had created pandemonium.

There was the block where the fiendish Var had announced the Cold Light would strike at nine o'clock of the following morning.

A few policemen were being overrun in their effort to keep order without resorting to the use of their sticks. Occupants of many surrounding blocks were joining the general exodus.

There were perhaps some two hundred families living in this six-story block. The street level housed small shops. All of the several hundred persons involved seemed determined to be the first out with their various belongings.

Monk, to gain entry, kept close to the police. The squad had discovered nothing that savored of a planted explosive. Monk aroused the policemen's interest when he produced his pocket chemical laboratory.

With a colorless liquid, an instantaneous reagent chemical, Monk made a quick analysis of each spot on the walls or elsewhere, when it seemed the stain had been recently made. He was aware that some of the most deadly explosive could be employed in liquid form. Perhaps even in the character of some powerful chemical that could be dried and still continue to send forth some vaporous element for many hours.

After several efforts, however, Monk wondered if all the scores of families in the block threw cups of coffee at each other.

A BOOMING voice announced Renny had arrived on the trail of Monk. When the big engineer swung his many pounds of brawn through a door, Monk was preparing to depart. He had been through all the block.

"Doc's worked out an idea to stop that Cold Light ray," Renny told Monk. "Doc explained it to Long Tom by radio-phone from a Red Arrow plane on the way to Washington."

"Now why would Doc go by one of the passenger planes?" wondered Monk.

"Don't know, but it's my guess he's laying a trap for somebody," said Renny. "Anyway, this thing he calls an ex-neutralizer may stop the explosions, if Long Tom can get the right gadgets together."

Long Tom, at the moment, was attempting to step up an electrical current to sufficient power for creation of an electromagnetic ex-neutralizer on the principal of the Hertzian wave. Long Tom was familiar with the practical application of the Hertzian wave, or ray. It had been employed for the killing of airplane motors at a distance.

No place remained where it seemed likely the smallest sort of bomb could have been hidden. Renny and Monk agreed the explosive force of Var was carried in his mysterious, terrible Cold Light.

"I'll stick here an' see if the cops give it another going over," said Renny. "You've got me worrying about Ham. All he ever carries is that trick sword cane, an' if they stick him in some robot like you say you were in, he wouldn't have much use for a cane."

Monk chewed thoughtfully on a gumdrop. Some child had left a paper bag of the candy on a sink drainboard in the hasty exodus. The thought of Ham in the hands of Var's ruthless agents turned the candy suddenly bitter in Monk's mouth.

"Dag-gone it! Nothin' even tastes right!" complained Monk, and he spat out the gumdrop.

MONK stopped on his way to the Hudson River warehouse hangar where Doc's private planes were kept, to phone Long Tom again. Long Tom replied impatiently.

"No, nothing new," he said.

Monk took off from the Hudson River in one of Doc's fastest amphibian planes. The cabinet craft shot across the murky night sky at a speed of nearly three hundred miles an hour.

Monk felt somewhat ill. He attributed this to apprehension for the safety of Ham. He had a bitter taste in his mouth. It had been there since he had left Renny with the police on the East Side.

The big chemist had the feeling he had overlooked something vitally important in the block threatened by the Cold Light. He felt it was something he should have recognized. Anyway, the sooner he got to Doc, the quicker the thing might appear.

Doc's uncanny power to read the thoughts and reactions of his five companions had been the salvation of Monk on many occasions. It was much the same with the giant fist-slinging Renny. Doc had extricated Renny and Monk from many hazardous spots.

In the East, slight streamers of light were telling of an early dawn. The dawn over Manhattan that was the beginning of a chaotic day.

Monk had planned to leave Doc's plane at a Washington airport and there take a taxicab to the vicinity of the address he had heard Wheeze McGovern give in the telegram sent to Ham.

Over the suburbs of the capital city, Monk angled to a lower altitude. On half throttle, the small plane skimmed along a couple of hundred feet above the tops of the trees.

Suddenly, Monk angled even lower. A blotch of bright yellow had appeared among the greenery. Monk took one of Doc's own inventions, an electronic glass, or, rather, powerful binoculars created by Doc on the electronic principle. The lenses of this telescopic device not only brought distant scenes close to the eyes, but they also amplified them in the vision much the same as radio tones are amplified for the listener by the loud-speaker.

One look through the glasses, as he held the little plane in a tight spiral and Monk growled in his throat.

"Howlin' calamities!" he barked. "I got here just in time! Hold 'em, you dag-goned shyster! I'm comin'!"

Monk shoved the plane into a dive. The staccato thunder of its direct drop awakened hundreds of Washingtonians before their usual hour of arising.

# Chapter 10
## HAM'S IN A JAM

BRIGADIER GENERAL THEODORE MARLEY BROOKS's arrival in
Washington somewhat preceded the coming there of Doc
Savage, and of Monk. If Ham had called Doc's headquarters
after receiving the bogus telegram from Wheeze McGovern,
the outcome might have been different.

Ham was a natty figure, as he yawned his way from a
passenger plane. He was wearing a spiffy topcoat, with a light
hat pulled with jaunty effect over one eye. He swung what
appeared to be a light walking stick.

In reality, it was the sheath for a sword blade of the finest
steel. Several inches of the sword tip covered with an anaesthetic drug. The smallest prick with the point was sufficient
to render an opponent temporarily insensible.

Ham, at this moment, knew little of the Var explosions.
Only the radio report of the Carberry blast and the warnings
of the expected attack upon Manhattan had reached him.

Though uninformed of his companions' connection with the
rapidly developing menace, Ham suspected this sudden call
in the night might have some connection with it.

Ham left the airport in a taxicab. He gave Dupont Circle as
an address close to the residence where he had been instructed to appear.

It was somewhat puzzling why Doc should have commanded
a meeting at the unearthly hour of four o'clock in the morning. Ham alighted at Dupont Circle and made his way toward
K Street. The yellow house was anything but modest. Its
golden-yellow bulk affronted its more decorous neighbors.

Heavy curtains were drawn at the windows, but knifelike
lines of brilliant light appeared at the edges. A dim light
burned in the entrance hall. The front door was set in a deep
alcove approached by a wide porch.

Ham's step was light as he crossed the porch. His fingers twiddled the cane in a flourishing circle.

IT was the mistake of an unseen man, that he growled a command to others instead of attacking silently. Ham's reaction to the menacing voice was instant. His heavy cane was traveling in a vicious arc before he had seen any person or any movement.

The swinging cane rapped the man flatly across one ear. The man grunted once and slipped to his knees.

Ham bounced the cane from the fallen one to a spot above a white face that loomed up from the alcove. A ringing rap of metal on hard bone and a howl of pain was the response.

If all of his unexpected assailants had been on the one side, Ham might have disposed of the four who had been in ambush. But two others were behind him. Ham heard their rush and attempted to draw the rapier blade from its sheath.

A hard-knuckled fist struck his spine a paralyzing blow at the base of his skull. A sinuous arm enwrapped his throat, snapping his head backward. The dim light in the entrance hallway danced, then it went out completely.

THE light came back, but now it was a painful glare against Ham's aching eyes. The lawyer was seated in an old-fashioned chair of the Victorian period. Before he looked into the faces of his captors, he noted the big room was furnished with articles antique collectors like to call "Early American."

Ham guessed shrewdly this old Washington home had either been leased or purchased furnished, for whatever purpose the gang surrounding him intended using it. Glancing at the nearest men, he quickly revised the thought of a "gang."

Ham counted eleven men. Voices of others sounded from another room in the rear.

"Quite a reception committee," Ham drawled.

One man, with mild blue eyes, blinked behind thick lenses.

"I can't say exactly what the chief may want," he volunteered. "You will be given a message later. You are to be informed that you are at the mercy of Var. Your friend—the chemist you call Monk—has been in Var's hands for several hours. The chief instructed you were to be told that Monk will be destroyed by the armored robot in which he is now imprisoned, if you refuse to do exactly as you are told. Your leader, Doc Savage, has been rendered helpless."

Ham's keen face sobered at the reference to Monk. The man's words were too sincerely spoken to have been an invention. But at the statement Doc had been rendered helpless, Ham grinned.

The speaker withdrew and the man swung into small groups. They talked in low tones. Ham's eyes had been busy every minute he had been speaking.

His sword cane, still intact, he noted was only a few feet away in a corner. Two buttons controlling the lights were plainly in view on the wall, a little to one side of the cane.

MORE than Ham's eyes had been at work for him.

On the middle finger of his right hand was what appeared to be a gold ring of heavy pattern. Concealed by his back, Ham had crossed his pliant fingers.

One crossed finger pressed a spot in the head of the ring. Ham suppressed a grimace. A sharp, tiny blade had darted along his palm and the wrist above it.

But the blade, operated on the spring forming the inside of the gold ring, had darted inside the cord tying his wrists together and, in turn, his body to the heavy chair. The deft finger worked rapidly. The spring recoiled and the blade dropped back. Again, it was sent darting along his palm.

Ham knew blood was oozing from the cut in his hand. He maneuvered to keep its dripping from being noticed by pulling his hands well upon the chair's cushion. The cord parted. There were still several wrappings to be sliced.

The front door buzzer burred viciously. Ham risked severing an artery with his swift play of the blade of the ring. He was still tightly held as four men moved in a group toward the door.

"It will be Var's messenger, but take no chances," warned one of the men.

"I wouldn't know if it were Var himself," growled another. "I've never seen him."

"None of us have, except Wheeze," the first man replied. "But make sure of the password and the card."

The four men were in the hallway. The eyes of all the others were fixed in that direction. Ham's hands were slippery with blood, but he was free. He waited tensely until he heard the outer door's bolt being drawn. Now or never, he decided.

Heaving his body forward, he kicked the heavy chair sidewise. It caught the nearest man in the stomach. Ham's lithe figure reached the wall. One hand was clicking the light buttons as the other grasped the sword cane.

THE room was plunged into darkness. One of the buttons had also switched off the dim light in the entrance hallway. The outer door had opened and a heavy voice had muttered, "Rav rules!"

For three or four seconds no one moved, except the man who had got the chair in his stomach. Ham grinned to himself over his temporary advantage. Though dawn was breaking outside, the heavy draperies over the windows excluded all light.

Ham played his sword blade, sharp as a razor, in experimental thrusts. The point contacted a yielding body. A man grunted with pain. He thumped to the floor on his face. This terminated the breathless suspense.

Ham could hear the rush of bodies. His sword blade became a darting tongue. It barely pinked two more men. A couple of others fell over this pair as they went down.

"Look out!" cried a voice. "He's got the sword out of that cane!"

One man started dragging back a curtain to let in light. Another man knocked him aside.

"Keep 'em closed, you fool!" he commanded. "Get him quick!"

The order was easily given. Laying hands upon the waspish, elusive figure of the fencing lawyer was much more difficult. One man had filled his hand with a silenced automatic. A yellowish-blue tongue of fire licked across the room.

At that instant, one man became distinctly visible to Ham. Or, rather, his eyes could be seen. They seemed to float into the room without a body. They glowed with the luminosity of a cat's eyes on the prowl at night.

"Put up that gun!" said a high-pitched, strident voice. "He isn't to be hurt, understand?"

The gun ceased to flame. The eyes came directly toward Ham, as if their owner could see the lawyer plainly in the darkness. A door opened toward the rear of the house. Faint light from somewhere above revealed a narrow stairway. Ham shifted sidewise and pinked another man. Two of the gang rushed, and collided with each other.

Ham was backing toward the narrow stairway. He figured if he could reach it he could stand off an army, as long as the order held against shooting him. The room he was leaving was filled with milling men, seeking him in the darkness.

The luminous eyes floated to one side. Apparently this man was withdrawing. The eyes vanished.

Ham had his feet on the bottom stair. Here, he could be plainly seen. He started backing slowly upward.

From the gloom of the space Ham had just vacated came an eerie, mellow sound. It was like the low piping note of some rare tropical bird. The softly whistled cadence filled all the rooms for an interval of a few seconds.

"Who did that?" rasped a voice.

The short puzzled oaths following, filled Ham with elation. Doc Savage was among the men in that room. None had ever before heard the peculiar emanation of sound that came from the bronze man.

The realization of Doc's presence strengthened Ham. Whirling the sword point, he retreated up the stairs. A dozen men crowded after him, but carefully maintained a discreet distance. Ham found two more flights and backed up these.

One of the men below him laughed.

"Let him go!" he ordered. "He can't get off the roof! We'll have him! Where's the little persuader?"

HAM had determined to make a stand in the narrow stairway below the skylight leading to the roof. Only one man at a time could reach him. He had hoped he would be safe. Nothing but bullets would ever get past the shimmering sword blade.

Something did get past it. This was the "little persuader" the man had mentioned.

Ham was smiling. He was really enjoying his position, especially since he was aware Doc was at hand. At any instant, he expected a tornado to break loose. He waited hopefully, prepared to launch himself downward as soon as Doc went into action.

Ham could picture the amazement when the bronze man exploded in the midst of these men. Not even the gigantic Renny, or the apelike Monk, was half the equal of Doc when he started using his mighty fists. But the group clustered at the foot of the stairs remained intact.

Suddenly, there was a sizzling stream ascending. It was being shot from a small, circular affair; such as would hold a steel tape line. Ham gasped. He was compelled to use his left arm to shield his face and eyes.

Ammonia fumes were clogging his nostrils. He couldn't breathe. Then he heaved himself upward and his shoulder carried away the window sash of the skylight. Inhaling a long breath, Ham bounded to the roof.

As other feet pounded on the stairs, Ham sprang to one side. He was confident he would discover a near-by tree or some other means of descending from the four-story roof. He realized his mistake too late. He should have held his opponents at the top of the narrow stairway.

Now some ten men were in the open on the roof. They were grimly determined on recapturing their prisoner. Half the men carried short clubs and other improvised weapons. Ham spotted a chimney and backed up to it.

His enemies ringed him closely. In the dawning light, they were able to keep clear of his flying sword. Ham was deliberately refraining from taking the offensive.

Doc was there somewhere. He wished he knew Doc's plans. The bronze adventurer always had carefully calculated reasons for his every action. That Doc had done no more than apprize Ham of his presence was proof he had some definite goal.

Ham wished he knew more to guide his own play. He scrutinized the faces around him. He was fairly sure two persons were missing from the ring of men now closing in.

From the stairs came a high-pitched voice. There was a scuffling sound. A body bumped in the hallway below the roof. Almost at once, an ugly, malformed face appeared in the skylight.

A deep voice complained, "Some guy down there made a mistake! He swung for me, but when I tried to grab him, he got away!"

"It's all right, Gobo!" ejaculated one of the men, quickly. "That probably was Scraggs! I was taking you to him when this sword slinger broke loose! Come here and help grab this fellow!"

THE hulking man who came onto the roof had puffed, unhealthy cheeks. His tow-colored hair was matted and his nose was broken. Of all the men Ham had seen, this was the only one who had the marks of being a bruiser. Ham smiled inwardly. He knew this man to be Doc Savage. Ham knew now whence the whistle had come.

It had been this man's voice at the entrance giving the password, "Rav rules."

Without glancing at Ham, the new arrival said, "Circle the chimney and get him from behind! The chief said he didn't want him injured. He wants to use him!"

Ham judged he should make a final pretense of fighting his way out, then permit himself to be overwhelmed. The bronze man had not looked at him directly. In fact, Doc was warily closing in on him from behind.

Ham deliberately pinked another man. Then a club was flung at him. His sword arm took the blow and Ham staggered.

Low overhead, a small airplane suddenly roared in a dive. It was Monk, coming in from New York.

AFTER sighting the vividly yellow house, Monk pulled Doc's small amphibian into a tight spiral.

Two maple trees grew beside the four-story house. They were spaced so near each other, their leafy branches seemed to be interfaced. Monk drew in one long breath, shifted the plane elevators and dived.

He clicked off the ignition as the trees, the house and the lawn leaped up to meet the hurtling plane. With wind screaming in the wires, the diving ship thrust between the trees. The silvery wings stripped off. The speed of the cabinet fuselage was slightly checked.

The next instant, Monk was being carried through the wall of the yellow house with the speed of a stone thrown from a catapult. The forward part of the cabin was crushed. Through this aperture, the body of Monk continued onward.

Monk's rebound to his feet was fast. It was as if his ungainly body were made of rubber. He was in an upper room of the house. Dashing through the first doorway, Monk glimpsed two men dropping down the stairway from the roof. Each carried a short club.

The big chemist's cry was one of delight. One man threw his club. He was not quick enough. Monk's long arms had reached. The men were of average size. Both were taller than

Monk. But their heads took the impact of the hallway wall at the same instant.

Monk had heaved one over each shoulder. Plaster and laths scattered under the blows from their skulls. Monk's broad shoulders filled the narrow stairway and the skylight. He gained the roof.

Two other men were quick enough, one with his fists and another with the flat side of an automatic pistol. They hammered at Monk's head as he came up. The chemist's breath hissed through his teeth. He caught an ankle and twisted once. The owner squealed with pain and dropped the gun.

BACK in Manhattan, Monk had been given no chance to replace the super-machine pistol Wheeze's men had taken from him. Now he caught up the automatic from the roof. He was about to shoot at another man rushing toward him, but he refrained.

There now were only six men on the roof around Ham. Monk contented himself with rushing into the attackers, the automatic swinging as a club.

To Monk's disgusted amazement, Ham had dropped the point of his sword.

"You would bust in on a gentlemen's party!" came sharply from Ham. "Can't that ape brain of yours understand when one is just practicing!"

Monk's short legs pivoted him to a stop. His homely face went blank with amazement.

"Well, I'll be flabbergasted!" he jerked out. "You tricky low-down shyster, now what are you——"

Ham's surprising words pulled his eyes away from his closest enemy. One of the short clubs smacked him viciously behind the ear. Monk folded to his knees and fell forward. His hard skull had barely resisted the impact. His senses had faded out.

Ham groaned. He hadn't meant that to happen. He had hoped to see Monk seized. But it was too late for regret, now. The broken-nosed man with the washed-out blue eyes had glided swiftly between Monk and the man with the club.

"Don't hit him again!" he commanded in a guttural threat that got instant respect. "The chief doesn't want these fellows hurt!"

It had been Doc's unspoken order that had caused Ham to prevent Monk from finishing the job of cleaning up the roof.

Ham had seen the lips of the broken-nosed man moving just as Monk sprang into the encounter. He had read the brief message. All of Doc's men were expert lip readers. Doc had said:

"Hold it, Ham—stop Monk—let them take you—escape police—we want Var."

Doc believed he was on a trail that would lead quickly to the Cold Light murderer. Perhaps they could discover Var in time to avert the menace over Manhattan.

## Chapter 11
## VAR BLINDS HIS TRAIL

HAM and Monk, securely bound, were shoved into two closed cars. There were three cars in waiting. These leaped away along an alley.

Ham and Monk were unloaded at the rear of an isolated, tumble-down house at the northern edge of Washington. Nine men, with Doc, had accompanied the cars. Behind these cars, trailing them until the prisoners had been taken inside, was a small, battered roadster.

The driver of this car was the little man with the scraggly face and clothes. He halted his small car a block away and made his way cautiously forward. Unseen, he slipped through a window into the basement of the old house. In the darkness of the cellar, his eyes took on the luminous propensities of a prowling cat.

Keeping to his rôle, Doc Savage saw Monk and Ham deposited temporarily in a small room with boarded windows. The other men assembled in a larger room with cheap, rough furnishings. High, narrow windows gave forth a little light.

As Ham was dumped unceremoniously on the floor, Doc made an excellent pretense of handling him roughly. At the same time, he was whispering:

"Follow all instructions. These men mean nothing. They seem expecting this Var himself."

Ham was astute enough to play his part.

Though Doc's rôle of the broken-nosed thug had been a surprise, his actions had been cleverly carried out. The men of the Var ring apparently were unsuspecting. Doc's swift analysis of their character led him to believe that several were far more intelligent than the average type of criminal.

The bronze man was confronted with the problem of being almost sure two or three had never before engaged in a crooked enterprise. It made their association with Var all the more puzzling.

ALL had the air of expectant waiting. This was suddenly rewarded by the tones of a high-pitched voice. This came from a ventilator leading up from the basement.

"Brothers of the ring! Our action here has been deferred! The chief has decided to wait until after the Cold Light has fallen upon New York! Then Doc Savage's man will receive the message he is to deliver to the White House! The Manhattan explosion will make certain a commission will be formed as Var wishes! Coming from Doc Savage, the word to the White House will be impressive enough to gain attention! Bring in this man Ham!"

Ham's legs were now tightly bound, as well as his arms. He was carried in and placed in a chair.

Doc unostentatiously shifted his position closer to a door he had marked as leading to the cellar of the old house. He was convinced he knew the owner of that voice. His character study brought before him a skinny neck in which a nervous Adam's apple would be jumping up and down.

Doc knew these men never had seen their chief, the man called Var. The strangely delivered message was the first direct link that seemed to connect with the perpetrator of the Cold Light explosions. The voice spoke again briefly:

"Five of you will remain here to guard the prisoners! The others will go at once to the place designated! We will then——"

The speech was cut off abruptly by a smash of Doc's mighty fist. A panel of the locked basement door was shattered to splinters. The door was of ancient, flimsy construction. The lock was torn loose and went flying down the basement stairway.

Though the bronze man apparently made no leap, his feet were on the damp concrete floor of the cellar when the lock banged with a ringing sound. His surprising movement and his quickness converted the room he had just left into roaring confusion.

In the basement's gloom, Doc flashed the searching ray of his generator flashlight. His other hand held a stupefying capsule no larger than a small glass pill. He located the cold-air shaft leading from the dead furnace.

Doc had expected to see the figure of the scraggy little man crouched somewhere close by. He was surprised to see no one. Swinging the light around, he discovered the small basement room seemed to be empty.

One more glance was sufficient to reveal the clever trick performed by this elusive emissary of the man Var. The cold-air pipe had been dislodged close to the outer wall of the foundation. One stone had been removed. The aperture led into the ventilator located in the room above. Var's messenger had apprently been crouched on the ground outside the house.

THE man had ceased speaking when the basement door crashed. He had vanished so swiftly Doc could not hear his running feet. Before Doc could reach the stairs, the men above were descending upon him.

Doc flipped a gas capsule and it .fell at the feet of the foremost man. But the rush carried the men over the gas before it could become effective. The bronze man was holding his own breath. Then an automatic pistol slashed its blaze into the gloomy basement. And a sizzling stream of ammonia searched for Doc's eyes and nostrils.

With his eyes tightly closed, Doc charged directly into the members of Var's ring. Though he was not breathing, the ammonia was pungent in his nostrils. Two men crashed into opposite walls under fists so fast and so effective they had no chance to use their weapons against them.

But one man had fallen, locking his arms around Doc's legs. The bronze man staggered. He was free in an instant, and the other man had rolled over limply. Doc's thumb had simply pressed into a clotted nerve group in the ringster's neck. The man would be paralyzed for several minutes.

Five men in all cluttered the basement floor, as the bronze man reached the top of the short stairway.

In a determined effort to free himself and go to Doc's aid, Ham had succeeded only in upsetting the chair. He was squirming on the floor.

As Doc reached him, a car roared away outside. Doc sprang to a window. In the space of seconds, he was back and had sliced the cords from Ham's arms and legs.

"The other room, Doc!" gasped Ham. "They've done something to Monk! If they've put him out, I'll run them to the end of the world!"

But apparently the men who had escaped had not put Monk out. They had taken him with them. The room was empty.

Doc and Ham got to the outside. Two of the three closed cars were still there. But the hoods of both motors were thrown open. The ignition wires had been ripped loose from the instrument boards.

The fleeing car was just disappearing on a side road, headed in the direction of the city.

Doc's deduction was almost instant.

"Wherever they had Monk a prisoner, he saw too much," he stated. "Var needs your legal experience for some purpose, Ham. But this probably upsets his idea. He'll go ahead now with that explosion in Manhattan. We must return at once!"

"But how about Monk, Doc? I could make a try at——"

Doc looked thoughtfully into the sky to the eastward.

"I'm very sure Monk right now is on his way back to New York," he stated.

He did not explain his reason for believing this.

Before they had reached a corner where a taxicab could be summoned, the thin glass shells had been removed from over the eyes of flaky gold. Their hypnotic pools again stirred with little whirlwinds.

Doc was thinking the luring of Ham and then himself to Washington had been for the purpose of making sure they would not be in Manhattan at nine o'clock this morning.

The taxicab was rushing toward the airport. Doc saw he would have just time to catch the plane that would arrive in New York at the time set by Var for the explosion of the city block.

He said to Ham, "You'll wait and take the White Liner back. It arrives an hour after the Red Arrow. If there is a little man on board with a ragged haircut and a loose Adam's apple, we want to know where he goes. His clothes are as ragged as his hair; and if you happen to hear him speak, it will likely be the voice that came through the ventilator."

"Would that be the one I heard them call Scraggs?" Ham suggested.

"The name would fit, and you couldn't miss him," said Doc. "He'll be on one or the other of the planes."

Doc's conjecture was partly correct. The scraggly little man at that moment was preparing to board a plane. But it was neither the Red Arrow nor the White Liner.

VONIER, the explorer, was in the waiting room at the Red Arrow airport. His intense blue eyes lighted a little when his gaze automatically followed the turning of all faces toward the big man who came unhurriedly through the wide doors.

"I can well believe all the adventures credited to him," murmured the explorer. "He looks like a bad one to get in anybody's soup."

Ten seconds later, Vonier added, again to himself, "It's almost unbelievable, but I'd bet my last dollar Doc Savage knows I've been waiting here in the hope of catching him. And he hasn't even seemed to glance this way."

This was true. The smooth, bronzed face had not once turned in the explorer's direction. The eyes of flaky gold had not appeared to have observed any person in particular. Then Doc walked across the big room and stopped before Vonier.

"A man I've always wanted to meet," the bronze man stated, as if introductions already had been effected. "Your paper on your last trip into the Arctic afforded me great pleasure. I'm glad to meet you here, Vonier. You came here to meet me, did you not?"

Vonier fixed him with a steady gaze. Then he glanced down his thin nose and shook his head.

"That savors of the occult, Savage," he smiled. "No other person on earth, except my wife, knew I had it in mind to find you in Washington. Are you a mind reader?"

"Not at all, Vonier," Doc smiled in return. "By this time, all Manhattan is stirred by something of which it never before heard. That is Cold Light. You are one of perhaps only seven men in New York who has seen Cold Light, even though it is of a far different variety. The other six men are my five closest companions and myself."

"Yes," assented Vonier. "That is true, but how would that give you such absolute certainty?"

"You knew we had visited, months ago, the caverns of the

strange race in the Arctic ice field," added Doc. "You had learned that we have been drawn into the mystery of the man called Var. Perhaps you have learned something you believe I should know."

VONIER laughed shortly, a note of uneasiness. He glanced around as if making certain they could not be overheard.

"It may sound simple enough to you, Doc Savage, but the average man would suspect you of being linked up with the supernatural. However, it is something more vital to me than you think. Something that impelled me to reach you as quickly as possible."

"Then you've had a message from this Var," Doc stated. "It is perhaps his idea that he can use your vast knowledge."

Vonier spread his thin, bony hands.

"I give it up," he said. "Probably you know all that is in the message."

"Hardly that," the bronze man smiled. "But we've only two minutes. I must be in New York at nine."

"I knew that, and it was why I was waiting here," Vonier said. "As soon as we are aboard the plane, I'll show you the note that has kept me awake and which seemed unbelievable until last night. I am threatened with death if I do not join Var's organization."

The pilot grinned down at Doc Savage as he climbed aboard. Because of an emergency, the same flier was taking the early morning Red Arrow plane back to the Newark Airport.

Vonier had maneuvered a seat next to the one Doc had thoughtfully reserved on his arrival in Washington. The seat just ahead of Doc was vacant. He thought the passenger had missed the plane, if it had been engaged, for the door was being closed.

Then the door reopened and a breathless man came in. The pulsing blood had reddened the bald spot between tufts of white hair. Doc recalled that only a few hours before that same bald spot had been the color of gray chalk.

The man was Carberry, the retired financier.

CARBERRY's pale-bluish eyes, slightly protruding, seemed to jump with recognition at the sight of Doc Savage. He extended one thin, blue-veined hand.

"I wish I'd have known you were in Washington, Doc

Savage!" he exclaimed. "I'd have asked you to go with me to the Federal agents! Even with all that has happened, the government agents don't want to take this thing seriously!"

J. Afton Carberry was shaking. His hands jerked continuously. He had apparently not noticed the explorer, Vonier, until the latter had spoken.

"I believe we've met, Carberry," he remarked. "You may recall I had occasion to congratulate you on your book dealing with the origin of species."

"Yes—oh, yes!" admitted Carberry. "That is right. We were on the same program at the museum. However, Vonier, I've never taken my own theories seriously. I've made a hobby of many curious things. After a man's made his money, that's about all he has left."

Doc apparently was watching the preparation for the take-off. He was studying both men. They were the direct opposites of each other.

Vonier might perish in any one of countless ways, but his nerve never would be shaken.

Carberry was of a volatile disposition. The menace over him had apparently unnerved him to the point of physical discomfort. His blue-veined hands continued shaking.

"I thought you had planned to take Mrs. Carberry away," suggested Doc.

"Yes—oh, yes—I have," the financier replied. "She is perfectly safe where she is. I'll admit, though, I'm gravely concerned over this thing. This man Var's a dangerous maniac!"

"That's not my idea," disagreed Vonier. "So far as I've learned it, his scheme of destruction is too perfectly planned in detail to be the work of a lunatic."

Carberry seemed to be fumbling for a reply. The Red Arrow plane had taken off and circled with the wind on its tail. It was already making up the lost time of departure in the direction of Manhattan. Then came the voice. Thin, but stridently clear, it filled the space of the passenger cabin: "Doc Savage—Carberry—Vonier——"

Eyes of those in the seats leaped from one to another. All had heard of Var's mystic warnings.

Vonier looked steadily at Doc Savage, a slight smile on his lips. There had been a pause in the voice.

"Yes, Doc Savage," he said, calmly. "I think this Var is dangerously sane.

## Chapter 12
## DEATH OVER MANHATTAN

IN the passenger cabin, the first excited murmuring of the inmates hushed. Only the steady beat of the motors could be heard.

Then the voice again:

*"This is my final warning! Doc Savage, you will forget what you have learned! One of your men is in my hands! Vonier and Carberry—you will do as already instructed! This is my final word! For I am—Var!"*

The voice seemed everywhere. It had the elusive quality of direction which a good ventriloquist imparts. Doc's hypnotic eyes had observed Vonier and Carberry in turn.

Carberry was shaking as if with palsy. Vonier was calmly rubbing one finger along his thinly arching nose.

Then Doc was on his feet. Swiftly he directed the stewardess, "Go through every article of the women's baggage." There were four women aboard. "I'll take the men myself."

The stewardess hesitated. The broad-faced pilot had given the controls over to the co-pilot. His mirror had shown the excited movement in the cabin, though he had not heard the voice.

Taking a cue from the attitude of the stewardess, a male passenger started to say, "By what right have you——"

"You'll do as Doc Savage directs!" snapped the pilot. "He has full police authority on the Red Arrow lines!"

The bronze man's hunt was quick but thorough. The stewardess aided as best she could.

DOC and the others missed seeing a hand steal through a two-inch opening of a window ventilator. A small object started on a mile drop to the gliding earth below.

185

Vonier suddenly exclaimed, glancing at his wrist watch, "We're a little late, aren't we, pilot? It's two minutes to nine o'clock."

The pilot, moving back toward his cabin, sighted through a window. The sky needles of Manhattan were shining in the brilliant sun only a few miles ahead.

"Ten minutes or so off schedule," the pilot grinned. "We've been held up a little. Figured maybe you folks would appreciate a grand-stand seat in the sky for the big blow-off down there—if there is one."

Clearly, the pilot was doubtful of the reason for all the madness in Manhattan.

"For Heaven's sake, man!" gasped Carberry. "You mean we'll be over Manhattan at nine o'clock?"

"Correct, brother!" The pilot's grin broadened. "It oughta be worth an extra fare!"

"I'd say we are in the safest possible spot," stated Vonier, calmly.

"Perhaps," said Doc Savage.

Vonier leaned closer to him.

"When we get down, Savage," he said in a low tone," "I believe I have something new on the formula for Cold Light. I'd like you to see it."

The explorer's lips were drawn back from his skeleton hard jaws. Even with his coolness, the smile was gruesomely reminiscent of a bony death's-head.

"I'll appreciate that greatly," Doc replied.

Doc Savage, during the flight to Washington, had worked out and transmitted to Long Tom the formula for creating the ex-neutralizer with which he planned to combat the destructive Cold Light.

While in the rôle of the broken-nosed man, he had employed the plane's radiophone to good advantage. His instructions to Long Tom had been detailed and explicit.

Doc had brought an advanced theory into practical working form with less than an hour of thinking.

Back in Manhattan, Long Tom was at work in the creation of a machine that would build a wall. Doc had enlarged upon an idea of a ray to meet a ray. He had so analyzed the explosion at the home of J. Afton Carberry as to become positive it had a double origin.

From some inexplicable source, perhaps from the magnetized earth itself, a gigantic destructive force had leaped to meet the ray of Cold Light. Therefore, a neutralizing ray to clash with that other ray in its death-dealing path would hardly be sufficient.

Doc judged the force must be something more like a wall. That would be the answer. An electromagnetic wall which the Cold Light ray could neither penetrate nor cross.

Just now, with the Red Arrow plane flying toward the sky line of Manhattan at a speed of more than two miles a minute, Doc was hoping Long Tom might have the new machine ready for its first test.

And the explorer, Vonier, was calmly telling him he had something new to offer on the formula of Cold Light. The bronze man studied the intensely blue eyes of the man. Vonier's eyes were the exact shade of the bright blue ink on the passport card that had admitted him to Var's inner organization.

An aquamarine blue. The kind of a blue that only the occasional artistic genius can capture in oils on a canvas.

The financier, Carberry, his thin lips twitching, also was observing Vonier closely. Though Vonier's words regarding the formula had been directed at Doc only, Carberry's straining ears had caught them. The financier apparently was in that state of extreme fear which led him to suspect any person who might be familiar with such mysterious elements as Cold Light.

As the island of Manhattan swam closer, with the broad Hudson widening into the harbor below, the Red Arrow plane was between five and ten minutes behind its schedule. The good-humored pilot angled the plane lower.

It was exactly nine o'clock.

Around the Red Arrow passenger plane the sky was empty. Plainly, other pilots were not interested in occupying grandstand seats for the explosion. The police commissioner, taking every precaution, had issued an explicit order grounding all aircraft in the Manhattan area.

But that order had failed to reach the Red Arrow pilot. Apparently, another pilot also had disregarded it. But this second plane was at so great an altitude as to be indistinguishable against the sun from the ground level. If it was seen at all, it appeared as only a possible tiny black speck in the observer's eye.

It was a small plane and it was flying at an altitude of more than four miles high.

As Carberry announced the time as nine o'clock, a steely-blue ray knifed downward from the higher heavens. Though the daylight was clear, this spikelike band could be plainly seen. It struck instantly all the way to the earth below.

Crowds back of police lines blocks from the heart of the threatened area gasped. To these hundreds of thousands of spectators, it seemed as if the fiendish hand of the destroyer above had directed the Cold Light ray directly upon the Red Arrow passenger plane.

The hushed crowds saw this. Simultaneously, a chilling blast of air swept across all of the central Manhattan area. The normal breathing of the terror-ridden, but curious, multitude of citizens was sharply interrupted. The air was sucked upward in a mighty cyclonic whirlwind.

Then the air came slapping back with the force of some tangible substance. Thousands of those closest to the explosion area would have been blown from their feet, had not the packed mass of the crowd kept them erect. The whole sea of upturned faces seemed to rock in a slow, rippling wave as individuals fought to maintain their balance.

THE six-story block designated by Var instantly ceased to exist. In its place arose an intense blue cloud. This was seen by those at a distance as a gigantic pyramid with a pointed apex reaching toward the sky. The blueness of the sky seemed dim in comparison to the color of the geometrically formed blast of vapor.

From this leaping, single tongue, wreckage spewed over many surrounding blocks.

The island of Manhattan swayed. New York was given a brief demonstration of what it feels like to be caught in an earthquake.

In the Red Arrow plane, Doc Savage has seen the first flash of the Cold Light. So highly keyed were the reactions of the bronze man's senses, he had seen something so clearly that he had arrived at a new conclusion in the infinitesimal part of a second.

Some force more definite than the magnetic response of the earth itself was leaping to meet the chilling ray of deadly Cold Light.

From below, the strange blue vapor of the blast was

rushing upward. All of the sustaining air had been instantly sucked away from the propellers and wings of the Red Arrow plane. Debris was riding into the sky on the aquamarine pyramid.

All the air seemed to return upon the passenger plane with cyclonic assault. The Red Arrow ship was whirled over and over. It became a mere helpless leaf blown by a hurricane.

# Chapter 13
## MONK BAILS OUT

AT the moment the Red Arrow plane plunged into a seemingly fatal spin, Monk was awakening to aching consciousness. Though his skull was hard as granite, the battering of the past hours had been such as to have given a stone monument a headache.

Monk's first impression was that he had been carried away in a boat. Then he quickly realized the jerking lurches of the floor on which he was lying could mean only one thing. He was traveling in an airplane.

Monk flexed the muscles of his long arms and short legs. All of his bones were intact. Moreover, his feet and hands were free. Clearly, some one among his recent enemies must be foolhardy.

Then Monk became aware his freedom of body did not afford all the opportunity he had believed. He was breathing with difficulty. All his body was cold. When he moved his arms, he discovered they were numbed.

This was no phenomenon. For the huge, apelike chemist was slowly being frozen. The temperature about him was several degrees below zero. The plane was riding at a high altitude. The rarefied atmosphere did not provide oxygen enough for his unaccustomed lungs. This and the frigid bath prevented his greatly abnormal strength from returning quickly.

Twisting his head, Monk peered through narrowed eyes under his gristly, jutting brows. He was in a small cabin plane. The ship had twin control seats. A man occupied each of these.

MONK could see their faces in a cabin-view mirror above the instrument board. The man then handling the plane was smoothly sleek and dark-skinned. He had not been among either of the groups Monk had encountered.

The pilot was stamped mostly by a gold-toothed smile—a fixed smile of evil, as it showed in the strip of mirror.

The man in the other seat was scraggly of person and clothing. Monk did not know this, but it was the mysteriously moving Scraggs. Doc had guessed Scraggs might be returning to New York on either the Red Arrow or the White Liner plane. For this, Ham's departure from Washington had been delayed in the hope of picking up the trail of the elusive messenger for Var.

Monk lay quite still, watching the two men. The plane was still taking on more altitude. The chemist gritted his teeth to prevent their chattering. He was gathering strength for an attack.

His big hands cautiously explored his clothing. Not a weapon or device had been left upon his person. He must depend upon his bare hands alone. Monk grinned to himself. There were only two men.

The luminous dial on the instrument board showed a few seconds to nine o'clock. The gold-toothed man muttered, but his words were snatched away by the thundering beat of the propeller.

Scraggs's long, wraithlike hands took over control. Monk saw the other man was bringing forth a flat instrument. This was somewhat the shape and size of a large-calibered automatic pistol.

But the metal was of steely blue. Monk judged it was some new alloy of which he did not know.

The gold-toothed man pressed one side of a series of buttons appearing on one side. From the device came a vicious whirring, much the same vibrant sibilancy as that of a rattlesnake about to strike.

Monk identified the sound as coming from some tiny, but powerful, generator. The gold-toothed man pressed another button.

The scraggly little man drew Monk's gaze. He had cried out sharply, as if in warning. The plane's motor had missed. It was coughing in the midst of what had been a smooth rhythm of power.

Monk crouched. His chance was at hand.

THE little plane was staggering with a slowing propeller. An oath ripped from the gold-toothed man. His thumb pressed a trigger on the side of the steely blue instrument.

Monk could not have told if the air in the small cabin suddenly took on more frigidity. The cold about him already was under the zero mark.

But his skin suffered, a tingling, prickly sensation. Thousands of tiny needles seemed to be thrusting into him.

Monk saw an edged ray of light directed at the floor of the plane's cabin. Though knifelike, it had a weird, intangible quality. For it was passing directly through the metal that formed the plane's fuselage. The gold-toothed man was pointing it downward.

One second or five, Monk could not have told.

Some tremendous, invisible force was lifting the whole body of the small ship. It was as if the blue Cold Light itself was a motive force impelling the plane upward.

At that instant, the motor died.

Monk was in the act of springing at the two men. But he was held back. The support whirled from under his feet.

The scraggly little man at the controls dived into the metal frame of the windshield glass. His thin body collapsed between the seats.

The gold-toothed man had shut off the cold-producing beam. This was a convulsive, automatic act, rather than one of intent. The sender of the explosive ray into the heart of Manhattan was hurled into the roof of the plane.

MONK felt as if he were in the exact center of a whirlpool. His body shuttled this way and that, twice banging his hard head. But he kept his senses.

The plane did a complete wing-over and went into a tail spin.

Monk, fighting against being knocked out, could tell the convulsions of the ship were due to something far different from ordinary air current. The plane seemed to be plunging into a vortex, a vacuum of the sky.

This was in reality the vaporous burst shooting upward from the heart of Manhattan. Even in that flashing instant, the Cold Light having been flicked off, the cloud began to recede.

Below, bricks and metal were raining upon the city. Thousands of skyscraper windows were being smashed. For blocks around the center of the blast the windows and many walls of older buildings had buckled.

Monk got a grip on one of the control seats. His mighty muscles held him until he could get into position. The bucking, whirling plane at first resisted every effort to throw the ailerons and elevator into neutral.

Without much hope, Monk pressed the inertia starter. To his immense surprise, the propeller whirled and the motor caught. He battled the ship to a level keel.

Monk then had time to notice his battered, unconscious airmates. The scraggly man had a deep cut across his forehead. His sunken cheeks looked bloodless. But one long-fingered hand moved at random over his skinny breast.

The other man could no longer indulge in a gold-toothed smile. Nose, mouth and chin had been flatly smashed. Blood seeped over his chin. But he was still breathing heavily.

From one of the wings came a crackling, tearing sound. The plane staggered and fell off. It was temporarily out of control with a flapping aileron. Monk shifted the side sticks to compensate for the drag.

Monk saw the plane had dropped nearly two miles in its dive into the turmoil of the explosion. All possibility of gliding to a landing field was removed.

Ten thousand feet below loomed the green expanse of Central Park. But now, only the greenery of the trees was showing. Monk had hoped there might be space enough on one of the lawns to land the plane. All these areas were black, packed with terrified humanity.

Monk could mark the sea of white, upturned faces. To attempt a landing would kill and injure many persons.

As packed mobs sometimes will, the thousands now in Central Park saw doom rushing downward and remained motionless. It was the individual thought, also as crowd madness, that death would hit only the other fellow.

Monk set the stabilizer device on the controls. This could not compensate for the damaged wing. The plane started a slow, circling drop.

The two unconscious men were wearing seat-pack parachutes. In a cabin rack were two other 'chutes.

Monk did not hesitate. Before he slipped into the harness of the air life preserver, he lifted the limp form of the gold-toothed man. Pushing him through the door, Monk ripped the man's 'chute as he sent him hurtling into space.

Five seconds later, Monk muttered, "I done all I could——"

The parachute of the monster whose hand had rocked Manhattan had only halfway blossomed. Some of its cords had tangled. The small umbrella only partly checked the descent of the body, then it was torn apart by the rushing wind.

Var's side, probably his chief lieutenant, fell nearly two miles. The body struck the cornice of a skyscraper. Dismembered, every possible identifying feature of the man was lost.

Nor was there about his clothing any mark or papers by which he might have been traced.

The plane continued its crazy circling, as Monk pulled back beside the slight figure of the scraggly little man.

"Dag-gone it!" muttered the big chemist. "I wouldn't wanta see that happen again!"

Once more, he tried the controls. The whirling motion had disrupted the plane's tail assembly. The elevator was tightly stuck.

The packed vista of Central Park was rushing upward. Monk made a quick, determined effort. He let go of the controls when he had made sure the plane would crash among some of the trees, well away from the densely packed crowds.

With a growl, he caught up the light figure of the scraggly man. The ground was still nearly a mile below. A strong wind had whipped up following the explosion.

Monk stepped off into space. The light little man was in his huge arms. Their bodies cleared the gyrating plane by only scant inches.

Monk was somersaulting, but his head was clear. One thick finger hooked into the little man's parachute ring. He ripped the pack. The 'chute spread. As it checked their momentum, Monk let go his hold. He feared their combined weight might tear the umbrella apart.

He pulled his own ring when he was still two thousand feet up. The 'chute billowed and danced under his weight. Caught by the wind, it drifted rapidly south.

With some satisfaction, Monk saw he would fall below Central Park. He was dropping toward the Seventh Avenue hotel section around Fiftieth Street. Just before a flat roof offered the best chance of landing safely, Monk could see small, blue-coated figures rushing along the avenue.

Then it came to him that he was falling from the plane that had brought madness, destruction and death to Manhattan.

"Dag-gone it!" he mumbled. "Now I'm in for it!"

His feet struck the roof of a hotel some three blocks from Central Park only a few seconds after the Cold Light plane tore itself to fragments in a treetop. As Monk regained his balance and struggled out of the chute harness, all of the hundreds who could reach the spot were tearing away the loose parts of the Cold Light plane.

When police arrived on the scene, the Cold Light-ray gun had disappeared.

Monk made for the nearest skylight and pried it open. It had been locked, but lock, bolt and all the fastenings came loose in his ponderous grasp. They might as well have been made of papier-mâché. Monk was in a hurry.

He slid down the steep stairs leading to the roof. Numerous brawny arms of the law were waiting to receive him.

Regardless of Monk's protests of innocence, they took him to headquarters on suspicion of being connected with the Cold Light.

## Chapter 14
## A GIRL SEEKS SCRAGGS

As the Red Arrow passenger plane winged over in the first mad hurricane of the explosion, the dozen passengers were pitched from their seats. All except the seemingly cool and imperturbable man of Bronze.

Doc Savage had set his cablelike tendons for the shock. His fingers were locked in the back of his seat.

Doc saw the pilot had been conked. The co-pilot was a limp bundle under his own wheel in the control room.

The motors threatened to tear themselves loose from their mountings.

The pilot had been flying low. That is, rather low over the sky-piercing masses of Manhattan. Doc had a glimpse of thrusting towers. The superb heights of the Radio City buildings glittered near. They were dangerously close.

Even under his stress, the bronze man's eyes of flaky gold got camera flashes. He was seeking reactions of those closest to him.

His bony legs thrust out as braces, Vonier, the explorer, was calmly seeking to prevent himself from being tossed about with the other passengers. And across his skeleton-hard mouth lay a faint smile.

The financier, Carberry, was jammed between another man and the roof of the cabin. The roof was now under their feet. Blood oozed from a cut in Carberry's forehead.

The man's countenance looked as if every drop of life fluid already had drained through that single gash over one eye. The scared chalky pallor had been replaced by the grayness usually seen only on the face of a corpse.

Carberry did not seem to be breathing.

THE man lying beside Carberry was evidently a traveling salesman. For he still clutched a sample case by its handle. He was very much alive. His free hand clawed for some new support, as the plane winged completely over for the second time.

With this new somersault, Doc saw the towers of Radio City rushing upward. A bare thousand feet more and the Red Arrow ship would be split into fragments over one of the edges of the cornices.

The bronze man's movement toward the control cabin was neither a leap nor a hurried swinging of his body. Everything within the big plane was topsy-turvy. The stricken passengers were huddled lumps either of inert flesh and clothing, or squirming bodies seeking some relief from the pain of many hurts.

The man of golden bronze glided through and over all of these. The motors were threatening to shake the fuselage to bits. Upside down though it was, Doc performed the feat of getting into the pilot's seat.

Gripping the control wheel with one hand, he got the safety belt around him. The pilot had not been using it. His co-pilot had been hooked into his own. His raglike body still clung there.

Now the earth, or the tangled, menacing part of it that was

Manhattan, was for the moment the bronze man's sky. As he took the controls, the air of the explosion rushed back. The propellers bit into the atmosphere as if it were a swiftly flowing stream.

Looping a passenger plane, even with the combined power of its motors, is among the unrecorded feats of the world's greatest pilots. But the Red Arrow ship had succeeded in winging over on its back.

Doc played the controls with hands as strong and sensitive as those of some master pianist. The motors had more than full power now. The ship was a leaf apparently in the rushing wind from the Cold Light blast.

Doc started the nose climbing into that turbulent river of air. The wings screamed. It almost seemed as if no human agency could have constructed materials capable of resisting the tearing strain.

But the bronze man put the plane up and over. Bumps and groans rolled from the passenger cabin. Those still conscious suddenly found their positions reversed. The floor once more was under their feet.

With the plane upright, Doc was forced to throw the ship into a bank that almost stalled its motors. Even Vonier's eyes flickered then. One wing tip had come so close it appeared to brush the sharp corner of the tallest Radio City tower.

Doc leveled off. The plane was shooting directly toward another clifflike skyscraper. The distance was only a matter of yards. Similar masses of gleaming granite and glass hedged the ship in on two other sides.

Doc saw he was trapped. No human hand could ever pilot a plane over these heights. There was no space in which to circle in even the sharpest stalling bank.

Only parts of seconds separated the Red Arrow craft and all in it from crashing head-on into one or the other of the buildings. The speed was terrific. There could be but one answer to that.

Doc's golden eyes flashed downward. This was well within the area that had been deserted. Some scattered débris from wrecked buildings had fallen to the streets.

Doc was thankful this was Manhattan. In almost any other city there would have been interlacing wires, phone and power poles. Here there were none.

The spread of the big plane was so nearly the width of the

street that the wing tips grazed the buildings on either side. Doc, without apparent anxiety, without a tremor of those bronzed, sure hands, was coolly flying the Red Arrow ship along a street.

Doc had no time to think about what street it might be. The signs flew past in a blur. He saw only that a wider space loomed ahead.

The nearest open space was the widening triangle of Broadway and Seventh Avenue between Forty-third and Forty-seventh Streets.

Doc depressed the elevators suddenly. The nose whipped up. The big plane seemed almost to hang suspended by only the power of its motors. The wide wings were flat against a vertical wall of air.

THE Red Arrow ship dropped. Its landing wheels were in the exact middle of Broadway. One wing tip was over a sidewalk. The plane shot forward. A deserted bus had been left standing in the middle of the street, just before the explosion.

On one side reared the curved, cave-like entrance to a subway station. Between the bus and this obstacle, the wings were trapped. One wing struck the bus and half of it was sheered off. The cabined fuselage skidded on one side.

Those of the nearest crowds behind the police lines were breaking through. Ambulances and police squad cars that had been held in readiness before the explosion racketed into a combined screaming of sirens.

Doc was out of the control room of the plane. Lifting a woman in his arms, he carried her to the door. The metal frame had jammed. Two men were frantically trying to pry it loose. The door was unyielding.

Without releasing the burden of the woman, Doc's cabled hand closed on a metal part where the glass was broken out. The tendons of the arms stood out like whipcords. Metal crunched and ground. The two men gasped as the door twisted out of its frame.

Vonier was just behind Doc. He was carrying the limp figure of Carberry. The financier's eyes opened. He moaned and tried to stand. Supported by the explorer, he succeeded.

Vonier was looking directly at Doc. The bronze man was making his third trip from inside the plane. Two police doctors were working over the victims.

"It's a miracle!" said one of the medical men. "Nothing but shock, concussion, three with minor fractures and bruises."

Some ten minutes elapsed before all were out and the medical men were ready to start these patients to the hospital. Doc stood flexing his muscles. Not a mark, bruise or scratch marred the smooth bronze skin. He was glancing around the circle of faces of those who had been in the plane.

Suddenly, the voice that had startled all in the plane, that had put a whole city in terror, spoke:

*"Doc Savage—my power has been proved! The world is in my hands! Stop before it is too late! You and your friends will be the next to go! One of my own aides is close beside you! I am—Var!"*

The financier, Carberry, gave a great convulsive gasp. Vonier uttered a low, short oath. He and Carberry were darting sharp glances at the others who had been in the plane.

THE man who had been carrying a salesman's kit grew suddenly pale. His eyes were widening upon Doc. The bronze man's lips had not moved. His flaky, golden eyes now were turned upon this man. They were hypnotic orbs, that seemed for an instant to hold the man.

Then Doc moved slowly toward him.

Doc had simply applied his ventriloquistic talent. So adept was he in this especial ability that none would ever have known the latest voice of Var had issued from his own motionless lips.

The voice had been thin, strident, but clear. It might have come from any spot within a fifty-foot radius. But upon that one man who knew of only one source from which the real voice of Var might be summoned, there was the immediate palsy of fear.

Doc was beginning to believe that the voice also fell with dire significance upon the startled ears of another man within the passenger group. Because of this second theory, he permitted the salesman passenger to recover enough to begin edging back through the crowd.

The bronze man's eyes again were upon Vonier. The explorer was smiling, but his lips were drawn back from the skeleton teeth.

"Pretty good," he murmured. "In fact, almost perfect, Doc

Savage. I wonder if the doctors have finished with the others, if one would have a look at my arm? I think it's broken in two places."

Doc was forced to admire the man's stoical calm. His left arm was not only broken, but in one place a sharp splinter of bone had been pushed through the skin.

Doc shifted his eyes back to the salesman. He saw only his back. The man was getting away. Doc took one step.

A girl's anxious voice inquired suddenly, "I'm looking for a passenger named Scraggs? He was to have arrived on the Red Arrow plane at nine o'clock. Have any of you seen him? He is a little man, wearing very old clothes. His hair is long and kind of ragged."

Doc pivoted slowly. He was instantly struck by the woman's clear-cut beauty. Her face was as perfect as an etching, as a carved cameo. Perhaps it was her apprehension for the safety of the man she sought. Her voice was edged by a sharp, metallic quality.

The pilot had recovered consciousness.

"We had such a man booked, miss," he said. "He went down with us on the Washington flight, but I guess he missed the plane coming back. He had his seat reserved, but at the last minute another man came with a note and took it. Maybe he knows; he's that——"

The pilot to whom Doc Savage had amply repaid the favor extended to him on the Washington flight, gave a quick look at his grounded passengers.

"Why, I guess he's gone," added the pilot. "He looked like a salesman. He was here a minute ago."

This clicked with Doc. He was sure the pseudo salesman had been the medium of bringing Var's voice into the plane. Now it was indicated he had been in the seat reserved by the man called Scraggs.

The bronze man pondered deeply. Who, then, really was Var? And who was the woman whose voice had murmured in accompaniment to the first manifestation of Var's ghostly tones on the New Jersey highway?

"Oh, then he must still be in Washington!" the girl breathed. Then, unexpectedly, she looked at the bronze man and said, "You're the famous Doc Savage, aren't you."

Did the girl's wide-spaced eyes express fear or were they

merely widened in wondering awe at being brought in contact with the world famed adventurer? It was difficult to judge.

Doc quickly decided she was a rare combination. The girl had unusual beauty. Her quick glance was one of keen discernment. Not often had the bronze man been thus studied and measured by a woman.

In the brief space of seconds, this girl had weighed him. Her brows contracted in a little frown. The bronze man read in her clear eyes what might have been either a great grief or a lurking fear.

Doc inclined his head and replied, "I am Doc Savage."

At that, the young woman turned, as if she had lingered too long. Her slender figure, cloaked in a coat of light blue seemed to melt into the crowd. Vonier and Carberry, watching Doc, scarcely detected the movement which took him from their view.

One second, the girl and Doc were there. The next, both had vanished.

Doc had suddenly determined the loose and puzzling end of the Var mystery lay with the little man Scraggs. He did not think the strange girl believed Scraggs still to be in Washington. She would know where to seek him next.

The girl's forward progress seemed impeded by the pressing of the crowd. The bronze man suffered no such impediment. His lithe body passed through the river of humanity without the touching of any other person.

The girl disappeared around a corner. Doc stepped aside to the curb to evade a packed group of chattering bystanders.

"You have something to explain, Mr. Savage!" rapped a commanding voice. "One of your men was in the plane of that blasting devil up there! We've got him! The commissioner wants to talk to you!"

Several hundred policemen in uniform, and others in plain clothes, were in Broadway and adjoining streets. They had been called in from outside precincts to serve as explosion guards. Four of these blocked Doc's progress.

The force held Doc Savage and his men in the greatest respect. These men were respectful. But their manner showed firm intention to carry out the order they said they had been given.

Doc considered quickly. Had it been Ham recaptured, or had it been Monk in the Cold Light plane?

Before he had time to question, the four policemen, guns pressed to his sides, were indicating he should get into a closed squad car standing near by. Doc made no protest.

The bronze man was quick to sense a deception. These men were not policemen. But he decided the command to attempt the trick must have come directly from the controller of the Cold Light.

Being taken to Var would be much more important than following a will-o'-the-wisp trail of the girl in blue.

The bogus squad car jerked ahead. Then quick hands closed the curtains. Revolvers were jammed viciously into Doc's sides.

"Step on it, Smoke!" one of the men snarled.

## Chapter 15
## THE MAGNETIC WALL

A SHORT time before the crash, Long Tom had been working at headquarters, as directed by Doc. Multiple coils, amplifiers, condensers, compact generators and other electrical appliances were scattered about.

Before the Cold Light blast had struck, Long Tom had believed Doc's experiment was on the verge of success. At this time, Renny had been with the electrical wizard.

Long Tom grinned up at him. His face was jubilant.

"We've got it!" he exclaimed. "Doc's ideas always work! Now why couldn't I have thought out this one myself?"

Renny grunted. He knew all about his own profession—engineering. But Long Tom's gadgets always filled him with suspicion, until he saw them in operation.

"Now watch this!" Long Tom directed.

THE box the electrical expert had created was covered with a variety of indicator needles. It was about one foot square, but barely three inches thick. It was packed with amplifying coils and Long Tom's own special generators of diminutive size.

When he threw a switch, there was a whirring sound. But there was no visible ray.

"Holy cow!" grunted Renny. "How would I know anything about something I can't see?"

It was true. The ray or emanation from one side of the box was invisible.

But Long Tom knew the electromagnetic ray had been created. It was more than a mere ray. It spread invisibly in the shape of a mammoth fan. At the distance of a few yards, it became a wall extending from floor to ceiling of the laboratory.

Renny grunted several times in the following few minutes. It was his way of displaying appreciation. For he saw the ex-neutralizer cut off in turn the violet ray, the X ray and a dozen other such electrical manifestations.

The interruption of a high-frequency current was disastrous. A polished globe exploded and rained fragments among the retorts and tubes of fragile glass. A fuse went out, and for a few seconds the laboratory was in darkness.

"Take it easy, Long Tom," advised Renny. "Maybe this thing will kick back on you."

"It's absolutely harmless!" insisted Long Tom. "Wouldn't hurt a fly!"

With the lights on, he again turned on the ex-neutralizer. He directed it as a dividing wall across the laboratory.

There were two rats in a cage. On these Monk had been testing the effectiveness of certain anaesthetic, but non-injurious, chemicals.

The invisible electromagnetic wall was projected toward the cage. Without special intent, Long Tom shifted the box.

"Holy cow!" grunted Renny. "Now you've done it! Wouldn't hurt a fly, huh?"

The rats didn't even squeal. Both dropped as if bullets had been imbedded in their scanty brains. When Renny reached the cage, they were still and dead.

"Don't let that thing touch me!" cautioned Renny, hastily. "The rats went out like a light!"

"Now what could have done that?" muttered Long Tom.

His homely face registered deep gloom. His tone indicated he would have liked to put responsibility elsewhere. But it was his job. In some uncanny fashion, the ex-neutralizer had become a death ray.

Long Tom set to work with frantic haste. He wished

heartily that Doc were here to advise him. In a few minutes, he believed he had found the flaw, and remedied it. But just then, he had no further opportunity for proving his theory.

Renny was glancing at his watch. He went through the door to the window of the outer office.

"Nine o'clock, Long Tom!" he called. "If there's to be fireworks, they're due right now! Holy cow——"

His words were snatched away by the reverberating blast.

"Good gosh!" exclaimed Long Tom. "There's the Red Arrow plane! Doc was coming back on it!"

The pair saw the Cold Light ray, steely blue in color, seeming to cut through the big passenger plane. Renny seized a pair of the electronic binoculars. His breath hissed from his big chest, as the Red Arrow ship winged over and over like a leaf in a cyclone.

Immediately after the crash of the plane, Renny and Long Tom had sought to trace Doc Savage. Contact with the police proved to them the bronze man had apparently been duped and taken prisoner.

They also learned that Monk had been aboard the Cold Light plane and had been taken by the police. In the meantime, another man also was trailing Doc's captors.

THE little man known as Scraggs, who had escaped with Monk, was running along a street on the East Side.

Scraggs's progress was much like that of a fleeing rat. His thin body slithered through holes where there didn't seem room for a man to pass. His frayed hat was pulled low.

Scraggs was abruptly halted. It was the girl in the bright blue cloak.

"Oh, it's you!" she exclaimed. "I was at the plane that fell! You weren't there! I started for the old houseboat hangar! You said you'd meet me and that——"

Her words tumbled out. Scraggs pushed off her detaining hand.

"Go back to the house in the woods!" his thin voice commanded stridently. "I haven't time to explain! You'll have to wait for me there!"

"But, Scraggs, I saw Doc Savage!" the girl insisted. "We've got to do something quick! We've——"

Scraggs interrupted impatiently, already moving away.

"I know more about that than you do!" his thin voice rasped. "And that's what I'm on my way to do!"

The girl remained motionless for a long minute after Scraggs had disappeared. Her perfectly chiseled features were as set as a marble mask. The paleness of either deep despair or implacable purpose only enhanced the cameolike beauty of her face.

Doc Savage had hoped the police trick, on the part of the crooks, would lead him straight to the man known as Var. Even after the car curtains were drawn, Doc permitted his captors to think he had been tricked.

Doc knew nothing of the man Scraggs having witnessed his departure from the wrecked Red Arrow plane. Nor did he know of Scraggs having been in the Cold Light plane and having been saved by Monk.

From Scraggs's dash toward East River, the little man evidently knew more of Doc's destination than the bronze man himself could have guessed.

But the bronze man's thought was that this was the quickest and surest way to come face to face with the Cold Light destroyer.

Doc's conjecture was roughly shattered. The car was jouncing along a water-front street on East River. Without any warning, one of the guns was whipped from his side.

The weapon crashed on his skull with stunning effect. Fighting back a swimming black cloud, Doc felt his arms gripped to his sides. A hoodlike affair was pulled swiftly over his head.

Under ordinary conditions, the bronze man had defeated the purpose of assailants who sought to administer an anaesthetic. His ability to hold his breath was that of the longest-winded pearl diver of the South Seas. Some of these divers had been known to remain under water for periods of three to four minutes.

Only half conscious, suffocated by the sack over his head as well as by the etherizing vapor clouding his throat and nostrils, Doc lost all knowledge of what was transpiring.

As he slowly recovered, the bronze man had no means of knowing how many hours had elapsed. He was only sure the day had passed. The pall of night was relieved by twinkling stars he could see through a slitted window.

Under Doc, the floor quivered, jerked. Thunder beat upon

his ears. His first effort to move convinced him a thorough job of tying had been done.

Rawhide thongs had been expertly bound, not only around his arms and legs, but another had been passed around his throat. This had been secured by spikes or staples to the floor, or to a wooden crosspiece.

The long, coffinlike space in which he lay was moving. Up and down. Speeding ahead. The dipping motion was sickening.

Doc knew instantly he was in an airplane.

There was no pilot at the controls. Twisting his head with great effort, Doc could see no other person in the cabin. He was alone. A side roll of the plane revealed rows of long white wave tops not so far below.

The bronze man was hurtling out to sea on a one-man flight. But no other man controlled the plane and Doc had been rendered powerless.

## Chapter 16
## THE DIVE OF DEATH

Doc attempted to roll over. The rawhide thong around his neck cut off his breath. So rigidly were his arms and legs bound with many wrappings, the bronze man could obtain no leverage against the choking cord.

He tensed his throat muscles and put his weight against the rawhide. This prevented the cord choking him, but his weight was insufficient.

Now he could see the lights of the plane's instrument board. He saw that his fate had been made cleverly, fiendishly sure. The plane was controlled by an automatic radio device. But in this plane the alternative hand controls had been removed. Only the special mechanism which operated the small cabin ship on waves of sound, was flying it.

The monster Var had taken no chances. Even were Doc Savage by some of his almost supernatural powers able to free himself, no means had been left for controlling the ultimate destiny of the plane now far out over the ocean.

The plane suddenly dipped in a breath-taking dive. But it only swooped down close to the surface and then zoomed for altitude. Doc put all the strength of his neck against the binding thong. It would not yield.

Even in this terrible predicament, Doc was thinking back. There was this Scraggs. Furtive, elusive, ratlike Scraggs. Afraid of being identified with his own efforts. Scraggs had acted at first as if he was trying to avert the explosions of the Cold Light, to stop the evil workings of the mysterious Var.

Doc pondered another item. Who was this girl seeking Scraggs? When Var's voice had first been heard, a feminine voice had murmured with it. Circumstances, as yet, had led to no definite conclusion.

Doc could almost feel the landing gear of the plane slapped by the tops of the ocean swells, as the little ship dived again. The rawhide thong was slowly lessening his freedom to breathe.

Up again. Higher this time. Doc had been awaiting the moment when the plane would be sent farther up. He could almost see the brain reasoning out the finish. For the last dive, the Var operator, perhaps Var himself, would cause the plane to take on more altitude.

This would make certain the disrupting effect of the final drop. If Doc's throat muscles had not been held as rigidly as a bar of iron, the drying rawhide would have throttled him before this time.

The plane was still climbing. Doc's super-sense put every nerve on the alert. Slowly, he forced his head over. The bronze skin rasped from his neck as he turned. He was looking into the shadowed space at the rear of the coffin-like cabin.

From the darkness a voice spoke. It was thin and strident.

"I guess you've had enough to know Var is ruthless! He will stop at nothing——"

What seemed to be a bundle of disreputable, unkempt clothing rolled into view and stretched into a skinny, little man.

IT was Scraggs. In the semidarkness of the plane's cabin, his eyes glowed like a cat's.

Doc eyed him closely. Scraggs had a pointed knife in his hand. It moved toward Doc's throat. The bronze man was helpless.

But the furtive, elusive Scraggs had only good intent in this movement. The edged knife slit the tightening rawhide thong at Doc's throat. The plane still was climbing.

The knife slid down along the other bindings. Doc stretched his cramped arms and legs, got to his feet.

"Thanks," he said. "That's a good turn I'll not forget. But how did you happen to be here?"

Scraggs's tongue licked along his bloodless lips.

"I overheard what had been planned when you returned to Manhattan. There were too many for me to try to rescue you. I beat them to the plane and hid in the cabin. I thought I could get you out before it was sent off, but now—well, now there ain't anything we can do."

Scraggs's explanation sounded sincere. Anyway, it was clear the furtive little man was in the same tight spot as Doc.

The nose of the plane suddenly dipped. The struts screamed in a full-powered dive. Doc pushed Scraggs ahead of him. He forced open the door of the plane against the terrific pressure of the wind.

"Jump from the door!" commanded Doc. "You will have to hurry!"

"But I can't! We'll be killed! No! No!"

Scraggs pulled away. Plainly, he feared the plunge into the open sea. Doc's strong hand gripped his shoulder and the little man winced. He was powerless to resist the viselike hold.

Then the plane suddenly leveled off. The swells were again so close, the white teeth of the combers could be seen plainly.

Doc let go of Scraggs and sprang to the radio mechanism. His corded hands fastened on the machinery. With one wrench, he had ripped the controls loose. Wires snapped under his super-human strength. Ailerons flapped. The tail assembly jerked loose, erratic weaving.

With crumpling, devastating force, the ripping propeller smashed into the sea. The plane's tail, went up and the little ship went far under the surface in its final dive of death.

## Chapter 17
## SCRAGGS JOINS DOC

Doc could easily have freed himself. His enormous lung capacity made him as nearly an amphibian as it is possible for any man to be. As the plane cracked up and sank, Doc had absorbed enough air to keep him alive for several minutes.

Instead of pulling himself out he let go his supporting hold. Scraggs's first scream died in a gasping gurgle. Doc groped his way to the confined space where the little man was trapped. Gripping fingers fastened on a bony ankle.

Fortunately, the amount of air in Doc's lungs increased his own buoyancy. Pulling Scraggs's shoulders into a scissors hold of his locked legs, the bronze man used his hands to drive them toward the surface.

Even Doc's tremendous lung capacity was tested. When his head emerged, the first long breath pierced him like many tiny knives. He rolled, treading. Scraggs was shifted over one arm.

From the bronze man's clothing came a special restorative chemical. Doc's trained hands forced the water from Scraggs's lungs. A tiny needle pierced the little man's muscles near his spine.

With briny water slapping and stinging his eyes and nostrils, the little man gasped and started kicking. Doc turned him on his back. Perhaps one man in a million could have fixed direction as the bronze man accomplished it.

Lying too low in the sea to glimpse the lights of shore, Doc simply made a quick study of the stars. He fixed the position of the Great Dipper. This lined with the North Star. Doc rolled and commenced swimming shoreward with the moaning Scraggs.

One hand held the little man. The other arm and his legs beat the swells with churning impact. Doc's progress was much like that of the porpoise. To gain speed, his mighty body plunged under some of the swells.

The distance may have been two miles or five. Doc's tireless limbs moved with the speed of motor-driven pistons. Even so, nearly an hour elapsed before he was pulling Scraggs from the frothing wash onto a landing of flat rocks.

Scraggs's thin body was draped with clinging kelp. The weeds gave the little man the appearance of some drowned sea animal. Doc worked him back to consciousness again.

STRANGE combinations were forming theories. Scraggs's appearance. The Cold Light of the explosion and the blast itself, with the queer coloring of aquamarine. The few words, in the plane, of the explorer, Vonier, and the financier, Carberry, over some of their theories.

All of these seemed to trend to the sea. They touched upon the mysteries of the vast, little-known life of the oceans themselves. In the analytical brain of Doc Savage, they became a directly separable quantity.

The greatest source of life lay in the sea. Therefore, why not the most terrible forces of destruction!

Scraggs began talking in a hoarse, strained voice:

"Who—who saved us?" he stammered. "Who—who got us out?"

"We had luck," Doc stated. "The tide was with us."

Scraggs sat up, staring at him. The man's eyes glowed with a hint of phosphorescent light. It was this made him resemble a cat in the darkness.

Doc's own flaky eyes also were glowing. He shot a question.

"You're safe now. Who is Var?"

Scraggs cringed as if he had been struck a blow. His thin lips trembled.

"I—I can't tell you that," he mumbled. "Because I don't know. I've never seen him. Yes, you believe I've been working for him. I have, but never directly."

The little man clearly was on guard. There was something he did not intend to reveal. The bronze man's hypnotic eyes held the sunken orbs of the other.

"No!" the little man almost shouted. "You're trying to make me tell something I don't know! I never saw Var, I tell you! But he murdered my best friend—the scientist, Jackson—and I was his helper!"

There now was sincere grief in Scraggs's voice.

"Jackson was the man killed in the first explosion?" the

bronze man suggested. "Before he could talk over the telephone? You put a message in my pocket, then I conjecture you went back to the house in the marsh."

Scraggs stared at Doc.

"No—yes, I did go back," he said. "I saw Jackson killed. I couldn't stand it. I ran away. I didn't dare be found there. Jackson was the best and kindest and smartest man that ever lived! He was inventing this explosive for the man who called himself Var."

"DIDN'T Var come to the house in the marsh?" questioned Doc.

"Yes; but only at night, and I was never permitted to see him," insisted Scraggs. "I knew some experiments were planned. Jackson told me where one test was to be made. That was one in the woods near Carberry's home in Little Neck. That's how I happened to be out there."

"The message indicated Jackson was afraid," Doc said.

Doc knew part of what Scraggs was telling must be the truth, but only part of it.

"Yes," said Scraggs. "At the last, Jackson was afraid. The chief kept him a prisoner in the house. There was no way out, except by the one road and it was guarded."

"Var seems to have many men," said Doc. "They are not ordinary criminals."

"No—I don't know—well, yes, you are right," stammered the little man. "Var has a big organization. All of his men are smart. Jackson told me Var had first planned to use his explosive for establishment of a new social justice."

"Jackson told you all of this?"

"Yes, yes, he told me!" exclaimed Scraggs. "I'm being honest with you. Jackson sent me with the message to find you. It was too late. Var's plans were complete. He had no more use for Jackson."

"You want to avenge the death of your friend and employer, is that it?" said Doc.

"Yes, that's it," replied Scraggs. "I've tried to help you all I could. Can't you see—I even hid in the plane to try and rescue you; then we were both trapped and you saved me——"

"Are you sure there wasn't some way to have controlled that plane without the radio, some way that you knew?" Doc quizzed.

"No; I expected to get you out before the plane was sent off East River."

Doc pondered this quickly. Had Scraggs a reason of his own for wanting to appear as the bronze man's rescuer? It might be a part of Var's plan to establish a closer contact with Doc's movements.

Scraggs suddenly interrupted his flow of thought.

"But I want to have your help," Scraggs said. "I'll go with you and your men. I know much I can tell you. There are several places you would never find alone. I'll help you, if you'll let me stay with you."

Doc considered this a moment, without speaking. Then Scraggs seemed to recall something important.

"Doc Savage!" he cried. "While you have been here, some of your own men may have been wiped out! I've heard of a new plan of Var's. He intends to get your men in your headquarters, maybe blow up the building!"

Scraggs was trembling. There was evidence of desperate sincerity in his warning.

"You can come with me," the bronze man decided. "We will find an automobile."

At about this time, Ham was arriving by a White Liner plane at the Newark Airport.


## Chapter 18
## HAM GETS POISON


HAM was his usually natty-appearing self, as he alighted from the passenger plane. The waspish, well-clothed figure took on a hasty stride. He pushed impatiently into the crowd awaiting arrival of other planes.

"I might have known I wouldn't have any luck!" he muttered.

Scraggs had not been aboard the White Liner. Ham believed the man he wanted would be on the Red Arrow.

The excited comment of those around him and screaming headlines informed Ham the Manhattan explosion had taken place on schedule. Ham seized a paper as he entered the limousine used by the air transport company to carry passengers back and forth between Manhattan and the airport. Reading avidly, he groaned.

"Good heavens!" he grunted. "It can't be possible! Not Doc!"

The edition of the newspaper he had bought had been issued within a few minutes after the Manhattan blast. This story had it the Red Arrow plane had crashed against a building in Radio City.

Ham felt for his handkerchief. A small box was in the pocket. The box had been slipped into his coat either on the plane or in the airport terminal buildings.

Across the box were printed a few words:

I TAKE THIS MEANS OF GETTING THIS STRANGE POISON GAS TO DOC SAVAGE. WHEN PLACED IN WATER, THESE PILLS FREE ENOUGH POISON VAPOR TO KILL HUNDREDS. I BELIEVE ONLY DOC SAVAGE CAN ANALYZE AND DISCOVER THEIR FORMULA. WHEN HE HAS DONE THIS, HE CAN COMMUNICATE WITH ME AT BOX 1131, QUEENS POST OFFICE.

A FRIEND

Ham opened the box. It contained four round pills, about the size of small marbles. These were of jellylike substance.

Ham carefully replaced the poison gas pills.

But more recent editions of the newspapers in Manhattan caused Ham to forget the pills of poison gas. He read that Doc had saved the Red Arrow plane. But his jubilation was short-lived.

For the papers had reported the manner of Doc's disappearance. The police were futilely searching for four phony coppers in a bogus squad car. Monk had been freed by the police and had joined his companions at Doc's headquarters. Ham hastened directly there.

Monk and Ham might have been expected to congratulate each other on their separate escapes from Var's clutches.

Ham's mouth twisted into a sneering grin, as he looked at the big chemist.

"So they got one look at that classic profile of yours in the explosion plane," said Ham, "and then they jumped out. Well, that mug must have been a shock!"

"Howlin' calamities!" squealed out Monk's high-pitched voice. "An' it takes a smart shyster like you to get me conked

when all I'm doin' is tryin' to save your worthless skin! Tellin'
me to quit on that roof! Sayin' you're just practicin'!"

Monk referred to the encounter on the Washington roof
where Ham had heeded Doc's instructions and stopped the
battle with Var's men.

"What's the latest news of Doc?" inquired Ham, anxiously,
of Long Tom and Renny.

"That's just our trouble," grunted the worried Renny.
"There isn't any. Nothin' to start on or get a hold on. Do you
suppose we'd be coolin' our heels here, if we had a lead?
We've been hoping every minute the police would report
something to start us off."

"So the fake police car went up in thin air?" mused Ham,
aloud. "Went toward East River?"

"Yeah," said Long Tom, "but the river patrol hasn't reported
a thing."

The day's shadows lengthened. Toward night, a much
subdued and unusually timid Broadway was flashing its first
lights.

"I've got it! I've found it!" Long Tom suddenly proclaimed.

"Found what?" groaned Renny. "A way to discover where
Doc's gone? That's all I want to know right now!"

"Well, no," admitted Long Tom gloomily. "Nothing like
that. But his electromagnetic wall is O.K. I've fixed it so it
wouldn't harm a fly."

"You said that before," complained Renny. "An' look what
happened to Monk's rats."

"Aw, rats!" muttered Long Tom. Then he brightened visibly.
"That's the idea," he added. "Monk, how about getting us
some more rats?"

Grumbling that something might happen, Monk finally
agreed and departed.

THE three companions left in the laboratory made a con-
certed spring for the front office when the phone buzzed.
Ham picked up the instrument.

Thinly, stridently, a voice started speaking:

*We have Doc Savage! You will never see him again!
Tomorrow, the afternoon Washington-New York express train
will be next to feel the power of Var! Tell Ham, the lawyer, he
must go back to Washington! If Ham goes to Washington
and follows instructions, the train will be saved! I am—
Var!*

With a bitter invective, Ham jiggled the receiver bar. A half minute later, he replaced the instrument.

"The operator says it's a dial phone in a public booth somewhere and can't be traced," he informed the others. "Brothers, we're faced by a situation that seems to be beyond our control. Only one thing: the voice didn't say Doc had been killed. And if he hasn't, we'll see him again and it won't be long."

Monk came back, bringing two rats in a wire cage. They were common, gray rodents.

Monk set the cage at one end of the long, spacious laboratory. He joined Renny and Ham at one side, watching Long Tom.

"Now," said Long Tom, "the Hertzian ray already has been perfected to the point where it will kill electrical force at a great distance. It can be used to stop airplanes in the air. But this is the first electromagnetic force to neutralize any other electrical ray."

Long Tom moved a switch. Generators whirred in the square, flat box. The ex-neutralizer wall formed an invisible partition across the laboratory.

"Dag-gone it!" squeaked Monk. "Even if they was rats, y' needn't've murdered 'em! I was wantin' 'em to try out a new kind of poison gas!"

Long Tom stared mournfully at the wire cage upon which the ex-neutralizer was directed.

The pair of gray sewer rats had rolled on their backs. Their legs were rigid. They hadn't even kicked.

"Holy cow!" barked Renny. "See that you keep that thing turned off the rest of us!"

Long Tom's hand was moving to switch off the ex-neutralizer. Monk started over to examine the rats. The apelike chemist jumped back as if he had been stung.

"Howlin' calamities!" he ejaculated. "Wouldja look at that! Keep that death machine on, Long Tom! Keep it on!"

A mysterious, deadly ray of Cold Light sliced through the thick stone and steel of the Manhattan skyscraper as a knife might have passed through soft cheese. It penetrated half of the laboratory.

Seen close up, it was like an edged, flat band of bright blue steel. Long Tom backed hastily toward the open office door.

Thus the box in his hand cast a fanlike ray that covered every inch of the test room from floor to ceiling.

"It works! By heavens, it works!" he shouted.

The skins of every one prickled with the sensation of cold.

But the deadly, explosive Cold Light did not reach its objective, whatever it might have been.

Its frigid band reached Long Tom's invisible electromagnetic wall. There it was abruptly cut off. The magnetic insulation converted half the laboratory into an impregnable refuge. Ham, Monk and Renny were within this haven.

For a long minute, the Cold Light remained fixed into the room. In the streets below thousands of persons saw it shining across the night.

Crowds scurried for shelter.

Then the Cold Light disappeared. A traffic policeman had fixed its origin in a near-by skyscraper. Within ten minutes squads of policemen were scouring this building. But they found nothing.

The Cold Light then was being reported from farther uptown. In reality, it had come from several miles. Its penetrating ray had pierced scores of office buildings, mostly emptied for the night. Nothing had interfered with its progress until it had encountered Doc's electromagnetic wall.

The four men felt as if they were freezing. The Cold Light had vanished, but the temperature of the room rose slowly.

Monk found chattering speech. The ex-neutralizer had been switched off.

"Lookit!" he shouted. "The rats! They've come back to life!"

WITH Long Tom's ex-neutralizer turned off, the gray rats were frisking about as if they had never been laid cold.

"Dag-gone it!" squeaked Monk. "That's nothin' but a hypnotizin' machine! Long Tom, you try it on me! Betcha it won't knock me out!"

Ham laughed derisively.

"Hypnotism takes effect on the brain, Monk. That wouldn't be much use as a test," he suggested. "Rats have got some brains."

"Howlin' calamities!" squeaked out Monk. "Maybe you think that shyster brain of yours would help!"

"I suggest we test it together," remarked Ham. "Suppose we both walk through it?"

Long Tom demurred. But the rats apparently were wholly unharmed. He figured he could switch the electromagnetic wall off, if the two bickering friends showed any evidence of succumbing.

Again, the invisible wall partitioned the laboratory. Long Tom directed it deliberately upon the rats' cage. The rodents blinked their beady eyes and promptly curled up their toes.

Side by side, Ham and Monk walked around the long table filled with globes, retorts and a variety of tubes. Monk edged a little ahead. Part of his great bulk was in the invisible wall. Ham's own waspish body was touching it.

"Don't feel a thing," asserted Monk, and moved across. "C'mon, shyster. You scared?"

Renny and Long Tom had their eyes fixed on Ham and Monk. The latter two were looking at each other, keeping up a fire of sarcastic conversation. Thus none of them saw the Cold Light ray suddenly reappear.

The blue-steel band knifed through the skyscraper wall. Monk's big hands went to his face. He was almost blinded by chilling cold. Ham, seeing something was wrong, reached for him. His own body had not yet crossed the protective ex-neutralizer.

The door opening into the outer office burst open.

From the doorway came the weird, mellow warning of Doc Savage.

THE bronze man was standing there. His wet hair and skin were smooth and sleek. Just back of him stood the sodden figure of Scraggs.

"Stay where you are, all of you!" Doc commanded.

His flaky gold eyes caught and followed the shifting Cold Light. He saw it dissolve in the electromagnetic wall.

Long Tom moved to flick off the ex-neutralizer switch. Doc seized Long Tom's wrist.

"Leave it on," he directed. "Wait until the Cold Light stops. It would get all of us!"

Monk staggered back to the safe side of the electromagnetic wall. His huge body shook as with an ague. He felt as if he were freezing.

Monk's bulk struck Ham and sent the slighter figure of the lawyer to his knees.

"You big, blundering ape!" sputtered Ham. "Look where you're going!"

"I think Monk just saved our lives," Doc said, calmly.

Scraggs's mouth twitched, as he stared at the Cold Light ray.

"It didn't explode," he muttered, amazedly. "But I was right, Doc Savage. You see, I was telling you the truth."

Ham walked toward him. "You were in that house in Washington. You know what all this is about."

"I'm not so sure Scraggs does know all about the Cold Light ray," said the bronze man. "Perhaps he helped to save your life. If you had crossed the ex-neutralizer, all of us would have been annihilated."

## Chapter 19
## PLOTTED POISONING

AGAIN, the Cold Light had been withdrawn. For the second time during the evening, the police were unsuccessfully seeking its source. It had been directed upon Doc Savage's stronghold from a new direction.

Doc directed Long Tom to set about duplicating the ex-neutralizer at once. Scraggs watched silently. The bronze man apparently ignored him, but he was studying the little man's reactions closely.

"We'll probably need as many machines as we can get together," he advised. "At least, we'll need two to try and save the express train you've told me about."

Ham had told Doc of the threat against the train, but had made it a point to keep Scraggs from hearing. Now Scraggs looked up with quickened interest.

"You know about the train?" he exclaimed.

Ham looked intently at Scraggs.

"Perhaps, Doc, if Scraggs stays with us there won't be any need to save the express," he said, significantly.

"It wouldn't make any difference," Scraggs muttered. "But if you could prevent an explosion here, you could do it there."

"That's what we hope to do," Doc stated.

Doc produced a thin book from inside his shirt. Fingers flicked through the pages.

Monk could see the riffled pages. The little book was illustrated by brightly colored plates. Monk grunted and peered more closely.

"Dag-gone it!" he exclaimed. "I've seen somethin' like that picture there!"

Doc glanced at him quickly.

"Sure of that, Monk? When did you see it?"

"Can't seem to remember where or when I saw it, Doc, but I know I did."

The book's illustration was a picture of marine life. It was done in intense blue. The figure shown was apparently half human, half crab. Gold letters gave the name of the author.

The writer was Vonier, the explorer.

Clearly, Vonier had had good reason for his admiration for and his disagreement with Carberry, the financier, over a treatise Carberry had written. For Carberry's one plunge into science had dealt with the cellular origin of the human species.

Such a study must necessarily lead to the established origin of all life; that of the sea.

THE phone rang. It was Vonier, calling from a booth in the building lobby. Doc invited him to come up at once. If Vonier recognized Scraggs, his impassive face gave no hint. But Doc marked Scraggs staring intently at the explorer.

Vonier's arm was neatly bandaged in a sling. His bony face was as calm as ever. He announced he believed an attempt had been made on his life.

"When I reached my home and went into my office," he explained, quickly, "I found these in my desk top. I couldn't have missed them."

He produced two jellylike globules, no larger than marbles.

"A note was with them," Vonier said. "It was signed just, 'A Friend.' It directed me to analyze them for a mysterious poison, and said the pills possessed a rare form of germs that could be employed to pollute the whole water supply of a great city."

Ham was staring at the man. Scraggs arose and walked nervously about the laboratory.

"The note said they contained germs to be released in

water?" Ham questioned. "Then the first thing you probably would do would be to put one of the balls in water to see what would happen. Then why didn't you?"

Doc said, "Perhaps that was what was wanted, Vonier. To have you place them in water."

"I thought of that," remarked Vonier, dryly. "That's why I came to you. You are reported to be a wizard on the safe analysis of any form of poison."

Ham took his own "poison pills" from his pocket. He laid them on the desk. Then he produced the note he had received. Doc read it at a glance.

Vonier's lips were drawn in a smile over his skeleton teeth.

"I would say the whole thing's the work of our good friend Var," he stated. "I've heard the Cold Light ray has been jumping about again to-night. Something has gone wrong. There has been no explosion. So Var seems out to get us by a more devious device."

Doc said, "I'll analyze these pills." He glanced at the nervous Scraggs. "In the meantime, I'll place them in the laboratory safe where I keep my radium. Even poison gas can't escape from that."

This safe, heavily insulated with lead and a special rubber-like composition, contained Doc's radium. It was one of the largest amounts in the world in the possession of a single individual.

Scraggs watched the pills being locked away. His eyes glowed as if a sudden idea had struck him.

"I'm going out for a while," he said. "When I return, I may have something important to tell you, Doc Savage."

Doc merely nodded. Ham's face was dark with suspicion, as Scraggs sidled toward the elevators.

Doc apparently gave the matter no further attention. He turned to Vonier.

"Did any one of your household observe any suspicious person?"

"No," said Vonier. "Only the Japanese houseman was there. Mrs. Vonier has gone to our house on the shore. I'm convinced this Var means business. You are more of a threat to him than I am, Savage, but I haven't the slightest intention of complying with his demand that I join his organization."

Another phone call came from the skyscraper lobby. It was the hoarse, strained voice of Carberry, the financier.

"In heaven's name, let me come up and stay with you tonight!" came the excited voice. "I don't believe Var intends to wait forty-eight hours. He has learned I was in Washington. Now there has been an attempt to poison me!"

Doc's flaky golden eyes glinted strangely.

"Come right up, Carberry," he invited.

He told the others what Carberry had said. Vonier seemed about to impart something more of importance, then he merely said, "I think perhaps when you get to the bottom of this Cold Light thing, you'll find yourself mixed up with some of the mysteries of our little known marine life."

Monk gulped, started to speak, and changed his mind. It had come to him where he had seen the picture of the half-crab and half-human creature. It had been one of those done in oil on the walls of the room where he had fought Wheeze McGovern's men!

Doc had slipped Vonier's book on marine life into a drawer of his desk.

CARBERRY was a shaking figure when he entered. His protruding eyes appeared ready to jump from their sockets. The bald spot between his white tufts of hair had a ghastly hue.

"What? You here, too, Vonier?" were his first words. "I'm glad to see you're safe! I was afraid to stay out at my home, and I don't dare risk being trailed to where my wife is hidden!"

"You said an attempt was made to poison you?" suggested Doc. "It would be some sort of pill?"

"How in heaven's name did you know that?" exclaimed Carberry, producing a little box.

"Holy cow!" grunted Renny. "They're different! Look like sugar cubes!"

"Yes—yes—that's it—and that's where they were!" stammered the financier. "In the sugar! A houseboy got hold of one. The butler found him dead. He had turned purple. After the butler went through the sugar and found these, I thought you could find out more quickly, Savage, what they are."

There were two square cubes. Though they were white and shaped like sugar, a close inspection proved them to be less granular. There was a smooth crust hardened over a jellylike substance.

In a few seconds, the new poison pills were behind the thick, insulated door of the laboratory safe.

Long Tom came in, announcing he had the second ex-neutralizer ready. Doc invited Vonier and Carberry to witness a demonstration on several different electrical rays.

"Could one of them be made for me, Savage?" questioned Carberry. "I'll let you name your own price if——"

Doc interrupted. "We never accept pay for what we do, Carberry. But you're welcome to any safeguard we can devise. I would suggest both you and Vonier remain here tonight. You shall sleep between invisible walls of the ex-neutralizer."

DURING the night, Doc Savage perfected a plan for saving the Washington-New York express from the Cold Light threat. In the early morning, Long Tom and Renny left the headquarters. They were carrying the ex-neutralizer boxes. Their destination was the Hudson River hangar where Doc's planes were kept.

Ham and Monk were on their way to the warehouse hangar by a different route. Doc Savage followed another direction.

Carberry had left with Vonier, saying he would stay with the explorer during the day.

"Daylight braces me up," the financier announced. "But when night comes, I begin to get the jitters. And my forty-eight hours are up to-night," he added.

"We'll be back late this afternoon," said Doc. "Meet us here again to-night."

Though Carberry seemed to have some doubt as to Vonier, it was apparent he did not want to be alone.

Doc had not informed either the explorer or the financier of their destination. After communicating with the railroad offices, Doc had advised that the Washington-New York express be allowed to come through on schedule. He had suggested, however, that a regular train for passengers be run as a second section.

Only the necessary crew was to be carried on the first section.

Doc was at the controls of the plane. Long Tom was making sure the ex-neutralizers were in perfect order. If the warning from Var had been genuine, and none thus far had failed, the

Washington-New York express would have one invisible passenger.

The name would be Death!

About the moment Doc's special cabin plane was taking off from the Hudson River, a window was softly raised high in the tower of Manhattan's tallest cloud-piercer.

The afternoon had seen the advent of a slow, drizzling rain. It had misted over the city with the usual smoky fog. No person in the street below could have seen the slender rope swaying from the high window.

Nor did any person observe the slim, shadowy figure coming down. The man was light, his body almost wraithlike. Though supported only by his hands, he swung out over space with a confidence of movement which proved he was accustomed to great heights.

The man's feet poised lightly on the ledge of an eighty-sixth floor window. A blunt instrument appeared in one hand. The glass crashed inward to the rug without much sound.

An instant later, the intruder had raised the sash and admitted himself.

In the office, he produced a case of small instruments. The locked laboratory door yielded to a control electroscope like that used by Doc Savage and his men.

From his clothing came a flat, metal case. A button was pressed and a tongue of purple flame was reflected. This flame increased in intensity.

The insulated laboratory safe was not burglarproof. The insulating composition and the lead were relatively soft materials. After two minutes, a square opening appeared under the flame.

The intruder chuckled. Again the purple flame licked out. But this time, it did not seem to be of a destructive nature. Rather, the cut square of the safe door had been replaced.

The flame curled over the surface. The figure emitted another ironic chuckle. The square was being "healed" into place.

Afterward, an observing eye might have noted the rewelding of the crevices, but the average person, would not have known the wall of the vault had been tampered with.

Shortly thereafter, the outside door of Doc's headquarters opened. A man came out and took the stairway upward.

From the window a few floors above, the thin rope was drawn in. The window was closed.

The "poison pills" were no longer in the vault. They were close to a water faucet in the laboratory. Perhaps it was only by chance that a faulty valve caused dropping water to dampen the surface of the metal on which the "poison pills" had been laid.

## Chapter 20
## THE WALLS OF LIFE

EVEN while the mysterious visitor was in his laboratory, Doc Savage was piloting a cabin plane over the eastern Pennsylvania hills. He was following a train to set the plane down. He selected a flat field where a paved highway paralleled the railroad track.

Apparently a worried engineer had been expecting them, for the air brakes started steel grating on steel as Doc and his four companions appeared on the track ahead. The youthful fireman's eyes rolled as Doc's bronze figure swung up on the grabiron into the cab.

"You get up front," Doc told Long Tom and Monk. "One on each side of the pilot. It's a ticklish spot for riding, but we'll want every possible inch of the train covered by the ex-neutralizers. Turn on the machines and keep the rays playing. They're effective for at least a thousand yards; perhaps more. Renny and Ham and I will take the rear end."

Monk growled and grunted as he clung to a pilot standard with one arm and worked the ex-neutralizer wall.

"I'll betcha," he squealed above the rush of the wind and the pounding of piston heads, "that fashion-plate shyster has found himself a soft seat on the cushions!"

"You keep that box working!" shouted Long Tom. "And slant it straight back!"

The invisible walls formed two magnetic shields, as the Washington-New York Express gathered speed.

Instructing Ham to continue a patrol through the coaches, Doc took Renny with him to the observation platform on the rear car. He had judged the Cold Light, if and when it came, would have to be directed from an airplane or from some automobile on the highway.

In case the danger came from above, Long Tom had been instructed to swing to the locomotive stack and cover the top of the train. This feat Long Tom was ready to perform.

By Doc's instructions, the engineer kept the train to the low speed of around thirty miles per hour. Renny and Doc on the observation platform were scanning every passing auto and every distant plane in the sky.

The cars of the express poured into a shallow grade cut. It roared out onto a long straightaway. Half a dozen cars were in view on the highway.

Making sure his own special grenades—a powerful chemical explosive—were at hand, Doc scanned each of these cars in turn. Nothing out of the ordinary showed for some time.

WHEN the Cold Light ray flashed on, it came from a distance. The edged band, blue-steel in color, was striking across the country from a wooded spot nearly two miles away.

The knifelike emanation played along the sides of the speeding cars. Doc breathed with relief.

For when the ray struck the invisible wall of the ex-neutralizer on that side, it seemed to waver, then dissolve.

But a big closed car between the train and the wooded spot was not so fortunate. The driver of this automobile was speeding. His car was passing the train.

The Cold Light played upon the driver. It seemed to jump along with the automobile. Doc saw the driver stiffen in his seat.

Then the man reared up, took his hands from the steering wheel and clawed blindly at his face. He pitched forward, his head striking the windshield.

The automobile left the highway. Careening down the bank, it somersaulted twice and came to rest on flattened wheels. Two men were hurled out.

The first person to reach the scene of the crash reported, to the unbelief of others, that the driver and his companions seemed to have been frozen stiff. Three were dead. The other was seriously hurt.

The bronze man waited neither for the slowing of the train or for inspection of the wrecked car. Dropping to the ground, Doc's feet seemed to glide along the gravel. He was upright when he let go, and landed on his feet with a single bound over the right-of-way ditch.

Renny followed. His huge body lacked the springy resiliency of the bronze man's.

Renny failed to compensate for the speed of the train. His big feet tangled. With an enraged bellow, he started rolling. It was well his muscles were iron-hard and his neck was thick-sinewed.

After the third somersault, Renny managed to stagger to his feet. He was close behind Doc.

Following orders, the train proceeded on its way. Ham, Monk and Long Tom stuck by it. Monk saw Doc and Renny speeding across the near-by field over the highway.

There seemed to be no side road leading from the wooded spot to the main highway. Doc noted the square mile or so of bushy expanse appeared to have no visible outlet. Renny was forced to give all he had to keep up with the bronze man.

Doc did not seem to run. His speed was evolved from a gliding, sinuous movement in which all of his trained muscles coördinated. In even the crisis of this seeking of the maker of Cold Light, Doc's brain was working on other angles of the problem.

Monk had informed him of his recognition of the illustration in the Vonier book on marine species. In Vonier's well-done treatise on little known elements of the deeper oceans were many direct references to as yet undiscovered atomic energy greater than anything the world's leading scientists had revealed.

Doc could readily understand how Vonier might be valuable indeed to Var. The man who, according to Scraggs, had started out with the idea of reforming world society and now wanted world domination, might well find an individual of Vonier's erudition immensely valuable to his further schemes.

Var also might fear Vonier possessed a knowledge that would enable him to solve the mystery of the Cold Light force.

Doc considered this point. How much did Vonier really know of the elements that might have gone into the creation of Cold Light as a destroying agency?

The bronze man also pondered the actions of the mysterious Scraggs. The presence of Vonier, or something connected with the failure of the Cold Light to explode in the laboratory, had caused the little man to invent an excuse to get away. Doc was sure of this.

Then there was the girl in blue who had been seeking Scraggs at the wrecked Red Arrow plane. There had been a woman close to Var, as he had uttered his message after the first of his explosions.

Each of the suspects had a woman closely related to him or his activities.

THE bronze man and Renny arrived at the fringe of woodland.

They paused a moment, listening. Birds trilled in the brush as if nothing had been there to disturb them.

The strip of woods was about a quarter of a mile in width. Its extent in the other direction could only be guessed.

"You take the other side," directed Doc. "Keep under cover of the trees and move quietly. If you run onto anything, fire the pistol."

Doc was gone, slithering through the bushes. His progress was that of a jungle cat or a deer.

Renny's woodcraft was not nearly so skillful. Doc heard the huge engineer crashing into the brush.

Doc weaved from side to side. His swiftness covered half the wooded strip thoroughly. Under the trees the ground was damp and mossy.

Only a keen eye would have detected the dull coppery shining of a bit of metal at the bottom of a shallow pond. Doc scooped up the small object.

It was a narrow cylinder of brass. It much resembled some form of cartridge, open at one end. It seemed to have contained a sort of explosive powder and had been recently fired.

The empty shell bore no imprint of hammer pin. If it had been exploded, the force had been other than by impact. He instantly decided the cartridge had contained some element employed in the Cold Light machine.

The mystery of this was heightened by the absence of any footprints or marks around the edges of the little pond.

Doc's gaze roved upward. A freshly broken leaf dangled on its stem. Bark had been slightly scraped on a branch. The stunted trees here were close together.

It was plain enough some acrobatic individual had swung along from tree to tree. A second later, Doc was in the branches.

A few yards above the ground, he followed a trail in the

trees that led toward the other side of the woods. Pausing, he listened for Renny. There was only silence.

Renny must be near. He called cautiously. He received no reply.

WHEN Renny parted from Doc, he proceeded to the opposite side of the wooded strip. The air was balmy. The whole scene was peaceful. Renny plunged into the trees. Underbrush impeded his progress.

He had covered perhaps two hundred yards. Birds hushed into silence close around him, but when he paused the distant ones resumed their trilling. Apparently, nothing had disturbed them.

Suddenly this was changed. Renny came upon a robin on the ground. The red-breasted bird was hopping about aimlessly. Sometimes it fell over.

When Renny pursued, the robin seemed not to see or hear him.

A half-grown rabbit lay on its back kicking. The little creature appeared to be recovering from a blow. Renny picked it up. The body felt icy.

The rabbit had been almost frozen.

Recalling the effect of the Cold Light in the laboratory, Renny was instantly on guard. Still no sound or movement disturbed the bush. Renny pushed through a tangle of berry bushes.

Directly in his face, an icy wall sprung up. The Cold Light ray filtered through trees as if they did not exist. Renny was bathed in an icy chill. The effect was much the same as liquid air.

The engineer had seen no one. He had heard no movement. Instinctively, he attempted to draw his supermachine pistol. His fingers clawed stiffly. His arms were almost instantly numbed.

Renny tried to shout. His throat was constricted. His tongue was powerless to utter a sound. The engineer was the first person upon whom the Cold Light had been directly played.

Renny felt as if his whole body were being frozen. But he tried to struggle onward. He went to his hands and knees. He crawled slowly.

Blurred figures came from the bush around him. Tape was slapped over his mouth and eyes. Thongs enwrapped his arms and legs. His stiff form was lifted and carried to an automobile.

Warmth returned to Renny. This was a warm wave. Renewed circulation brought tingling pain all over his body. Much the same as when frostbite is being relieved too quickly.

The automobile jounced and jumped over the rough road.

"Why didn't we wait and grab Doc Savage himself?" growled one harsh voice. "With him at liberty, anything might happen!"

A hoarse voice, strangely familiar, replied curtly.

"Keep your advice, Smoke! He's being saved for the big blow-off! The world may suspect, but none will ever be able to prove what became of this so-called invincible bronze man!"

Renny strained at his bindings. The effort availed nothing.

PERHAPS five minutes later, Doc Savage came upon the spot where Renny had been seized. Tracks of the auto ran out to the highway. By this time, there were many cars moving.

The man of bronze whipped back to the spot where he and his men had landed their plane before boarding the train. Trailing the car in which Renny was a prisoner was impossible. But Doc was convinced he could quickly gain a lead to the place where Renny would be taken.

## Chapter 21
## THE WOMAN IN IT

DOC SAVAGE had instructed Monk, Ham and Long Tom to join him at the Hudson River hangar, when they arrived back in New York. The man of bronze planned to visit the penthouse apartment where Monk had first been held prisoner.

He had his own reason for delaying this visit until nightfall. Likewise, the bronze man wished his companions to remain away from the skyscraper headquarters. For this, he offered no explanation.

Vonier and Carberry had said they would not return until darkness. Vonier had not yet imparted his own theory of the Cold Light.

Leaving his companions at the Hudson River hangar, the bronze man vanished. During the late afternoon, he was engaged in visiting various real estate offices handling properties on Manhattan's East Side.

He was especially interested in the block destroyed by the Cold Light explosion. Darkness was falling over the city when Doc returned to the hangar.

And the coming of night was bringing another moving angle of the mysterious Cold Light.

THIS new angle revolved around an isolated house, buried deep in a wooded section of Long Island.

The furnishing of this obscure house was exotic. A raftered room with a high ceiling had heavy window drapes tightly drawn.

A woman sat in this room. Her features were flawless, of chiseled perfection. But the face lacked any warmth. Grayish-green eyes were like bright agate. A mask of a face. It might have been cast of plaster of Paris. The mouth was a pallid curve of bitterness. When she spoke, the name was hissed.

"Doc Savage! The luck of the devil's with him! The luck of Satan's own imps! I should have used a knife in a crowd, as I suggested!"

She drew a thin, stiletto blade from a silver sheath in the bosom of her dress. The blade was needle-pointed.

Somewhere in the back of the house was the tinkle of silver and dishes. A soft-footed servant was moving about.

The woman walked with a sinuous movement to one of the heavily draped windows. She pulled aside the corded cloth.

Overhead, the sky was speckled with coldly winking stars. The calm peace of the night apparently stirred her to tigerish fury.

"The fool!" she said, venomously. "We're not safe until this Doc Savage is put out of the way!"

She moved back to one of the chairs.

"He had the greatest power in the world and he can't get one man," she said in a low, brittle tone. "And now what is he doing? Since the first night, I haven't been in on any of it!"

She crossed the room and pulled a silken cord. Two dark-skinned men appeared from a rear room.

"Tako," the woman said, commandingly, "I want you and Scov to find your master at once! Try the river place, and if he isn't there he may be in the uptown apartment. You are to bring him here to me. Understand?"

"I understand," said the man addressed. "And if he doesn't want to come?"

The woman smiled, but it only made her mouth harder.

"You will bring him to me," she repeated, softly. "I will wait no longer!"

The two men withdrew.

Sparks glinted in the woman's grayish-green eyes.

"After all," she mused aloud, "the creator of the killing ray is dead. He can never come back. Our supply is almost inexhaustible. The secret of its origin is lost forever."

A GLASS clinked in another room. The woman arose and closed a pair of heavy double doors. She turned a key in the great brass lock.

Crossing the room, she came to an alcove containing a case of books. It appeared to have been built solidly into the structure of the house.

The woman glanced at the draped window. She touched a light switch and all but a single, dim eye faded out.

The woman moved one book. The bookcase swung silently outward. Back of it appeared a solid steel door. She whirled the knob of a combination.

A little light showed in the vaulted space behind the door. This was high enough to admit the woman's figure.

There were a dozen piled cases. Each was about a foot long, and possibly four inches in width and depth. They were like small caskets of a dull, lusterless metal. Each casket was fastened with screwed steel clamps.

The woman's long fingers sought one of the clamps. She swiftly unscrewed the casket fastening. The lid lifted. Under the raised top she could see the contents of the little casket. She lifted it. The weight did not appear to be great. Not as if the queerly devised boxes contained jewels or other treasure.

Yet the movement of the woman's hands was almost caressing.

For perhaps two minutes, the woman stood motionless. Her lips moved without sound. Whatever her ruthless purpose, it no doubt involved the contents of the dull metal caskets.

As she stood thus, she could not see the key in the ponderous brass lock of the double doors. This key was turning slowly. In the room at the rear of the house had sounded a muffled blow. It had been followed by a sighing moan.

The key was being turned so slowly from the other side of the door, its movement was almost imperceptible. But, as it caught the tumblers of the brass lock, there was a sharp *click*.

Without waiting to screw down the clamp of the small casket, the woman sprang back into the room. The double doors were swinging back on silent hinges.

In the aperture appeared a moonlike face. The small mouth was merely a hole above a thick, double chin.

"You!" gasped the woman. "What's happened? What are you doing here?"

WHEEZE MCGOVERN leered at the woman. His darting eyes had confirmed his belief. She was alone. His gaze fell upon the open door of the steel vault.

"Perfect! Better—*siss*—than I'd hoped for!" he wheezed. "Now just don't move!"

The woman was transfixed for an instant.

"Where—where is Var?" she stammered. "Why——"

"Sent me to get 'em!" cut in Wheeze. "An' I see—*siss*—you were expectin' me!"

"No! No!" The woman gave a little gasp. "You're lying! Var——"

Her slim hand pushed at the vault door. It was heavy. Two other men crowded the door behind Wheeze. He rolled his fat body across the room with incredible speed.

One of the woman's hands was caught and squeezed in the door she fought to close. Wheeze McGovern's pudgy fist struck her under one shell-like ear. The blow staggered her.

But with a furious hissing breath, she flung herself upon the stout figure of Var's aide. Curved fingers clawed at his face. The nails welted a bloody track across its moon-shaped surface.

"I know what you're after!" the woman screamed. "I'd been expecting it to happen! Others have brains, if Var hasn't! But you'll never get them!"

Wheeze snarled, and caught the woman's neck in a twist of his heavy arm. Disregarding her clawing fingers, he forced her body to the floor.

"You listen to me—*siss*—an' maybe we can get together on this!" he wheezed. "With the stuff we've got, we can have millions!"

The woman was breathing rapidly. Her eyes widened.

"Yes! I'd thought of that!" she said.

232 / A DOC SAVAGE ADVENTURE

One hand was sneaking to the bosom of her dress.

"What would you do with them?" she added. "What do you think could be done?"

Wheeze McGovern laughed softly.

"What? Collect millions!" he gloated. "Why, I'd make the big boys pay plenty! The time's ripe to collect!"

He had relaxed his hold on the woman. She came to her feet with the quickness of a cat. There was a silvery, flashing glitter in her hand.

For all of his apparently clumsy weight, Wheeze leaped aside with agile speed. He ripped out an oath as the stiletto pierced the cloth of his coat and ripped a furrow along the flesh of his arm.

"Why, you—*siss*—hellcat!" he grunted. "If you'd been only halfway reasonable—well——"

He was chopping out the words, even as his fingers closed on the woman's throat. His strength bent her downward and backward. He twisted the stiletto from her hand with a brutal force that cracked a bone in the woman's slender wrist.

She tried to scream, but the grip on her throat was inexorable. The face of chiseled marble turned slowly a greenish hue. Wheeze threw her limp body to one side.

"Take her, Smoke!" ordered Wheeze. "An' tie her up plenty!"

He pushed into the vault. He rapped out a command to another man. Wheeze's hands trembled a little, as he started passing out the small caskets. Then he came to the last one.

This was the dull metal box the woman had partly opened. The lid was up a few inches in the screw clamp. Wheeze gazed at the contents of the casket.

"Not a bad idea," he muttered. "Might as well leave it like it is."

WHEN all the caskets were in the car standing in the driveway outside, Wheeze reëntered. The woman's slim body lay in the cool, green depths of a seaweed rug.

With her hands tightly secured and her ankles lashed to a heavy, shell-like chair, the woman was powerless to move. Across her mouth tape had been fixed.

"Not that it matters," grunted Wheeze. "Won't anybody be comin' along this forsaken road. Nobody but Var would have the idea, and that won't mean anything."

The woman's bosom was heaving convulsively. Her eyelids fluttered open. In the gray-green depths of her orbs glowed killing hate. Wheeze shivered and looked away.

Then he smiled a little. He went into the big vault. When he came out, he had made sure the lid of the one casket remained open. He left the heavy steel door slightly ajar. As he went out, he pushed a button.

The oddly furnished room was plunged in darkness.

In the darkness, the bound woman was staring at the partly open door of the vault. None could see the terror that had replaced all other emotion.

WHEEZE MCGOVERN'S closely curtained sedan swung onto the main, paved highway about a mile from the house hidden in the woods. For persons leaving the scene of a crime, the occupants of the car seemed in no great haste.

Once the car speeded up, Wheeze laid his hand on the driver's arm.

"There isn't any grand rush," he cautioned. "Nobody's chasin' us, and this is one of the times—*siss*—we don't want to be picked up by any speed cop. Take it easy."

The car proceeded at a sedate pace. It was a mile up the concrete from the side road to the house in the woods. Two or three cars had passed in the opposite direction. A couple had sped by toward the city, where myriad lights were reflected in the sky.

Another car, with weak headlights, appeared, meeting the sedan. The face of this driver was white and strained. The car was a roadster, old and almost paintless. The man was driving fast.

In the darkness, Wheeze and his men could not distinguish the face. If they had, their controlled speed toward the city might have been altered.

The driver of the roadster was the furtive, mysterious Scraggs.

Though Wheeze McGovern had not guessed the identity of the man in the roadster, it was apparent Scraggs had recognized the other car. A short distance down the road the little car squealed to a stop.

Turning, Scraggs was perhaps half a mile from the sedan. His foot pressed the gas and he sped toward it.

It being early evening, traffic from the city showed a dozen dancing headlights at the same time. Three other cars passed Wheeze while Scraggs's car was creeping up behind the sedan.

The driver of one of these cars also slowed down. Only a minute later, a big car whizzed by both Scraggs and the sedan, coming from the rear.

Out of the night, from the midst of the blazing headlights, another light suddenly appeared. It was blue and cold. The Cold Light. The happenings of the succeeding moments were so fast, an observer would have had no time to fix details in mind.

Only it seemed the Cold Light had been directed at Wheeze McGovern's big car. The blue-steel ray must have missed, for the sedan abruptly spurted ahead.

The long beam of the Cold Light shifted from the highway. The sender undoubtedly was seeking to pick out Wheeze. The knifelike ray laid a silver pathway that could have been seen for miles. But for only a second. Perhaps only a fraction of that.

The Cold Light picked out the wooded area from which Wheeze and his men had lately emerged.

The following roaring explosion had the might of an unleashed volcanic crater. Vivid blue flame rushed through the trees toward the highway. An excavation the width of the East River was being ripped across the formerly peaceful countryside.

For miles, the earth rocked and trembled.

THE suction of the tremendous blast was so great that a dozen cars were caught in the fury of the air stream. They slid from the highway, catapulting into the ditches. Two automobiles were deposited up in the edge of the field through which the lurid blue blaze had rushed.

The Cold Light was flicked off. Instantly, the tumult and fury of the main explosion died. Only the reverberations and echoes remained.

At the scene of the apparent origin of the tearing explosion, when the first State police arrived, was only an immense crater. Here the woods and alll the surrounding territory had been gouged out to great depths. An area of more than ten acres was a deep excavation.

Not a stick or even the splinter of a tree remained. It was

as if the house, with its exotically furnished living room, had never existed.

Though the Cold Light had deliberately sought out the sedan of Wheeze McGovern, the car had escaped its direct force. Other cars near by had hurtled from the highway.

Even before the tearing chaos of the explosion had begun to die down, globules of sweat were popping from Wheeze McGovern's forehead. His double chin trembled and shook.

"It—*siss*—got her! Step—*siss*—on it! No, wait!"

Ahead of the sedan, a closed car had turned over in the ditch. A woman was crawling from a window. She was screaming. Blood ran from a cut on her forehead. One arm dangled.

Wheeze sprang from the car. The woman moaned.

"Oh, my son! Please, my son's down in there!"

Wheeze got down and pulled the inert figure of a boy from the crashed auto. The youth was undoubtedly past all human aid. Wheeze opened the rear door of the sedan and got the body inside.

Then he helped the woman get in. He followed.

"Now you can—*siss*—step on it plenty!" he wheezed.

The sedan whirled cityward. The speed crept up past seventy miles an hour. Two motor cycle cops flagged the car down.

"All hell's busted loose back there!" rapped Wheeze. "Maybe a dozen people killed! We're getting this woman and the boy to a hospital!"

The coppers saw five respectable-looking citizens. The woman with the bloody face was an argument.

"Right!" assented one of the cops. "Hope you make it in time!"

The motor cycles sped on toward the scene of the explosion.

The policemen did not know when they passed a furtive figure behind the fence over in a field. They did see a paintless roadster upended on its nose.

The little man known as Scraggs crouched close to the yawning gash of the Cold Light explosion. His luminous eyes glowed with hatred. His tongue licked his thin lips with seeming satisfaction, as he looked toward the place where the house had been.

# Chapter 22
## SHADOW OF DEATH

DOC SAVAGE used a plane to arrive at the scene of the latest Cold Light explosion. He instructed his companions to be on their guard and await his return to the hangar, before going to headquarters.

Havoc wrought by the new blast was such as to have destroyed any further lead to the mysterious Var. A Long Islander divulged the information that a woman with a number of servants had occupied the house.

The woman had been there only a short time. The house had been privately built. Several hours' check-up would be necessary to discover its owner.

Doc judged the Cold Light ray had been projected from an automobile. The word of frightened witnesses bore out this theory.

The bronze man spent no more time here. He was convinced that a woman had died.

Returning to the Hudson River hangar, Doc announced, "We'll go first to headquarters, then have a look at that penthouse west of Central Park where Monk was imprisoned. Var's men might not use it again, but there are some things there I should examine. We will take the ex-neutralizers with us."

Reaching the skyscraper headquarters, the four men ascended in the private, high-speed elevator.

In the foggy street behind them, a tall shadow moved from a doorway. The man's hat was pulled low. His eyes burned in the darkness.

Waiting until Doc and his companions had vanished, the man drew out a cigarette case. Gently, he tapped the smoke on the silver box. He was watching the window of a tall building only a block away.

Other windows in the row on that floor were lighted. This

one was distinguishable by its darkness. But in its square, black space glowed for an instant a tiny light. It was as if a man had just lighted a cigarette.

The man in the street was computing the time required for one of the regular skyscraper elevators to reach the eighty-sixth floor. Unfamiliar with Doc's own speedy, private cage, the man had loitered in the building lobby for some time previously. He had made a careful check on the elevator indicators. He was sure he had the lifts timed to the second.

A full minute passed, then seven seconds more. The man flicked on his cigarette lighter. He swung it in three small circles past his face. Then he stepped back into a doorway and applied the flame to his own smoke.

His next movement was fast. With a bound, he crossed the pavement and entered a low-slung car. The gears screamed protest. The driver took the first corner recklessly. The car gathered speed. A red traffic light loomed ahead.

The driver disregarded the signal, shooting across between a car and a truck. He heard a policeman's whistle, but he only smiled. For he had timed everything to make sure he would be at a sufficient distance. By the time the angered traffic cop overtook him, if he did, he was sure the policeman would have something else to take his attention.

Doc and his men were a good three minutes ahead of the furtive man's carefully plotted schedule when they reached the eighty-sixth floor.

The outer door leading into the reception room opened. Doc stepped inside. The bronze man's eyes went to the broken window. His calculation and reaction was lightning fast.

Doc glided to the inner door leading to the laboratory. The door opened.

Doc was carrying one of the ex-neutralizers. His hands moved with incredible speed. The electromagnetic ray laid its wall across one side of the big room.

"Cover the other side, Long Tom," he directed. "We are about to entertain the Cold Light ray again."

Before he had finished speaking, the Cold Light had sliced the laboratory. The blue-steel ray cut through the thick wall of the building as if it were a fog bank.

"Howlin' calamities!" grunted Monk. "That fella Var don't seem to know when to quit!"

But the Cold Light was effectively blocked by the ex-neutralizer wall spreading its invisible fan from Doc's hands. Against the strange electromagnetic force it wavered and dissolved. It played with weird effects across the retorts and polished spheres of the chemical and electrical equipment.

"Hold it," said Doc, calmly. "Here, Monk, take the box. We've had a visitor while we were gone. If he had been able to replace that broken window, I fear, brothers, we now would have joined the long list of Var's victims."

While the Cold Light still played futilely against the invisible wall, Doc strode across the laboratory. His eyes searched among the clutter of tubes and glasses on the laboratory tables.

"Not anywhere here," he stated. "Keep the ex-neutralizers at work, even after the Cold Light leaves. He might think to surprise us and flash it back."

Doc's surmise was correct. The Cold Light vanished. It was gone for a minute. The bronze man continued his search. Finally he shook his head.

"We've had a visitor," he said slowly. "But he doesn't seem to have left a calling card."

The Cold Light came back for a second visit. Its play was briefer this time. Then it was switched off. Doc directed the ex-neutralizers be set to protect the laboratory while they armed themselves.

HAM walked over to the laboratory sink. Immediately, he called out to the others.

"Quick! Get out before the water hits these things!"

He was scooping up the four globular "poison pills" and the two cubelike ones. The dampened area from the dropping water was within an inch of touching the first of these. Ham had no doubt but that a trap of deadly gas had been set for all of them.

"Our visitor had it figured too closely," said Ham. "In another few minutes, the place would have been full of the gas, if that's what these things are intended to do. We arrived just a little ahead of the killer's schedule. Say! Scraggs knew where you put the poison pills!"

Doc looked at the white pellets lying in Ham's palm.

"Yes," said Doc. "Vonier and Carberry also knew. The Cold Light might have been a diversion to keep our minds elsewhere. I'll take those pills, Ham. We must find Renny."

Doc's assured manner informed his men he had arrived at some definite conclusion which he was not yet ready to divulge.

Long Tom was bending in front of the leaden safe. His nervous, long fingers were rubbing across the door.

"Used the torch on this to get them out," he remarked. "Neat a job as I ever saw."

Doc wrapped the pills in a silk handkerchief and placed them in his pocket.

DOC SAVAGE'S intention to investigate the penthouse where Monk had whipped a robot might have been a great relief to Renny, if he could have known of it. For Renny was conscious when he was carried up a stairway. His eyes and mouth were taped, but sound and his sense of direction informed him he was near Central Park.

Renny had counted floors while on an elevator.

"Holy cow!" he grunted. "You wouldn't think the boobs would be that dumb! It's the same place they had Monk, or I'm no judge of descriptions! This will be the first place Doc will make for!"

Renny's elation at the apparent dumbness of his captors was only short-lived. He was dumped roughly into a room. This was so small it seemed to be little more than a narrow closet. Renny's huge body required considerable room.

The tape was suddenly and roughly torn from his eyes. Renny mumbled a bellow of rage through his sealed lips.

"Go on and howl, big fellow!" said a hard voice. "You'll be glad in a minute we're letting you look everything over!"

The man stepped back. Renny was amazed to discover he was looking through a doorway where there was no door. The sides of the frame were of gleaming copper strips. Renny had been placed far back in the little room. He was perhaps ten feet from this metal-sided entrance.

The man who had spoken was standing with several others on the rug of a curiously painted room. The walls were of aquamarine. Renny stared at the opposite side.

Monk's story of the metal man he had ripped apart was proved. A glass door had been shattered. An armless, broken robot stood in the room back of the smashed entrance.

Renny stared at one of the weird oil paintings. It was that of the half-crab, half-human figure depicted as arising from the coral-strewn botttom of the sea.

So this was the picture on one of the colored plates in Vonier's little book? Renny wondered how Doc had come upon that angle of Vonier's activities.

RENNY was sitting now, with his back propped against the back wall of the closetlike room. He looked sharply at the men outside. He judged that Var was not among those present.

One of the men said, "And right now, big fellow, you're figuring how you might roll yourself outta that nice, little cell. Well, just in case you try it, I'll give you something to think about!"

The man was at least six or seven feet distant from the copper-plated entrance. He walked over to the far wall, threw an electric switch and returned. In his hand he held an ordinary walking stick with a thick, rubber tip.

He reached with the cane and pressed on the rug several feet from the copper doorway. Instantly, there came a wicked crackling. An electrical current of high voltage leaped across the space of the entrance. It played with vivid flashes.

"You'll notice it's the works," said the man with the cane. "And if my foot or your foot were where this cane is, there'd be nothing left but to bring on the lilies. Now, big fellow, it's about six feet from where you are to the doorway. The plate on your side starts only a few inches from where you're sitting."

Renny could see he was hopelessly trapped. His mind leaped to another angle of the ingenious death trap. Had Var's monstrous crew thought of that? He wasn't left long in doubt.

"And now," continued his tormentor, "we will leave you. No doubt, your brainy chief will think of this penthouse. He'll figure we wouldn't be dumb enough to come back here after your ape-faced partner escaped. But he'll want to have a look, anyway."

Renny tried his muscles against the multiple cords.

"So, Doc Savage will be along presently," the man went on. "We won't be visible, but we'll be close by. Naturally, he'll make a hunt for you. Probably won't believe you're here until he sees you in this closet. That will be pretty.

"There you are. You can't talk or move. You can only use your eyes. We'll leave a light on, so you can't be missed. No doubt, the smart Doc Savage will immediately suspect the copper doorway is a trap. But he can't know how far the plates reach under the rug.

"So your chief will walk up close enough to inspect the device." The man used the cane again—"Like this!"

The walking stick was sheathed with metal. The rubber tip had been worn thinner than the man using it had noticed. A blue electrical spark suddenly played along the cane. It writhed and twisted around the man's hand.

With an oath frozen on his lips, the victim succeeded in heaving himself free. He rolled to the floor, cursing wildly. Renny detected the odor of scorched skin and flesh.

The man got to his feet, his body shaking. He rubbed his burned hand. His face was white.

## Chapter 23
## DEATH THREATENS DOC

RENNY could only stare at the fiendish trap. His tormentor had presented only facts. Even Doc could have no reason to suspect other than that the doorway itself was highly charged. Renny groaned under the gagging tape. He hoped Doc and the others would believe it useless to visit the penthouse where Monk had been held.

But at this moment, four figures were emerging from the skylight of a roof less than half a block from the penthouse.

"So up here's where you chewed up an armored robot?" grinned Ham maliciously at Monk. "And it didn't seem to make even a dent in that prognathous jaw."

"Dag-gone it!" squeaked Monk. "I'll bet that's an insult!"

Doc cautioned silence. Long Tom was following him closely, as they kept near the coping walls along the street side of the roofs. Long Tom was carrying one of the ex-neutralizers and Monk was burdened with the other.

Doc expected to find the penthouse deserted. He reached the shelter of a chimney where he could see the structure rearing above the apartment house roof. To his surprise, the windows of the penthouse glowed with mellow light.

Directing the others to keep back in the shelter of the shadows, the bronze man glided forward. In the vague light his movement could hardly be detected, so swiftly he moved from one shadow to another.

Doc flattened himself beside one of the windows. He was looking into the room with vivid blue paintings. He saw the illustration about which Monk had exclaimed in Vonier's book.

He saw another painting. The same figures had been in Vonier's book. It looked as if the author had caused the room to be created. The bronze man considered the relation of this room to the emotionless explorer.

Doc was using one thumb against the window casing. With only the pressure of this, he was slowly raising the sash.

The room was in confusion. The drawers of a desk had been pulled out. A few papers were strewn on the floor. There was other evidence that several persons had taken a hasty departure. A door which apparently led to a stairway was partly open. A man's hat and one glove lay on the floor near this exit.

A bottle of ink had been spilled on the expensive rug. It was logical the Var men might have fled hastily after Monk's escape.

Though a night had passed, if no person had visited the penthouse, it was not unreasonable to suppose the lights might have burned all day. Doc's instinctive senses put him on guard.

One bronzed hand gestured his companions to stay back. He eased himself into the room.

Doc's figure was fully revealed. He judged if this were a trap, the time had come for it to be sprung. Nothing happened.

The bronze man studied the marine paintings intently. From an inner pocket, he brought out Vonier's thin book. After a brief comparison, he nodded. From another pocket came another book. This second volume was not illustrated. It was a leather-bound volume. But its text was printed in bright blue ink.

Looking at the picture of the half-crab, half-human figure, Doc started reading the accompanying text, when, from across the room, came a muffled, guttural sound as if some one were strangling. Doc sought its source. He saw the closet-like room into which Renny had been crowded.

His keen eyes saw the engineer's hunched figure. Though bound hand and foot, his mouth taped, Renny was going through queer contortions. Doc strode across the larger room.

Now he could see Renny's position more clearly. The big man's eyes were blinking rapidly. His head shook violently. He was trying to warn Doc of something.

The bronze man moved closer. He was only about eight feet from the doorway. Renny moaned under the tape. He reared to his heels. He lunged forward, heaving his big body directly toward the concealed death plates.

In his loyalty to the bronze man, the giant engineer counted his own life a slight sacrifice. If he could only strike the hidden peril in such manner as to prevent Doc Savage being electrocuted, Renny felt it would be much more than worth the price.

Instinct developed in many situations of extreme danger, brought instant understanding to Doc. As Renny hurled himself toward the doorway, Doc's own springy body left the floor.

The almost simultaneous action of the two men carried their leaping bodies clear of the floor. They were, for the moment, as agile and fast as two great apes of the jungle. Two bodies cannot remain suspended for more than the fraction of a second. Renny, knowing the truth, groaned deeply in mid-air. He had accomplished nothing. Doc would die along with him. The striking of their weight would make the fatal contact.

MONK, as ever venturing beyond where he had been instructed to go, had reached the window opened by Doc. He had watched the bronze man as he paused in the face of danger to read a book, examine the paintings.

Now he witnessed the inexplicable action of his chief. Monk could not possibly reach either of the flying figures. To his awe-struck senses it seemed as if the bronze man and Renny were bent upon annihilating each other. The purpose of this, Monk could not fathom.

His own instinct told him this was his cue to do something. It was not within human possibility to reach either of the men. Monk did the next possible thing. He had no conception of what it would accomplish.

The ex-neutralizer box was in his hands. Monk flicked the switch. The focussing slot of the invisible wall was pointed directly at the copper-lined doorway.

Renny and Doc collided in mid-air. Big as he was, the breath hissed from Renny's lungs. He strove to make his weight hurl Doc backward.

They dropped together upon the rug between the deadly copper plates. There was a lurid, blinding flash of high-frequency current. Like the bursting of a freakish floating ball of lightning, the side of the room where the switch was concealed exploded in blue smoke and yellow flame.

Renny and Doc rolled over together. Renny's breath was gone. His ankles and his wrists were still tightly bound. He had leaped with the propelling force of his corded leg muscles. Doc's quick hand pulled the tape from the engineer's mouth.

"Holy cow, Doc!" Renny gasped, as darkness enfolded them. "Are we dead?"

"I'm all right," replied Doc, bounding to his feet. "We'll remove these cords. We're due to have visitors."

Monk stood for a moment in petrified silence. As yet, he hardly realized what he had done. Then he heard Renny and Doc speaking, and the apelike engineer exhaled a mighty breath of relief.

"Howlin' calamities!" he grunted. "Somethin' sure busted somethin'!"

The something had been the invisible wall of the ex-neutralizer. Before either Doc or Renny had hit the concealed plates intended for the bronze man's electrocution, the electromagnetic ray had flashed through the closet doorway.

The invisible wall had the effect of interposing an insulating, nonconducting element in the space across which the high-voltage current would have jumped. This intangible, yet powerful, force had cut the circuit in such a manner as to short circuit the high-powered wires at the hidden switchboard.

Fuses and a part of the board had gone out. With these went the house lights. The strange room with its aquamarine paintings was instantly a dark cavern.

EVEN as Doc's fast hands were slitting the cords off Renny, men were pouring into the room.

"It didn't get 'em!" snarled a voice. "I heard them speak! We can't take chances now! Let 'em have it!"

The bronze man's shoulder struck Renny and heaved him far to one side. They rolled to the far wall on the deep rug.

Half a dozen flashes mingled with the vicious, whiplike crackling of silenced pistols. Leaden slugs were ripping into the copper-sheathed door frame.

The bronze man was holding one of the anaesthetic gas capsules.

The gas capsule would have rendered any number of men helpless. But Var's force was strong. Doc divined that not all were in the room. Before Renny and he could make their way out, Renny might be hit by the gas. The engineer was not capable of holding his breath half as long as Doc.

More bullets were being poured across the room. Doc felt the searing touch of one across his neck. Renny grunted. A slug was buried in his shoulder. The bronze man caught Renny and made another gliding change of base.

There came the sound of crashing blows. Monk was shouting. "I'll pulverize y' for that!"

"Look out!" warned one of Var's men. "There's another one here——"

The speech was sliced off with the cracking, splintering impact of a blow. A box was shattered.

Monk had swung the ex-neutralizer box as a weapon. The man who had spoken, and another man, crashed down in the darkness. The unexpected landing of the apelike chemist into their midst was the beginning of a frenzied battle.

Var's men were striking each other in an effort to put their unseen foe out of business. Monk's long arms reached out and enfolded victim after victim. When he drove them together, some heads were irreparably damaged. Others were merely knocked senseless.

Var's men had ceased shooting. They were so tangled and scattered by Monk's steam roller attack as to lose all sense of direction. Those still on their feet could see only the dim square of light coming from below. It marked the secret stairway from the penthouse.

A few of Monk's victims were breathing heavily from the floor. Then Renny let out a bellow.

"Stop it, Monk! You wanta break my neck!"

Renny heaved once. He was more than a match for the apelike Monk. The chemist smashed into one of the oil paintings. There was momentary silence.

THE whole battle had taken up less than two minutes. Doc's pencil of light from his generator flash picked out eight men huddled on the floor. The bronze man gave several faces a brief study.

"The only way, brothers, we can help these men is to remove the temptation that drew them into this," Doc stated. "They're men of brains. Surgical treatment would do them no good. Remove the power of Var and they'll return to their professions."

The sound of the retreating survivors of the encounter was dying out.

"There's only one thing here we want," Doc stated.

Using the flashlight, he slit one of the oil paintings free from the wall with swift strokes of a knife. It was the picture of the half-crab, half-human form. The oil work was on canvas, secured by its edges to the wall of the room.

Then Doc said, "It's strange, Long Tom and Ham aren't here. They must have heard the shooting."

The three men hurried through the open window to the roof. Doc called out. Neither Ham nor Long Tom replied.

The bronze man led the way, gliding over a roof coping. Three bodies were lying near an open skylight. It was quickly revealed that none of the three was Ham or Long Tom.

Bending over one of the bodies, Doc pointed out, "Ham's sword got him!"

The unconscious man's cheek had been pierced by the keen point of Ham's cane sword blade. The anaesthetic drug had done its work. The same treatment had been parceled out to the other two.

Examination showed the skylight of this roof had been smashed. There was a small pool of blood near by.

Excited voices were coming up from the floor below. Doc led Monk and Renny in a swift descent. Panicky residents of the apartment house were pouring into the hallways.

Doc quickly learned a number of men had tramped through the upper corridor. They had pushed their way to the roof. One man had heard the scuffling noises of a fight.

"Then they came tumbling back down!" this man said. "They were carrying one man! He had a camera box in his hands! They had handcuffs on another man! He looked like a gentleman! Funny! Come to think of it, all of them looked like gentlemen!"

"The other ex-neutralizer!" groaned Renny. "That lays us wide open to the Cold Light ray, doesn't it, Doc?—since

Monk smashed our other ex-neutralizer in the fight."

"We'll not worry too much about that," said Doc, quietly. "We've first got to find Ham and Long Tom. Come on, brothers. I have a feeling we shall have visitors very soon at headquarters."

## Chapter 24
## THREE VISITORS

THE visitors to Doc Savage's headquarters numbered three. The explorer, Vonier, was the first.

Doc noted that throughout all of the crowded events of the past forty-eight hours, the explorer's fixed expression of cold detachment had not varied.

Vonier drew the bronze man quickly to one side.

"Just in case something happens we can't control, I'd like you to know one or two facts that might help you," he offered. "This Cold Light, or the destructive force it represents, contains one element to be found only at the greatest depths to which man has ever descended in the ocean."

The explorer's smile gave him a derisive, cynical look.

"I'd guessed that," Doc replied, quietly. "I got the hint of it directly from a book."

Vonier started perceptibly. His intense blue eyes became like sword thrusts.

"Yes?" he said. "From a book? You've known then that I knew?"

"Could hardly avoid that," said Doc, "seeing you wrote the book."

"Marvelous!" murmured Vonier. "For the past two days and nights, you haven't slept. You've been threatened by death from many directions. Yet during that time you've read a book."

"Two books, to be exact," smiled the bronze man. "They are oddly alike in many parts, though others are dissimilar. By the way, Vonier, do you count artistic conception among your other varied accomplishments?"

Vonier's reply was surprisingly direct, defiant.

"No," he said. "I'm not an artist. I didn't paint the pictures in the penthouse, if that's what you mean? Now you'll be asking——"

"Well, yes," interrupted Doc. "Where have you been during the day, and thus far to-night?"

"Many places. And alone mostly. I've been very busy."

"I judged you had," said Doc. "So you haven't been much comfort to Carberry. I imagined he would stick by you."

"Carberry had several phone calls," Vonier stated. "He went away to attend to some important business. He was still greatly scared, but he said he would meet me here to-night."

Just then, the headquarters had a visitor. It was the financier, Carberry.

Carberry's first words were, "I hear there's been another big explosion. I'm almost afraid to walk in the streets. I've called the police commissioner and asked for a special police bodyguard. I think he'll be sending them up here."

"We will give you all the protection possible," Doc stated. "We employ our own methods, and call upon the police only when some matter should be brought to their attention."

"Indeed—well—you see—Savage, I'm terribly sorry," stammered Carberry. "I'll call the commissioner at once. I feel safer with you than I would with a squad of coppers. Let me have——"

"Never mind," interjected Doc. "I've been in touch with the commissioner. He told me of your request. I've already instructed him not to send his men. The commissioner himself is paying us a visit in a few minutes."

"Oh, that's all right then," mumbled the financier. "I suppose then you've turned those poison pills over to him?"

"No," stated Doc. "I shall analyze them myself. Some one tried releasing the poison gas to trap us, so I'm carrying the pills with me."

Carberry gasped.

"Carrying them with you, Savage?" His protruding eyes rolled. "Don't you fear—well, mightn't something happen?"

The immediate entrance of the police commissioner interrupted Doc from giving an answer.

The police commissioner was a stocky, red-faced man. For good reasons, involving countless past services, his faith in Doc Savage was boundless.

He had met both Vonier and Carberry. While he did not

ignore the importance of the financier or the cause of his fear of death, the commissioner's attitude was abrupt.

After all, though he was a world figure, Carberry was but one individual. The safety of millions had now been in the balance for two days and two nights.

"We've got those men from the penthouse," the commissioner announced. "We've been checking. Not one has ever been mugged. We find they are doctors, professors and the like of that. Only two have any kind of records. We believe they have been international spies in Europe."

Doc nodded. This confirmed his quick analysis in the penthouse. None of these men had the kind of brains requiring the usual treatment for the reformation of crooks.

Carberry arose. His terror seemed to be returning in force.

"I just remembered," he said. "I think I should go out and put in a call to Mrs. Carberry. I want to know she is still safe."

"You could call from here," suggested Doc.

"Wait a minute," interrupted the commissioner. "I think Mr. Carberry should stay with us. In fact, all of us have something we ought to do at once. I've a dozen carloads of men on the way, but I came directly because I have to admit I'm afraid they can't stop this one."

"Holy cow!" muttered Renny. "Aren't things never goin' to quiet down?"

"We haven't any clue to your two men, Mr. Savage," the commissioner went on. "But we have a phoned report that the Hudson River warehouse where you keep your planes is to be the next spot visited by the Cold Light."

"WE must proceed to the hangar at once," Doc stated. "We'll have to do what we can to get the employees to safety. Some of the workers are too loyal to flee from any danger."

"I know," said the commissioner. "We tried warning them by phone."

"Get out the extra bulletproof vests," Doc instructed. "Commissioner, you and the others need the protection. I believe this is much more involved than a mere threat to destroy the hangar. It is a deliberate scheme to have us go out there."

"If you think it is a trap——" began the commissioner.

"We shall go," said Doc, quietly. "Perhaps Vonier and Carberry would rather remain here."

"Wouldn't miss it for a million," Vonier said, promptly.

"I wouldn't feel safe anywhere but with you, Doc Savage," declared Carberry.

Doc was holding an extra bulletproof vest in his hands.

"We've all got our vests, Doc," said Monk. "Why are you taking that one?"

A thin voice interrupted from the doorway of the outer office.

"Your Hudson River hangar is the next place Var intends to hit, Doc Savage."

Scraggs was standing there. His thin face was gray.

"I have been expecting you," replied Doc. "This vest is too big for you, but you will be wise to put it on."

Scraggs's sunken eyes were staring now at Carberry, much the same as he had looked at Vonier a few hours previously.

With Ham and Long Tom missing, there was ample room for the four extra man in Doc's armored car. The bronze man sent the motor at high speed across town.

ALL streets in the vicinity of the hangar were deserted. The commissioner had caused police lines to be drawn several blocks from the innocent-appearing old warehouse.

This building housed Doc Savage's latest in planes, his dirigible and two types of submarines.

As they passed the final police line, Doc glanced at Vonier, Carberry and Scraggs.

"I would suggest you leave us here. I will go ahead with my men and have the watchman and the other men get out."

"I'd prefer to be in at the finish," remarked Vonier, crisply. "I've a funny hunch this will be some sort of a showdown."

"I—I—wouldn't want to stay here alone," Carberry quavered. "I mean with the police. I'd like to go along."

"I'm seeing this through," came the positive voice of Scraggs.

Doc never wasted words in argument. The strangely matched pair, the explorer and the financier, had made their own choice. If they could have seen Doc's flaky-gold eyes at the moment, they would have guessed the bronze man was not ignoring their safety as much as it seemed.

For Doc Savage had arrived at a direct conclusion with regard to the Cold Light ray and its explosive effect. By simple elimination of certain facts, he had reached the point of knowing much more than the men accompanying him would have believed.

Doc was convinced there would be an explosion.

But right now, he was equally sure he had discovered the means of controlling the blast and its effect. And he had no intention of seeing the hangar destroyed.

The police lines took in a half circle about a half mile distant from the warehouse hangar. More than five hundred coppers, all heavily armed and instructed to permit no one to pass, formed the guarding ring. Police patrol launches guarded the river side.

The coppers looked apprehensively at the dark canyons of near-by deserted streets close to the hangar. The round-up had been made.

But this had not included buildings which seemed vacant. In the lower part of another old warehouse were four automobiles. Each of these cars carried eight or ten men.

Doc swung the car in front of the hangar. He regularly employed a crew of a dozen mechanics and others.

Entering the hangar, Doc ordered all his employees to depart from what he considered the danger zone surrounding the hangar. All excepting one mechanic.

"The rest of you wait here," Doc instructed his companions. "I'm sending up a plane. It's just an idea that came to me."

"You mean, you're going up?" queried Carberry.

"Rather a big chance to take, isn't it, Savage?" came from Vonier. "Remember what happened to the Red Arrow ship, or would have if it hadn't been for you?"

"No, I won't be going up," said Doc. "Just the plane."

Accompanied by the mechanic, the bronze man quickly moved one of the amphibian planes. The little ship was equipped with a radio-controlling robot. But unlike the plane in which Doc had been sent out over the ocean, this ship had alternative hand controls.

The radio robot could be cut off at any time by a pilot in the ship. He then could handle the plane in the usual manner.

THE police commissioner went back with the departing hangar employees to issue further instructions to his police lines.

Renny and Monk started an immediate prowl of the building. Apparently, no one remained. Vonier and Carberry were left standing together. Carberry, especially, seemed to prefer being where the light was brightest.

Scraggs glanced furtively around. Then he vanished with the quick movement of a scuttling small animal.

Carberry remarked to Vonier, "Savage seems invincible. Nothing gets by him. But I'm afraid this time he hasn't much of an idea what makes the Cold Light."

Vonier smiled thinly at the financier.

He said, "To put Doc Savage out of the running, you'd have to get inside his mind. For example, right in the middle of this turmoil and threats, he stops to read a book."

Carberry's eyes protruded more than ever.

"Read a book?" he queried. "What book?"

"Oh, the little thing I did on marine energy," replied Vonier, lightly. "Perhaps he thought he had something there."

From the near-by warehouse, men were moving. They were keeping in deep shadows. Doc Savage had ordered roof and river landing lights of his hangar on at their brightest. Carberry and Vonier remained near the open street door.

IN a nearer shadow inside the hangar, Scraggs was moving to concealment. He watched intently as Doc Savage and the mechanic got the small plane into its dockage ready for a take-off from the broad river. Scraggs watched until he saw the man of bronze climb into the plane's cabin.

The mechanic wound up the inertia starter. Apparently, it was Doc's hand on the throttle. The bronze man revved the motor with a warming burst. He remained in the cabin several minutes. Then he idled the motor and emerged.

"We'll leave it idle," the bronze man stated. "I'll give it the gun with the radio controls when I'm ready."

With the mechanic beside him, Doc started back across the hangar. Sudden shouts, harsh oaths and the sound of blows broke from the vicinity of the street door of the warehouse.

Doc glided into a run. The mechanic was close at his heels.

Half a dozen men swooped into the light where Carberry and Vonier were standing. A blow sent the explorer to his knees. Two men had seized his arms. He was being propelled toward the shadows.

Carberry was putting up a stiff fight.

Though a man of slight weight, the financier was surprisingly effective. Nor, now that he was in physical combat, did he seem afraid.

With catlike movements, Carberry had disposed of two of his attackers before Doc and the mechanic could make it halfway across the floor. Another man seized the financier, only to go somersaulting over Carberry's head.

But more men were pouring into the building. Carberry saw them coming. Suddenly, his nerve seemed to desert him. The financier turned and darted across the inside of the warehouse.

Vonier had shaken off his two attackers. To Doc's amazement, the explorer also took to his heels. He ran after Carberry.

Renny and Monk came bursting from behind a plane. There were now more than a score of men. They had started to pursue Carberry and Vonier.

RENNY's sledge-hammer fists disposed of four men in quick order. Monk whooped shrilly and his long arms flailed a disconcerting broadside of knuckles and elbows into the leaders of the rush to grab Carberry.

Then a pistol flashed, and another.

"Let 'em have it!" wheezed a high voice. "Look out! Here's Doc Savage himself!"

Over the arm of the moon-faced man with the rathole in the middle of his countenance for a mouth appeared the snout of a machine gun. He turned it directly upon the bronze man.

Any one looking on would have sworn Doc merely sidestepped the stream of slugs without great effort. The fact was, Doc's reactions under a pointed weapon were a split-second ahead of the gunman's trigger finger.

Wheeze McGovern cursed, and sought to bring the machine gun directly upon the slithering figure of the bronze man. The mechanic groaned with pain and sank to the ground. Some of the bullets had got him in the stomach.

Doc became a moving streak, hurtling himself straight upon Wheeze and his crackling gun. With all his massive weight, he dived under the tearing streak of death. One shoulder struck Wheeze's stubby legs.

There was a sharp crack. Doc rammed his head upward. With one leg broken and all the breath gone from his body, Wheeze dropped his weapon.

As Doc came to his feet, he saw that Renny and Monk were being overwhelmed by numbers. Renny was handicapped already by having a bullet in one shoulder as the result of the penthouse battle. Now he had a furrow across one temple and he was staggering groggily.

Monk cracked the heads of two men together, his favorite pastime. Then he sprang to Renny's assistance. A pistol butt crashed down on the chemist's head and sent him to his knees.

Doc Savage exploded suddenly in the midst of the attackers. His arrival had about the same effect as a cyclone ripping through a field of dry corn.

Doc's iron knuckles played at the ends of his corded arms with a speed too fast for the human eye to follow. When his knuckles landed, one man stayed down.

Though there had been some shooting, the invaders of the warehouse were now too closely packed to use their pistols. Nor did Doc or his men attempt the use of weapons. In the bright light it was mêlée for fists and muscles.

A group of six men remained on their feet. Seeing their leader, Wheeze McGovern, was out, they started a retreat. As they withdrew, two men drew their pistols. They now had a free play at Doc and his two companions.

They snarled hard laughs as they aimed the guns.

Two figures came lithely from the street outside. They were disheveled objects. Cords still trailed from the legs of one. Handcuffs held the wrists of both men. The mistake of Wheeze McGovern had been that he had not manacled the men's hands behind them.

Long Tom was a slight specimen of manhood. He looked frail compared to any other of Doc's men. But he could make the average man very sick indeed in a fistic encounter.

This time, Long Tom had an advantage. He swung the heavy handcuffs in sweeping arcs. Two men were mowed down with bleeding heads.

Ham, the lawyer, was quick as light. His favorite weapon was his trusty sword blade. Lacking this, the steel handcuffs seemed to serve very well. The manacles crashed on three heads before the men could get themselves set.

Almost abruptly, there were only four or five men left of the gang, and these were running toward the street.

"They won't find the cars they're looking for!" panted Ham. "Long Tom tore out their ignition wire!"

Doc was starting toward the door of the lighted radio control room.

"Keep an eye on all of these men," he instructed. "You needn't trouble about the one with the machine gun. He has serious trouble with his legs."

Doc was in the door of the control room. A slim figure ran past the edge of the lighted area.

The running man was Scraggs. He vanished in the direction Carberry and Vonier had taken. Neither the explorer nor the financier had reappeared, although all pursuit was definitely ended.

Doc stood before the radio controls. He closed a switch. In its take-off dock, the motor of his small plane roared on fuller throttle.

The bronze man's hand moved over to the impulse that would control the take-off. His hand never reached it.

The little ship suddenly lifted its tail and moved out upon the river. Gathering speed, its nose lifted under an expert hand.

Some one was in the radio-controlled plane. It was being zoomed into the air in the direction of the ocean by a human hand.

Doc's eyes held little golden whirlwinds of light.

He knew the mystery pilot of the zooming plane believed him still to be carrying the "poison pills" in his pocket.

# Chapter 25
## THE RUNAWAY PLANE

THE police commissioner was in the doorway of the radio control room. He stared at Doc Savage. Doc's feet were braced wide apart. He was looking up at the sky through the observation window.

"You're sending up a plane with the radio robot?" questioned the commissioner. "What's the idea, Mr. Savage?"

"It was my idea to send up a plane with the radio," stated

Doc, tersely. "Now, it's another idea altogether, and I don't know but it's a good one."

Renny appeared beside the commissioner. He was mopping blood from his long, solemn face.

"Holy cow, Doc!" he exclaimed. "I thought all the time that skull-faced explorer would bear watching. He's in that plane! I saw him run over that way."

Ham pushed his way in.

"You're wrong, Renny, this time," he interposed. "It's that ratty little fellow Scraggs. I was watching him making for the plane when Doc came in here. He's making a get-away!"

Doc smiled a little.

"Time will tell us that, and it won't be such a long time either," he said. "Has Carberry returned?"

"Not him!" supplied Monk. "The last I saw of him he was high tailin' for the police lines!"

Doc was watching the riding lights of the small plane. The ship had been sent steadily upward. It was nearly two miles high and its lights had faded in the fog. Only the thin drone of its motor could be heard.

"Hope he stays that far up," said Doc, crisply. "Just the same, I'd advise all of you to get back toward the police lines. I could switch off the hangar lights, but I'd rather have him come back over the river than try landing some other place."

"Why? Do you think he'll come back?" said the commissioner, doubtfully. "I think whoever it is, he's making his get-away. He'll probably land somewhere up or down the coast. I'll get to one of the cars and send in a radio warning to be on the lookout for him."

"That will hardly be necessary," smiled Doc.

THE others obeyed the suggestion. They listened. They heard nothing. Only Doc's keenly tuned auditory nerves had detected the thrumming of the plane's motor growing steadily louder.

In fact, Doc was the only one among them who had not lost the vibration altogether. Even at its farthest point away, the bronze man had judged the plane to be nearly two miles high and still climbing.

The enigmatic smile deepened across Doc's bronze jaws.

He alone knew that the mysterious pilot of the runaway plane was expecting to hurl destruction upon the warehouse hangar. That the man at the controls was Var himself.

Var, at this instant, was sure he had the means of striking one mighty blow. A blow that would not only wipe out Doc's hangar, but end the lives of all of Doc's men and the police commissioner.

Moreover, Doc was now sure that Var's own men had turned upon him. He could read only one answer to the attack of Wheeze McGovern.

McGovern, Var's chief aide, had made an effort to steal the Cold Light gun. He lacked only this to complete the combination that would make him the master of the shattering annihilator.

Once in possession of the gun, Wheeze McGovern had planned to embark on a career of crime with his own selected companions. They had seen the chance to extort millions from fear-crazed millionaires.

Doc was sure Wheeze McGovern never would obtain that gun. Its owner was flying high, high in the sky over the man he most feared and hated—Doc Savage and his four valiant companions.

By a change of wind, the others now could hear the increasing beat of the plane's propeller.

"Making for some inland field," said the commissioner. "He's taking on altitude, thinking we'll have planes after him."

"He's taking on altitude," replied Doc, "but not through fear of any other plane. He believes he's putting himself far enough up to be beyond the danger of his own deviltry."

"I don't understand——" the commissioner began.

His words were lost in a shattering explosion. Only Doc had seen that instantaneous flash of the Cold Light ray. It was no more than the thousandth part of a second. For the Cold Light had no distance to travel to reach its objective.

A lurid cloud of blue flame spread across the heavens. Its weird illumination made all faces in the group seem pock-marked and gray. Indeed, the face of the commissioner was a chalky gray.

The blue cloud was only a momentary flash that lighted the sky from horizon to horizon. The blast was like the impact of a battleship broadside.

The air about the group in the warehouse chilled. All of the hangar lights went out as if a master switch had been pulled.

Then the silence was so complete each man thought his eardrums had been hopelessly shattered.

Doc's radio plane had totally dissolved, as if it had never been. From the lack of any tiny bit of falling wreckage, it was conceivable that the terrible, close-up force of the Cold Light explosion had disintegrated the ship into all of its component atoms.

And with the ship, the man whose ghostly voice had announced, "*I AM—VAR!*"

RENNY was the first to find speech.

"Blazes!" he muttered, hoarsely. "So that's the last of our friend, Vonier!"

Ham found his voice and spoke in the darkness.

"That rat Scraggs, you mean!" he rapped out.

Two voices murmured close by. Footsteps approached slowly.

"Who is speaking of us?" inquired the calm voice of the explorer. "We're here to talk for ourselves."

The eyes of Vonier were like bits of shiny blue glass against the light. Beside him was the thin, shambling figure of the little man, Scraggs.

"I rather thought you would be around somewhere," said Doc Savage, quietly. "I admit I was quite a bit mixed up for a while. But after I discovered Carberry had written his book on the cellular origin of the human species from oil paintings he had copied from your book, Vonier, I made some other inquiries."

"Howlin' calamities!" squeaked out Monk. "And he was with us most of the time!"

"Some of the time," corrected Doc. "But at no time when he was trying to explode the Cold Light bombs."

"What do you mean, Doc, Cold Light bombs?" questioned Ham. "I've never seen anything but the Cold Light itself."

"You carried some of them in your pocket for quite a while, Ham," said Doc. "I seem to recall you rescued all of us from being poisoned by gas. You thought the intention was to kill all of us in the laboratory by having them dampened."

"Good gosh!" exploded Monk. "And that shyster tries to pulverize all of us with that weak brain of his!"

"I wonder," mused Renny, who had just thought of something. "Say, Monk. Maybe Ham didn't do so bad. Come to think of it, you tried eating one of the bombs in that Manhattan tenement. You thought it was only a gumdrop."

Long Tom broke in.

"Listen, Doc!" he exclaimed, excitedly. "You had six of the things in your pocket!"

"That's what Carberry thought," said Doc, calmly. "In fact, I had them when we came here. It was my idea to send them up in that plane and dive it into the ocean. I had hidden them in the plane. And Carberry thought it was his chance to destroy his enemies.

"You see, some of his own men were double-crossing him. If I'd had the Cold Light bombs in my pocket, it would have wiped them out as well as us. In a way, he was driven to it, for this Wheeze McGovern had turned on him."

THE little man, Scraggs, was muttering.

"And I discovered who Var was just too late," he complained. "I was almost sure, and I learned where his wife was hiding. I was on my way out there tonight, when Carberry met Wheeze McGovern's car on the highway. I guess Carberry suspected Wheeze and tried to stop him with the Cold Light."

"You knew there was something more, some element other than the Cold Light ray that caused the explosions?" Doc suggested.

"Yes, I knew there was some sort of combination, for Jackson had told me that," admitted Scraggs. "But it was only after I saw in your laboratory those pills you thought were poison that I got a real idea what the bombs might be. That's why I started out to find Mrs. Carberry. I had a hunch the supply of bombs would be wherever she was hiding. McGovern must have grabbed the bombs from the woman."

Scraggs shook his head sadly.

"That was a terrible thing!" he went on. "The Cold Light missed McGovern's car. McGovern had the rest of the Cold Light bombs, thousands of them, in insulated boxes. But the ray would have exploded one of the uninsulated bombs if it came within a ten-mile radius. That's why Carberry's wife never knew what happened. I imagine McGovern had left some of the bombs open with that purpose."

"But," interposed the police commissioner, "how about the explosion at Carberry's mansion? The voice he heard, that every one heard?"

"Among other things, I learned Carberry had been an actor, a character man before he became wealthy," Doc stated. "He married a young actress. After the murder of Jackson, the old chemist, they had it all fixed to put on a show, a red herring across any trail the police might pick up."

"That's right," said Scraggs, eagerly. "Only they had me fooled. Jackson had told me there was to be a test in the woods at the Carberry place, to frighten the millionaire."

A FLUTTERING figure came running from the street door. It was the same lovely girl who had appeared at the smashed Red Arrow plane, looking for Scraggs. All were amazed when she threw her arms around the disreputable-appearing little man.

"Scraggs, honey!" she exclaimed. "Are you all right?"

Scraggs looked at the others sheepishly, but his thin arms went around the girl.

"Meet Muriel Jackson, gentlemen," he said in a thin, proud voice. "You see, it was her father—well, I had to get his murderer."

The girl's face was bathed in tears. She hugged the scraggly head to her bosom.

"Well, I'll be dag-goned!" sputtered Monk.

The homely chemist had a weakness for beautiful women. Doc turned to Vonier.

"You suspected Carberry from the first, didn't you?" the bronze man questioned. "But you weren't sure?"

"Right again, as usual, Savage," said the explorer. "Old Jackson read my book and came to me to explain his experiments with an element I had mentioned found in the depths of the sea. I told him it would be best to let it alone. He said he wanted the army and navy to have it. I wasn't sure he had gone to Carberry, but he mentioned having read the man's book and how like my own it seemed to be. So I suspected he went to Carberry."

"Strange what angles a normally intelligent brain will take," Doc said, slowly. "Carberry had a rich man's traditional respect for property rights. He owned that Manhattan block he blew up. He was one of the biggest stockholders in the railroad and he tried to blast the express. In trying to cover up his trail, he laid the broadest possible one for his own detection."

"He was especially good at laying false trails," added Vonier. "He used a special bright blue ink in writing warning notes. It happens I had used that same sort of ink. I have a bottle of it in my study. Carberry adopted it."

"That clears that up," Doc stated. "I have seen the ink on your desk, Vonier."

"Saw it? On my desk?"

"Yes," replied the bronze man, "when I visited your study to confirm a few deductions arising from your rather remarkable book."

"Is there anything on land or sea or in the sky you overlook, Savage?"

Doc's quiet bronze smile was his only reply.

To the world at large, Doc Savage is a strange, mysterious figure of glistening bronze skin and golden eyes. To his fans he is the greatest adventure hero of all time, whose fantastic exploits are unequaled for hair-raising thrills, breathtaking escapes, blood-curdling excitement!

☐ 20934    **SECRET OF THE SKY #20    $2.25 and COLD DEATH**

☐ 14616    **THE WHISKER OF HERCULES $1.95 #103 and THE MAN WHO WAS SCARED #104**

☐ 14916    **THEY DIED TWICE #105 and $1.95 SCREAMING MAN #106**

☐ 14901    **JIU SAN #107 and    $1.95 BLACK BLACK WITCH #108**

☐ 20573    **THE SHAPE OF TERROR    $1.95 #109 and DEATH HAD YELLOW EYES #110**

# OUT OF THIS WORLD!

That's the only way to describe Bantam's great series of science fiction classics. These space-age thrillers are filled with terror, fancy and adventure and written by America's most renowned writers of science fiction. Welcome to outer space and have a good trip!